Praise for

THE BUTCHER'S DAUGHTER:
THE HITHERTO UNTOLD STORY OF MRS. LOVETT

"Perfect for those who love to escape back in time with a dark atmospheric story with that unmistakable Victorian gothic vibe. It's told from the perspective of the young woman destined to become the infamous Mrs. Lovett, and she certainly has a chilling and disturbing tale… *The Butcher's Daughter* paints a vivid picture of a secretive world filled with enigmatic characters with lots of sinister intrigue."

CLARE WHITFIELD, author of *People of Abandoned Character*

"Your fingers may bleed with paper cuts as you tear through *The Butcher's Daughter*. Retailed with consummate confidence, this novel draws out of the foggy demimonde of Victorian London all manner of mayhem. I am spellbound. You will be too, should you attend the tale."

GREGORY MAGUIRE, author of *Wicked*

"Engrossing and exquisitely detailed. A twisty tale worthy of the enigmatic Mrs. Lovett."

KELLEY ARMSTRONG, *New York Times* bestselling author of *Bitten* and *I'll Be Waiting*

"Bloody and beautiful, *The Butcher's Daughter* is a visceral novel that grips the reader and refuses to let go. David Demchuk and Corinne Leigh Clark brilliantly reimagine a classic, giving it new depths, new horrors, and new layers to peel back by centering the character of Mrs. Lovett and rightfully letting her tell her own tale in her own voice. The moment I started reading, I didn't want to put it down."

A. C. WISE, author of *Wendy, Darling* and *Hooked*

"Grisly, spellbinding, and oddly touching . . . Demchuk and Clark get their arms bloody to the elbow reaching deep into the carcass of a story about life at the margins and the gruesome allure of wanton violence."

GRETCHEN FELKER-MARTIN, author of *Manhunt* and *Cuckoo*

"A consistently clever and harrowing fin-de-siècle horror, *The Butcher's Daughter* draws its eerie narrative harmonies from a cacophony of documents. Demchuk and Clark are equally adept in blending genres, creating a unique mixture of sensation fiction and literary horror. Tremendous fun."

NABEN RUTHNUM, author of *Helpmeet*

"A Victorian nightmare. Demchuk and Clark present an assembly of communications and reports that together form temporal windows to a slaughterhouse, turning us into voyeurs glimpsing the edges of carnage. All the ingredients of a macabre treat."

HAILEY PIPER, Bram Stoker Award©-winning author of *Queen of Teeth* and *All the Hearts You Eat*

"A wonderfully sophisticated horror. *The Butcher's Daughter* is a gloomy, disgusting, and suspenseful rollercoaster ride, brought to vivid life by two exceptionally talented writers. At its heart, it is a tale about bodies—especially women's bodies—about freedom and agency, and those who wish to control other human beings down to their guts. An historical novel, yes, but very much spun from this current bloody moment. Bleak, witty, and disturbing."

RICHARD MIRABELLA, author of *Brother & Sister Enter the Forest*

"The seedy underbelly of Victorian London comes to life in this deliciously dark novel, with mad scientists, murderous cults, merciless madams, and, of course, meat pies. If Sarah Waters had written penny dreadfuls, it might look something like this, but only David Demchuk and Corinne Leigh Clark could make me hungry while reading about cannibalism."

NINO CIPRI, author of *Dead Girls Don't Dream*

THE HITHERTO UNTOLD STORY
OF
MRS. LOVETT

DAVID DEMCHUK &
CORINNE LEIGH CLARK

TITAN BOOKS

The Butcher's Daughter: The Hitherto Untold Story of Mrs. Lovett
Print edition ISBN: 9781835410844
Broken Binding edition ISBN: 9781835416310
E-book edition ISBN: 9781835410851

Published by Titan Books
A division of Titan Publishing Group Ltd
144 Southwark Street, London SE1 0UP
www.titanbooks.com

First edition: June 2025
10 9 8 7 6 5 4 3 2 1

This is a work of fiction. All of the characters, organizations, and events portrayed in this novel are either products of the author's imagination or are used fictitiously. Any resemblance to actual persons, living or dead (except for satirical purposes), is entirely coincidental.

Copyright © 2025 David Demchuk & Corinne Leigh Clark.

The authors assert the moral right to be identified as the authors of this work.

No part of this publication may be reproduced, stored in a retrieval system, or transmitted, in any form or by any means without the prior written permission of the publisher, nor be otherwise circulated in any form of binding or cover other than that in which it is published and without a similar condition being imposed on the subsequent purchaser.

A CIP catalogue record for this title is available from the British Library.

EU RP (for authorities only)
eucomply OÜ, Pärnu mnt. 139b-14, 11317 Tallinn, Estonia
hello@eucompliancepartner.com, +3375690241

Design by Richard Mason.

Printed and bound by CPI (UK) Ltd, Croydon CR0 4YY.

Inspector A—

As requested, this dossier contains
the letters, documents, notebooks and
miscellaneous papers gathered from Miss
Emily Gibson's rooms after her mother's visit
to Whitehall. The housemistress expressed
surprise that Miss Gibson's door was left
unlocked and could not attest with confidence
that the premises had remained inviolate in
the days preceding. I detected no evidence of
theft or foul play, no obvious sign of violence
or struggle. Nothing of value appeared to
have been taken. Many items that I would
have considered among her prized possessions
were in their proper places in plain sight,
including a few coins and a small cache of
jewellery on her dressing table near her
bedside. None of the other residents could
recall any recent visitors. They were unaware
of any suitors, romantic involvements or close
companions. This is a curious one! The rooms
are now secured and will remain so until you
approve the release of their contents to the
family. Mind the feather.

—Dew

ST. ANNE'S PRIORY
Hampstead, London

APRIL THE 3RD, 1887

Dear Miss Gibson,

I am in receipt of your three letters to Mother Mary Angelica, our Prioress, which had been held for consideration in the offices of St. Anne's Priory here in North Hampstead. They have been released to me for reply. I see that you are a journalist, in search of Mrs. Margery Lovett—a wanton woman, a murderess, whose name we daren't speak aloud for its profanity. A half century has passed since her dark deeds! You believe her to be secreted here at the Priory, working in the kitchen or as a housemaid or possibly as a nurse. What has led you to this conclusion? You do not say. You present a rough and unflattering description of her, which no doubt befits such a monstrous creature. You do not elaborate on your interest in her whereabouts or well-being, though given your occupation one can surmise the worst.

Three letters! You are persistent, I will give you that. I suppose it's a vital quality in your profession and serves you well for the most part. However, we do not know your Margery Lovett nor do we know where she might be found.

St. Anne's is a community of Sisters of the Church, living

in quiet contemplation. I can assure you the pious women on these premises would have nothing to do with someone as depraved as your Lovett, let alone provide her with shelter. A hundred and fifty gruesome murders! Baking human flesh into pies! Perhaps she was more diabolical than her vile confederate Sweeney Todd, that malevolent barber of infamy, for who could conceive of such a thing. The Sisters here are innocent of such horrible stories as are told to children to frighten them under the covers. They have no knowledge of these ghastly crimes, and they are better for it. One of our youngest, Sister Catherine with her fine and delicate hand, has been assigned to assist me in crafting this reply. Poor soul. The names of Lovett and Todd had never touched her ears until this moment. If only I could be as unspoiled as she.

I wish you had been here with me in the minutes just after dawn when I was out in the yard with the cook's maid, gathering eggs from our three nesting hens. I take on such tasks as the need arises, and will sometimes top a plumped-up bird to make our Sunday supper. As we had our basket filled and our backs to the runs and were dithering with the kitchen door, a windhover lurking in our ancient oak saw his chance to strike and swept down to seize one of the hens. Unexpectedly, the old girl put up a tremendous fight, screeching and thrashing with beak and claw until the maid and I could grab our sticks and drive the creature off. The hen may yet die from her wounds, poor thing, but not without having torn a few feathers from her assailant. I know some of how she feels. Young as you are, and more fair than fowl, I wonder if you do as well.

Why don't you turn your attention away from the gutter, to

more worthy journalistic pursuits? I have read your inspiring piece in the Daily Post on the suffragist Helen Taylor, and your series of articles on the Malthusian League, abandoned mothers and unwanted children. Why seek out the worst of women, when those who suffer legitimate injustices need your passion, when we need you to shine a light on the struggles we face in every turn of our lives, at every station, at every age? Even the Priory has faced hostilities over decades: accusations of succumbing to papacy and rejecting women's natural obedience to men. You are not the first to write to us enquiring after vagrants, cutpurses, dissolutes, harlots and worse.

Ours is an order of Christian charity. I myself have suffered greatly, decade upon decade. I have endured many abuses, faced horrors at the very height of London society and among the very dregs. In these, my final years, I am grateful that the Sisters and the Prioress, Mother Mary Angelica, took pity on me and accepted me into their fold so that I could escape the turmoil of the world. Your time and effort would be better spent on noble works, on acts of bravery and benevolence, than on a ghoulish tale which has been glorified in penny bloods and gaffs. In any event, the last I heard of your Lovett was that she died in her cell at Newgate Prison, poisoned herself I believe, which by all accounts was the best possible outcome. Certainly, poisoning is more merciful than a hanging.

With this, Sister Catherine and I must leave you, as we are being called to dine before Vespers. This is a time of great unease for us at the Priory. The Reverend Mother, God bless her soul, was taken to hospital early yesterday evening; we understand her to be direly ill, and do not know if she will ever return. Our Sister Augustine is acting in her place, and is at sixes and sevens with her new duties, as you would expect. Might the Post consider a portrait in prose of the Reverend Mother as a beacon of benevolence in the capital? It would send an inspiring message to the populace, even as she lies on what may be her deathbed.

We wish you the best of luck in your endeavours, but please know this is not the right rock under which to look. Margery Lovett is no doubt at the bottom of a pile of bones in a pauper's grave, and that is better than she deserves. Leave her to rest with the dead, if rest she can. You would be chasing phantoms.

I enclose for you the windhover's feather, speckled and striped. A memento between us.

> Always look forward, never look back.
>
> Margaret C. Evans (Miss)

From the London Evening Post

APRIL 3, 1887   10 PAGES   {ONE HALFPENNY

HAMPSTEAD PRIORESS TAKEN ILL

Hampstead Heath, England: Mother Mary Angelica, age 71, of St. Anne's Priory, fell ill unexpectedly last night, and was transported to the Royal Free Hospital where she is under careful watch in the Victoria Wing. Doctors suspect an inflammation of the heart. The Sisters of St. Anne's request the prayers of our readers to hasten the Reverend Mother's recovery.

ST. ANNE'S PRIORY
Hampstead, London

APRIL THE 14TH, 1887

Dear Miss Gibson,

Thank you for your kind enquiry after the health of the Reverend Mother. Sadly, she remains at Royal Free Hospital in a most desperate state, watched over day and night by the fine nurses in the Victoria Wing. Despite all our prayers, we are told that she is unlikely to recover. It is only a matter of time. Sister Catherine is beside herself with grief. She and the Reverend Mother had grown quite close in recent months.

As for your other queries, your determination is admirable but remains misdirected. We regret that we do not permit visitors to the Priory. Ours is an order of peaceful observance that benefits from being at a remove from the troubles that surround us. As the acting Prioress, Sister Augustine would be the one to receive guests on our behalf. If you have questions, she would be pleased to assist, though I doubt she has the answers that you seek. Even if your Lovett had been here in decades past, our files are unlikely to be of much use, and are not available for your perusal.

I do see though that we have piqued your curiosity about our order and Mother Mary Angelica. Allow me to take a moment to tell you about the Priory. St. Anne's was built as Hunt House, a huddle of mottled black brick and grey stone along the northeastern edge of the cemetery. It was built by Sir Charles Marten shortly after the ascent of George I, and was so named for its proximity to the Bishop's Wood, now known as Brewer's Fell. He died fifty years after, leaving the house to the Church which first fashioned it as a convalescent home for those leaving hospital, and then as an attachment to the St. Milburga's Abbey in North London. Our Sisters number twenty-nine at the moment, the eldest aged eighty-one and the youngest sixteen. To this, we add six lay workers who tend the kitchen, the refectory, the oratory, the dormitory and chapel, and the ice house; the Sisters and I tend to the chicken shed where we get our eggs, the small glass conservatory, the laundry, the garden and grounds. There is also the Prioress, may the Lord bless and protect her. And, of course, they also have me. When my strength is with me, I assist in the baking of altar breads between Matins and Lauds; these are offered up to churches throughout London. On the harder days, I join the elders in the parlour and embroider handkerchiefs, table linens and altar cloths, and help with the mending of socks and mantles and robes. One must strive to be useful in this life, and through usefulness find purpose. My loving Sister thinks I see the world queerly, and perhaps I do. While the women here are gentle with me and hold me among their number, it is at an arm's length at best: I sleep and eat alongside them; I watch them as they rise and wash their bodies, pale and freckled and soft with womanly down; I listen as they chant and pray; but I am not of their realm, not truly, nor am I of the world beyond the gate. I admit I keep a certain distance as well, and do not invest myself in their whispers and their tiny daily dramas.

Sister Catherine's face is already flushing, she knows what I'm about to tell: yesterday after Terce, one of the youngers, Eleanor, went to fetch her sewing kit and found her thimble was missing, an enameled silver bauble set with tiny white beads. Eleanor came to us a merchant's daughter, well-to-do, just turned twenty-one and twice as vain as she was pretty. She refused to surrender this token of her father's affection and now it was gone: not in the basket, not under the bed, nowhere on the floor. Vanished. An hour of wailing while the others searched the dormitory; then one of the others, Estelle, two years older and two feet taller, she came in laughing from outside to say that she had tossed it in the sluice where we all dump our chamber pots, and no doubt was on its way down to the Thames. Eleanor ran out into the morning fog in just her tunic, hurried to the sluice and combed through the clots of muck with a stick until she saw the dainty item lodged against the iron grate in the Priory wall, stopping it from sliding out and down into the gutter. She scurried back in, sobbing and sniveling, flung herself down to the cellar and into the laundry, and washed and scrubbed the filthy object as best she could. Sister Augustine, meanwhile, took Estelle by the ear, pulled her up the stairs and confined her without meals to the bedchamber that we keep aside for those who are unwell. She remains in there at this hour, and likely through the night. As if all that would not suffice, one of the kitchen girls, a rude and ruddy sort, muttered to the others about "Sister Stinkfinger." We were two twips away from a bare-knuckle brawl. None of this would have happened, of course, if the Reverend Mother was well and with us. It is in our grief and fear that our tempers flare; pettiness takes hold of our hearts, and we lower ourselves to foolishness that would be frowned upon by bone-grubbers.

I say all this to you, but to the others I say little. Sweet Catherine here has never heard me speak so much. Her eyes are wide as saucers! I keep to myself, and wisely so, and know my company is true. I am more alone here than I have ever been, yet I cannot claim to be lonely. I have never been safer than I am in here, yet my heart still quickens, seizes, at the thought of the dangers I've left behind. If you are reluctant to share the story of our Reverend Mother with the world, perhaps you would find something of interest in mine, here at the Priory or in my life before. I have come to virtue late in life. I enjoy a simple existence, and have ample time to reflect upon it. Your readers might do well to join in that reflection.

I wonder, Miss Gibson: Have I seen you at the gate, in those moments after Prime when we gather ourselves to break our fast, when the streets outside are calm and still? Have I seen you standing there, watching our windows, imagining our lives? I have caught a woman lingering there more than once these past few weeks. A smart, sharp, curious girl, perhaps from the village, imagining a life of solitude and service within these walls. Young and strong she is, cheeks aflush with the first light of dawn, a feathered green postilion perched above her auburn curls, emerald dress ruffled and pleated with a jet-black bodice, taffeta and silk, blouse clutched tight at the neck. Could this be you? Would you tell me if it was? Her soft black glove frothed with white lace at the cuff, she clasps one bar and then another, stares intently through the refectory window, strains to see inside. Fleeting figures shuffling in and out of the shadows. Is that you watching, Miss Gibson? Have you seen us? Have you seen me?

Walk worthy of the vocation wherewith you are called.

M.E.

ST. ANNE'S PRIORY
Hampstead, London

APRIL THE 29TH, 1887

Dear Miss Gibson,

A fortnight has passed since your last letter. I fear that my tone has offended you, and for this I must offer my apologies. This was certainly not my intention. I have sat and stood by the window, morning and evening, day upon day. The strong young woman has not returned to the gate, at least not that I have spied. She may well have watched us and she may have seen enough, her fancies of a cloistered life dispelled by glimpses of the dull reality: a gaggle of geese clucking and squawking as they trundle from psalms and prayers to barley soup and potato bread. I know I shouldn't talk this way, the Sisters have been very kind to me. But merely being alive is not much of a life. All that aside, it grieves me to think that I, or that we, might have frightened you off. We are barely kind to each other, no wonder they shut us up away from the likes of strangers.

Sister Catherine is here with me, as she is most days, wrinkling her nose at my rudeness and rightly so. She is delicate and fine and fair, where I am coarse and stiff like an old bristle brush. She comes to me in the afternoon between None and

Vespers to help make my words pretty for you. She thinks I was born to tell a story, and that my tales would give your readers at the Post a window through which they could observe our devotion and works of mercy. I wish I had her grace. I went for a few years to the charity school at St. George-in-the-East, near Ratcliff, where I was born and raised. My father was a butcher on the Row, and he needed me to be good with numbers and to read and write a little; to help my mother, who stood out front hawking while he worked in back salting and hanging and smoking and carving the meat. I only ever learned a little but I make use of what I did. My tender Sister has been so kind to me, and in such times of trouble. The Reverend Mother is still in care, her days are surely numbered, and we are all beside ourselves in despair. Young Estelle has left us; her nasty prank on Eleanor turned back upon her like a wave, all the youngers refused to sit with her or speak to her. Sister Eleanor remains, and has passed her silver bauble on to Sister Augustine for safekeeping. She uses a plain brass thimble like the rest of us now, every one the same as every other. Some of her vanity has been passed off as well. No longer a giggling girl, she sits alone most days, and at odd moments displays a quiet dignity. An improvement.

Have you found another avenue to pursue in your quest to unearth your murderess? I expect if we are to have newspapers then we must have them sold. Unlike the odious Lovett, I am alive and present, and would gladly unburden my soul to you if I thought it would uplift another, if only someone might listen.

I doubt you've ever been to the Row. A different world for you. I can see you in a clean corner shop, picking out a neatly trimmed joint, getting it all wrapped up in paper and tied nicely with a length of string, tucking it under your arm as you step out into the sunshine. No stink, no filth, no vermin, no screams and squeals. You can forget that something's throat was slit to make its flesh your supper.

Growing up as I did, I learned quickly about man's place in the world, and the place of all our lessers. Meat was meat, you were lucky to have it, and you didn't enquire too deeply whence it came. Life was not so precious then. Creatures lower in the natural order were beasts of burden, food on the table, and little else. They weren't to be pitied, even though they led miserable lives and met gruesome ends. They were better off dead, all things considered. At least that's what we tell ourselves.

Little went to waste in our shop. There was barely a scrap left at the end of the day, apart from what fell to the floor. Every part was good for something, from the ends of the ears to the tips of the tails, blood, gristle and bone.

Each day I would awaken well before dawn to the bleating of terrified sheep being strung up and slaughtered, to the smell of blood and muck flowing out into the gutters. My father was always hacking and sawing big hunks of mutton and beef, striding about with a whole side of cow slung over his shoulder. I would watch him pierce the slabs with massive iron hooks and hang them by the window where they swung all red and dripping into the fresh sawdust strewn across the floor. Then he would sharpen his knives, saws, cleavers and skewers, and ready the buckets and bowls to collect the offal. My mother and I would don our aprons and wash down the butcher's blocks, stained pink and slashed with deep knife cuts, and sweep the gore-soaked dust out of sight of the customers. Some mornings my mum would call for me to help her make short crust for rolls and pasties, stuffed with scraps that we had chopped and seasoned and baked into brawn. Then when we opened she would stand out front shouting the wares of the day: pork loin, side of beef, tender leg of lamb, a chant not unlike those you hear in the oratory. I'd hang back and watch her without her knowing, to see how she dealt with haggling housemaids, belligerent hawkers, drunks and beggars and thieves.

In the last few years that we had the shop, we received carcasses that had been slaughtered elsewhere, but it was not always so. When I was a child, we had a steady stream of calves, lambs and piglets through our yard and shed that my father would kill and hang and drain and skin himself, or in exchange with Mr. O'Brien, who often needed help with his chickens and geese. I would help by collecting offal, picking it up with my hands off the killing shed floor, and dropping it into tin buckets to either be cleaned and washed and ground into sausages or, if it was poor or diseased, to be fed to the other animals. It was beastly, messy, smelly work, but I accustomed to it soon enough. I do recall one time, though, when I was just seven or eight years old, my father was in the shed with a stout young finishing pig, a thrasher and a biter. He was in the pen kicking and squealing and sending the other animals into a frenzy. My father shouted and I came running. He held the pig tight by the neck while I slid under and around and pulled the rope harness tight over his front legs, then up around the back of his head. He grabbed the rope and hoisted the creature about a foot in the air while I held its back legs still. He then tucked a blood bucket between its legs, grabbed his long, thin knife, and slashed the animal across its throat. The pig screeched once more as the blood spewed onto my hands and into the bucket. I still remember how it steamed in the freezing shed, the stench and the thickness of it. Once the animal was finally still, I wrung the blood off my hands into the bucket and then went into the back of the shop to wash myself while my father tied the hind legs together and raised the carcass onto a hook for skinning and gutting. I caught a glimpse of my reflection on the side of a kettle. I looked like a mad murderous fiend: I raised my hands and clutched my fingers like claws, bared my teeth and growled, leaning in towards my distorted face, then giggled, having scared myself. My father hired Ned soon after, the O'Brien boy, as he was six years older than me and better suited for such things. I was very proud of myself though, that I had been so helpful when my father needed me. I would spy on Ned from time to time and watch my father teach him how to tie and stun and hang and bleed and split and dress an animal, things I already knew. It was only much later, once I was with the Sisters, that I thought back about the death we delivered to so many innocent creatures.

Life can end at any moment, for any of us. Cut short in one of a thousand ways. It can be cruel or merciful, painful or peaceful. Sometimes we choose our ending, oftentimes we can't. If you had to choose your own end, Miss Gibson, what would it be? Do you believe in a divine saviour, like the Sisters around me? What sort of end does each of us deserve? Are we judged ultimately by all we've done in this life? I have considered these questions myself, and don't yet have a good answer. This is that strangeness that Sister Catherine sees in me. I want to know my heart, yet there are times when it feels like it is wrapped in thistles and thorns, impossible to touch.

Another day comes to mind, not so different from the ones before. I would have been just sixteen. I was out in front with Mum, selling chops and sausages, shooing away boys carrying sacks of onions and potatoes. Already carriages crowded the street, their muddy horses riding shoulder to shoulder with mere inches between their clattering wheels. The rhythmic clopping of their hooves blended with the cries of the costermongers and their rumbling carts. Cross sweepers and newsboys wound their way through the crowds of pedestrians streaming in every direction. Skinny, mangy dogs nosed through heaps of guts and refuse. The sky hung low and grey over the crooked rooftops, spitting and grumbling. A trio of gulls wheeled and soared above us, seeking out scraps to fight over, their cries scraping at our ears.

I saw it out the corner of my eye—a child, a boy, rushed out of one of the shops next over and chased a ball into the street. Quick as a flash, knocked to the ground, trampled by a carriage horse, pulled under the wheel, the screams, the screams were terrible. My mother and I, we were right there, we were the first to reach him. He was nearly a baby, just three or four years old. Not dead, thank God, but his leg was crushed and the bone-flecked blood poured out like water. We pushed our way through the gathering crowd, lifted and carried the boy into the shop, back to where my father was. A half-dozen men rushed in with us, jostling my mother as she waved back the women and the children and hurried back to the street to keep the thieves at bay. The tallest man, with a silk top hat and frock coat and silver-crowned cane, he was the one who had followed from the carriage, his face was as grey as the scarf around his neck.

My father had slaughtered countless lambs and calves, but when he had to save this screaming boy, he froze, he could not make a move. I hollered for him to hold the boy down on the wide wooden table while I tore a strip of waxed linen from the roll and tied it round his leg above the knee, pulled it tight and tighter still. The boy was bucking and thrashing, the tall man from the carriage pressed forward to join us, he stood with my father and held the boy down. I took the flesh-choked meat saw from the sink, wiped it across my apron, jumped up on the table and, with one knee on his ankle, I dug the metal teeth into his flesh and dragged and pulled with all my might, six long hard strokes, until I felt the bone give way and the flesh tear off with a snap. At last, the boy was silent. Had I killed him? No, he was breathing still, eyes wide, trembling, in another world from our own. Behind me, someone spewed their breakfast on the floor. I called out for another square of waxen cloth, a length of twine. I wrapped the oozing stump like a mutton shank, leapt off and cried, "Hospital! Hurry!" My heart was pounding half out of my chest. The tall man seized the boy from the table, cradled him against his chest, and flew through the shop and out into his carriage, which roared through the street as if chased by the devil. The crowd untangled and withdrew. My father showed more emotion in that moment than he ever had. He wasn't one for crying—no Englishman is. But he let out a heavy, hard, guttural sound. I realised he had choked back a sob, and turned away so no one could see his face. I stood there, staring at him, unable to speak, unable to comfort him. I raised a blood-crusted hand to touch him, but then thought better of it. He would not want to be comforted by me; it would humiliate him. I turned instead to the sink, plunged my hands into the pinkish water, scrubbed them clean, then wiped them dry on my apron. They were ruddy and raw and blistered and sore from the work I had done, but alive. So alive.

I turned round and saw the boy's severed leg on the table, blackened and oozing. So did my father. "Take that round the back," he said quietly. I stripped off the tattered pants cloth and the single bloodied shoe and tossed them into the bin by the sink. I knew by dusk the dogs would have it. Meat was meat, after all, and they were none too picky about where it came from. What luck for them.

Two days later, the tall man returned, on foot this time. He took my mother aside and told her that the boy had died on their way to the infirmary. Despite our efforts, he had lost too much blood. He had likely been doomed from the start. The man thanked and commended us, then proffered his card and told my mother that, if at any time I sought a servant's position in a fine household, he wished to have me come and work with him. For he was a physician, north of the city, and was often in need of help in the kitchen and perhaps in his office as well. He turned the card over and drew a strange symbol, an eye enclosed within a triangle, then told us to take it to any cabman stationed at the corner of Commercial Road; whomever we asked would take us direct to Highgate without charge. Surprised and saddened at the news of the boy, my mother curtsied, bid him good day, and placed the card under the foot of the counter scale. It remained there for one year, until I turned seventeen, when we found ourselves with an urgent need to make use of it.

I do remember wondering that night, as I lay in my bed: If he was a physician, why hadn't he helped us? Why hadn't he helped me? Why did he just hold the boy down and watch?

It is time. We have been called to prayer. Gloria Patri, et Filio, et Spiritui Sancto. I do hope I will hear from you soon.

M.E.

Miss Gibson: I believe your father is Sir Hadley Gibson? The Reverend Mother was taken by his generosity toward the less fortunate. I will hold you both in my heart. Your servant in Christ. —Sr. C

From the London Evening Post

MAY 6, 1887   10 PAGES   {ONE HALFPENNY

PRIORESS DEAD.
BELOVED NUN PASSES AWAY

London, England: A beautiful, saintly life ended at the London Free Hospital, Friday evening, 5th May. We are joined in grief at the passing of Mother Mary Angelica, 71, Prioress of St. Anne's. We know that the Reverend Mother, in her gentle humility, would, if she could, forbid this loving testament to her memory. But, in our deep sorrow, we must allow ourselves a few words in tribute. Truly one of "God's chosen" on earth, we confidently know she is with Him now in Heaven. She is fondly remembered for her kind, inexhaustive patience; devotion to her Sisters; and dedication to the betterment of the less fortunate. On the grievous night she was taken from us, she was struck down breathless after evening prayers. Despite the finest care these past four weeks, she has found her rest in God. May perpetual light shine upon her, O Lord. The well-attended funeral procession was held at St. Mary's Church, Hampstead, headed by the children of the London Oratory School, dressed in white with mourning scarves, on Saturday morning following the Requiem Mass. Canon Arthur Purcell officiated, attended by the Rev. J. Evans of Archbishop's House, Dundee; the brother of the deceased; and a large group of priests and nuns. Sincere and warm condolences are still offered daily to the melancholy community of St Anne's; many are mourning with them from outside the Priory walls. Let our anguished hearts take comfort in the presence of our Lord. Blessed be His name. Amen.

ST. ANNE'S PRIORY
Hampstead, London

MAY THE 7TH, 1887

Dear Miss Gibson,

We were touched to receive your note expressing your condolences for the passing of the Reverend Mother from our earthly realm. It truly is a tragedy, but at least she suffers no longer and has found her peace with Our Heavenly Father. The Sisters are overwhelmed with grief, and their mourning suffuses every aspect of our lives in the Priory. They will observe forty days of fasting and continuous prayer, and then will return to their regular offices on the 15th of June, when we will observe the Feast of St. Vitus.

Did I detect your subtle hand in the phrasing of the notice in the Evening Post? It was most generous and kind. As was true of my own mother, Sister Augustine's strength is not in disquisition but in compassion. "Let us not love in word, neither in tongue; but in deed and in truth" (John 3:18). I was pleased as well to receive the card you left at the funeral service at St. Mary's. It was with great sorrow that I could not attend. I was asked to remain at the Priory to help with the duties that the Sisters were unable to perform while in mourning. I am glad that you are interested in maintaining our correspondence, and that my insights into the history of hardships of Londoners in the East End may be illuminating to your readers. Sister Catherine's availability is limited at the moment; she and I will meet in the early hours before she begins her vigil or during the brief respite when she takes her afternoon meal.

These last few days of profound sadness have reminded me of my father's death. It will be fifty years this June, just before Victoria ascended the throne. It was a terrible time, one that tore apart our family irreparably. I cannot fault him, nor my mother. We suffered a series of grave circumstances and navigated them as best we could but, well, I will try to tell the story in a way that will spare Sister Catherine some of the harsher aspects of his demise while remaining truthful to the plight in which we found ourselves.

It was not unusual for men to die at such an age, forty-eight as I recall, but the manner was unexpected. No doubt you'll think it was consumption or cholera, but in fact it was an injury due to his trade. He had always been careful with his knives and saws, and only ever weathered a nick or two, which healed quickly and with little pain; however, on the day I'm picturing now, a cleaver slipped while he was slicing through a side of lamb, and he gashed the fleshy web of his hand between the thumb and index finger. It was a deep, clean cut which immediately began to bleed, more heavily than either my mother or I noticed and that he was willing to disclose. I was at the sink with my back to him, I heard him curse when the blade sank into his flesh. He dropped the cleaver, I turned and saw him squeezing his hand, his blood mixing together with that of the carcass he was breaking down. I could see he wanted to keep working and I thought he would, but instead he took up a length of cloth and wrapped it around his hand very tightly. However, a moment later, a crimson bloom soaked through the fabric. I shouted for my mother and she peered into the back, confused. She thought I was the one who had been injured. When she saw the rag on my father's hand, now sopping and dripping onto the floor, the colour drained from her face leaving her pale and gaunt as a ghost. She told me to take over the counter where a clutch of customers waited, some of them impatiently. She wiped her hands down her apron and hurried towards him.

"A nick is all," he grumbled before she could speak. "Never mind me, Clara. Take care of the customers." He spoke with such briskness my mother couldn't argue. He called to young Ned, across the shop, "Finish with that mutton, eh? I'll be back as soon as I give it a wash." He left through the back with a slam, and I heard his heavy boots upon the stairs as he climbed up to our rooms above. I imagined him sitting down on the edge of the bed he shared with my mother, the bedsprings groaning under his weight, then examining the wound and cursing some more. Perhaps he had a jug of water that he splashed over it, made a tourniquet to staunch the bleeding. I have no doubt he was infuriated by his situation. We had meat to butcher and customers to serve.

He returned to the shop half an hour later, wearing a heavy leather glove on his left hand, one of the pair he wore for wood chopping. I could see folds of wet bloody fabric peeking out the bottom of it. He fumbled his knives a bit, it was awkward cutting the meat like that. I knew he'd rather die than admit he couldn't keep working, and he wasn't one to stand back and bark orders at others. I caught his eye and he scowled at me, then turned his face away. He didn't want to seem weak to me a second time. He pushed through the rest of the day until the shop door closed, and if splashes of his blood mingled on the table with that of the carcasses he split and dressed with Ned, well, we had much worse things to worry about.

That night, as Mum put the kettle on the stove to make a pot of tea, she turned and reached for his hand: "Tobias. Let me see it. Please." I thought he would wave her away with his usual bravado, but instead he slipped off the glove, wincing, unspooled the red-stained fabric from the base of his thumb, and held it out to her. She gasped, and my eyes went wide, when we saw how deep and wet it was, wet and red like a baby's mouth and, all those hours later, still bleeding. He shuddered a little, from pain or fear or from the sight of the wound. It didn't matter which; he knew, and we knew, just how bad this could be.

My mother grabbed her shawl from the nearby chair, draped it around her shoulders. "Father, keep your hand wrapped and rest by the fire. And make the tea, will you, Meg? I'll be back before the clock strikes." I saw her slip a few coins in her pocket.

"Where are you going?" I asked her. It was getting late and growing dark. Soon it would be too late for a woman to be out alone.

"I'm going to fetch a doctor." She knotted her bonnet under her chin. I cringed at the thought of my father protesting but instead he sat in silence. We watched her leave and I heard her boots patter down the stairs, much lighter and faster than my father's had been.

A doctor. Did she mean the physician from Highgate? I shook the thought from my head—that was impossible, he was much too far away, ten miles by cab at the least. She would have to settle for someone nearby and that was a frightful thought. Still, we had little choice. I bustled about the kitchen, my hands trembling as I filled the kettle with water and put it on the stove to boil. My father watched me move to and fro like a metronome, then closed his eyes. He was glistening with sweat. I feared he would faint and fall to the floor. I measured out a spoonful of leaves and dropped them into the old tin teapot. Pushing the curtains aside that overlooked the road, I watched the lamplighter move from post to post, discomfited when tears blurred my vision. I turned away and poured the water into the pot, and as it steeped, allowed myself a glance in my father's direction. His head was tipped back against the wall and his breathing was ragged. I doubt he even knew I was with him.

Again, there were boots on the stairs, and the murmuring of my mother's voice, answered by one with a deeper resonance. She threw the door open and hurried into the room, followed by a stooped older man leaning on a cane. His features sagged as though he was made of wax and had stood too close to a fire. Greying hair sprouted from his ears, and the buttons down the front of his coat strained against his bulging belly. He wore a shabby top hat and carried a small leather bag. His nose was red, and not from the evening chill. Three cooling cups of tea sat on the table next to the old tin pot. I hardly remembered pouring them. The clock struck nine, a harsh clanging sound, and my father stirred at last. He looked around slowly, vaguely. His face was flushed and shiny, and he was shivering slightly. All bad signs.

The doctor gingerly lifted my father's beefy hand, turning it over and back again, squinting at the laceration. He put the back of his hand to my father's forehead. "There's a fever here." He pushed his hand into his pocket and pulled out a small brown glass bottle. It was laudanum. "He'll need that for pain," he said to my mother as he set it on the table. "A surgeon is required to stitch that hand up. We must take him to the hospital." A noxious cloud of gin wafted from his mouth as he spoke, and I noticed a small egg stain on his sleeve.

"I've got to be back at work tomorrow," my father slurred, meek as a lamb. "I can't close up the shop. Fix it." He held out his gashed hand. "Please."

The doctor puffed his cheeks out. He knew he wasn't sober enough. We all knew, I think. "I've done a stitch or two in my time," he said, "but never on such a wound as that."

"I'll pay you extra," my mother said. Her eyes were so pleading and desperate, I had to look away. I couldn't bear it. Then I thought of the small tin of coins I had been saving to buy a new bonnet. I feared I'd be throwing it away for the same result, but I couldn't help myself.

"I've got money," I blurted. Before anyone else could speak I rushed into my bedroom to retrieve the tin I had stashed beneath my bed frame. It was an Indian tea tin, yellow and orange, with an image of an elephant led across the sands by a man with a scarf wrapped round his head. I forced the lid off and tipped the money into my hand.

When I returned to the kitchen the doctor and my parents were just as I had left them, frozen with worry. "Here," I said, offering the coins to the doctor. He gazed at the pennies and shillings on my palm. I hoped the gaslight made them shine a bit, to tempt him.

"No, Meg, you can't," my father barked. "That's yours what you earned in the shop. How could I let my child pay for my own foolishness?" But he looked even weaker, if that was possible, his eyes struggling to stay open. Beads of sweat lined his upper lip. I had never seen him like this.

"Please, Doctor," I said, tears welling in my eyes again. I shook the coins lightly. "He's a proud man, a strong man. He needs to work. We don't have time to take him to hospital and wait a week for him to get better. And we can't close the shop."

The doctor sighed. "Give us a shot of gin, then," he said. He looked at my mother keenly. Her eyes narrowed. I thought he meant for my father, but she knew he intended to drink it himself. She turned, pulled open one of the cupboard doors, and reached into the back. Glass and crockery clinked together. She pulled out half a bottle of pale yellow liquid that I'd always been told not to touch, and a small white enamel cup that was chipped around the edges.

The doctor gave himself a generous pour of the alcohol and tossed it back in one go. He winced, wiped his lips on the sleeve of his coat and reached into his bag. After riffling through it he emerged with a dirty vial of catgut and a large needle in a case. It looked like the ones my mother used to darn socks. "We'll need a stick," he said to my mother. "For your husband to clench between his teeth."

My mother fetched a wooden spoon and held it up to my father's mouth. "Bite that as hard as you can, Tobias," she said. "And close your eyes." The doctor squinted as he threaded the needle. My mother turned away and crossed the room, then stood at the window I had looked out of moments before. She tried to stay silent, but we could all hear her weeping.

My heart was pounding in my ears. I was frightened for my father, but I was also curious about what the doctor was going to do. I moved closer and peered over his shoulder. "More light, girl," he said. I took the oil lamp off the table and held it above my father's hand, as close as I dared. I could easily imagine my father slapping it away and starting a fire.

"Hang on, my good man," the doctor said. "I'll do it as quick as I can."

I watched, slightly sickened but also enthralled, as the doctor forced the needle through the fleshy part of my dad's hand. My father grimaced and threw his head back, gripping the wooden spoon so hard between his teeth I feared it would crack. The doctor pushed the needle in and out five times till he had made a crooked seam. He snipped off the end of the catgut, took the spoon from between my father's clenched teeth. The straw-coloured thread stuck out gruesomely against my father's flesh. A trickle of greenish pus and blood had begun to ooze from between the stitches, the skin around the wound inflamed and hot to the touch. The doctor gestured towards the laudanum. I brought it to him and he gave my father a few droplets on his tongue. His forehead and cheeks were red and shining with sweat. His breathing was harsh and shallow. My mother returned to his side, making soothing sounds and brushing her hand through his damp hair. I had never seen her be so tender with him. With anyone. I gave the doctor my handful of coins, and the rest of the bottle, and led him to the door and down the stairs and out into the thickening, darkening night.

Of course, the shop never reopened and my father never recovered. He lay in the bed for hours, slick with sweat and racked with fever, his breath ripe and sickly sweet like fruit on the turn, and then he slipped away just as the clock struck noon. Blood poisoning, the doctor said, when he returned to make the pronouncement. A terrible death. A mercy he passed so quickly.

The following day, the butchers and their wives all came to pay their respects, crowding into our small rooms in the late evenings, after they had closed their shops. The undertaker and his assistant came by early the next morning to carry him away, wrapping his limp body in a linen shroud and gently depositing him into a rudely crafted pine box, then loading him into the back of a cheap hearse, a grim black cart on wobbling wheels, drawn by a single horse.

Fortunately, my father had paid a penny a week to a burial club for several years, which entitled him to as grand a funeral anyone in the East End could hope for, including an elm-wood casket ornamented with punched tin corners and a cross on its face, and a stone with his name upon it for the graveyard. Loving father and husband.

The service took place on a sunless Sunday, grey and dull and leached of colour. My father was to be buried at St. Mary's in Whitechapel, on the high street not far from our shop. The small, cramped churchyard at St. Mary's was already crammed with the dead, sometimes two or three to a plot, but there was nowhere else to put him. It had rained in the early hours and the air was ripe with coal smoke and the smell of the mouldering dead. How eerie it was to see the majestic stallion emerge from the haze, with two rows of solemn butchers in their finest suits trudging alongside the glass-sided hearse.

My mother had bought herself a mourning gown made of Albert crape, black as pitch with not a hint of shine to it, ruched across the bosom and gathered simply at the waist, with nary a ribbon nor a bow nor a sash. We could not afford a new dress for me, so instead my mother took my best frock, a pale blue wool with fine white stripes, and had it dyed black by a dressmaker. The damp in the air made the wool clammy and heavy, and the sleeves stained my wrists like soot.

As my father's coffin passed by, carried by the men whose shops were closest to ours, she wept into a black lace handkerchief that she threw into his grave as the first clots of dirt were thrown into it. The sky gave a growl, and flung a few droplets at us as a warning. By the time our carriages returned to the Row, the rain was pelting down and we hurtled ourselves through the doors of the shop. Ned was there, as was Millie from across the way, and they had set out a small feast, two chickens and a well-trimmed shoulder of mutton, a stew of barley and carrots and parsnips, two loaves of still-warm bread and a seed cake from the baker around the corner on Ratcliff Cross. Millie forced Mum to sit on a chair near the stove while she and Ned and I served the guests, filling plates and bowls and setting out pitchers of punch and pots of hot tea. Everything was borrowed from one place or another, but no one seemed to mind. Once everyone was inside, the room fell to a hush and all eyes turned to my mother, wanting her to say something. Her tears, which had stopped ever so briefly, began to flow again. "Go on, love," she said to me, and gave me a tiny nudge. I stepped up onto a little stool we kept behind the counter to reach the top shelves, and I cleared my throat and spoke.

"My father was a good man," I said. "A strong man," I added, looking from face to face around the room. "The strongest I've ever known. He worked hard, he was honest. Butchery is a rough job but it needs to be done, and there was none as clean and quick as he was. He stood with everyone here on the Row. I never much heard him complain, except maybe to God, and only because he knew God would keep his thoughts to himself. He liked a drop of gin. He liked a good cigar when he could get one. He loved us, my mother and me. He loved the Row. People don't live too long here, the work wrings it out of you. And once you're gone, you're gone. But it's a good life while you've got it. If he was here, he would thank you for all you've done for him, for our shop and for our family, and for coming to visit today." I looked back at my mother who nodded, wiping at her eyes with her handkerchief. I realised then that mine were dry. I had shed no tears, had held back no sobs. I loved my father, I mourned his loss, but it was as if my grief was outside my body, a phantom that walked alongside me with a hand upon my shoulder. Ned reached up to help me down from the stool. I thanked him and moved back to my mother's side.

One by one the guests stepped up to share their quiet remembrances of our father, with Mr. O'Brien, Ned's father, at the last. He said something close to my mother's ear. I couldn't hear it but I could see it. "Time to go." She nodded, her tears catching the firelight and glistening as the room grew darker. What did he mean? I couldn't ask, not then. He and Ned departed, and so did the rest of the others. I locked the door behind them, helped my mother up to her bed. I noticed as we passed that the card for the physician whose carriage had injured the boy was now out on the counter. It had been many months since I'd last seen it. I remembered the doctor's interest in having me come to work for him, and knew then that we would be calling upon him the following day. All that I knew of my life would be changed, and perhaps not for the better.

For now, we will know this man only as Dr. C, as his identity must be held in strictest confidence.

Augustine has scurried in. She has asked for Sister Catherine to join her. It seems a doctor has come with a constable and they're scratching around in the Reverend Mother's quarters, searching for something. For what, they haven't said. I'm frightened to think what they'll find.

Let Him be our refuge and our shield,

M.E.

I have seen you. I know I have. I know it is you at the gate.
I hope you are reading this. I have put these words down with no help.
I have left them outside the wall for you.
Please see this. Please.

No one will tell you but the Reverend Mother killed herself. They found a note and a bottle of poison in a locked drawer in her room.
Eleanor's thimble is gone. I am frightened.
I am a prisoner here. Someone pays to keep me here.

Do not tell this to anyone.
Do not say anything in your letters to me.
They read everything. They watch me.

Miss Gibson, please, you must help me.
    You must find my son.

POST OFFICE DIRECTORY OFFICE.

16th of May, 1887   Post Office Directory Office
                                     51, Great Queen Street,
                                     Lincoln's Inn Fields

Dear Miss Gibson,

Thank you for your recent enquiry. We have consulted the Street, Commercial and Trade Directories for the period you have requested. We do have a listing for Evans, Tobias Giles, butcher, 14 Butcher Row, Ratcliff, in 1820; it seems he remains there until at least 1837. In 1838 the shop changes hands and remains in the possession of a poulter, O'Brien, Edward, until approximately 1846, at which point it is taken over by McLean, Norman, owner of the Turk's Head Public House, 2 Butcher Row, as a beer and wine merchant. We have no listing for Evans, Tobias, after 1840, nor is there another Evans listed in Ratcliff, Limehouse, Whitechapel or St. George-in-the-East.

Further, we unfortunately do not have any records for a Mrs. Evans or a daughter, either at the Butcher Row address or at any other, nor do we have any listings for gentlemen or ladies by the name of Lovett. If Mrs. Evans took over her husband's shop, it could not have been for very long.

Finally, we found several doctors in Highgate and Hampstead during the years you have noted, as well as a number of surgeons. (You did say that the gentleman in question was described as a doctor?) Of those whose surnames began with C, we found Dr. Ian Carstairs, who lived on Hampstead Lane at No. 17, but he died in 1840, just after the dates you mention. I have no account of a wife or children; the house changed hands directly after his death. Dr. Noel Cavanaugh was at 18 Jackson's Lane. He continued his practice until 1868; the house was demolished two years later. He may still live somewhere in Highgate, or perhaps in London, if indeed he lives at all. He would be quite old at this point.

We do hope that this has been of some use in your research. Please let us know if we can assist you in any other way.

Yours sincerely,

Martin Padgett

MAY THE 21ST, 1887

Dear Miss Gibson,

My apologies for the abrupt conclusion to my last letter. As I mentioned, a police constable and a doctor who cared for the Reverend Mother whilst she was in hospital came to investigate her quarters. They had developed the suspicion that she had taken her own life, with poison, a horrific suggestion that none of us could bear to contemplate. They forced the lock on the cupboard at the side of her writing desk, and there they found a small vial of cyanide and a handwritten note, in which the Reverend Mother, may God have mercy upon her, confessed to a life of thievery and deception, perverted lust and treachery. The list of whorish activities to which she confessed would scald your eyes and ears. It was in this note that she made clear her intention to bring an end to her sinful life to prevent the contamination of her licentiousness from reaching the rest of the order. She sold Sister Eleanor's thimble in order to pay for the poison.

As you may expect, these revelations shattered the Sisters of St. Anne's who had already been consumed with grief, offering up their prayers for weeks on end in hopes of healing Mother Mary Angelica's body, and elevating her soul. However, on this, the Scripture is clear: there is no hope of Heaven for those who curse in the face of God and take the lives that he has so generously given them. The poor woman is damned to the darkest of the black pits and is enveloped in the fiercest of fires, and there is naught we can do to help her. We have abandoned our forty days of mourning. She is better forgotten. We can only turn our prayers inward, silently, for His Mercy, and her eventual peace. Please join us in these prayers, if you can, and hold her with love in your heart despite her grievous transgressions. We are all the wayward children of the Lord and to the Lord alone we entrust our final judgement.

Sister Catherine and I are heartened that the tale of my dark and tumultuous past continues to be fascinating and illuminating for you. She is seated next to me, poor soul, and is taking down my words as best she can. She was the one who found the poor Reverend Mother collapsed on the floor of her office. She asks that we be patient with her, and I know you would gladly grant that patience knowing what sorrow she suffers.

In a terrible coincidence, our last letter to you was about my father's terrible death, and my mother's fateful decision to leave the shop and to dispatch me to work for the physician in Highgate. Mum woke me so early that morning that I opened my eyes into darkness and wondered if it was a dream. Had my father really died? Were we really to leave the shop, leave the whole Row behind? I asked her and she confirmed that, yes, it was all true, and that we were to take advantage of the physician's kind offer if he was still able to have me. As I lay there, I couldn't keep myself from wondering about what new life awaited me. A strange house, so far away from where I had grown up, with people I'd never met. A mysterious gentleman who knew of me only what he had seen when I was struggling to save a child's life. I had no education, no fancy manners; I had never lived in a proper house, a house with servants. I had no experience maiding for anyone either. Working in a butcher's shop was all I knew: hanging sausages, wrapping chops in brown paper, taking money from customers and counting out change, and, towards the end, helping my father dress and carve a lamb for Easter, a few piglets and calves, and prepare some smaller cuts of meat to particular customers' tastes. How would I go from having my arms up to the elbow in offal to being a kitchen maid in a doctor's house? It seemed almost impossible.

I sat up, still bleary-eyed, then threw back my scratchy grey blanket and forced myself out of the bed. The room was bright and bare. I scarcely had time to wash and dress before we had to be out the door. Mum was sitting at the kitchen table in her mourning dress, black linen shawl and bonnet, a fine lace veil streaming down the side of her face. Her case sat at her feet. She barely looked at me. She gestured at a couple of biscuits she had saved for my breakfast. They were gone in an instant; I'm not sure that I even chewed them. I wondered how I would make it to the doctor's house. It was at least two hours away by carriage. As if she had heard my thoughts, or more likely my growling stomach, she spoke. "We'll stop at Covent Garden on the way and get you a pie to carry you through." Covent Garden! I hadn't been since my fifth Christmas. I remembered it as a magical place. How different would it be now, without the eyes of a child?

I tugged on my wool cloak and bonnet. I see now that after my father died my mother had to do something with her life. And I had to do something with mine. I wasn't a child anymore, it was time to fend for myself. But I was furious that my fate had been chosen for me. "Why can't we keep the shop?" I asked her. If we couldn't run it, why couldn't we lease it and keep living upstairs? Were we not the owners?

"Don't be silly, Meg," she answered. "It's not ours to keep." I realised as soon as she said it that, yes, we were not the owners. It was Mr. O'Brien who owned the shop, Ned's father, the poulter up the Row from us. The shop, and the flat above it. I had seen my father passing money to him, and my mother asking for help with one repair or another. And after the funeral, I had seen him whisper to my mother: "Time to go." I had thought he was my father's friend, but in fact, he was our landlord. We had been paying him rent all this time. And Ned—Ned had come as a butcher's boy, had learned what he could from my father, and now the shop would belong to him and his family. There would be no women in the shop who were not married to the men.

My mother's voice interrupted my thoughts. "We have to leave, Meg. Mr. O'Brien will be round soon." We carried our bags up to the cab station at the end of the block, on Commercial Road. My mother took the physician's card from her purse and showed it to the first cabman she saw. He glanced at it, turned it over, nodded, gestured for us to enter. He didn't jump down from his bench to help us, but watched as we climbed into the cab and slammed the door shut. We put our cases down by our feet. The space was so cramped I knew my legs would fall asleep by the time we reached Highgate. I glanced out the window at the street, at the shop. I hadn't realised that our farewell meal for my father had been a farewell for us as well. The cab lurched forward and I grabbed onto my seat, struggling not to cry.

A physician's house. I had never been in one. I had never thought about working for anyone other than a butcher, and only ever for my father. But I remembered in Covent Garden there had been a sweet shop, and from time to time I pictured myself running one just like it. A little sweet shop where I would sell candied fruit, jelly-babies, sugar mice and toffees in twists of coloured paper. Children would come in with coins pressed into their sweaty palms. They would point to the sweets they wanted in the gleaming glass jars, and I would scoop them into little brown paper bags. I might even give an extra one now and then, if a child was very good.

A child shrieked in one of the alleys, and the cab lurched in and out of a pothole. A vision of the bleeding boy ran through my mind like a bolt of lightning. The vision of my sweet shop vanished.

"What is it like to work as a kitchen maid, Mum? Do you think they'll be happy with me?"

She glanced at me and turned back to the window. A tear glinted in the corner of her eye. "I'm sure you'll be a very good maid, Meg. You're young and strong and you do what you're told. Not afraid to work in the muck if that's what needs doing. I think they'll be very happy with you."

The muck. Off in the distance, a church bell rang out six o'clock. The city was still asleep, except for thieves, and cabmen, and the men who kept coffee stalls in the heart of the city, their braziers glowing orange in the darkness. I leaned my head against the window and watched my breath bloom and recede on the glass as we rattled onto the Ratcliff Highway.

"Why can't I come with you to Leeds to stay with Aunt Lillian?" I asked.

This time she didn't turn her head at all, she just stared rigidly out the window. "They haven't the room," she said quietly. "They barely have space for me. Please, let's not talk about it. There's nothing more to say." She reached her hand out to me blindly, and I took it and held it tight.

The highway was all but empty. The shops along the streetsides were still shuttered and dark, the old buildings sagging against one other for support. A man smoking a pipe leaned against a burnt brick wall, a shadow in the shadows between two glowing streetlamps. He barely noted our presence.

When we rolled past the docks, I saw a line of men dressed in fustian trousers and jackets, smoking and shuddering, breathing warmth into their hands, waiting for a chance to be given day work. The line snaked far down the street. Each was as still and quiet as he would have been standing alone. Why be friendly with someone who might take a day's pay away from you? Behind the warehouses, the lightening sky was pierced with the masts of hundreds of ships gently bobbing on the dark water, and the air was ripe with the smells of tobacco, rich coffee and exotic spices. Between the warehouse buildings, I could see slivers of the Thames beyond, slick and dark and pungent. "People have died in there," my mother always cautioned. My father would grunt and nod in agreement, then sip from his cup of tea. A policeman raised his lantern in the gloom to watch us pass, his eyes locking with mine. I shivered.

We passed the ancient Tower of London, the White Tower at its heart looming over the rings of fortified walls, and turned onto Lower Thames Street, where the rank smell of fish and salty water stung our noses. We rocked and rattled down towards Billingsgate Market, a cluster of booths and sheds sloping from the street down to the river. Already it was teeming with crowds of grubby fishermen and fishwives lugging baskets and carts laden with scaly goggle-eyed creatures of every description, and haggling noisily with costermongers who were barking out their wares.

Before long we were at London Bridge, which was a mighty sight, outstretched from one bank to the other with boats of every shape and size ducking in and out of the arches below. Although the day had just begun, the deck was thick with carriages and carts and droving animals. Soon it would be hopelessly clogged, threatening to come to a standstill. I wondered how anyone was meant to get through. I looked back at my mother. She and I had barely spoken. Her leg was pressed against mine, her warmth and presence a comfort to me, as mine perhaps was to her. I thought, then tried not to think, that this might be the last time that I would see her. She glanced at me and gave a sad smile, and I wondered, not for the first time, what was going through her mind. I knew she missed my father terribly, and that his sudden death had been a shock. Her drawn face was ghostly pale against the faintly dusty black of her mourning bonnet.

"Don't worry, my girl," she said, giving my knee a gentle pat. "It'll be all right, you'll see." I half-wondered if she was reassuring herself more than me. I wanted to give her a small smile back, but I couldn't muster one. I placed my hand on hers for a moment; she slid hers out from under and coughed into her glove, then dropped her hand back into her lap. After a moment, I withdrew mine. I wanted to cry—tried to will myself to cry—but no tears would come. I was numb from all that had happened, from all that was about to happen. It was sit still and be silent, or scream and scream and scream.

When I allowed myself to look back out the window, I saw that we had turned away from London Bridge and its seething swarm of carts and carriages and crowds, and now were heading up to Cheapside, but the traffic was not much better. As we merged onto the wide thoroughfare, several roads converged and brought yet another stream of carriages, cabs, dray carts and omnibuses thundering in from every direction. Shutters rattled down from the fronts of the shops, revealing jewellers and watchmakers, tailors, stationers and silk merchants. I saw an elegant millinery with an assortment of silk and velvet bonnets trimmed with ribbons and feathers, and imagined my fantastical sweet shop nestled in next to it.

The sun was beginning to peep over the city's rooftops, and the forest of chimneys that stretched in every direction were coughing columns of black smoke into the sky. Despite the gloomy surroundings, the lead-covered dome of St. Paul's Cathedral shone like a paragon over the teeming streets below. We traversed Fleet Street, rattling past its banking houses, taverns and inns, gin palaces and public houses. I struggled to take it all in. Pedestrians of every sort now clogged the pavements and the narrow spaces between the thronging vehicles.

Our progress halted abruptly amidst a burst of shouts as

we approached Covent Garden, the streets surrounding the market blocked by rows of farmers with donkey-carts stacked with piles of papery onions, deep green cabbages and bright orange carrots, and barrows filled with strawberries, red apples and plums—things we rarely saw on the Row. Men with towering piles of baskets on their heads marched through the crowds, and women with enormous wicker hampers on their backs frothing with colourful blooms trudged towards the steps of St. Paul's where they would sell their biedermeiers, posies and nosegays.

Just outside the colonnade, I spotted a man with a cart which had a painted tin sign fastened to its front. Wm Thomas—Champion Pie Maker. "Two pies for tuppence!" he bellowed. "Fresh meat pies! Hot, hot! All hot!"

My hunger returned like a sudden sharp pain. I turned to look at my mother just as she turned to look at me. I hoped that she remembered her promise. She glanced down at her little purse, opened it, took two pennies out and pressed them into my palm. "Get us one each."

Just as I poked out my head to call to our driver, a farmer struggling with his overloaded cart of potatoes pulled out in front of us, blocking our way. Our carriage bounced to a stop as our horse snorted and squealed in protest.

"Please, sir, please!" I shouted up to the cabman, then clambered out of the carriage, ran up and told him I was going to grab a pie, and that I'd be quick.

He shrugged. "We ain't movin' anyway." He brought out a flask from under his coat and took a long swig.

I raced towards the pie man, weaving through the crowds

flowing in and out of the market. Ladies in lively frocks and gentlemen in chestnut-brown suits strolled amongst street merchants, labourers and feral children begging for food and coins.

As I moved closer, the pie man spied me and smiled, recognizing the ravenous expression on my face. I saw he had a charcoal brazier to keep his pies hot. The smoke stung my eyes, but the smell of peppery gravy and onions pulled me closer as if I were mesmerised.

I handed him my two pennies. "Two kidney pies, please." He reached into his hot can with his bare hands, blistered and calloused, and pulled out the two steaming treats, one in each fist, their crusts as thick as crockery pots. He handed me a greasy paper to wrap them in, then turned his eyes back to the crowd. "Hot pies, hot pies," he shouted behind me as I turned back towards the cab. The smell of those pies made my knees wobble. Poor Sister Catherine and I are practically salivating as we write this.

I made my way back across the street, dodging hawkers and beggars and dogs. Mother swung the carriage door open for me just as the farmer inched his potato cart forward and the road ahead began to clear. I handed one of the pies to her, then greedily tucked into mine, taking care to use a scrap of the paper to wipe my mouth and chin. "Slowly, Meg, slowly," she said. "You'll make yourself sick." I glanced over at her; her pie sat on its square of paper in her lap, untouched.

"Don't you want it?" I asked.

"Maybe later," she said quietly. "We still have a long journey ahead."

She was grieving, I remembered; grieving, tired, and she was sending me away. I was sad to be leaving, and sad to be leaving her, but more nervous and fearful than anything. I lifted the pie and took a few more bites, tucked the last bit of pastry into my mouth, then crumpled the paper and dropped it out the window for the pigeons to tear at. It wouldn't be the worst thing to fall on that road. I looked out and saw the sign at the edge of the Regent's Park. The cabman steered the carriage north alongside it, and I caught glimpses of the conservatory and the zoological grounds through the stands of trees. Somewhere behind us was Buckingham Palace. It was said that King William had fallen direly ill after the death of his daughter in the spring. Change was all around us, at a distance and close at hand. I could feel that change was coming within me too; it frightened me, I hated it, but that could not halt or slow its impending arrival. I leaned my head against the glass and watched the trees in the park speed past, the carriage rocking like a child's cradle, until my mind grew weary and my eyes grew heavy and sleep washed over me like a wave.

A hand squeezed my shoulder and I awoke with a start. At first I couldn't make out where I was, then I realised I was still in the cab, my mother seated beside me. "We're nearly there," she said. I turned back to the window and saw that the tidy stands of trees in the park were far behind us, now replaced with the unkempt heath and unruly woods that foreshadowed our ascent into Highgate.

As we wound our way through the village streets, I gazed out the window at the people strolling along the leafy laneways. They weren't walking at the frantic pace that the people in the heart of the city did, with sombre looks upon their faces, furrowed frowns, striding so fast and with such purpose that they'd knock you down if you got in the way. The refined people of Highgate moved at a leisurely pace. The women glided past in their dresses shaded in lilac, rose and blue, trimmed with ruffles and flounces skimming the tops of their little slippered feet; they peered out coyly from under their wide-brimmed bonnets, which were lightly decorated with silk flowers and ribbons. Alongside them walked the men, smart and sharp in checkered trousers, gleaming top hats, and flattering frock coats nipped in at the waist; they had an arrogance about them, with their chins in the air and their silver-tipped canes tapping the stones as they sauntered. No one in the East End walked like that. I touched my own shabby bonnet, and looked down in dismay at the patch on my sleeve.

The other thing about Highgate was the quiet. No teeming traffic, no clattering hooves, no bellowing costers hawking their wares. The streets were leafy and green, and wild birdsong floated down delicately from the trees. In the city, the only song you heard came from the markets, from the bedraggled finches and canaries and linnets trapped in their tiny cages.

We turned away from the village high street onto a lane lined with box-shaped houses of brick and stone. I'd never been so grateful to reach the end of a journey. I reckoned we'd ridden in that carriage for nearly three hours. My bones ached—even my teeth ached—after rattling over the roads that brought us here. The cabman dropped down from his seat to offer us his large, workworn hand so that we could steady ourselves as we climbed out, as though we had come from the city to visit our close relations. Despite the gesture, we felt awkward and out of place.

The driver stood by as we stared at the front of the doctor's house, awestruck. It was part of a row of townhouses, its front face crisply composed of red brick with large, elegant windows that peered over the road. A set of very white steps led up to a gleaming black door with a polished brass knob, crowned with a fan-shaped window, and the whole thing was surrounded by a low fence wrought from black iron. The streets were swept, the gutters were washed. This is what struck me the most: how clean it all was, especially compared to the East End, which was perpetually grey and black, smothered in soot and chimney smoke, and the noxious brown fogs that crept up from the Thames.

"Come on," my mother said. "We didn't ride all this way to stand and gawp."

We stepped up to the front door as if we had come for a proper visit. Mum took a deep breath and smartly brought the brass knocker down against the striker, twice. A few moments later the door swung wide to reveal a middle-aged woman in a long, dark blue dress, simple and unadorned, her wiry curls tucked up into a matching dark blue bonnet. She was round and flustered, with very red cheeks. She looked at us, then looked at the cab and driver behind us. My mother pulled the engraved white card out of her little purse and showed it to the woman.

"Mrs. Clara Evans and Miss Margaret Evans to see the doctor," my mother said, softly.

The woman's eyes widened and she let out a squeak. She took the card from my mother's hand. "Please wait one moment."

She closed the door. She didn't slam it, but it felt like a slam. We stared at the gleaming brass knocker, afraid to move or even speak. After a moment, the door swung open again. Standing there was the doctor in his vest and shirtsleeves, wiping his hands on a linen towel. He was as tall as I remembered, with a longish face and a sweep of dark hair with whiskers growing partway down his cheeks. I barely noted his features in the turmoil of the accident. I saw now that he was handsome in a sharpish sort of way, with silvering hair, dark brows, crow's feet stretching out from the corners of his eyes, and a small brown mole high on his left cheek.

"Oh, of course!" he exclaimed. "Mrs. Evans. And your lovely daughter. Thank you for coming all this way." He signalled to the driver, who scampered over to join us. The doctor reached into his pocket, pulled out half a crown. "Here you go," he said, handing it to the man. "There's another half-crown in it for you if you wait. We won't be too long."

"Yes, sir," the cabman said eagerly. "Yes, sir, I'll be here. I can wait all day if you need."

The doctor turned his attention to us. "Please," he said. "Follow me." He led us into a grand hallway with doors on either side, a corridor leading back and a staircase rising upward. He led us down past the stairs to a door on the left, which turned out to be a drawing room. The far wall featured a black slate fireplace with bookshelves set in on either side. Dozens of books were stuffed into it, every which way, their names pressed into the spines in gold. A cheerful fire crackled behind an ornate brass screen. A fancy parlour settee in yellow silk was perched against the wall. Another half-dozen mismatched chairs dressed in satins and brocades were scattered throughout the room. "Here we go. Please have a seat, anywhere you like." He turned and locked the door behind him, which I thought was strange, then dropped the key into his vest pocket. We planted ourselves side by side on the settee, and he pulled one of the chairs closer to us. He placed the linen towel on one of the dainty side tables. I saw then that there were faded spots of blood on the corner of the cloth. Was it his, or a patient's? Was it fresh, or from days or weeks in the past? Human blood was somehow different in my mind from the animal blood I was used to seeing. I thought once again of the boy, the saw, the leg. I thought of my father and the gash on his hand. I looked up and saw that he had seen me staring at the cloth. I turned away, and took in the rest of the room.

It was a strange but elegant space, its walls covered in Paris green paper, lacquered to a shine and lined with shelves; some had stuffed birds and reptiles mounted on blocks of wood; others had framed engravings and miniatures, still others had more books in heaps and stacks and tumbling in rows. The air was lush with the scents of brandy, cigar smoke and lemon balm. There were portraits and landscapes in oils, some very old and in need of dusting, hanging from a picture rail high up on the wall; a human skeleton wired together stood in the corner, reaching out with one arm, one hand, as if in greeting. One could hang a hat from it, I suppose. It may have been meant to be lighthearted, but I found it quite unnerving. I felt Mum squeeze my hand to signal she found it so as well.

"I'm sure your mother told you why you're here," the doctor began. "I've been hoping to expand my household staff, and I think you'd be a fine addition to the kitchen. You've met our housekeeper, Mrs. Dawson. She would not say so herself, but her strength is in decline and she could use the assistance. You would start as a maid-of-all-work to see how you get on. I'd also like your help with some routine medical tasks, nothing too strenuous, and, if you are interested and have the aptitude, possibly guide you towards becoming a nurse."

My eyes grew wide as he spoke. A nurse! Helping the doctor with his patients, assisting with wounds and treatments and surgeries. I wouldn't have to be a kitchen maid forever. "Yes, sir. Of course, sir," I said quickly. "I'd be very interested."

"Most unfortunate about that boy," he added with a sigh. "But I must commend you. You showed courage and determination, clarity in a critical moment, substantial inner strength, and a sterner stomach than most men possess." The doctor, as it turned out, was not afraid of sharing his opinion on things. "You would not have known his veins needed tying off, or that his wounds needed to be cauterised. It was inevitable that he would bleed to death. If we had been closer to my surgery, or even to the hospital, it may have ended differently."

I felt my cheeks grow hot under his penetrating gaze. If he had known these things, why hadn't he done more? Why had he not pushed me aside and taken over?

"But please know, it was not your fault that he died. You did all that you could, and more. It is a sad fact. Death is with us everywhere; it meets us at every turn."

"Yes, sir." I nodded. I wondered, not for the first time, what happened to the boy. Had he died in the carriage, at the hospital in London, or in the surgery down the hall? We never heard tell of his mother and father, nor mention of a funeral. What had his parents thought when he never came home?

"So, my dear Margaret, a few things of note. This is our drawing room. Behind me is the morning room where I take my breakfast. Across the hall is the dining room. At the front is my office, where I meet with patients and colleagues, conduct my research and prepare for my appointments. I'm never to be disturbed there, unless you have been summoned. That is the first rule. The most important one. Do you understand?"

I nodded. "Yes, sir." My mother nodded along with me, and then caught herself.

"The second door leads to the surgery, where I examine and treat my patients. When I say I am not to be disturbed in my office, the rule extends even more strictly to the surgery. You are never to set foot in it except with my express invitation. I know young girls are innately curious creatures, but I must preserve the dignity and privacy of those who consult me. They rely on our discretion. If you greet a visitor at the door or see one in any of these rooms, you are to promptly forget the encounter. Mrs. Dawson alone is responsible for both my office and my surgery—she cleans them, arranges them to suit my purposes and attends to the lamps and fires."

Of course, once the doctor made me vow never to step foot in his surgery, my curiosity drew me towards it. I wonder now if that was his intention, if he already knew me better than I knew myself.

He continued, quietly but emphatically. "Whatever you see or hear in this house, you are never to discuss it, most especially with anyone outside the household. Not with tradesmen, patients, shopkeepers, not with anyone at all. That is crucial. If you violate that rule, or any other, you will find yourself on the street in short order and you will have lost my sympathy and assistance. However," he said, leaning forward, "if you follow the rules as you should, things will go very well for you. Should you earn my trust, you will find yourself appropriately rewarded." He picked the linen towel up from the table. "Your salary will be eight pounds a year, paid quarterly."

"Eight pounds a year," my mother whispered. In all our days on the Row, our shop had never made more than sixteen pounds in a year, and that was for the three of us!

"You will receive room and board," the doctor continued, "and a weekly allowance of tea and sugar. Mrs. Dawson will provide you with your uniform and will instruct you on your duties. I will draw up a contract for you tomorrow. Unless you need your mother to sign on your behalf."

"I can sign," I said. "When do I start?"

"You've already started," he answered. "I'll hand you over to Mrs. Dawson and she'll put you to work straightaway. It's a busy house with plenty to do. Tomorrow she will introduce you to my wife. I'm afraid she's very frail and needs her rest today."

A wife! I glanced up at the ceiling, wondering whereabouts she was, if she knew we were here. Why did I think he was unmarried? I glanced at his hand: he wore no ring. Not every man did, though. Perhaps because of his work, he'd be taking it on and off and forever losing it. Still. A wife.

"Thank you for taking her on," my mother said, rising to her feet. "I don't know what we'd have done otherwise." It was hard not to be bruised by this; it was as though I were a pup she could no longer care for. It was this or the street, she seemed to say.

The doctor walked across the room and tugged a rose-embroidered bellpull that hung from high on the wall. Within a few moments, Mrs. Dawson appeared in the doorway, her hands lightly crossed in front of her apron. "Margaret has agreed to join us. Please show her to her quarters, and then to the kitchen," he said. "I will see her mother out to the cab that's waiting for her. After that, I'd prefer not to be disturbed until supper is served."

"Certainly, sir." She gave a little curtsy, so my mother and I did the same.

"Oh no! I almost forgot." My mother reached into the inner pocket of her jacket and drew out a small glass vial decorated with a delicate blue and gold pattern. She pressed it into my hand. "This belonged to my mum," she said. "I wish she could have seen this day. Go on. I want you to have it." Her eyes shone with tears.

I turned the vial to see the tracings of gold glitter in the darkened room. It was the prettiest thing I'd ever seen, and I didn't know my mother had anything like it. It smelled of roses. I wanted to tell my mother that I loved her. But those words had never passed the lips of anyone in my family. In fact, I'd never heard anyone on the Row say it. It was one of those things you just knew.

"Are you sure, Mum?" I asked. Not just about the vial, but maybe that's how it sounded.

"You'll be all right, Meg," she said. "Make us proud, eh?"

The doctor tossed a look at Mrs. Dawson. She gave a little

tug on my arm. I nodded, clutching the vial in my hand, and followed her out into the hall. With that same penetrating gaze, the doctor watched us leave, my mother watching beside him, till the door was closed between us.

As I stood in the hallway, without Mum beside me, the silence and gloom of the house overwhelmed me. I felt like a small child again, lost among strangers. Mrs. Dawson held a finger to her lips, and motioned for me to follow. Neither of us spoke as she led me down through to the back of the house, so quiet I heard every one of our steps on the wooden floor. It was as if the ghosts of decades past crept alongside us, daring us to utter a sound. At the end was a door wrapped in green baize and studded with tacks. Behind it was a staircase so dark and steep I had to keep my hand against the wall to make sure I didn't tumble to my death. I was afraid my fingers would brush against something that would make me cry out in fright.

Once safely at the bottom, we passed through a scullery which smelled of root vegetables and damp, and then into a bright open kitchen with a long table in the middle of it, set with metal mixing bowls, cooking implements and a fat sack of potatoes. Next to the doorway hung the array of brass bells that were rigged up to the rest of the house. "Right," she said. "Here we are." I let myself breathe, and suddenly felt much more at home. The walls on either side were lined with racks of plates, and shelves crammed with crockery cups and bowls. Gleaming copper pots and pans hung from the ceiling, and a blazing coal-burning stove was heating up a kettle and a few bubbling pots. On the far wall was a hearth surrounded with an arch of bricks. Beside it, a boy about my age sat on a stool polishing a pair of men's shoes. His hair stood up in a mess of curls, and he had a streak of black on his cheek. He looked up as we came in.

"All right?" he said, by way of welcome.

"Tom, stand up when you're greeting ladies," Mrs. Dawson scolded.

"Right, sorry. Name's Tom." He jumped to his feet and extended his hand as though to shake mine, but I wrinkled my nose at his blackened fingers. He wiped them on his apron and thankfully didn't offer them again.

"This is Margaret," Mrs. Dawson said. "Our new maid-of-all-work."

"A new maid. That's the ticket," he said. "Me and Mrs. D are run off our feet."

"It's not as bad as all that," she replied. "But yes, it's been six months since we've had any help. The last one . . ." She didn't finish her sentence, but instead exchanged an awkward look with Tom. I couldn't imagine how the two of them had gone on alone for six months. I thought about my lavish eight pounds a year, and wondered what could have happened to make "the last one" leave the house.

"Right, let's get you up to your quarters and settled in, then I'll need help preparing lunch for the missus." She hung her damp apron on a hook by the door, then took me back to the dark staircase, which still felt as narrow and treacherous as a ladder.

We climbed three flights up to the attic, where Mrs. Dawson let me into a little room with a tiny window in the ceiling. Where the basement had been cool, the attic was hot and airless, and the little window I mentioned was painted shut. Pushed against the wall was a small iron bedstead with a patched woollen blanket spread over it, and a painted green cupboard for my clothes. There was a straw-seated chair and small table, a chest at the foot of the bed, a speckled looking glass on the wall and a chipped jug and basin to wash myself with. Oh, and the tiniest fireplace I'd ever seen. Twigs and straw and feathers on the grate—the chimney was likely choked with birds. It probably hadn't been used for years.

"What's that you're wearing?" Mrs. Dawson looked me over disdainfully, head-to-toe.

I looked down at myself, wondering if I had ripped the dress or dirtied it getting in and out of the cab. "Begging your pardon, missus. My father died a few days ago."

"You have my sympathies," she said drily. I couldn't tell if she was offering them for my father or for the dress. "Dyed, is it? Well. You can't wear your own clothes in any event. Except when you've got a half day off, but I'd burn that one if I was you." She opened the cupboard and took out two printed frocks: one blue, and one mustard colour; two pair of black stockings; a black frock; an extra petticoat; two white caps and half a dozen aprons. "The coloured frocks you wear in the morning with an apron over top, the black frocks are for the afternoon, and you must always wear a cap."

"I have to change into a new dress in the afternoon?"

"Of course," she said, as though I were daft. "The morning dresses will be dirty from clearing out the fireplaces and washing the stairs. You can't wear those to serve the family." She puffed up her chest as she spoke. "The black dresses are to be worn when you serve meals," she continued, "and when you are in the company of the doctor or the missus. And it's your job to keep your own clothes clean and mended." She laid the frocks on the bed. "It's a good thing you're about the size of the last girl, otherwise the cost of your uniform would have come out of your pay." She must have been fired for laziness, I thought, or for breaking something, or maybe she had been caught stealing. I knew that younger maids were often hired out of the workhouses, and could be undependable.

"You've never worked belowstairs, I reckon."

I shook my head. She sat down on the corner of the bed and patted the mattress next to her. I perched myself on the edge and faced her.

"Every house has rules, and you will do well to mind them. The first is to be quick and quiet. Move in and out of rooms like a mouse, don't speak unless you're spoken to, and then the less said the better. No need to talk when a curtsy will do."

She paused, then nodded for me to respond. "Yes, Mrs. Dawson," I replied. I had never been this formal with my family, my neighbours or our customers.

She nodded back, then reached over and pinched the fabric of my dress, rubbed the cloth between her fingers. "Second, if you meet the doctor or his friends or a patient in the hall or on the stairs, always stop and stand to the side. Clasp your hands in front of you and look down at the floor, like you're saying a little prayer." She let go of my dress, looked at her black-smudged fingertips.

"Yes, Mrs. Dawson," I replied. My face flushed hot and red. The longer I stayed in my mourning dress, the more humiliated I felt.

"The last one I'll tell you for now is: don't be sullen, and don't fuss and fidget like a bird in a cage. When someone is speaking to you, stand up straight, keep your face and your hands still, and look them in the eye when you answer. That goes for Tom and me as much as anyone else." She reached over with her finger and raised my chin up to look at her. "Is that understood?"

"Yes, Mrs. Dawson," I answered. I felt the tears welling in my eyes, and I fought to keep them back.

"I know how hard this is, all alone, everything new, your life turned upside down in a moment. And whatever you've done before is child's work compared to here." I thought of the calf, the boy, the leg, my father's festering hand. "Most girls never get a chance such as this, to be a maid in such a fine house to a respected doctor and his wife, with room and board. Plus sugar and tea."

"Yes, missus, I'm very grateful," I said, though truthfully I wasn't sure how I felt.

"See that you are," Mrs. Dawson said pointedly. "Now, it's past one, so change into the black, don't forget your cap, and meet me back in the kitchen. You can take a moment to unpack, but not much longer." She closed the door, and I listened as her shoes thumped back down the stairs; I heard her pause for a moment, and then continue down slower, step by step into silence. It was comforting in a way to hear she had as much trouble with them as I did.

I pulled my small bag up onto the bed, opened and unpacked it, not that there was all that much inside: a spare petticoat and shift, extra stockings, and a dress I had thought was all right but now saw how raggedy and dismal it was. Worse than the one I was wearing, the one that should be burned. I hung my clothes in the cupboard and pulled on the black frock. It did fit surprisingly well. I pulled one of the caps on over my hair and tied a clean apron around my waist. My feelings of despair changed with my clothes. Now I wanted to show them that I could do the work, that I could be better than the last girl, that they would regret ever doubting me. I wanted to stand on the chair and look out the window, but there was no time for that. Instead, I gave myself a quick check in the mirror, then left my little room and went down the treacherous staircase back to the kitchen.

I heard one of the servants' bells in the kitchen as I was making my descent. I would have to learn which was which, I realised. I stepped into the room and found Mrs. Dawson rushing around like a whirlwind. Her face was even redder, if that was possible. Tom had cleaned his face and hands, and was wearing a clean checkered waistcoat. The two of them ducked and dodged around each other as he fetched a bowl and a plate, grabbed a handful of cutlery, and placed everything on a silver tray which sat waiting on the table. She in turn pulled one of the pots off the stove and ladled a thick stew from it into the bowl. "We must let the stew cool before we serve it to her ladyship," she noted, then pointed to a loaf of bread on the counter. "Margaret, cut a few thin slices, will you? And put a bit of butter on."

I looked around for a bread knife, but was mystified as to where it could be. Tom saw my predicament, and without being asked, he fetched one from a drawer and handed it to me. I began to saw the bread as carefully as I could, but I was flustered and the slices came out uneven, narrow at the top and thick at the bottom. Mrs. Dawson saw what I was doing and gasped. "We can't serve bread like that to the doctor's wife!" She elbowed me out of the way and began to slice the bread herself, muttering under her breath. "Fetch the butter," she barked at me. I scanned every surface in the room but couldn't see butter anywhere. "In the larder," she snapped. Before I had a chance to ask where the larder was, Tom ducked into it and came out with a butter dish. He set it squarely on the table in front of me, and I spread a thin layer on each piece of bread while Mrs. Dawson carefully arranged them on a plate next to the steaming bowl of stew. "Tea!" she ordered, wiping her hands on her apron. I moved towards the kettle and picked it up then poured the boiling water into a flowered china pot. I was about to spoon the tea leaves in when Mrs. Dawson stopped me again. "Leaves first and then the water!" Her mood turned foul as she shooed me away, and I stood at a safe distance, feeling utterly useless. I vowed to find a spare moment to examine the kitchen and larder and scullery to learn where everything was.

Once the tea was brewed to Mrs. Dawson's satisfaction, and the food was ordered prettily on the silver tray, she took off her apron and motioned me to follow her. My heart squeezed with fear at the thought of meeting the doctor's wife. What would she be like?

We climbed back up the dismal staircase and passed through another of the green baize doors; directly across was her bedroom. Mrs. Dawson held the silver tray in perfect balance, though it must have been very heavy. She motioned towards the door with her head. "Gently," she whispered. I gave the door a tap, then opened it as smoothly and quietly as possible.

I wanted to do at least one thing right. Mrs. Dawson called out cheerfully, "Good afternoon, milady. I've got a bit of lunch for you." She swung the tray around to the side and stepped into the room, but as I began to follow her, she turned and gave me a black look, mouthing "Stay there."

I froze on the spot, my heart tight in my chest, but I was able to see a good portion of the room from where I stood. I had never been anywhere so soft and pretty. The walls were the same creamy yellow as the butter on the bread; they were hung with restful country landscapes and what seemed to be family portraits and silhouettes; the furniture was lean and elegant, with clever little chairs and stools, a dressing table and a mirror. There was a blue patterned rug spread on the floor, a washstand near the foot of the bed, and a copper hip-bath next to the blazing fireplace. I was desperate to get a better look at the doctor's wife, but she was little more than a shadow behind the muslin curtains surrounding her canopied bed. I did see that a lovely lace-trimmed nightgown was draped over a nearby chair with pleats and ruffles running up and down the front. Closer to her, on a dainty bedside table, was a burned-down beeswax candle in a silver holder, a stoppered glass bottle with an orange label that I knew to be laudanum, and an elaborately engraved brass tube that I later learned was a clyster syringe.

Mrs. Dawson put the tray down on another small table close to the bed and spoke so softly to the woman that I couldn't make out what she was saying. I leaned forward, trying to hear the exchange, but all that met my ears were quiet murmurs, the way one would speak to a baby. Before long, Mrs. Dawson retreated and shooed me away from the door. She closed it behind her so slowly and carefully you'd have thought it was made of glass. "Shh," she warned, then softened her demeanour. "Hopefully the missus will eat something. Poor thing doesn't have much of an appetite. Then she'll rest a bit."

"What's wrong with her?" I asked, as we made our way back to the stairs to the kitchen. If I thought Mrs. Dawson had given me a dark look earlier, this look was absolutely black. She stopped walking and put her face close to mine. "I'd have thought the doctor would warn you never to speak of anything you see or hear in this household. Not to me, not to anyone."

I dropped my gaze, sheepishly, because I had in fact been given that warning, not an hour earlier. I wouldn't make that mistake again. I was so innocent that first day. I thought I understood something of human nature. I came to learn I knew nothing at all. By the time we climbed back down the staircase, it was time to prepare for supper, and the incident was forgotten.

Sister Augustine has summoned Sister Catherine for reasons unknown. Our time has been cut short. It's strange of me to ask, I know, but please hold Mother Mary Angelica in your prayers. Let her not be abandoned and forgotten as are so many troubled women. Bless us all in our time of grief.

M.E.

Miss Gibson—Something terrible is happening here at the Priory. You are not the only person asking questions about Margaret. Horrible rumours are swirling. I cannot say more at the moment. Do not let her be lost. —Sr. C

May 26th, 1887

Dear Miss Gibson,

I have received your letter of the 16th soliciting personal and professional information about Doctors Ian Carstairs and Noel Cavanaugh and their respective practices. My apologies for the lateness of this reply.

You make a most unusual request. The privacy of the members of the Royal College of Physicians is paramount, but I am inclined to provide you as a representative of the press with a modicum of information so that you may proceed with your enquiries. I trust that you will treat this with absolute discretion.

You are correct that both Dr. Carstairs and Dr. Cavanaugh were members of the Royal College of Physicians, and that both lived in Highgate in the years that you propose. Dr. Carstairs began his medical career as a surgeon, then received further training in order to earn his licence as a physician. Dr Cavanaugh, on the other hand, was fully trained as a physician and licenced by our college, and subsequently sought education in matters of the surgery.

I can confirm that Dr. Carstairs passed in 1840, and that Dr. Cavanaugh retired from his practice in 1868. Dr. Carstairs did leave a wife and daughter; Dr. Cavanaugh was a lifelong bachelor. I regret that this is the extent of the information available to you.

At your urging, I will have your contact information submitted to the doctors, or their surviving families or their estates, as the case may be. I will do my utmost to fulfill your wishes but can make no promises in this regard.

Yours very truly,

Dr. Philip Montague

THE ROYAL COLLEGE OF PHYSICIANS
THE REGENT'S PARK, LONDON

St. Anne's Priory
Hampstead, London

MAY THE 29TH, 1887

Dear Miss Gibson,

I am Sister Augustine, acting as Prioress of St. Anne's as we await the appointment of a permanent replacement for Mother Mary Angelica, whom we surrendered to the mercy of the Lord just weeks ago.

I have met with Sister Catherine, who has been assisting in your correspondence with our visitant. I believe that your exchange has reached its natural end, and there is no need of further communication between you. Please do not write again.

Our best wishes to you. Go with God.

Respectfully,

Sister Augustine
St. Anne's Priory

Something is wrong.

You are silent. I have seen you at the gate of St. Anne's. Two days, three days. You stand and stare at the windows.

The Sisters pray without ceasing. Catherine prays without ceasing. She will not sit with me.

Augustine will not see me. She has done this. I know she has. What has she said to you?

I have so much more to tell you. I will leave this for you on the hinge of the gate. Please God let it find its way to you. My son must know me.

None will stand in my way.

M.E.

June 11th, 1887

My dearest Emily,

Not even the battle at Majuba Hill could prepare a man for the tribulations I have faced as a tender and devoted husband. Your mother is hovering over me like a portentous cloud, enquiring once again if you will be joining us at Kestrels on the 19th and through the week-end, as she insists on throwing this ridiculous party for me and inviting half the country. The whole thing is already intolerable and will only grow more so; I will understand completely if you have made other, more pleasurable plans, such as having clusters of boils scraped from the soles of your feet.

Good, she has flounced out of the room, no doubt to devise more cakes and festivity with which to besiege us.

I have interceded on your behalf as you implored and have called upon the bilious Sister Augustine at St. Anne's. I knew to prepare for the worst, but her comportment was better suited to a kennel than to a convent. It took a full day's journey by cart and a great deal of my very limited charm to gain the woman's grudging co-operation, not to mention the contribution of a small fortune for the purchase of a rather hideous brass plaque for one of the chapel alcoves. The result: she will permit you to resume correspondence with "the resident at St. Anne's." The letters will pass between you unopened and unread. She will not interfere with the contents therein unless and until you pursue publication, at which point another brass plaque will no doubt be required. Please accept this as a testament to my confidence in your vexatious career, and not as a sudden fascination for brass plaques and chapel alcoves.

Sister Dogsbreath did obligate me to pass on an amusingly dire warning, and so I repeat it here word for word:

"Miss Gibson must be on her guard. She should be aware that the visitant is confined to St. Anne's as a measure of safety for the village, the capital, and for the resident herself. Whatever else she may have confided in her letters, she is a fantasist, a dissembler, a criminal. Her many years in our care have done little to dim the foul light that burns within her. I cannot overstate the dangers inherent in these matters: they extend in all directions, from the Priory gate to the heart of London, from the heights of our society to its very depths, from decades past through to the century's imminent end, and back to the woman herself. Hers is a deserved silence and a welcome obscurity; God save anyone who would incautiously release her voice upon an unwitting world. Some stories, Miss Gibson, are best left untold."

What a remarkable expenditure of energy.

I did not mention the symbol on the physician's card to her, nor did I feel the need. I am well aware of what it represents. This, however, will have to wait until next we meet: your mother has returned with ever-more vicious proposals to celebrate the onset of my dotage. May Death deliver me from these unending torments.

Always your loving father,

Sir H.

ST. ANNE'S PRIORY
Hampstead, London

JUNE THE 14TH, 1887

Dear Miss Gibson,

    I feared I would never hear from you again. These have been dark days; our grief has raked its claws across these walls of stone. Imagine my shock when Sister Augustine came to me to tell me I would no longer have to submit my responses for her approval, and that Sister Catherine was to assist in whatever way I desired. As well, she said that I am moving from the wing I share with the Sisters to the room we have set aside for the Bishop and other visiting members of the clergy. She handed me a fine leather folder tied with a silk ribbon, in which I found several of your unanswered letters that she had withheld, as well as your very kind note from yesterday, unopened, untouched. With that, she threw me a scorching glare, then turned on her heel and left the room. It is a wondrous day, and I am grateful for whatever influence you have exercised to make it so. I will strive to be kind to Sister Catherine and not unduly burden her with reams of dictation and transcription, but I do want to tell you my story in as much detail as our time allows, for fear of forgetting some insignificant item or gesture that could illuminate the entire narrative.

I would like, if I may, to tell a little more about those first days at the doctor's residence. I remember how little I slept that first night in the attic, so quiet compared to my bedroom in London. Every twist and turn on the mattress unleashed another cloud of dust, urging me to sneeze. More than once I thought I heard someone in the attic creeping about in the dark, but it was only the house settling around me, the floors creaking and cracking, a burst of starlings from under the eaves, the wind whistling around the roof and rattling the chimney pots. I was used to the steady clopping of horses' hooves as carriages rattled down the street beneath my window; the barking dogs; the church bells striking in the distance; and the costers and shop boys singing and laughing as they staggered home from the tavern up the street.

Well before the sun rose, I would hear the floorboards squeal when my mother got up to lay the fire and put the kettle on. My father would hop up soon after, shave and dress, and trundle down to the shop where I heard him moving around, then the slam and jingle of the shop's front door and Ned's husky voice, still wet and raw from the pub, would drift up the stairs. Those mornings were familiar, and all I'd ever known. But in that big house in Highgate, I lay cold and alone in a narrow little bed in a house full of strangers. My own family was no more. It was the first time I felt truly alone in the world.

I had no clock, but I knew it was early. It was still pitch dark outside and my room was cloaked in gloom. I turned onto one side, then onto the other, then surrendered and climbed out of bed. I felt around for a candle and a match, and by its wavering light I changed out of my nightgown, pulled on my underclothes, stockings and boots, then pinned my hair up under my cap and tied on one of the aprons. Soft and silent, I left the room, candle in hand, pulling the door closed behind me. I struggled on the staircase, my footsteps loud and echoing although I crept downward slowly. There were very small windows at intervals, I suppose to let in a bit of daylight, but in the early hours they were useless. The firelight danced and jumped on the wall as I made my way down to the basement.

I pushed open the door at the foot of the stairs and made my way through the scullery to the kitchen. Both were empty. Mrs. Dawson had her own room somewhere down the corridor, and I could hear Tom snoring in the servant's hall, where he slept on a mattress on the floor. I put my candle down on the long pine table, casting a timid, hazy glow in the darkness. A pair of windows high up in the wall let in enough moonlight for me to see the gleam on the copper pots. There is something eerie about an empty kitchen: the hulking shapes in the darkness, the chairs and table, the range in the hearth, the shelves of bowls, the racks of plates. I looked all about me, unsure of what to do, warming my hands by the candle and rubbing my arms to warm them. I jumped with surprise when the door swung open and Mrs. Dawson flew in. She carried an oil lamp and caught me in its wide circle of light.

"Oh, Margaret!" she said. "I almost didn't see you there. You're the first girl I've ever had to appear in the kitchen before I was awake." She was wearing another dark blue dress, this one patterned in a light grey stripe, with a large white apron tied over top, and a white cap on her head as before. She set the oil lamp down on the table and lit another. "It'll be a busy day today. You'll be tired at the end of it, until you get used to all the work. You'd best start by cleaning the range and rekindling the fire."

As Mrs. Dawson bustled around the room, fetching things from the larder and pantry so that she could start the doctor's breakfast, I approached the range and noticed a scuttle of coal and a pile of wood next to it, a wad of straw and twigs, along with a very dirty hogshair brush. I couldn't let on that I didn't know what I was doing. I waited till she went into the pantry again before I reached in and gave the range a good scrub with the brush. She was right; it was a dirty job. Between this and the dusting and sweeping, I'd soon be covered in muck and soot.

A great blaze would be needed to heat the oven and boilers. I had seen Ned and my father light the butcher shop oven dozens of times, so with this I felt more capable. I stacked the tinder and wood and coals and pushed them into the modest flame that had lingered through the night. Very soon a hearty fire rose and flared and licked at the fuel. I splayed my hands out in the warmth to thaw my icy fingers.

Mrs. Dawson looked pleased as she returned from the pantry with a tin of tea leaves. "It's not every girl who can tend a fire. We'll have a speck of breakfast before we get to work. Would a bit of toast and tea do you? Maybe an egg?"

"Yes, please," I said, trying not to sound too ravenous. Eggs were for week-ends at home on the Row, and sometimes not even then.

"There's boiled eggs in racks in the larder, and bread over there in the bin, if you would fetch them, please." As I retrieved the things for our breakfast, I heard the door swing open again.

"Hallo, hallo. How's you both this mornin'? Sleep all right?" It was Tom. He was dressed in decent clothes, trousers and a waistcoat and had a cap pulled down over top of his round dark curls.

"Well enough, thanks," I replied. "Just getting used to it all."

"You'll figure it out soon enough. You're more clever than I am, that's for sure." He went out back to the courtyard where there was a pump and returned a few minutes later carrying two enormous buckets filled to the brim. He set one down next to the range, and though the water sloshed, not a single drop ended up on the floor. He opened a door on one side of the oven and filled it with water to heat it. When he was out of the way, I filled the kettle and put it on the hob.

While I made the tea, Tom toasted the slices of bread over the fire. Together we set out the dishes, including the plates and teacups from the shelves around the room, and Mrs. Dawson joined us at the table. It was quite nice, to sit together like friends as the sun came up and began to light the room. I scraped a bit of butter on my toast and took a bite, savouring the flavour of it. The tea was hot and fresh, and warmed me from my fingertips down to my toes.

After only ten minutes, Mrs. Dawson said, "Time to make breakfast for the doctor and her ladyship. Tom, see to the fires, please."

Tom picked up the coal scuttle and put an apron on over his clothes before disappearing up the servants' staircase. Tom, it turned out, laid the fires in all the upper rooms. Normally it would be one of the maid's tasks, but things were done differently in that house, as I soon learned. The only fire he didn't lay was her ladyship's, as it wouldn't have been appropriate for a young man to enter her private rooms. But he did a great deal for the doctor, sometimes helping him shave, and dress. That was the way the doctor wanted things.

Mrs. Dawson made eggs and rashers for the doctor and a thin grey porridge with raisins for the missus. The smell of the sizzling bacon reminded me of the Row. Being a butcher's daughter, I often had slivers of bacon and scraps of ham, which my mother would fry up in the mornings and serve with dripping and bread from one of the shops up the street.

Everything had to be served hot, Mrs. Dawson told me, as she ordered me to make a fresh pot of tea and more toast. I knew where the pantry and larder were now, and where the crockery and cutlery were kept, so I guessed how to find each thing she asked for, committing their places to memory so I would be quicker next time. Mrs. Dawson watched me as I dashed about, and checked a little watch hanging from a chatelaine around her waist, which made me more anxious.

At last, I had everything laid out on two silver trays. The food was hot and ready to go. I hoped Mrs. Dawson would praise me, but she said nothing. I thought she would have me accompany her to serve the meals, but to my disappointment, she told me to wash up the dishes and peel potatoes for lunch.

Tom had his own chores to do, so I was left alone to clear the table, do some washing up in the scullery and then sit with my bowl of potatoes and a thin black knife and an old rag to catch the peelings. I thought again about the Row, and how busy it was. There wasn't a chance to be lonely with people always around. My mother and father; Ned; the shopkeepers from up and down the block; the hawkers out on the streets shouting their wares; the customers popping in and out of the shop. I got to chat with all of them, and have a laugh now and then. I would step outside to get a bit of sunshine on my head, being careful of where I put my feet. In the doctor's kitchen, the snick and scrape of my knife seemed loud, and every time I sighed, it drifted out into silence.

I wondered if Mrs. Dawson would always be the one to serve the doctor and the missus. Would I get a chance to go into the rest of the house, or would I always be in the basement, washing and peeling and chopping, and making tea? And when would I be allowed to assist the doctor with his patients? I didn't realise how many jobs there were in the house, all the cleaning, sweeping, polishing, airing out. We kept our rooms clean enough on the Row but we never worked so hard at it. As I soon learned, the doctor kept mainly to his rooms: his office and his surgery during the day, the drawing room in the evening. He wasn't a stickler, as Mrs. Dawson would say, but he did like the rooms kept neat. We never bothered to lay fires in the rooms outside his office unless he expected visitors.

As I was lost in my thoughts and already feeling sorry for myself, and minding not to cut my thumb off, I heard a loud knock and was confused. I realised it had come from the tradesmen's entrance. I wiped my hands on my apron and hurried to answer it. I pulled the door open and saw a portly man with a florid face and a basket under his arm with a tea towel over it.

"Three loaves of bread, mince pie, and a teacake," he said, without greeting. He foisted the large basket into my arms.

"Account needs settling today. It's already been a week and I'm owed three shillings."

"Right," I said, awkwardly holding the basket. "You'll be wanting Mrs. Dawson then." We stood staring at each other for a moment. "Well? Go on and get her then," he said, as though I were a child. "And hurry it up. You're not the last on my list."

I didn't want to close the door in his face and leave him standing outside, so I stepped aside. "Well, come in," I said, trying not to sound as impatient as he did, though I was annoyed by his arrogance. He followed me into the shadowy passageway and down the corridor to the kitchen where Tom was sitting by the fire about to polish a pair of the doctor's boots. He looked up.

"All right, Mr. Grady?" he asked.

"Twill be once I'm paid." The baker surveyed the room, probably looking for Mrs. Dawson.

"She's gone upstairs to deliver breakfast," I said. "But she'll be back in a blink, I'm sure."

"Go on and fetch her then, I ain't got all bloody day." He made a sweeping gesture with his hand, which I found very rude. Would Mrs. Dawson want me to fetch her, or should I wait? Perhaps she'd be more cross if I didn't fetch her. "You can tell the good doctor there'll be no teacakes for the rest of the week unless'n I'm paid. And I won't be made to wait long." He folded his arms across his chest. I looked over at Tom. He made a face behind the baker's back, which was decidedly unhelpful.

"All right," I sighed, and headed up the back staircase. I assumed the doctor wouldn't be happy to be short of teacakes. I didn't know where exactly to find Mrs. Dawson but I decided to give it a go.

As I got nearer the first floor I heard her voice but I couldn't make out what she was saying. The doctor's reply, though, I heard clear as a bell. "Yes, a shame about the other," he said. "But this one seems more suited to the job. I think she'll rally from her recent troubles and find her place in the household." Mrs. Dawson murmured something again. "Once we know she can be trusted," the doctor replied. "She's a dab hand with a bone saw, I'll tell you that. I'll put her to work in my office, if she has a mind for it, and possibly the surgery. I have no doubt she will be of great use to us both."

"Yes, sir," Mrs. Dawson said, rather more clearly, and then I heard the tap-tapping of her shoes heading towards me. I froze for a moment, then decided it was best to meet her head-on so she didn't think I'd been eavesdropping. I made a lot of noise tramping up the last few steps and greeted her at the top of them. "Excuse me, Mrs. Dawson."

"Margaret!" she exclaimed. "What are you doing up here?" She sounded irritated and suspicious. "You'll have to learn to use the stairs quietly. It will be most disturbing to the doctor and her ladyship if you clomp about like a dray horse." There wasn't a trace of cunning in her expression. She didn't realise that I'd been listening.

"I'm sorry, Mrs. Dawson," I replied, looking embarrassed. "It's just that the baker is here, and he's upset about his account not being settled."

She sighed. "He's rather a bully," she said, as she descended the stairs in front of me, quiet as a ghost. "Did he threaten to withhold the teacakes again?"

"He did, in fact," I answered. She threw the basement door

open and soared through the scullery, with me scuttling along in her wake.

"Mr. Grady," she said warmly when we reached the kitchen. "How nice to see you again. Thank you for bringing our goods personally. I've no doubt you're wishing to be paid, and I thank you for your patience with our new maid, Margaret."

"You do go through 'em, don't you," he grumbled. "I'm owed three shillings."

"Yes, yes, I've got the account book. Come with me." And with that, she led the baker back down the passageway to her sitting room. He whinged all the way.

"Are they all as rude as that?" I asked Tom.

He shrugged. "Don't let it bother you. It's all bluster."

I went back to the table to continue peeling potatoes, wondering how much Tom knew about what went on in the household.

"What's wrong with her ladyship?" I asked, trying to sound casual.

The brush in his hand stopped mid-swipe, then resumed. "Don't know," he said, sternly. "Ain't none of my business. Best not to ask any questions about what don't concern you." He had an odd look on his face, and it made me wonder if he was in on any of the doctor's secrets, or if he knew Mrs. Dawson was in on them too.

"And what happened to the last maid?"

"Can't really say." He shrugged. "One day she was here, next day she was gone." He turned the boot in the light to see if he'd missed any spots. "Didn't care for the work, I expect. It happens, 'specially girls from the workhouses. You'd think they'd be happy and they are, for a time. Anyway, I never heard no more about her, and I wouldn't say more if I did."

When Mrs. Dawson returned, she unpacked the baker's basket. The bread looked pale and doughy to me. The pie crust was shiny with grease, and the teacakes looked coarse and dry. They weren't near as good as the stuff we got from the bakeries on the Row, which was odd seeing how posh the village was. Maybe the richer houses had their own baking done inside. But the scent of the mincemeat met my nose, and the bread smelled yeasty and slightly sweet. How different from the odours of the butchery: the metallic tang of blood, organs and sweetbreads. Muddy sawdust, mutton fat and salted beef. The faintest threat of rot.

"Can you bake, Margaret?" Mrs. Dawson asked.

"A little," I replied. "Some simple cakes, a pie or two. My mother showed me."

"I could teach you how to make bread and scones," she said. "Have you work up a tolerable crust for pastries, mix up a fine dough for sweet buns and savouries. It's all in the fingers, you'll learn it all by touch. Perhaps we won't have to rely so much on Mr. Grady. Best to be self-sufficient if we can." I looked at her fingers which even at her age seemed limber and dextrous. Mine were stiff and clumsy in comparison. I wished I'd paid more attention to my mother's handiwork with the tasty treats she made for customers' lunches and teas, instead of the chopping and grinding and carving that had become the sole province of my father and Ned.

Mrs. Dawson dropped a large book down in front of me and flipped the pages to one that said "Introduction to Bread

Making and How to Make Yeast." "Tom and I are going to the shops. We'll be stopping in at the butcher's and greengrocer's, and I'll bring us some fresh flour and soda and yeast for our lessons. You take a look at this and see what you can gather from it."

I felt a bit of sadness rise within me at the mention of the butcher's. I wished I could go with Tom and Mrs. Dawson, and compare the shop to my father's. Would they have calf and lamb cut up as neatly as my father did? Was their shop tidy? Was it busy? Did they sell chops and sausages, roasts rolled and trussed in twine? But it was only my first day. Once I settled in, perhaps Mrs. Dawson would let me go with her. Once she and the doctor trusted me.

Tom put on his jacket and Mrs. Dawson tied her bonnet under her chin. "The doctor's gone up to Kentish Town, so he won't be here for lunch. We'll do up some beef tea for her ladyship when I'm back. In the meantime, sweep the back staircase, the steps at the tradesmen's entrance, and the main stairs down to the front door. Quiet as a mouse, mind you. We won't be more than an hour. And if anyone knocks, don't answer. No one's expected."

I fetched the broom and dustpan as they left, but all I could think about was that I was alone. Mrs. Dawson, Tom and the doctor were all out. The missus was up in her bed—asleep or awake, it hardly mattered. I had the house to myself. I knew to do the sweeping first, and quickly, if I didn't want to be scolded; I did wonder, however, if I might have a bit of time to do some exploring.

I started with the main stairs, at the very top, right where the attic door opened outside my room. These stairs were easy work, broad and polished and well lit, a far cry from the back staircase which I dreaded. I made my way down to the first floor, building up a little mound of fine grey dust: in from the sides and forward, step down, in from the sides and forward, past the bedrooms of the doctor and the missus, and down towards the ground floor. Sometimes, as the afternoon light began to fade and the house slowly filled with shadows, I would hear a sound from elsewhere in the house, a squeak or a groan from the attic or the parlour, or from behind the heavy wooden doors of the office or the surgery, and my heart would jump in my chest. Had the doctor come back early? Had Mrs. Dawson forgotten something? I couldn't fathom why I had such fear of them, when they had behaved so kindly toward me. I felt at times like I was being watched. Once I reached the bottom of the stairs, I did a general sweep of the entrance hall towards the front door, unlocked and opened the door and pushed the now sizable pile of dust down the steps and into the bushes on either side. I stepped back into the house, checked the old clock in the hall: twenty minutes. If I could do the back stairs just as quickly, I'd have at least fifteen minutes to poke my nose around. I hurried to the rear of the house, opened the door to the back staircase and tiptoed my way up to the top, careful not to disturb her ladyship who I hoped would be sound asleep.

Even with the attic door open it was very nearly black as pitch, but I could feel the grit on the steps under the soles of my shoes. These stairs were narrower and shallower, and I had to put my hand on the wall to keep myself from falling forward. I began sweeping the dirt downward, pausing every step to feel my way along. It wouldn't surprise me to have Mrs. Dawson check my work with a candle in hand, so I was determined to be thorough. As I swept, the dust began to cloud up in front of my face. I was terrified to sneeze and lose my balance. As I reached the first floor, I passed one of the windows placed high on the wall. The light from it caught something under the stairway door opposite, the same door I'd hovered behind just a few hours before. I opened it a crack and looked on the floor: right there before my eyes was a shiny silver crown, King William IV in profile. In all my life, I'd never seen one before. I turned it over and saw the royal crest. The coin was marked 1831. I thought about him lying ill on his bed in the palace. They had said on the Row that he was going to die soon, and that young Victoria, just a year older than me, was poised to take the throne. I whispered a "God bless," picked up the coin and tucked it into my apron. Then I shut the door and continued sweeping my way down.

Finally, I reached the door at the garden level that led out into the courtyard. I released the lock, stepped outside, and pushed the dirt down the steps. I was about to head to the tradesmen's entrance when I heard an odd sound, a kind of mewling. I couldn't tell what it was. I turned and looked back across the yard and saw a woman crumpled on the ground near the ice house. The doctor's wife! She was wearing the same lace-trimmed nightgown I'd seen draped across the chair in her bedroom. "Help me," she sobbed. It was nearly a whisper. "Help me, please."

I let out a little shriek and ran to her, knelt down and lifted her by her arm; she was as thin and light as a wounded dove. Had she fallen from a window? It didn't seem possible. She couldn't have passed me on the back stairs. How did she get out here? She rose on one foot, then the other. No shoes, no stockings, shivering from the cold. Had she gone out the front door and around the side? I peered down the edge of the house. A dense privet hedge blocked the way. I pulled her close to me, brought her up the steps and into the scullery. "Who are you?" she asked foggily.

"I'm the new maid, milady," I said as I pulled open the door. I couldn't be sure, but I thought she said:

"Oh no."

"It's all right," I assured her. "Let's get you up into bed. Did you come down looking for some lunch?" I locked the door behind me, then pulled open the door to the back staircase. She recoiled as soon as she saw the darkness. "I'm here, I can help, you've no need to worry." I took her hand and led her up, step by step, both of us using the wall to guide us forward.

"I was in the surgery," she said softly, "and I got lost."

I was sure the surgery was locked, and even so, how could you get lost in it? "Come now. We'll get you safe and warm." Her hand was as smooth and cold as ice, it made me shiver to touch it. I couldn't imagine how long she'd been out there. We reached the first floor and I pushed the door open. Thankfully her bedroom was right across the hall. I half-carried her across the room, dusted her off and tucked her into the bed, then pulled the blankets up over her. As I turned to leave, she seized my wrist and pulled me close with a startling burst of strength. "You can't tell them what happened," she said. "You can't tell them we spoke." There was a terrible stench to her breath, like she was rotting from the inside.

"Of course not." I nodded, and helped her settle back into the bed. "I won't say a word to anyone, I promise."

"You must go." She sighed. "You must leave."

Only now do I realise that she didn't mean I should leave the room. She meant I should leave the house. As I turned to close the door, I saw that her cheeks were streaked with tears, glistening in the glow of the fire. I hurried across to the back stairs and fairly scampered down to the bottom just as I heard Mrs. Dawson's key turning in the lock.

"And there you are," she exclaimed as she and Tom stepped over the threshold. "All done with the sweeping, I trust?"

"Just finished," I said, which wasn't strictly a lie. "Let me help you with some of those things." She handed me a cake of ale yeast, a basket of eggs, some carrots and onions and potatoes and currants to take to the larder, while Tom set his sack of flour and packages of meat onto the large wooden table. As I came back into the kitchen, I remembered the coin. "Mrs. Dawson," I said, reaching into my apron. "Look what I found. It was up on the first floor, right near the door. It must've fallen out of the doctor's pocket." I showed it to the two of them. Tom's eyes went wide with surprise. If I'd never seen a silver crown before, it was likely that he hadn't either.

"Tom," Mrs. Dawson said, turning to him. "Be a love and leave the two of us for a moment. Go to my room and put your feet up." He scurried off down the hall. I wondered if I was in trouble.

Once Mrs. Dawson heard the door click shut, she turned to me with a grin that stretched from ear to ear. "Margaret, my dear, you've made me so happy. So many other girls would have kept that coin, or at least would have made me ask for it. You're the first in many years to offer it willingly."

I was dumbfounded. "Was this a test?"

"It was," she replied, "and you've passed, with flying colours." She took my hand in both of hers and squeezed it tight. "You're a good girl, Meg, if I may call you that. I'm so proud of you right now."

"I'd be so pleased if you called me Meg." I could feel the tears welling at the corners of my eyes. My encounter with the missus flashed through my mind, her shoeless feet, her nightclothes, her hands of ice.

"We should heat up that beef tea." Mrs. Dawson poured a jar of salted broth into a small copper pot while I pulled down the silver tray, one of the flower-painted plates, and a matching cup and saucer. Then she took the loaf of bread and the knife and carefully cut two slices, even all the way through. Once the broth was poured and Mrs. Dawson was on her way up to the missus, I took a peek inside the book she'd set out for me, and resolved to become the best baker in any house in Highgate. I should have been annoyed to have had my loyalties measured in such a way, but I was not: I had made Mrs. Dawson proud of me, and I was determined to make the doctor proud of me too. I hesitate to say this, but it might be that I want to make you proud of me as well.

Your grateful friend,

M.E.

June 15th, 1887

Darling, thank you for coming to my hateful party. Here is the text I mentioned while we were out chasing after peacocks with croquet mallets. I have marked the page that would be of the greatest interest. Use this information wisely and discreetly. The passage has not specified the signs, symbols and passwords that the Freemasons employed, as that would have been a breach of confidence, but it should not be difficult to confirm some of what you've already surmised.

Interesting that your correspondent mentioned the Turk's Head on Butcher Row. It was used as a meeting place by Freemasons for many years. This may be why your mysterious physician was down in Ratcliff ten miles from his house. I doubt he travelled all that way just to have a pint!

Be well,

Your loving father

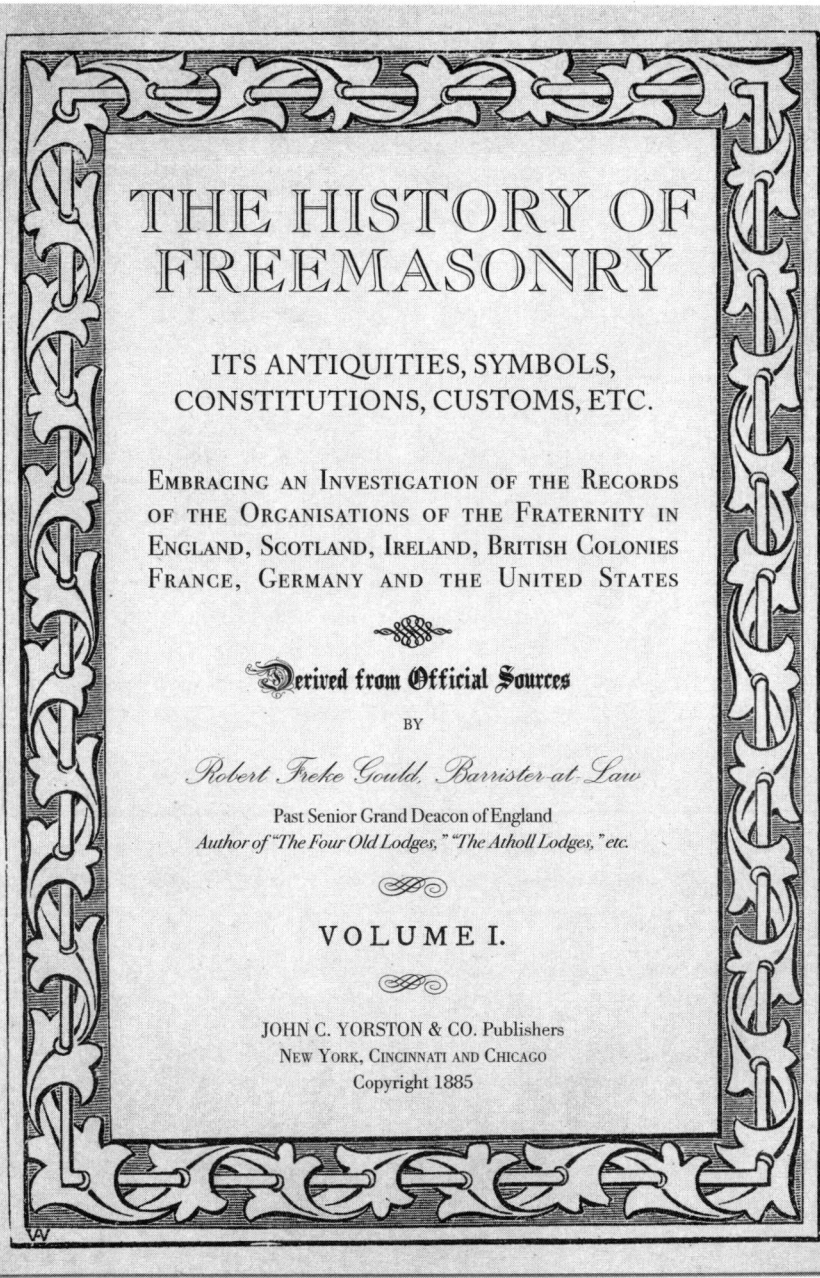

THE ANCIENT MYSTERIES

Amongst the Pythagoreans there were similar gradations. It was an old maxim of this sect, that everything was not to be told to everybody. It is said that they had common meals, resembling the Spartan syssitia, at which they met in companies of ten, and by some authorities they were divided into three classes, "Acustici, Mathematici, and Physici." It also appears that they had some secret conventional symbols, by which members of the fraternity could recognise each other, even if they had never met before.

That, in all the Mysteries, the initiated possessed secret signs of recognition, is free from doubt. In the "Golden Ass" of Apuleius, Lucius, the hero of the story, after many vicissitudes, regains his human shape, and is initiated into the Mysteries of Isis; he finds, however, that it is expected of him to be also instructed in those of the great God, and supreme father of the gods, the invincible Osiris. In a dream he perceives one of the officiating priests, of whom he thus speaks: "He also walked gently with a limping step, the ankle bone of his left foot being a little bent, in order that he might afford me some sign by which I might know him." In another work (Apologia) the author of the "Metamorphosis" says: "If anyone happens to be present who has been initiated into the same rites as myself, if he will give me the sign, he shall then be at liberty to hear what it is that I keep with so much care."

Plautus, too, alludes to this custom in one of his plays (Miles Gloriosus, iv.2), when he says: "Cedo Signum, harunc sies Baccharum." *Give me the sign*, if you are one of the sevotaries; literally one of the Bacchæ or votaries of Bacchus. These had a sign or password—symbolum or memoraculum—by which they recognised each other.

*

June the 16th, 1887

Dear Miss Gibson,

I am writing in response to your enquiry, passed to me by Dr. Montague at the Royal College of Physicians. Dr. Noel Cavanaugh was my mother's brother. He died just two years ago, at a most advanced age.

I understand that you are a journalist, and are not bound by requests for discretion. Still, I am hoping you will keep private the information that I am about to impart, as it could cause some embarrassment for my mother, my brother and certain other members of the family.

My mother is ailing but she still has her wits about her. I have brought your questions to her and this is what she can recall.

My uncle never married. He had no discernible interest in the institution and rebuffed any encouragements from my grandparents and other family members. He lived what I would describe as a solitary life. He never had a housekeeper named Mrs. Dawson, nor any maid by the name of Margaret or Margery or Meg. No women at all, in fact; not as servants nor as patients nor as friends. His only household staff were a longtime butler named Perkins, an African, with whom he was quite close; a footman named LeRoy, who was apparently deaf; and a young houseboy named Billy, who ran off at some point never to return.

You may infer from this what you will.

I did ask my mother if these names sounded familiar to her, and she seemed to recall a doctor at the other end of the high street named Desmond. Dr. Clive Desmond. He may have had a housekeeper named Dawson, and there may have been a boy. She could not confirm any other details.

I do hope this is helpful. We appreciate your attention to the sensitivity of these matters, and we wish you all the best in your pursuits.

Mr. Henry Boulton

Bell House,
Norfolk Street,
Mayfair

JUNE THE 19TH, 1887

Dear Miss Gibson,

The Jubilee is upon us! I hope you will be taking part in the festivities. We hear little of the turmoil down in London but we are aware that Her Majesty has been out of the public eye since Prince Albert's death, God rest his soul, and that many are questioning the need for the monarchy in the modern era. This would make for an interesting article in your newspaper. Perhaps you should suggest it, or venture to write it yourself.

I am unaware of any celebrations planned near the Priory, though I expect some of our neighbours will gather on the heath to watch the fireworks over the city, and perhaps set a few off themselves. I've never seen such things outside of Guy Fawkes Day, which seems nothing but a feeble excuse for drunkenness and chaos and clamour. I don't much care for crowds or noise, so I will join the Sisters here in quiet prayer for Victoria's continuing health and strength in body and spirit. If only we all could live so long in service to our country and to the Lord.

I remember the day the King died, the doctor was kind enough to ask Mrs. Dawson and Tom and myself if we would like to take the following day to go down to St. James Palace to welcome the new Queen. I knew that Mrs. Dawson would have loved to go, but it was so far away that, even if we rode down by carriage, we still would have had to walk miles through the crowds that were expected. Who would have imagined that, not even two years later, while those same streets were still dressed in flags and bunting from Her Majesty's Coronation, I would find myself in an utterly desperate state: a fugitive, escaped from the doctor's house with just the clothes on my back, destitute, bereft and abandoned. But more on that soon enough.

I have written about my first day with the doctor and the missus. The first day in any job is the most memorable, except, perhaps, for the last. The ones in between though, they mostly flow one into the other, especially if they are long and the duties seldom vary. Most mornings, Mrs. Dawson and I rose early. I would clear out the hearth and start the kitchen fire, then help her prepare breakfast for the doctor and the missus; Tom would stumble into the kitchen, wash his face and hands as Mrs. Dawson demanded, and then see to the fire in the drawing room; I would serve the doctor in the morning room or take a tray to his office door per his request, and Mrs. Dawson would bring her ladyship a very light meal of weak tea or clear salt broth and buttered bread or toast, then tend the fire in her room and help her wash and change into a fresh dressing gown. Once I was back belowstairs, I would hurry to the scullery to do the washing-up while Mrs. D cleaned the kitchen and organised the larder, making note of any supplies that needed refreshing. Some days the doctor liked an early luncheon; other days, if he was in meetings or with patients, he liked to take tea in the afternoon with scones and small cakes and sandwiches. Mrs. Dawson would bring another light meal to the missus in the late afternoon and then help her into her nightclothes; she was often back in bed just as the sun was setting. After that first day I stayed well away from the lady's bedroom, for fear that she would mention our encounter in the courtyard.

Every morning I would sweep either the front stairs and hallways or the back stairs and common rooms and basement. Once every few weeks we hauled the rugs and curtains out into the courtyard for a good beating. These were just some of the things that consumed our waking hours.

At Mrs. Dawson's urging, I did examine the bread-baking book, and she guided me in making my first loaves, a few of which were disastrous, and several batches of scones which were quite a bit better. After serving lunch, Mrs. Dawson would provide instruction while I prepared our yeasted dough and pastry crust, and then in the evenings after the doctor's supper we would return to the kitchen and shape and bake the loaves and cakes and tarts so they could cool overnight. It was torture for poor Tom to go to bed amidst the smells drifting out of the kitchen, but he knew that Mrs. Dawson was still strong enough to give him a hiding if he tried to sneak himself a snack.

There was one day, I think it must have been two or three weeks after I first came to the doctor's house, that I brought his breakfast first to the morning room and then to his office, and he was in neither place. Nervously, I gave a light tap on the door of the surgery. It was still forbidden to me, and therefore a source of continuing fascination. "Sir?" I asked. "Are you in there?" A moment passed before he gave a hullo and asked if there was a problem. I told him I had his meal ready and asked if he would like it there or in one of the other rooms, and he pulled the door open so sharply that I nearly threw the tray down in fright. He apologised, and took it from my hands, then placed it on a long wooden table near the centre of the room, a narrow table with an incline at one end, draped in a clean white sheet. I couldn't help myself, I peered in and took note of a wild array of drawings and diagrams and vessels and instruments and specimens. Some of it was ghastly, I fully admit, though my curiosity overwhelmed any shock or revulsion. The doctor watched my reaction, a corner of his lip curling with amusement.

"Would you like to come in?" he asked. "You have shown admirable restraint so far."

"Begging your pardon, sir. Just for a moment, if it pleases you. I must be mindful of my many tasks for Mrs. Dawson." He stepped aside and I crossed over the threshold. The first thing I noticed was that it was quite cold, nearly as cold as the attic. The room had no fireplace, which was odd; perhaps it was newly separated from the doctor's office. I rubbed my hands together and shivered, yet the doctor was in his shirtsleeves. There were many pictures around the room, engravings of various parts of the human body, cut away to show the veins and muscles and organs, like maps to strange cities and countries in faraway lands. On the shelves were many books, specimens and displays, illustrating a variety of ailments and abnormalities.

"Most young women wouldn't have any interest in what goes on in my surgery."

The corner across from the door where I stood was lined on two walls with a heavy green velvet curtain, presumably to block the draft from where a window or door had once been. In front of the curtains stood a folding privacy screen hung with white muslin; next to it was a small metal bathtub, a large bucket and a side table with a row of carefully laid-out instruments, gleaming in the early light. A nearby washstand held bowls and water jugs and a stack of clean cloths, much like the red-stained one he held when first we met. "I was in the surgery and I got lost," the missus had said. For the life of me, I couldn't see how.

"Much of the work I do is rather unpleasant," he continued. "There can be a lot of blood." He picked up a piece of toast from the tray and bit into it.

"I've seen more than you might think," I replied.

He sipped from his cup of tea and nodded, plumes of steam hovering in front of his face. "I suppose that's true," he said. "If anyone has the stomach for these things I do, it's likely to be you."

I moved to the far wall, where three deep shelves displayed jars with organs afloat within them, many of them diseased, some cut open to show clusters of growths or pockets of rot. Near the end of one shelf were four smaller jars which held what looked to be tiny babies, not yet born, foetuses they were called, each slightly larger than the one before, with the last jar marked "Matthew—nine months" in a spidery scrawl. They reminded me of the fist-sized piglets we sometimes found inside of sows. How had he come to own all these things? I looked closer at Matthew and saw that he had a hole in his side, out of which poked a tiny tangle of innards: his stomach, his liver, his bowels.

"Matthew is my son," the doctor said softly, placing his hand gently on the jar. "Stillborn. A mercy, it was. He could not have lived for long in that state, and would have suffered every moment. And my poor wife, you see, she was left barren after his arrival. Unable to ever carry another child." I looked up and saw he had a wistful, faraway look. A tear was glinting in the corner of his eye.

"Oh my goodness, sir, I'm so sorry," I said, flushed with embarrassment and sorrow. What a horrible thing to have happen! In my flustered state I moved away and caught my hip against something heavy and solid, a wooden table or some kind of low cabinet.

"Ah, careful now! That's something I'd like you to see," he said, relieved, I think, to move to another subject. I stepped back and realised that I stood next to a long, large object covered in a thick dark cloth, a navy-blue brocade. He pulled the cloth aside and revealed a case made of glass and oak, and inside what appeared to be the corpse of a woman, slightly older and taller than me, with jet-black hair and gentle features. It took me a moment to see that she was made of wax, and another to realise she was the very image of the doctor's wife.

"She's an Anatomical Venus," he said quite proudly. "She's very precious to me. She helps me with my work. Here, let me show you." He slid down one of the glass panels and reached into the case, turned several fasteners on either side of her belly and then removed her chest and midsection. Inside I could see her ribs, and underneath them her heart and lungs and stomach and innards. It was eerie how real she looked. He pulled the ribs up, as they were on tiny brass hinges. Now my view of her organs was unobstructed. "I have one more surprise," he added. He showed me a shelf underneath full of rubber tubes and bulbs. He gave one a squeeze. I jumped with shock as the woman's heart sprang to life and pumped a dark red fluid out into her arteries. He showed another bulb and squeezed it; the lungs filled with a gasp and then deflated with a whispery hiss. He squeezed yet another bulb, and fluid bubbled in her stomach. He handed the bulb to me and I tightened my fingers around it. The liquid swirled and gurgled as if she was alive.

"She's beautiful," I mused, captivated by her intricacy and complexity. I had never seen anything like her. He placed the bulbs back on their shelf, closed the rib cage, and refastened the front piece to her torso. I saw that his cheek was wet with the single tear that had fallen. His eye caught mine, and he used his shirt cuff to wipe it away.

"Margaret?" called a voice from the hall. It was Mrs. Dawson. I felt my heart quicken. She was sure to be furious. "Margaret, where have you gotten to?"

"It's all right, Mrs. Dawson," the doctor called. "She's in here with me, at my express invitation." He gave me a wink, but I was still not reassured. He pulled the blue cloth back up over the Venus cabinet, then smoothed it out with his hand.

Mrs. Dawson stepped through the door, wiping her ruddy hands on her apron. Her face was fraught with distress. "There you are! Doctor, I am so sorry. She knows not to be troubling you in here."

"No trouble at all, Mrs. Dawson. She was kind enough to bring me my breakfast, so I decided to give her a little tour." He finished his tea and the last of his toast, then handed the tray back to me. I bobbed a quick curtsy in response.

"You've been very patient, sir," she replied icily. "Come, Margaret. We are behind on all our chores." She turned on her heel to leave the room, and clearly I was to follow. It was only then that I saw what stood in the corner behind the door, the most unusual thing in a room full of such things: a child's skeleton hanging from a hook on a fine brass stand. It had a small, sharp, jagged hole in the side of its skull, and it was missing a leg.

"I will take lunch in my office at noon, Mrs. Dawson," the doctor called after us. "I'm done with this room for the moment. Perhaps you should bring the tray up this time." He closed the door firmly behind us. I heard the turn and click of the lock. Mrs. Dawson scowled at me and marched towards the back staircase. Glumly I followed behind her, knowing I'd done nothing wrong but feeling otherwise.

Another fortnight passed without incident, but then late one afternoon Mrs. Dawson and I were in the kitchen preparing the evening meal when we heard a quick, sharp knocking at the front door. Mrs. D dried her hands and hurried up the back stairs. I heard the door swing open, and a few words exchanged. It was a man, younger or older I couldn't say. There was an air of urgency to their conversation. The doctor must have stepped out into the hall, as I heard him speak as well. I carried on as best I could, continuing to fix the supper while catching a word here and there. Tom, who had been tending the fire in the drawing room, bumbled down the steps almost breathless. "They want you upstairs, the doctor and Mrs. D. You're to hurry as quick as you can." I tidied myself as best I could and followed Tom back up to the front hallway. The doctor was standing by the door, pulling his coat on. Mrs. Dawson came soaring towards me, as fretful as I'd ever seen her.

"Margaret, the doctor is being called away to see to a patient and he needs you to go with him. If you go up to the room next to the nursery, you will find a uniform you can wear—a blue dress, a white apron and a white cap. I'm to run downstairs to fetch a few things for you to take. Now, hurry!" I didn't hesitate a moment, I rushed up the front stairs to the attic and threw open the door to the musty old nursery, furnished but never used. The room was outfitted with a cradle, a rocking chair, a washstand. I peered into the adjacent room where the nursemaid would have stayed: a weary old bed not much better than mine, curtains scattered with faded flowers, an imposing mirrored armoire. I twisted and pulled at its knobs every which way until it finally sprang open. There was the uniform. I tugged off my maid's outfit and laid it out on the bed, then pulled on the nursemaid's uniform and cap. I took a quick peek in the mirror and scarcely recognised myself. It was not so long since I had left the Row and I had somehow changed from a half-grown child in patchy bloodstained clothes to a proper serious woman. And who knew with whatever might come how I would change again? I gave the cap a sharp tug and then scurried back down the stairs. Mrs. Dawson was there with a coat for me, and a large black bag like what the doctor carried. I tossed on the coat and took the bag from her. I was startled by the weight of it. What would I be doing? How could I possibly help?

"Perfect," the doctor exclaimed as he saw me, though I didn't feel perfect at all.

"Thank you, sir," I stammered. At last I saw the gentleman who had come calling. He was a distinguished man, close to the doctor's age. His face was grey and creased with worry. Mrs.

Dawson opened the door for us, then held me back by my arm and whispered.

"Be quiet and still, do as you're told and don't ask any questions. These are very important people, very private people. Now off with you."

She released me and I flew down the steps to the private carriage that awaited us. The doctor helped me inside and onto my seat, pulled the door shut, and off we sped. We hurtled down past Hampstead Heath and the Regent's Park and into the heart of Mayfair, stands of trees and spiralling nightingales waving us on our way. Neither the doctor nor the gentleman spoke the entire way down and I was too afraid to say the first word. I did notice the gentleman had a card clutched in his hand, one of the doctor's cards, and on the back was drawn the same strange symbol that had been on the card my mother had carried. I thought of my mother nearly every day, but the sight of this brought me close to tears. "Steady now, Meg," I could picture her saying. I swallowed my sadness and vowed to be brave, whatever it was that awaited me.

Eventually we slowed and stopped at a row of mansions on the edge of Grosvenor Square, fashioned of stone and brick, circled with a fence of iron. The driver hopped down and helped us out of the carriage, and we rushed into a door marked No. 16 where a valet stood at the ready to take our coats. Our gentleman companion left our side and entered a room at the right, the sitting room, where twelve or fourteen people, men and women and children of every age, sat in solemn silence. None would raise their eyes to look at us. "Come this way, please," the valet said, and led us up a grand staircase to the bedrooms on the first floor. As lovely as the doctor's house was, this was ten times more so. Golden wood, cream-coloured stone, sparkling silver and glass, shimmering brocades, and lightly flowered paper on the walls. Paintings and tapestries were scattered about, fields and forests and hunting scenes, dogs taking down stags by the throat. I wanted to touch everything but kept my two gloved hands firmly on the handles of my bag.

Outside the farthest door stood a servant girl who curtsied as soon as she saw us. She stood next to a long narrow table crowded with dainty ornaments. Among them was a tarnished brass handbell with a leather handle. The girl was all a-tremble, I had no idea why. The doctor thanked the valet, who returned to the family downstairs while we approached the room. "Stay here," the doctor told the girl. "You will ring the house when I tell you." She nodded, ashen-faced, and backed away from the door. The doctor reached into his pocket, then turned to me, proffering a small vial of oil of camphor. I'm sure I must have looked confused. He rubbed a few drops under his nose, and urged me to do the same. He then grabbed the knob, turned it firmly, then gestured for me to follow closely. I stepped inside with him and, I couldn't help myself, I gasped. Even with the oil of camphor, the stench of death struck me like a slap, that same sickly sweet smell my father exuded before he passed.

On the bed was a very old woman, skin stretched over bones, eyes sunken and cloudy, sparse strands of white hair tufting out from her skull. She was turned on her side slightly, bedclothes pulled up to her chest, her frail left arm poking out, spotted and scabbed and crooked up near her chin like that of a bird. If I hadn't heard the rasping of her breath, I would never have known she was alive. Had she heard us? Did she know we were there? I couldn't tell.

"Come," the doctor said as he moved to the side of the bed, standing in front of her face. She seemed oblivious to our presence. "Inside your bag are two bootlaces. Could I have them, please." This information startled me. Why would I have these, and what were they for? Still, I snapped open the bag, reached in and felt around until I found them and handed them over. He nodded, then said, "Prepare yourself." He reached down and carefully pulled aside the old woman's bedcovers, exposing her frail, colourless body. Something was nestled against her, wrapped in a damp white towel. My first thought was a newborn babe, though I knew that couldn't be possible. The doctor pulled the top of the towel back and revealed an enormous tumour, as large as the old woman's head, that had grown out of a split in her side that itself was dressed in gauze and cloth. The hole was seething with small white worms and glittering flies. The doctor waved them away absently, then took first one bootlace, and then the other, and tightly tied off the stalk that joined the tumour to the woman's body.

"We must work quickly," he said. He reached into his own bag, withdrew the engraved brass syringe I recognised from the bedside table when Mrs. Dawson had taken the missus her meal. "Have you ever given a clyster? It's fairly straightforward." He reached into the bag and brought out a stoppered glass bottle of dark brown liquid. I could read the bright orange label from where I was standing. Sulphate of Morphine. Poison. Two grains. He uncorked the bottle, drew the entirety of the liquid into the syringe and handed it to me. "Gently ease the tip into her backside until the length of the stem is within her, then squeeze until all of the contents are inside her bowel. Do you understand?" I understood the words but could not comprehend what we were doing. How were we helping this woman? I pulled the bedclothes further down, exposing the old woman's buttocks. They were as grey and withered as the rest of her, with barely any flesh on them. I knelt down and inserted the tip of the syringe as far as it could go, then pressed the plunger as the doctor had asked until the syringe was empty. I carefully removed it and handed it back to him. He wrapped it in one of his surgical cloths and placed it in his bag. In a moment, the old woman's breathing abruptly changed, becoming hoarse and heavy and slow.

"Mrs. Dawson has placed a copper bowl in your bag. Could you pass it to me, please?" I reached into the bag and, yes, found the copper bowl, one of the kitchen bowls we used for mixing our bread and pastry dough. I took it out and handed it to him. He took a scalpel from his bag, which glittered in the firelight, and placed the sharp edge on the stem of the tumour between the two shoelaces. He sliced through it in short, even movements, until the tumour was separated. A gush of blood and murky fluid spilled out onto the towel. He pulled it up and around the tumour, wrapping it tightly, and slipped it into the copper bowl. He then passed the bowl to me. The stink of the cancerous flesh was overwhelming, as if I had been plunged back into the Row with all its rancidness and rot. "Into the bag with that," he said. "Close it tight, and do not open it again until we get back to the house."

The doctor turned his attention back to the old woman,

whose throat was now thick with phlegm and rattling with every slowing breath. The corners of her mouth were flecked with foam. She would not last much longer. He pulled down the dressings, tucked the stem of the tumour back into the wound, and untied the bootlace. Now what little blood and fluid she had left in her body would leak into the cavity until she died. He placed the dressing and cloth back over the opening, pulled the bedclothes up to her chest, and then gestured for me to seat myself. He remained standing, watching the old woman carefully until she gave her last breath, a lengthy guttural growl, approximately seven minutes later. He pressed his fingers to her wrist, her neck, consulted his watch, then pushed the lids down over her eyes. He went to the door, opened it, and told the servant girl, "She has passed."

I picked up my bag and joined him in the hall as the servant girl lifted a brass bell from the hall table and rang it till it echoed throughout the house. I heard rustling downstairs as the family members rose as one, and then strode up the stairs toward and then past us without a glance in our direction, and entered their separate rooms to dress for mourning. The sole exception was a small child, a girl, who looked up longingly into my eyes as she came towards us. At the end of the procession was the man who had fetched us, and with him an older woman in a dark grey dress and head-covering. I realised then that they were not members of the family, but very likely an undertaker and a layer-out of the dead. "Time of death, half past eight in the evening," the doctor told the gentleman. With nary a whisper they glided into the room where the old woman's body awaited. The doctor gestured towards the stairs, and together we made our way down to the front hallway, where the valet had begun to drape the mirrors in heavy black cloth. He turned to us, nodded. The doctor reached inside his coat, handed the valet a rather fat envelope. I remember how odd this was to me, him paying them and not the reverse. Only later, when I saw the tumour in its jar on the shelf alongside his other wonders, did it occur to me that he had purchased this tumour, and perhaps had paid the family to allow it to grow unimpeded. But it was too ghastly a thought for me to dwell upon.

"Thank you," the doctor said. "And please convey our deepest condolences. She passed without pain and was welcomed peacefully into the world beyond our own." The valet nodded once more, then led us out the front door to where the carriage awaited. The horse snuffled, pulled his head away from us. He could smell what was in my bag. He knew what that smell meant. The doctor led me well away from him to the side of the carriage, helped me inside, seated himself and shut the door. The carriage pulled away sharply and sped back down the road, back down towards Highgate.

The following day, the doctor welcomed me back into his surgery to show me his newest specimen, preserved in formaldehyde in an enormous glass jar: the old woman's cancerous tumour. Glued to the side of the jar was a label, written in the doctor's own hand, listing the specimen's measurements and weight. A smear of blood stained the corner of the paper.

That night, after a full day's work in the kitchen, I lay awake and wondered if the tumour lived still, somehow, independent of its host, if it somehow housed the soul of the old woman who grew it, nurtured it, surrendered it. In the rest of my time in that house, I was always aware of that jar, in that room, and measured my location wherever I was, farther, closer, above, below, by its proximity.

I disgust you, I fear, with these letters, with these tales of mine that turn, always, to flesh and blood and bone. Yet still you write, often enough, and still you ask for more. I know you still seek your Mrs. Lovett, turning stones in the mud to see what vermin might crawl out. But now, tonight, with the moon at wane above us, I have a question for you: What would you be, if not a journalist, if not the child of a wealthy man, in a well-appointed house, with hats and dresses and servants and suitors and social engagements? What sort of creature, if you were born and grew up in a place where it seemed the sun didn't shine? And when it did shine, it was filtered through a veil of smoke, and smothered under a cloak of fog? Where soot floated down like snowflakes in summer, and snowflakes came down grey and sullen in winter? What would you be, if every day you heard the cracking of skulls, the mournful lowing of cattle, and the frantic bleating of sheep? Where the gutters ran red at dawn, and offal lay on the cobblestones. Where freshly flayed skins steamed into the early morning air, and everything was splashed with muck. Where children were nearly trampled by a thousand hooves, where meat was meat, where nothing went to waste, and you learned the value of every penny and every pound. What would you be then?

You might be me.

M.E.

22nd of June, 1887

Miss Gibson,

I have received your letter with your questions about my parents, their household, and my father's medical practice.

I do not appreciate your attention. My mother and father are long dead. My husband and I are private people. I have no desire to speak to the press on these or any other matters.

<u>Please do not write to me again,</u> nor to anyone in our circle.

Good day.

(Mrs.) *Marie Desmond Winstead*

Hycliffe House
Berkshire

JUNE THE 24TH, 1887

Dear Miss Gibson,

Begging your pardon, I didn't know what else to do or how to reach you. I pray your colleagues at the Post will treat this with the utmost urgency.

The constable investigating the Reverend Mother's death has returned with more questions. He is interviewing each of the Sisters in turn. I've no doubt I will be the last on his list, followed by Miss Margaret. There are dark doings here. They claim the Reverend Mother may not have taken the poison willingly, and the note that was found with her body may not have been written by her at all. A shocking suggestion! They say she has been done a grave injustice, that someone has committed a horrendous crime. It simply cannot be. It is beyond what any of us can bear.

I know that Margaret is innocent. She could not have written the note that Sister Augustine found. Yet all eyes are turning towards her. I feel powerless to intervene.

The night closes in upon us.

Sister Catherine
St. Anne's Priory

JUNE 26TH, 1887

Dear Miss Gibson,

What an intriguing letter you've sent me, asking about things I haven't thought of for an age. I'm not clear as to why you're asking about my great-grandmother, long dead and gone, or the doctor who attended her—whom I barely remember. My grandparents lived in the house you're enquiring about, throughout Nana's illness and beyond. Afterwards the house was sold, and the proceeds divided between my father and my Uncle Jonas. We lost touch with him after my father's death. Might you be his child, I wonder? No matter, she made no other provisions for heirs. I will see what I can recall of her last days and hope it is of some assistance. It is a pleasant diversion for me in any event as I am alone most days with only ma petite femme de chambre for company.

I believe that year I was nine years old, so the memories come to me through the eyes of a child, everyone tall and towering over me and quietly resentful of my presence. I did not see Nana on her final day, so I cannot recall the specifics of her death. I do remember being crowded into the parlour with an inordinate number of relatives. Everyone sat under a pall of gloom but I wonder, even now, how many of them were truly sad and how many made pretense of their grief. I have discovered that when one dies, their true feelings about each family member, and vice versa, are brought to light by what they leave behind and to whom. I've heard for some families the formal reading of a will is an ordered affair, with at least a veneer of civility; in ours, sadly, some of the wishes inscribed in such documents have caused such shock that the grudges they inspired were handed down through the generations, like an unattractive set of Wedgwood.

As I recall, my mother, father and I were to guest at her house in Grosvenor Square for a week. My father in particular seemed oddly impatient, as if he had expected her to pass away sooner; however, in keeping with her characteristic stubbornness, she hung on like the last withered leaf before the onset of winter. My parents were both irritable throughout our stay, and my father was even more distant than usual, if that was possible.

Our time in that house stretched on, and, I can tell you, for a nine-year-old, it was as dull as dust. There were no toys to play with, no other children for games, no books worth reading. My mother kept forcing weighty tomes of history on me, all from my grandfather's library, in an attempt to keep me quiet and out of the way. There was one book I had a bit of pleasure from: it was about Mary, Queen of Scots, and how her cousin Elizabeth had her head chopped off. Other than that, my only entertainment was to drift from window to window and look out at the people and carriages passing in the street. I remember it being eerily quiet as the carriages went by; usually they're noisy, rattling things, but to help relieve Nana's suffering, the servants spread the cobblestone road with straw to dampen the sound of the passing hooves and wheels. It stretched quite far in either direction, and was replaced at least once a day.

Desperate for some amusement, I hid behind the curtains from time to time so I could eavesdrop on my parents, aunts and uncles, but even they proved dull, at least to me. Funeral arrangements, invitation lists, teacakes and butter biscuits wrapped in waxed paper, and orders of oysters and sherry. The most interesting thing I heard was that Uncle Jonas, my father's brother, was a Freemason. At the time, the term meant nothing to me, but the hushed tones and dark intonations made it sound mysterious and exciting. There were mentions of meetings and secrets and symbols and obligations. Strange rituals. Very little, as I recall, about the actual laying of bricks. But I couldn't make any more of it than that.

The evenings at Nana's house were dreary in a different way. Looking out the windows ceased to be diverting as the streets quieted after dark, and in the house it grew too dim to read or draw or review the lessons Miss Sealey, my governess, had sent with me. So, instead, I sat near my relatives in the parlour, watching the fire, listening to my mother and aunts disparage other women in their circle, and complain about their husbands, servants and children as though I wasn't sitting right there. In those moments I envied the maids, who bustled about and kept busy, while I was left to sit still as a statue and do nothing.

Truly, nearly all my memories of the house on Grosvenor Square were of darkness and gloom. I had been assigned to a bedroom near the back stairs, where the servants thumped up and down at all hours. There was never a fire in the grate, so I was always cold, and there weren't enough blankets for so many guests. One of house girls, the plump one with the pink cheeks I think, she would put a warming pan in my bed for half an hour around eight o'clock. When it was time to turn in, I would dive beneath the covers, shivering, with my knees drawn up to my chest, huffing on my frozen fingers till sleep carried me away. In the morning, I got up and washed myself with warm water, which was brought up very early by the maids; they slipped in and out of our rooms without being seen or heard, like phantoms.

I suppose I've digressed from your initial query about Nana's illness and the days after her death. I will try to stay on course from this moment, though this is an enjoyable test of my memory.

The first time I saw the physician who came to visit Nana, he was with my Uncle Jonas. I remember this quite clearly. It was as if they were old friends, though I couldn't imagine how that would be. Jonas was somewhat roguish, but the doctor was handsome and refined, almost delicate. He had a slim, strong build and those fine slender hands. I thought him very dashing and enigmatic. I believe it was after his first visit that I heard my father and uncle discussing the Freemasons, because it turned out the doctor was one too. This might be how my uncle and the doctor knew each other. They said something about one of the public houses, the Turk's Head. I wondered what a Turk's Head looked like, and what went on there. I remember my mother clucking her disapproval as she did at any mention of ale or spirits and then excusing herself to retire to her rooms upstairs.

When they were alone in the parlour with just me in the corner reading about royal executions, I overheard the doctor offer my uncle a large sum of money in exchange for something of Nana's, but I couldn't tell you what exactly. One of her hideous porcelains, I imagine. I remember my uncle recoiling in disgust at the suggestion, but eventually acceding to the request.

The day my great-grandmother finally breathed her last, that day I do recall. Unlike the previous days when everyone was sullen and bitter and peevish, there was an air of sadness, of resignation.

Something had changed. There was the inescapable sense that the waiting was at an end. I recall that my grandfather went to fetch the Vicar from St. George's, who came quickly to pray with the family at the old woman's bedside. Uncle Jonas then jotted something onto his card and gave it to one of the housemen, instructing him to bring the doctor once more. A few hours later the houseman returned with the physician at his side and a young nurse trailing behind, rather plain and shy, and slightly terrified; I couldn't imagine what help she could be. The two of them rushed up the stairs; we heard some murmuring, then the bedroom door opened and shut. Everything went quiet. We all were gathered in the parlour, silent except for my mother's sighs and the snapping of the fire. It could not have been more than ten minutes when the upstairs girl rang the bell. Nana had finally passed, with the doctor and nurse at her side at just the right moment. The servants emerged as if out of nowhere and began to drape the mirrors with lengths of black cloth and stop the ticking clocks in every room. Life in that house would stand still and silent until Nana was in her grave.

A mere half hour after her death, the undertaker appeared at the front door, trailed by an apprentice with spotty cheeks. The older man was tall and thin, like a fireplace poker. Tufts of woolly whiskers sprouted down his jawline and along his brow, and he wore a black wool suit with black gloves, a black cloak and a black top hat. He was positively ancient. I found him to be quite eerie, gliding through the rooms, gazing upon every member of the family with the gravest solemnity and sympathy. When he did speak, his voice was as gentle as rain and twice as moist.

He and his apprentice vanished into the study with my father and uncle, shutting the door behind them. I couldn't press my ear against it or I would have gotten a smack. Instead, I watched the footmen crown the front door with black crape, and hang a boxwood wreath upon it so callers would know to knock softly, and not to ring the bell. Afterwards they swathed the parlour with black velvet drapes, spreading them out like raven wings, and set out a plinth for the coffin to rest upon.

Within the hour, the death knell sounded at Grosvenor Chapel. We all stood still for a moment as we heard the echo throughout the streets. A short time later, the undertaker's associates descended upon the house like a swarm of beetles. The first to arrive were two women in black dresses with white aprons, layers-out-of-the-dead, who were there to wash and dress the body. A pair of maids followed at their heels as they trudged up the stairs, and were instructed to provide anything the women required: jugs of warm water, clean cloths, a hairbrush, hair pins and Nana's finest clothes. Everyone in the house whispered and walked on cats' feet, as though the slightest sound might bring the old woman back to furious life.

Next came a flurry of seamstresses from a mourning shop on Regent Street. They arrived with tape measures, fabric samples and pages of designs so my relatives could order their mourning wear, to be delivered in two days' time. My mother and grandmother selected gowns of silk and velvet, all puffed and pleated, but inflicted a plain wool dress upon me, heavy and hot and itchy, ugly as a scowl, and I had absolutely no say in the matter.

Soon, we were all shooed out of the parlour into the drawing and dining rooms as more neighbours and acquaintances arrived, offering their condolences. Endless cups of tea and wedges of seedcake were served, while the maids scuttled about seizing anything soiled before it could touch the table.

For the rest of the afternoon, I positioned myself within view of the front door so I could watch the comings and goings of the funeral arrangers: the coffin maker, there to measure Nana's tiny, birdlike corpse; the florist, who would provide sprays of lilies and roses; and a watcher to sit with Nana through the night as if to keep her company. A stranger! I could only think what a ghoulish job that must be, to show respect to the dead, but also to watch over them, in case they let out a twitch or a gasp, to avert a premature burial.

That night, when I went to bed, all I could think about was Nana, one floor beneath me, in her bedroom, the watcher staring at her sunken face, looking for any sign of life. On the table next to my bed was a candle with a struggling flame, but its glow didn't penetrate the gloom. I knew I had to fall asleep before it went out or I'd be plunged into darkness. I couldn't help myself, though. I stayed wide awake, staring at the cloth-covered looking glass on the far wall, staring through the shadows to make sure it didn't move. My eyelids fluttered and for a moment I thought I saw Nana, crouching down near my feet, head hunched forward, glaring at me, but it was only one of the bedposts. The house was deathly silent; the candle whiffed out with a hiss.

For the next three days, a steady stream of mourners passed through the house. Friends, acquaintances, colleagues all filed past my great-grandmother's coffin. Every now and then I was forced to greet them, ordered to walk through the parlour and look appropriately grief-stricken. One glimpse of Nana in her silk-lined coffin, crowded with lilies and roses, was more than enough for me. She looked nothing like herself, with an oddly styled auburn wig on her shrunken head, and a shroud wrapped around her withered frame.

The stink of the room was awful, even with the hundreds of flowers, even with the body laid out on a cooling tray which the servants filled and refilled with ice. Most of the mourners pressed handkerchiefs against their noses as if they were weeping but really it was to stifle the stench. Now and then another child would hover nervously in the doorway, but they looked so wretched and afraid that I didn't want to play with them. I had thought the doctor and his young nurse might return to pay their respects, but they never did.

On the fourth day, the family dressed in our mourning clothes and filed out to a row of enormous black carriages lined up along the road, each pulled by a pair of black horses wearing plumes of black ostrich feathers on their heads. My mother, grandmother and I were not permitted to join, as our sensibilities were deemed too frail to attend such events. We stood at the kerb in our mourning clothes and watched the men climb into the carriages. I was startled to see the doctor appear out of nowhere, hurry up the street, take Uncle Jonas's hand and give it a hearty shake and join him in his coach near the front of the procession. Puzzled, I distracted myself by watching the feathers sway and bob in the wind as the carriages veered out into the street and trotted steadily around the square towards the cemetery. Paid mourners and pages carrying black crape wands walked solemnly alongside the glass-sided hearse, a spray of lilies on its roof. It was rather pretty, as I recall, in a melancholy way. I was sure Nana would have been pleased.

As the procession turned onto South Audley Street, carts and wagons moved out of the way, and pedestrians stopped to bow their heads in sympathy. I raised my hand to wave goodbye to Nana, but my mother gave me a sharp pinch under my arm and told me I was being disrespectful.

This was all so long ago. Well before you were born, I expect. It must all sound so strange compared to how we live today. I regret I could not be more helpful, but I hope it gives you a tiny window into the world of my youth. I do hope you will write again, with any other questions that come to mind. Of course, you are always welcome to visit! I have so few callers these days, and would be delighted to take tea with you on a day of your convenience.

Yours very truly,

(Miss) Eloise Chapman

Balfour Mews
Mayfair

P.S. I had wanted not to tell you this, but now I feel someone should know. In for a penny, I suppose. I did see Nana briefly, just two days before she died. I had been kept away from her for months at the end of her life. My mother had said that it would be too distressing and that I should remember her as healthy and strong, but I begged for a chance to wish her a final farewell. My mother relented and sent me up with one of the housemaids while she waited below. I think now that she was the one who couldn't face what Nana had become. We approached the bedroom door and opened it rather timidly. I could see the outline of her body on the bed, on her side, her breathing coarse and shallow. The maid held a finger to her lips, then gestured towards a chair at the bedside. As I crept towards it, I felt how stuffy and hot the room was from the blaze in the fireplace. My cheeks flushed when I walked past it. I wanted to ask the maid to open a window, but she had already slipped out, leaving me alone with a creature I hardly recognised.

I held back a gasp at the shock of her appearance. I was only a child after all, but I knew I had to be brave for her. I wanted her to be proud of me. I sat in the chair and whispered to her and told her I was there. She made a small noise, at the back of her throat. Her clouded eyes could not see me. Her crusted lips could not speak my name.

I should have taken her hand, or given her some sign of affection, but my childish terror prevented me from touching her. I was afraid I would hurt her, I'm sure that was it. A wad of blankets was clutched near her belly, wet and stained. The sound of her laboured breathing, the shuddering of her lungs, the rasp in her throat that didn't seem human. How had she lived so long like this? How much longer could she continue?

I stared at the deep lines that scored her face, and the spots scattered across her cheeks. She moaned and I caught myself. My mother had always taught me staring was insolent. But as I turned my gaze away, I saw a single tear track down onto her pillow. To this day, I regret that I did not wipe it away. —EC

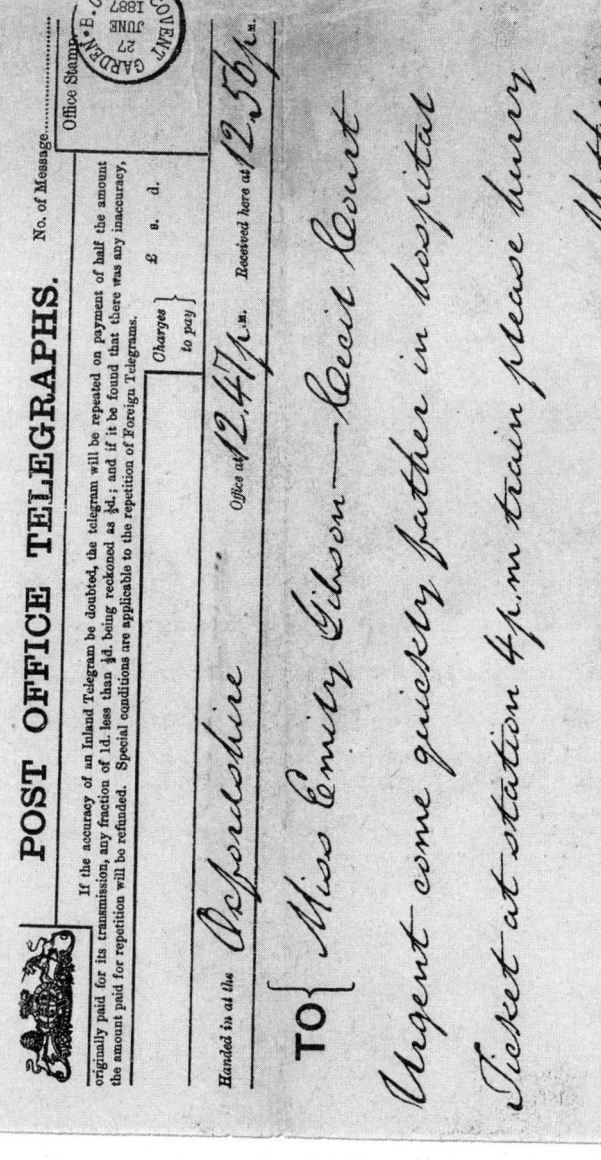

The Oxford Times

EDNESDAY EVENING
JUNE 28, 1887

E THE
me and
ode the
touched
d as a
splendid
threads
ss. The
t mere
rather a

SIR HADLEY GIBSON narrowly escaped death after he was shot on his Berkshire estate. Although out-of-season, a poacher is suspected. Sir H.G. is in capable hands at the Royal Berkshire Hospital, uplifted by our prayers for his rapid recovery.

REVEREND PEMBROKE

ST. ANNE'S PRIORY
Hampstead, London

JULY THE 2ND, 1887

Dear Miss Gibson,

The first thing you'll want to do, when you're making pies, as I have done a few times in my life, is to find yourself some good quality meat—not too fat, not too stringy, cheap if you can find it, and free is even better. You never looked too closely at what was inside, if you knew what was good for you, and in certain neighbourhoods you knew not to buy a pie when the streets were bare of pigeons, cats and dogs. I tell you this because a stranger, a huge man with a big beard and a sack coat with a funny felt hat, came to the Priory in the hour just after dawn; he brought a brace of pheasants, plump little things, to the kitchen door along with a few speckled eggs and wanted sixpence for the lot. The village merchants all know that the Sisters are sparing in their consumption of meat and fish, but the housemaids and the kitchen help are always starved for it. I had a few coins I'd set aside for some special thing or another, so I pooled my money with the cook and made us a nice leek and pheasant pie. I was worried that I'd lost the knack, but it was quite the tastiest thing, it was like magic had come from my own two hands. The pastry is always the test, but we had wheat flour and middlings and the fat from a bowl of pork scraps that we kept in the larder, so I was well set.

All I know about baking pies and cakes and breads is what I learned from my mother and Mrs. Dawson, and I am lucky to have kept that with me all these years. Even as the doctor brought me into his office on Thursday afternoons to learn about nursing and to help him with his patients, Mrs. D was with me Friday evenings after dinner showing me how to make the fancy cakes and tarts and little buns that the doctor liked to have with his breakfast or when his associates came to visit. This plus the regular work I had to do around the house, and some of Mrs. D's work when she was feeling poorly.

The doctor most wanted me in his surgery when one of his lady patients paid a visit, often with women's complaints or unusual pains or swelling. Most times it amounted to little of consequence: indigestion, irregular bowels or troubles with their monthly courses. The doctor kept a variety of pills, tonics and ointments for these various ailments, and prescribed them as appropriate. There were times, though, when he would separate himself from us behind the privacy screen and give me instructions for examination of the patient's private areas to ensure they were free of infection, discharge or disease; in nearly all cases, the women were sent home to rest in their beds and relinquish all domestic activities to their sisters, daughters and servants. I do recall several of his patients who were "with child," and came to us wishing to be examined prior to confinement to their lying-in rooms either at home or in the city, and in those cases we would administer purges or blood-letting to relieve the pain and assist in the child's safe passage from the womb. We were very lucky that not one of these women suffered a loss, nor were they stricken with poor health at any time before giving birth. Not every woman was as fortunate as these, and that misfortune continues even today with modern medicine and procedures at our disposal. Poor Sister Catherine, she is sitting here quite flushed at the turn our discussion has taken! I have a terrible story on this theme to relate, and I can only hope she doesn't faint dead away as I tell it.

It was early December of that same year, and the household was preparing for our annual Christmas festivities. I had been assisting the doctor in his practice for more than six months, with nothing but praise from him for my sensitivity, discretion and composure. This one particular evening, I was cleaning the kitchen after supper as Mrs. Dawson had taken to her bed a few hours early. A sudden, violent knocking at the door startled me and was sure to rouse everyone on the premises if I didn't see to it. I rushed upstairs and flung the door open, prepared to scold whoever was responsible, when I saw two finely dressed ladies standing on the steps, one older and one younger, though not resembling mother and daughter. The older woman had her arm around the younger one, who was flushed and sweating and seemed on the verge of collapse. I saw behind them to where their carriage awaited, and I saw also a trail of heavy dark stains that led from the door of the coach up the steps to where the young woman stood. I shuddered, dreading all the implications of that sight. "Please," the older woman implored. "Is the doctor in? We need his help most urgently." I did not even pause to call for him, I led them into the hallway and down the hall to the surgery. The doctor had heard the clamour and now saw for himself the emergency that was presented to us.

"Good heavens!" he exclaimed. "What on earth has happened? Please, help her up here." The poor young woman groaned and grimaced as we lifted her onto the doctor's surgical bed. The blood was coursing dark and heavy. I had not seen anything like it since my time back on the Row.

"Quickly, sir. May we speak in private?" the older woman asked, casting a glance in my direction.

"If you have something to say or ask," he replied curtly, "you can do so in front of my nurse. We cannot assist you otherwise." The older woman looked at me, her eyebrow raised. At that moment, I felt less like a nurse than a scullery maid. Just then the young woman let out a howl of pain. She was growing paler by the minute. We had to know what the circumstances were in order to be able to proceed.

"Very well," the older woman said grimly. "We come to you from Kensington, at the urging of our housemaster. My young lady serves as a companion at Her Majesty's court. She had reason to visit a midwife earlier this evening for a female complaint, but the bleeding began during the visit and has not stopped since. We could not turn to the Royal Physician in the circumstances. I am sure you understand the gravity of the situation, and the need for absolute discretion."

The doctor gestured to a collection of tonics on one of the lower shelves. I knew immediately what he required. I fetched the bottle of potassium bromide and wrenched the cork out of it. My stomach fluttered with nerves, but my hands were steady. I turned to the remnants of his dinner which we had interrupted, took a spoon from the tray, and put a small scoop of the salts into the glass of red wine I'd brought him, then mixed them together vigorously. I put the edge of the glass to the young lady's lips. "This will help calm you," I reassured her. She took a long sip and coughed. "Drink it all up." I tipped the glass till she had swallowed all of the wine. "Good girl," I said, as though she were a small child. In truth, she might have been three or four years older than me.

The doctor held open the door to his office. "Please wait in here," he said to the older woman. She turned, looked at her young charge, then stepped through into the other room. The doctor closed the door firmly behind her, then pulled on one of his large white aprons and retrieved a set of terrible-looking instruments from one of the desk drawers. There were scissors, clamps, scrapers and blades of various sizes and materials, along with a vial of catgut and several large needles, both straight and curved. The young woman's face blanched and her eyes went wide with terror. I removed her bonnet and found her beautifully curled hair dishevelled. It clung to her face and neck with perspiration. I gently swept a lock of it from her brow and untied her cloak. As I helped her onto the table, I saw a large crimson blossom on the back of her silk gown, and realised most of her undergarments had been removed, making her dress hang limply around her legs. She gripped my hand very hard and wept.

"I'm Margaret," I told her. "What's your name?"

"Helen," she said hesitantly, looking from me to the doctor and back again. It was likely not her real name, but something close to it: Heather, Hilda, Harriet. It was her secret to keep, of course, and that of her guardian.

"There now, Miss Helen," the doctor said. "What was done to you to cause all this?" He slipped off her shoes and pushed her skirts and petticoat up around her waist. Her legs underneath were bare and smeared with blood.

"A whalebone ... was put ... inside me," she whispered, tears streaming down her cheeks. "It hurt very much. It still hurts so much." A whalebone. An abortion. It was clear the young miss had visited a midwife to interrupt a pregnancy, and somehow it had gone terribly wrong. This sadly was as common then as it is today, maybe even more so. I'm sure you know, Miss Gibson, women die daily from such procedures, sought out in moments of desperation. Those who don't die can find themselves permanently damaged, unable to conceive.

"How far along would you say? Has the child quickened?" She could not speak, could not look at him. She gave my hand a squeeze. I looked up at him and mouthed the word: yes. The doctor nodded, reached for one of his instruments and leaned in to see if he could determine whether the womb had been emptied, and how the bleeding could be arrested.

Now, Miss Gibson, you might think me very hard for some of what I've written to you in the past, but I can tell you that when it came to Miss Helen, my heart went out to her. There was something about this young woman that touched me deeply. She lived what many would consider an untroubled life, cherished and cared for, in the presence of royalty. She spoke in a refined manner, dressed in the finest clothes of recent fashion, and her pale skin was so smooth, her fingers so soft and feminine. I knew she hadn't done a hard day's work in all her life, and yet I felt something for her. Were we so different, reduced as she was to lying on a stranger's surgical table long after dark, her life dependent on his ability to repair all that had been done to her?

In other situations, I might have turned my attention toward the doctor and indulged in my fascination with his procedures. In this moment, I wanted only to comfort the poor girl, and preserve her dignity. So instead, I stood near her head and held her hand, and let her clutch me so hard I thought my fingers would break. Every now and then she cried out, and wailed, and groaned. I talked softly to her, and swept tears from her cheeks while the doctor performed his operation. The bromide had calmed her a little, but not enough to blot out the horror of what she was going through.

"Please. I don't want to die," she whispered to me, choking on tears.

"You won't," I said confidently, though I couldn't know if that was true. But I wanted it to be.

After nearly three quarters of an hour, the doctor stepped away from her and wiped his bloody hands on a nearby towel. The poor young woman, her eyes looked glassy and she stared quite blankly at the ceiling. Her breathing was shallow and laboured, and she had slipped from whimpering and moaning to stillness and quiet. The doctor checked her pulse, replaced the cloths between her legs, removed the covering from the surgical bed then bade me to help her into one of the chairs near the door. It was unkind of me, but the first thing I thought was how much work it would be to clean it all.

The doctor rang the bell to summon Mrs. Dawson. She would have wondered why I hadn't reappeared in the kitchen after serving the doctor his dinner. If she had looked out the window to see the carriage waiting, and if she had passed the door to the surgery and heard the voices within, she would have realised it was a medical emergency of some sort and been in a lather of curiosity about it. I imagined her perched in the kitchen, clucking and fretting at poor Tom, waiting to be called upon. And so, within moments of the doctor yanking the bellpull, she appeared at the door of the surgery, a thin smile pasted over her irritation and nosiness.

"Mrs. Dawson," the doctor said, "we have two guests for the night, this young lady and her companion in the next room. I need you and Tom to lay the fires in the guest bedrooms and warm the beds. Our guests will need water to wash themselves, and I'm sure they would appreciate some tea and a light supper. The young lady would benefit greatly from some of the beef tea you prepare for my wife. Tom should go to the carriage out front and advise the driver to return at dawn. Margaret will stay here and help me till the rooms are ready. Let us know at once when everything has been arranged."

"Yes, sir." Mrs. Dawson looked in a daze, her eyes darting from me to the doctor to the young lady, now ghastly pale and looking very unwell. No doubt she had many questions on the tip of her tongue, but this was not the time to ask them. She let out a sharp sigh and hurried off to advise Tom of the tasks at hand.

The doctor opened the door between his surgery and his office, and described the situation to the young lady's waiting companion. I couldn't hear them clearly, but I knew from the tone of her voice that the woman was fraught with fear. She tried to decline the doctor's invitation to stay the night, but the doctor would brook no refusal. As soon as he brought her into the surgery to see her young charge, the older woman blanched and relented. It was clear that "Helen" had been through an ordeal, and should be moved as little as possible.

Mrs. Dawson and Tom had the guest rooms ready within half an hour. The companion and I helped the young lady up the stairs, and then into the larger of the guest rooms, before she installed herself in the room next door.

I closed the door behind us softly, and eased the young woman into a chair. I helped her out of her ruined clothing, and into a nightgown that Mrs. Dawson had laid out for her on the bed. As I helped slip the nightgown over her head and arms, I realised how tiny and childlike she was. Everything she had gone through that day could have killed her. I knew she would need to be watched throughout the night in case she ruptured, or showed signs of fever. It would be morning before we would know if the doctor's procedure had saved her.

Guiding her towards the washstand, I put a cloth in her hand, and told her she would feel better to wash herself off a bit. As she started to do so, Mrs. D brought the tray with the beef tea and some buttered bread. She finished her ablutions, then sat by the fire and sipped at the broth while I untangled her hair. It had been curled and pinned in an elaborate style with a dozen pink ribbons, which must have taken an hour to do. I carefully untied them and slid the hairpins out, dropping them into a small porcelain dish. She began to weep again, but didn't speak. I felt it was better to give her peace, so I stayed quiet, and brushed the curls out of her long hair, which shone like gold in the firelight. "There you go, pretty as a picture," I said as I finished, and then helped her into the bed.

I pulled the spindly old rocking chair out of the corner and sat down beside her, and lightly stroked her hair until she fell asleep. She scarcely stirred except for one strange moment, perhaps an hour later, when she twitched and twisted and shuddered and barked out a name in terror: "Jonas!" It struck me as odd, as one of the doctor's frequent visitors had the name of Jonas, and it was not a common name. Her eyes whirled around the room wildly, and only calmed when her gaze fell upon me. I gave her hand a pat and she smiled weakly, then fell back into a deep, still sleep. As dawn came, so did the carriage, and her companion spirited her out of the bed, the house, and Highgate, hurtling back towards London. Her bedclothes had a few small spots of blood on them but the worst appeared to be over.

As I made my way down to the kitchen to begin my day, I stopped on the stairs as I heard a voice—her ladyship's voice— calling from her room. It was odd, she had the bell pull next to her bed, she could have rung for assistance. I wondered if she was having words with Mrs. Dawson or with the doctor. I stepped out into the hallway, approached her room, gave the door a tap. "Is everything all right, milady? Do you need me to fetch someone?" I opened the door a crack and peered inside. The missus was alone on her bed, propped up on her pillows, staring directly at me. Nothing seemed to be wrong, but she did have a queer look about her. Perhaps she, too, had had a bad dream.

"Which one are you?" she asked. Her voice was hoarse. I wondered if she had been coughing instead of calling. Influenza, consumption—I still had no idea about the nature of her illness. Was she contagious? Was it something I could catch?

"I'm Margaret, milady. We've met before. I'm the maid-of-all-work." I almost mentioned that I'd found her outside, but thought the better of it.

"Yes, right, come here," she croaked. "Help me out of this bed. I want to show you something." Before I could even move, she began to lift the covers, to pull herself up and shift her legs. I could tell she was in considerable pain. I hurried to her side.

"No, no, missus, you shouldn't!" I tried to urge her back under the blankets, but she was adamant. What would Mrs. Dawson think? What was I supposed to do?

"I should and I will," she said through gritted teeth. "Slip your arm under mine and pull me towards you." I did as she asked, reluctantly and with great discomfort, lifting her up out of the bed and into my embrace. "Now do exactly as I say, quickly, and do not ask any questions. Reach down and grasp the hem of my nightgown, and pull it up above my chest, as if I were about to bathe." She saw the hesitation in my face. "Do it. Now."

Mortified, I did exactly as she asked. I knelt down and took the hem of the nightgown in my hands and lifted it up, past her legs and thighs and waist and bosom until I could see the whole of her body, naked as when she was born. From neck to knees she was crisscrossed with all manner of scars, the deepest slicing down from her throat to her sex, with other deep slashes across her belly and around her back. Surgeries. The one over her left kidney was freshly stitched, livid red, only a few days old.

"You see what he's done to me," she said, her voice hoarse and heavy, barely more than a whisper. "He'll do the same to you, or worse. Him and his friends. You must leave here, or you'll end up like all the rest, down the corse passage and into the ice house, and then sold and stripped and opened by some grubby student with a meat saw." She took the hem from my hands and pulled the nightgown down over herself. "Now put me back into bed." I lifted her legs and tucked them under the coverlet, then pulled it and the blankets up under her chin.

I didn't know what to think, what to say or do. "What do you mean, the corse passage?" I asked.

"Behind the green velvet curtain," she croaked. "That's how they take the bodies, through the curtain and down the stairs. That's how you found me, out in the courtyard. But I can never escape. He's taken my money, he's taken my child, he's taken things from inside me I can't even name." I thought of the jars on the shelves in the surgery, and shuddered. How much of what he displayed there had once belonged to her?

I heard a noise from the hallway. Mrs. Dawson was calling up the back stairs. I gave a quick curtsy and a soft "Thank you, milady," then hurried out the door just as Mrs. D emerged from the stairwell, carrying the morning tray of dry toast and beef tea.

"Her ladyship was calling," I said before she could even speak. "She was too weak to reach the bellpull. I tried to bring her a little closer, but I think she'd rather see you." Mrs. Dawson's eyes narrowed but she didn't respond. I held the bedroom door open for her, and then closed it behind them both.

It is late, Miss Gibson, and my trusty tallow has burnt to a smoking stub. I fear I've given Sister Catherine a sleepless night or two with this latest letter. I will write to you again soon with the tale of my escape from the physician's house, and the birth of my long-lost son.

May the angels hold you gentle in their loving hands,

M.E.

Miss Gibson, the rumours and whisperings continue unabated. There are some who feel that Margaret is too difficult and dangerous to remain here at the Priory. Strange men come at all hours to see Sister Augustine, neither from the diocese nor are they from Canterbury. One might be a doctor from Bethlem? And the other an officer from Scotland Yard? No one will tell me, for they know I will warn her. I fear they will take her away from here. Please, Miss Gibson, I could not bear to lose her. —Sr. C

Dear Miss Gibson,

We are not acquainted, but I hope you will regard me as a trusted friend.

Abandon these investigations and enquiries at once. You are placing yourself and your beloved father in peril, and no one will protect you.

Return to your anodyne tales of the unfortunates, and let the dead bury the dead.

Omnes una manet nox.

JULY THE 11TH, 1887

Dear Miss Gibson,

I've not heard from you for days now, nor have I seen you lingering at the gate. Sister Catherine read in the Evening Post that your father was injured in a hunting accident. I hope that he has made a full recovery, and that they catch the culprit if they have not already done so. What an ordeal for you and your family! You have my deepest sympathies.

I suspect that my recent letters may have shocked you with their vividness and candour, and that there were elements to my tale that could provoke nightmares of a vivid hue. Even though you are a journalist I sometimes forget that you are a woman less travelled in the darker aspects of our existence, and that I should be mindful of your more delicate sensibilities. Yet I feel I must press on and tell you of my final months at the doctor's house, grisly as the tale may be. The doctor plucking tumours and organs like ripening fruit. Her ladyship, bedridden, scarred, kept in a state of insensibility. Imprisoned in her own home. One would think that her warning to me would have been enough to send me out into the street, but I was young and stubborn and determined to prove my worth at almost any cost.

After the departure of the mysterious young lady and her guardian, several months passed without significant incident. I continued with my household duties, interrupted on occasion by a request from the doctor to join him in his office or his surgery to assist with a patient or to clean and organise his instruments and specimens. His wife's kidney was not among the items on display, which made me wonder if he had removed it as a remedy to some affliction. The doctor was nothing but kind to me, and I never saw him raise a hand or a voice to anyone on the premises. He seemed to be devoted to his wife, such that I wondered for her sanity. Perhaps, scars aside, this was the true nature of her infirmity.

I worked hard all that first year, and made great progress both in my baking and in my duties as a housemaid. Shortly after Mrs. Dawson and Tom quietly marked my anniversary with a lemon cake scattered with poppyseeds, I fell strangely and unexpectedly ill and took to my bed for several days. Mrs. Dawson delivered to me the very same beef tea that the missus drank daily but, despite that, my head was in a perpetual fog from which I struggled to emerge. Each evening I promised Mrs. D that my illness was nearing its end, and each morning I found I felt worse than the day before.

Then came that one indelible night, frightening in every aspect: a series of interlocking waking nightmares, each bleeding into the other, forming a vile puzzle with no apparent solution. At first, I was on my bed paralyzed and shivering, with a cloth sheet erected before me, across my waist, keeping me from seeing anything below. A circle of black-robed men towered over me, around and behind, chanting like in a church, words I could not understand. Some of these men were strangers, some were neighbours, and others were friends of the doctor that had visited in the days before. Centred among them was the doctor himself, robed but unhooded, looking down upon me, gazing where my legs were spread, holding something dark and gleaming in his gloved hand that I could not properly see. "The time is now," said a voice off to the side. I turned my head to see one of the robed men holding a red book open in front of him, its pages edged in glittering gold. My eyes were heavy and weary; I closed them against my will. Very shortly after, I could feel something cold and hard, metal or glass, pushing deep into my privacy. I cannot say why, but I was reminded of the syringe that I used on the tumorous old woman. I opened my eyes again. The doctor still stood above me, but he had turned away. He had placed his dark instrument aside and was wiping his hands with a crimson cloth. The others stood swaying and chanting. I knew I was not in the doctor's surgery, but I could not imagine where I was. Everything was real, and nothing was real. I had never been more afraid. I remembered what had happened to young Helen or Hazel or Harriet, and wondered if, wherever I was, the same was being done to me.

"Is she awake?" another of the men asked.

"No," said the doctor. "She sees, but only as a dreamer sees."

In my terror and humiliation, immobile and utterly helpless, I saw a flicker of movement at the edge of my eye, a shadow at the door. Mrs. Dawson stood there, watching, her face grey and grim. Then, a strange, ghostly movement behind her shoulder, a flutter of white silk satin, ribbons and lace. The doctor's wife.

Furious, Mrs. Dawson turned on her, her whispers slashing the air, and the door abruptly swung shut, sealing me in with the men. I closed my eyes, waiting for the slice of the knife, but it never came. Instead, I felt both lighter and heavier, tossed like a feather in a storm, and I drifted off on churning clouds toward a darkening horizon.

I opened my eyes and saw the light streaming into my room. I nearly jumped out of bed, but Mrs. Dawson was there, in the chair next to me, and she held me back down and told me that I had no choice but to rest. It seemed I had taken a terrible turn in the night and the doctor had worked hour after hour to save me. I was to stay under the blankets for three days at least. She and Tom would take care of the house, the doctor and the missus, and I was to put it all out of my head. I knew there was no fighting her, and I did still feel poorly, so I stayed the three days in my bed, with Tom bringing up a basket every morning with milk toast, weak tea and a soft-cooked egg, and Mrs. D coming up each evening with a bit of fish and a caudle to help me to sleep.

On the fourth day I was right as ninepence, and ready at first light to do my day's work, but even then Mrs. Dawson urged me to be careful, and had Tom do all the lifting and reaching and carrying so that half my morning was spent standing around. Finally, in the afternoon, Mrs. D relented and let me do the sweeping, but I felt like I was being watched over like a porcelain doll, that if I made a wrong move I would crack and collapse into pieces. By the following week, though, I was fully back into my duties, with only the occasional frown from Mrs. D or the doctor, and I was even let back into the surgery if only to dust and tidy and to gather the sheets and cloths and aprons for the laundry. I paused from time to time to visit the shelves of glass jars. I could see that some had been traded away and that new ones had arrived. The doctor's son, Matthew, had vanished, leaving only a faint circular stain on the shelf as a remembrance. I saw the other two jars at the end remained, the three-month foetus and the six-month foetus. I sometimes felt their eyes on me, or what would have been their eyes. I felt them slowly turn themselves to observe me as I worked. On those days, I couldn't leave that room fast enough.

In all that time, I never spoke of my strange illness or of the dream of the robed men. I suppose I thought that if I put them behind me, then that's where they would stay. Of course, I was terribly wrong.

It must have been nearly six weeks later, when I woke up to once again find myself direly ill. This time, I could keep down neither food nor water. I was bent over a tin pail for most of the morning, and then again the following day. Back into the bed I was flung with more milk toast and more weak tea; the doctor made daily visits to my side, checking on the strength of my heart and the depth of my breathing, pressing his hands on my belly and hips and nodding to Mrs. D who nodded back, and began the regimen of twice-daily beef tea, which put me back into the incapacitating fog. I realised too late that my monthlies were overdue and wondered in my haze if my insides were ruined somehow. Then it slowly dawned on me that I might not be ill at all, that inexplicably I might be carrying a baby. But how? I remembered the horrible dream, the men standing around me, the doctor looming over me, the instrument in his hand. The dark intensity of his expression. Could it be that the dream, or some fragment of the dream, had been true? I recalled the cold steel I felt inside me, and wondered if it had delivered the ingredients of a child and if the doctor, the man whose hand had held the instrument, was the father. I held my hand over my belly, feeling around for any sign that another life might be growing inside me. How could such a thing happen, and why would it happen to me? I dared not say anything, not to the doctor, not to Mrs. Dawson or Tom, not even in my prayers.

Nor did I need to. A few nights later, as I lay in that twilight state where I was neither asleep nor awake, I felt a warmth near me and then a cold and trembling hand pressed to my arm. I opened my eyes and looked to my side and saw that the doctor was seated next to me, in his shirtsleeves, his hair disheveled, his face flushed, his eyes unnaturally wide and threaded through with blood.

"Helen," he started. "My sweet young angel."

"Begging your pardon, sir," I rasped. "I'm Margaret. The maid-of-all-work."

"Ah yes," he said. "So you are, how foolish of me. Dear Margaret, maid-of-all-work. It seems you've gotten yourself into a bit of a predicament. I don't want to enquire too deeply, but it appears that you are pregnant, and have been for some number of weeks. Do you have some awareness of how this might have happened, or who the father might be?" He looked at me darkly, his stare sending a shiver right through me.

"No, sir," I stammered, hoping my nervousness sufficiently covered my lie. "I don't know what has happened to me or how. I thought I was just unwell. I'm so confused and afraid."

"There, there, my dear," he said, patting my arm with his clammy hand. "You've no need to fear. You are a treasured member of our household and we will give you the finest possible care. You are, I should say, quite frail. You will need to cease all your daily duties and turn your attention to maintaining your health and that of the child."

"Oh no, sir," I gasped. "Poor Mrs. Dawson, poor Tom! They already have so much to do. I can't just stay up here in bed. I need to help them however I can."

"You will, my dear, you will, eventually. But they will carry on with a modified list of duties until you are well enough to return to your post. They are aware of your condition and will assist me in seeing to your needs. We all want to ensure that you regain your strength in preparation for a successful delivery."

I thought of the row of jars downstairs: three months; six months; would my child be next on the shelf? "You are being very kind, sir," I said, looking down at his hand on my arm. "I don't know how I can ever repay you."

"Think nothing of it," he replied, giving my arm a squeeze. "I know in other households you would be stripped of your position and tossed into the street without a penny, left to fend for yourself. Unmarried, with child. You'd be facing the workhouse, the madhouse or the whorehouse, and who's to say which is worst?" His every word seemed laced with acid. I could not help but hear them as a threat. He brought his face down towards mine until I could taste a sweet rot on his breath. "You are very lucky to have us, dear Margaret, and we are so lucky to have you. You are a part of our family, and soon even more so." To my shock, he leaned in and gave me a kiss on the forehead, then drew back and stood up, steadying himself with the back of the chair. "Try to sleep," he said softly. "Let yourself dream. The sweetest of dreams for you both." With that, he stepped out the door and closed it gently behind him.

When I awoke the next morning, I found that Margaret the maid-of-all-work had ceased to be, and that I had become Margaret the mother-to-be. As my belly began to grow, the doctor had me moved down to one of the musty guest rooms at the other end of the hall from the missus so that, if something should go wrong, he would be able to attend more quickly. With Tom's assistance, I was permitted twice daily to walk the length of the hall and back and to look out the back window at the changing weather, and I was allowed to wash myself with a shallow dish of cold water and a rough rag. In what must have been a low moment for her, Mrs. Dawson was made to fetch and clean my chamber pots, to check for blood or any irregularities. My meals were changed seemingly at random, fish but no meat, meat but no fish, neither fish nor meat, only soft food, only white food, only boiled food, only raw food, until it felt like my insides were being torn apart. Finally, we returned to what you would feed an invalid, rice porridge and boiled pork and bread sopped in milk and the accursed beef tea. I tried to refuse it but it was no use; if I ended up soaked in it I would just have another cup forced upon me.

This was my life, for six more months, until my body was swollen and the creature inside was kicking and thrashing within me and I was too weak to whisper. I will say there were good days, afternoons when he would flutter and feather within me, when I would murmur to him and sing to him. I always knew he was a boy, just as the doctor wanted. He kicked like a boy, in every direction, but was quieter in the afternoons. I would lie in my bed with my hand on my belly, my eyes on the frosted windowpane, and I would sing a little tune my mother sang to me while she was washing up in the scullery: "Cable Street, Knock Fergus, New Road and Back Lane, Blue Gate Fields, Sun Tavern, then onto Brook Street, we're off to the Tower of London." I imagined my boy in a little pink frock seated by the fire, a golden glow about his cheeks. Mummy, Mummy. A smart curious boy, tender to his mother, with pretty green eyes and a light hiccupping laugh. So, I cannot say all the days were bad, not every single day.

Then came the evening, just after supper, when in my endless narcotic fog I heard a familiar voice from downstairs, ringing like a small glass bell. It was the palace girl, Helen or Hortense or Hagar, coming to call once more upon the doctor, in an even greater state of distress. She had come alone, much as I could tell from overhearing, heavily veiled so as not to be known. She had not seen the midwife this time, she had come straight here. Her courses were not as they should be and she was afraid. She asked after me, I heard this quite clearly, "the girl who sat and held my hand," and the doctor replied with regret that I was unavailable, that I was visiting my mother in Norwich, and if she could just come this way to the surgery. I don't think my mother had ever been to Norwich.

There was an odd tone about the doctor, something that insinuated its way into my bones and touched them with ice. I had heard some raised voices in the days previous, among the doctor and his friends, that young man Jonas among them, an edge of desperation. "We need more," one had cried out, refusing to be shushed into silence. "We need more and you must do more." I wondered if the girl would somehow be the "more" that he needed to do.

I, of course, was helpless, useless. I could not move, I could not cry out, I could only lie there and listen, every squeal of the door, every scrape of the furniture on the floor, every hiss and gurgle and muffled shriek and thud. And then a faint scuffle, pushing and pulling, and I heard the doctor cry out, "What are you doing here? Get away from here! Dawson, put her back in her bed at once!" The missus! Then sharp words between her and Mrs. Dawson as they came up the front stairs and the bedroom door slammed behind them. I settled into a fitful sleep only to be awoken hours later, in the dead of night, to the doctor's shouts, "What did you see? What did you see?" and then the strike of flesh on flesh and the weak cries of her ladyship escalating into high piercing shrieks.

I wished I could lift my hands to my ears to block out those screams. I could only imagine what he was doing to her, with Mrs. D watching from the doorway no doubt, and Tom cowering belowstairs like a damned dog.

It was then that I realised that something glinted on the night table next to my bed, something caught a fleck of moonlight and twinkled at me. I could just barely turn my head enough to see that it was a pair of bejewelled earrings, gold filigree with amethysts and pearls, and under them one of the doctor's cards, face down, with that strange triangular symbol on its back. The missus, she must have crept into my room and left them for me, it was the only explanation. I struggled and strained and finally pushed my hand out from under the sheets and coverlet towards the items at my bedside, clutched at them feebly until I had them in hand, and then pulled them back under the bedclothes. The earrings may as well have been made of iron. I was so exhausted from the effort that I gasped and shivered. But what was I to do now? Where was I to hide these gifts until the time was right?

I remembered that Mrs. Dawson insisted that each of the mattresses on the second floor be tied with a square of Holland linen, harsh and stiff, to protect them from soil and soot. This bed, which I had made and stripped and remade many times, had a split in the upper edge seam of its mattress just under the linen cover, into which I could slip the earrings and the card, if I could just get my hand up to reach it. I grimaced and pulled my arm up against myself, clutching the items as tight as I could, then slowly, painfully, moved my hand up to the upper edge of the bed, careful not to drop them over the top of the mattress and onto the floor where they would be lost to me. I was able to feel my way around to the open seam, then push the first earring and then the second into the matted horsehair stuffing, followed by the doctor's slender white card. I had just smoothed the linen cover under the back of my hand and pushed myself and the pillow back over it when the door swung open and Mrs. Dawson stepped into the room. She was shocked to find me with my eyes open.

"Hullo there. How long have you been awake?" She set the morning tray down on one of the occasional tables, then bustled about opening the curtains and tending to the fire, which had burnt into ashes well before dawn.

"I heard voices, shouting," I croaked. "Did a patient come in the night?"

"More of your dreams," Mrs. Dawson replied. "Finish all your caudle as the good doctor wants you to, and you'll sleep like a babe yourself." I don't know why, but at that moment I thought once again of the jars in the surgery: three months; six months; and the place at the end of the shelf where poor nine-month Matthew had been. I was nearing seven months, just over two months to go, if we avoided all disruptions. It was his baby and once he had it, he'd have no use for me. I'd be like the others the missus had warned me about, dragged down the corse passage and sold to some college, cut open by anatomists and chopped up like dog meat.

"What of milady?" I asked. "Is she well?"

"Oh, I see," she replied coolly. "I reckon you did hear some noise. Her ladyship took a terrible turn in the night. She's not doing well at all. Not to worry, though; the doctor is doing the best he can with her." Mrs. Dawson reached down and hoisted me up in the bed, the better to feed me my meal. She brought the bowl under my chin: boiled groats dotted with bits of fatty ham and apple, stirred with cream and sprinkled with cinnamon. "Here's a good girl. Open wide." She pushed spoon after spoon into my mouth, faster and faster until I could barely choke it all down. But I did empty the bowl and that seemed to please her. Then came a slice of buttered bread with marmalade, which I gulped down in three bites, and after that the dreaded beef tea. I knew that would send me off till supper, but there was no way to avoid it.

Except: "What's that smell?" I asked. "Is something burning?"

Mrs. Dawson turned and sniffed the air, looked out the door into the hallway. Wisps of smoke like tattered ribbons twirled past. "Oh God, help us!" she shouted, throwing down the cup of broth. "It's a fire!" She ran out of the room, shouted up through the whole of the house. "Tom! Doctor! There's a fire! It's in milady's room!" Tom came thumping up the stairs as the doctor burst out of his bedroom, and the three of them converged at the far bedroom door. The smoke in my room was thickening and warming, and I could hear the faint crackle of flames. The baby twisted and turned inside me, as if he could sense it as well. "Where is she? Can you see her?" I heard them rushing about, grabbing sheets and blankets and soaking them with water from the toilet cabinets and the ewers. "How did she get over there? Quick! Pull her out into the hall!"

Was I strong enough to stand up from the bed? Was I able to dress, to stumble down the stairs unseen and out into the street? No, not yet, but I could do one thing. I lifted the cup of beef tea and carefully poured it into the whistling crack in the corner of my window where the sash met the sill, letting it run down the outside wall and onto the jut of roof set over the back of the dining room. When the cup held just three small drops, I sipped them up and placed the cup on its saucer on the tray. Mrs. Dawson hurried back in and looked around the room. "The smoke!" she exclaimed. She rushed to the window by my bed, grabbed the sash and threw it upward, I was sure she would see the trickle of beef tea down the outside wall, but she did not. She waved her arms around to try to clear the air, then glanced down at the tray. "You drank it, good girl. Show me."

I hesitated, then opened my mouth. She leaned in, sniffed

my breath. "That's the ticket. You should get some rest now."

"What about the fire?" I asked. "How is her ladyship?"

"She has taken a bit of foul air, but she should be better soon," Mrs. Dawson said. "A spark must have leapt from the grate to the rug. It burnt a large black circle and caught the leg of her favourite chair. The doctor is a hero, I'll tell you that." She waved her arms around some more, then pulled the window shut. "Now, we've all had too much excitement, it's time to sleep. I'll send Tom up with your breakfast tomorrow while I take care of her ladyship."

"He means to kill me," I blurted, without even meaning to. I thought it, and I said it, and I couldn't take it back.

"Who? Tom?" she asked, shocked. "He wouldn't hurt a hair on your head!"

"No, not Tom," I replied. "The doctor."

An odd look came over her face that I couldn't begin to describe. "Well now, dear, I can't see why you would think that, what with the baby coming and all. Every child needs his mother, and this one will need you. I would think that's perfectly obvious." With that, she turned her face away from me, lifted the tray and carried it out the door. "Don't be giving yourself unpleasant thoughts," she said as she reached for the knob. "They are the cracks through which the devil slips his fingers." She placed the tray on the table outside just long enough to pull the door shut behind her, and then I heard her trundle and jangle as she made her way down, down to where sounds became silence.

No longer inebriated against my will, I lay awake until well after the clock chimed two. I knew I would have to be very brave to carry off what I was about to attempt. My first stop was down the hall past the doctor's bedroom to that of the missus. I pulled my door open swiftly and silently and then crept down the hall in just my sleep clothes, one hand on the wall and the other on my belly, minding those floorboards that I knew had a creak in them. I was especially quiet as I passed the doctor as I knew he slept on a feather's edge, and was trained to jump to attention to face any emergency. As I reached the door for the missus, I saw that it was open to let out the vapours from the glowering coals. Mrs. Dawson sometimes came up in the night to tend to the fire. I hoped beyond all hope that this would not be one of those times. I pushed it another inch or two, then slipped myself in, breath held all the way, until I was standing in the dim of the clouded moon not five feet away from her. The bed was heavily veiled. I could not see her face.

"Who's there?" she whispered.

"Just Margaret, milady," I whispered back. "I need to borrow some things."

"You must be quick," she sighed. "I'm never alone for long."

I opened her beautiful old Queen Anne wardrobe, fashioned out of cherrywood, and pulled out a morning wrapper of sixpenny blue calico and a hooded black woolen cloak. I swung the cabinet closed and was ready to leave when the missus whispered out once more: "Come to me."

I was so afraid, my heart was in my mouth. It could all be over at any moment. I whirled over to her, barely able to breathe from terror. "Yes, milady?" I gasped.

Her pale hand extended out from under the veils and she pointed her long frail finger at the portrait table kept near her bed. "Take this key." Nestled in amongst the framed cameos and cut silhouettes that cluttered its surface was a beribboned brass key, tarnished and worn. "Make good use of it. It opens every door."

I felt my eyes grow wide at the sight of it. "Yes, milady. Thank you, milady." I snatched it up and spun toward the hall. I just barely caught a glimpse of her face but I couldn't say what I saw; it was like it was half-gone somehow, faded into mist.

"Never, ever come back," she murmured. "You must promise."

I drew the door behind me and crept down to my room like a cat, back inside and back to my bed. I knew I had no time. I pulled the earrings and calling card out from inside the mattress, tucked them into the pocket of the cloak, buttoned it shut, then threw it and the wrapper under the bedcovers. I yanked on my shoes, heaving my belly this way and that so I could bend down and lace up my old prunellas. The baby, bless him, was still. I cringed at the thought of what my mother would say, but pulled my feet up onto the bed and pulled the blankets over them, and then over the rest of myself. I clutched the brass key so tightly that my hand began to go numb. It wasn't but a few minutes later that I heard the thud-thud-thud up the back stairs: Mrs. Dawson was coming to check on me, and check on me she would.

She pushed the door open, peered around the room, went to the fire and poked at the coals, making them hush and sizzle and smoke. She turned towards me, holding the poker in her hand. I shut my eyes and soothed my breath, waiting. Then I felt her face close to mine. I smelled her breath. I was shocked to inhale the same foul cloud of gin that I had sometimes whiffed from my father. Still, I held my face quiet and composed.

"You think that you'll ever get to hold your precious baby," she muttered, not so loud as to wake a soul, but enough to spray her venom. "You think that you'll ever get to see its face, push it to your teat and suckle it like a sow." She leaned in even closer, her spittle flecking my face. "I hope he opens you up and strips you from your guts to your gizzard."

I snapped my eyes open. "Oh no! My foot!" I exclaimed.

She jumped back in drunken fright, looked down at the end of the bed just as I flung my right leg up and kicked her in the face, knocking her head against the corner of the mantel. She dropped the poker and crumpled to the ground, blood leaking out from the wound on her temple. Was she dead? No time to find out. I lunged out of the bed, pulling the cloak and wrapper with me, and grabbed the poker and hurried out into the hall and down the back stairs. I paused halfway down to listen. From the other end of the house I heard the doctor's voice call out. "Mrs. Dawson?" As he started up the front stairs, I slipped down the remaining steps to the main floor and rushed up to the surgery door. I tucked the brass key into the lock and turned. It opened. I nearly dropped it with the shock. I stepped inside and relocked the door, then pulled the wrapper and cloak onto myself.

"Mrs. Dawson!" came the shout from upstairs. I was out of time. I looked around the room every which way until I saw the green curtain in the corner, concealing the corse passage, but not before I saw one other thing that made my stomach lurch: the newest addition to the doctor's collection, a small round jar that floated within it a pair of pale blue eyes.

I couldn't let myself think or feel. I grabbed the green curtain and pulled it aside, exposing a door with no handle, just a small slot edged in brass. Every lock, she had said. I pushed the key into it, turned it. It would not budge. Now I heard thundering from both the front and back stairs. The doctor and Tom would be on me in moments. I tried again, and again, and felt the tiniest give in the lock. With both hands on the key, I turned and turned, and with the slightest squeal the corse door sprang open. I threw myself into the passage, locking the door behind me. The stairwell was black as pitch, as steep as the one that led to the kitchen. I would have to feel my way down to the bottom. Slowly and carefully I descended, step after step, dizzy from blindness. The passage was so narrow I could feel the other wall brush against my belly. Finally my right foot touched the floor and my hand touched the door leading out. I felt up and down the edge of it and found an iron latch. Above I could hear the doctor shouting at Tom to check outside. I only had a moment. I unlatched the corse passage door, pushed it open, shoved it closed behind me and rushed across the frozen courtyard into the ice house, early light peeping in through the cracks between the boards in the walls. There I stood, legs crouched, poker raised and at the ready. "Please, Tom," I whispered. "Please don't be the one to find me."

I heard the corse door slam against the wall of the house and the frantic footsteps of the doctor. He ran right past the ice house, catching Tom running from the other direction. "No sign of her?" he shouted. Tom said something I couldn't quite hear, and then the doctor continued running, I assumed around to the front of the house and out onto the street. A silence fell like a stone. Then, a rustle in the patch of weeds right next to the ice house door. I recoiled and stepped back onto something soft and wet. I looked down. It was a hand, a frozen hand. My horrified gaze traced it up to its owner: Helen or Harriet or Heather, the young girl from the court, face blue, mouth gaping, tongue lolling. I couldn't help myself, I let out a small gasp and the door burst open. There was Tom, if anything more terrified than me.

"Tom," I whispered, "please don't."

"He'll kill me. You know he will." He looked up at the poker I held then looked back over his shoulder.

"Come with me, then," I urged. "We can leave this nightmare together."

"Tom!" the doctor yelled. He was running towards us, slipping on the frosty ground.

"I can't," he said, his face screwed up tight like an old rag.

"Then let me go," I begged him. Indecision was tearing at him, the doctor's footsteps grew louder.

"Tom, is she in there?" He was nearly upon us.

Tom shook his head furiously. "No, it's the other girl. She ..." He covered his mouth, stepped away from the door.

The doctor slowed, skidded on the ice-touched grass. "The other girl?" he asked, puzzled. "You mean the dead girl? What about her?" He poked his head around the doorway, looked me right in the eyes, and I caught him full in the face with the poker, striking him down to the ground. I hit him twice more across the head and shoulders when I heard a bloodcurdling scream from above. Tom quailed and pointed up at the house. It was the missus. She was standing in the window, hands pressed against the glass. I could see now why I thought her face was lost behind the veils: yellowed-crusted bandages crossed her face where her eyes used to be. I glanced back at Tom who looked sickened and mortified, then I threw down the poker and I ran.

I knew that they would picture me running along the high street, where I would be able to duck in and out of shops and hide myself in the alleys behind them. Instead I bolted up to the end of the lane, my breath heaving out my mouth in clouds, and turned north towards the Red Lion, where the drovers stopped their carts on their way into the city, and where coach drivers gathered for their morning repast. I strode up to the first coach I saw and, with great purpose in my demeanour, I waved over the driver. He had a fistful of bread and ham and a half-bitten boiled egg, and he was none too keen to be interrupted. Still, he leant down in my direction and cocked his ear. "Please," I begged, my teeth chattering, "I must hurry to London Hospital in Whitechapel. It's most urgent. The doctor is meeting me there." I pulled the calling card out of my pocket and presented it to him. When he saw the symbol on the back, he snapped to attention.

"Yes, milady. Whatever you say, milady," he declared, and tucked the last of the egg into his mouth. "London Hospital straightaway." He wrapped the end of the sandwich back up in its paper, wiped his mouth on his coat sleeve, pulled me into the carriage and grabbed the reins. The contraption lurched forward with an ominous wobble but righted itself soon enough. I heard shouts behind us in the distance and wondered if Dr. C and Tom would be able to give chase. I needn't have worried. Within a few minutes I had left all of Highgate and its horrors behind, and was hurtling like a comet towards the city. Not for the first time, I wondered what kind of world I was bringing my child into, and how I could possibly save him from all who would prey upon us.

Such terrors in these last few pages, so much evil, so much cruelty! Poor Sister Catherine is beside herself with fright, and I am so overcome by these ghastly memories that I can no longer speak. We will be lucky to get a fleck of sleep between us. Thank you for all you have done, for myself and for so many other women suffering at the hands of men. I will hold your father dear in my thoughts.

M.E.

July 15th, 1887

Daughter,

I apologise for the brevity of our visit, and that you were sent home so rudely. This "absolute bed rest" nonsense is ridiculous; there are infants with more autonomy than what I have at present. No matter. I will be well soon enough and then the doctors can be buggered. I trust that, for once, you followed my instructions and waited until you were on the train before opening this letter. There are some questions I could not answer to your face, some theories I could not volunteer, and certainly not while your mother was skulking about in the shadows like Spring-heeled Jack. I love her very dearly, but would prefer to do so from the opposite end of the house.

First, that burly half-wit with the musketoon who was flushed out of our back woods. I have concluded that he is innocent. He concedes that he was on our property, illegally, but he is adamant that he was on the other side of the pond, and I am inclined to believe him. What's more, his gun is fitted to fire single balls and I was struck with a spray of lead birdshot. Clearly, someone else was with me in those woods, someone who was determined to send me a painful message. But what? I agree that your embattled spinster does appear to have been at the heart of some intrigue, years in the past, but this pain in my posterior is more likely to be about property lines, hunting laws and water rights than mist-shrouded conspiracies from decades lost to time.

Speaking of which: our friends, the Freemasons. As you have surmised, they are, as a group, essentially harmless, using their arcane symbols and rituals and lore as the theatrical backdrop for their social gatherings and philanthropic activities. However, there has been, and may still be, an inner circle that acts against the stated desires of the order, exploiting their connections to further their ambitions both inside the fellowship and at the highest levels of society. Some could well have been physicians and surgeons; they may well have contributed to and benefited from the odious resurrection trade, that horrendous trafficking of corpses and body parts throughout the country as practiced by such villains as the monstrous Messrs. Burke and Hare. We cannot pretend such practices did not exist. They were lawless times, and many indignities were visited upon the dead and living alike.

This leads us to your mysterious eremite. I have reviewed the letter you showed me; it is certainly vivid, and persuasive. If any of her story is to be believed, she may well have crossed paths with someone truly dangerous, compromising their secrecy and placing herself at risk. I suspect that someone arranged her lengthy confinement at the convent as an effort of mutual protection. Now you have been drawn in and are receiving veiled threats at your own home. I do not pay much credence to these cowardly comminations, but I would still err on the side of prudence. I know it is tempting to try to visit this woman, to sit across from her and hear these stories from her own lips, and that you yearn to receive some confirmation of this fabled murderess that you seek. However, as your father and as someone who has travelled in the worlds that she describes, I would strongly discourage you from meeting her, engaging with her or continuing your correspondence. Whatever her struggles have been in this life, they appear to have left her in a fragile state; she may no longer know what is real and what is a figment of her fevered imagination, and your receptiveness to her missives may be unhealthy for her: poisoning her mind with vile phantasies, and inflaming her dark obsessions.

All that aside, I will accept her prayers for a swift recovery, and those of the Sisters at the Priory, and yours as well if you still know how to say them. I had best conclude this dispatch before your mother creeps up from behind me and snatches it out of my fingers.

Ever your loving father,

Sir H.

St. Anne's Priory
Hampstead, London

JULY THE 23RD, 1887

Miss Gibson,

I am growing concerned. Nearly two weeks have passed and I've received no word from you. I have watched the gate morning and night and you have not even so much as scurried by. Nothing more in the newspaper about your father, nor about the investigation into his attack. As far as I can tell, your last item for the Post was more than six weeks ago, that sad tale of the children in the poorhouses who rely on petty theft to survive. As brief as it was, it tore at my heart. I felt as if I knew those children. I hope you haven't forgotten about your dear friend Margaret. I still have much to tell, and tell it all, I shall.

Strange things are happening here. Twice now the Bishop has come up from London, gaunt and sinister, to meet with Sister Augustine behind closed doors. Both times he brought a retinue of timid little men and both times they glared at me before sealing themselves up in her chambers.

I hearken back to my arrival at the London Hospital in the back of the cab I hired in Highgate. I knew I would have to act quickly as the doctor and his associates were sure to be hard on my heels. The carriage swerved into a lane alongside the building, which spread out across Whitechapel like a bird of prey, a structure of brick and stone looming over us, with a regiment of tall, narrow windows in the front catching and swallowing the light of the afternoon. The driver kindly helped me out of my seat and down onto the footpath, handed back the doctor's card with its strange and powerful symbol, then stood watch as I walked up and through the heavy wooden doors that led into the main hall. Instantly the noise rushed into my ears, an unholy din as the sick and the injured and their families milled about, some moaning and wailing in great distress. Those who could not stand were outstretched on chairs and benches and some lay on the floor in puddles of sick, covered in pus-swollen sores, leaking blood and muck. It was a horrible sight.

The baby woke and turned inside me, thumping and stretching and pushing. I knew my escape required me to turn to the left and exit out onto Stepney Way, so I skirted the worst of the mayhem by walking close to the wall with my head lowered and my hood pulled forward, then followed the signs fixed to the walls, enamelled in the colours of butter and blood, ducking and dodging past nurses and doctors and students scurrying from one room to another. More than once I thought I saw one of the doctor's friends and jerked my head away so that I would remain undetected. Finally, with my breath catching at my throat, I found the east door and burst through it into the fresh foul air of the city, back in my home once more. If anyone had followed me from Highgate, I could only hope that I had lost them in the tangle of the hospital's corridors. Careful down the steps I crept, my arm cradling my swollen belly, minding the slippery cobbles and the careless carts and wagons, heaving and gasping, then down past the inns and taverns, the beggars and urchins, and then on to Butcher Row. The street I most urgently needed to visit, and was most direly afraid to attend. I had to try to find my mother.

Once I reached the St. Dunstan Church grounds, I turned southward onto Belgrave and strode alongside the stands of towering plane trees and mulberries that lined either side. As I left the green and continued south to Rose Lane, I saw evidence of the changes spurred by the ascent of our new Queen: new rowhouses, shops and amenities under construction, many impressed with the insignia of the crown; strolling gentlemen and couples in their winter cloaks and frock coats, pausing in front of merchants' displays and engaging in lively conversation with acquaintances and neighbours. A different life from what I was allowed to live. I felt as if my face was pressed to another pane of glass separating my existence and my yearnings from theirs.

As I reached the north corner of the Row, I gave a wave to the dollies posing and flirting from the benches outside, corsets tightened, hair loose and uncovered, shoulders bare under their shawls. Tuppenny uprights, my father once called them, much to my mother's horror. One of the trio, the prettiest one I thought, gave a little wave back, then hiked her dress saucily at me, all striped silks and velvet like a theatre curtain, showing off her slim stockinged ankle and the swell of her stockinged calf. "See something you like, love?" I felt a rush of colour blaze my cheeks, and a flutter of fear in my chest. That could be me if I'm not careful, I thought. The baby squirmed and jabbed inside as if he agreed.

I slowed myself, cast my glances from one side of the street to the other, from merchant to matron to hawker to sweeper to coster, wondering who would know me and who could help. The changes had taken hold here, too: so many shops shuttered, gutted, renamed, reopened. So many new faces, and others older and hardened. At last I came to the poulter's shop, Mr. O'Brien's, Ned's father. It was shuttered and dark, an ominous sign. I peered through the glass and saw rosettes of black crape and vases of withered white lilies, their petals strewn across the front counter down onto the sawdust floor.

"Still closed, after my dad passed," a voice said behind me. I froze. "More'n two months ago now. Mum's away north t'see our nan. She was to come back a month ago, but our Aunt Sis had a fall in the barn. Is there, might there be something in my shop for you? My wife and I are right across the way."

I made the slightest turn of my head, pulled the hood aside and caught his eye with mine. "Ned, it's me," I whispered. "I must speak with you, please, and quickly." He peered round at my face, glanced down at my belly, prominent even under the cloak, eyes saucer-wide, then pulled a key from his apron, twisted it in the lock and pulled me through the door, slamming it behind us.

"Meg!" he exclaimed. "What has happened? Where is your husband? How are you out on the streets alone?"

"I have come to ask after my mother. I had hoped she might have told your mum where she would be settling after we quit the shop."

"No, she said nothing. She never spoke to us after your father's do. I thought the two of you went off together." He pulled me away from the window, towards the counter, where the light was dim. He was jittery, words flying out of his mouth like startled sparrows. "She never stopped in to say goodbye to us. Not a word, not a wave. Do you have any kin who could have brought her in?"

"A sister in Leeds. I only know her as Aunt Lillian. I've never met her in all my life. I don't know where she'd be. They were born in Newcastle, but . . ." In the wake of his outpouring, my words were halting and hard-spoken. "I don't know," I sighed. "I just don't know." I was trying hard not to weep myself, but the tears were welling just behind my eyes. I knew I couldn't hold them off for long. "Ned, what am I supposed to do? I have nothing! I've run from the house where I was a maid. His Nibs is after me, no doubt, to take the baby and leave me in the dirt. They'll know I've come back here, because where else could I go?"

I looked at him pleadingly. His face was utterly blank. These were all just sounds to him; they had no meaning, and were not a part of his world.

"Marylebone," he said. "Edgeware Road. There's a place for women there." My heart tightened, clasped in fingers of ice. Marylebone. The slums of London. I had never seen it, of course, but I had heard about it. The almshouses, the workhouses, paupers and foundlings. The women's dormitory, a prison attached to a prison. Filth, violence, disease, despair, sticking to you like tar, grinding your bones until you fell face-first into your grave. Early, if you were lucky. I watched as he reached into his pocket, pulled out some coins, counted out two shillings, held them out to me. His elbow touched one of the faded lilies in the vase, knocking more petals to the floor.

"Couldn't I stay here? Just tonight?" Now it was my turn to unleash my words in a tumble. "No one will know. I won't make a sound. I'd stay in the back, or in the cellar, in the dark. I'll just sit and wait until dawn, and then I'd leave out the back, you wouldn't even see me go." I placed my hand on his arm. "Please, Ned. Please. I'm in so much trouble."

A woman's voice called out from across the way. "Ned?" she trilled.

He said nothing. His hand hovered between us, the coins in his palm shining softly in the window light.

I took them.

He led me through to the back of the shop, out into the yard where a few sad biddy hens scrabbled over some bugs in the dirt. Feathers and bones and dung, a blood-crusted chopping block off to the side, swarmed with flies.

"Ned?" the woman's voice sang out once more.

"Just getting some eggs," he called back. He stood back as I slipped the latch on the gate and let myself out to the alley, walked up along the shaded edge past the backs of the other shops, holding the cloak's hood low over my face. If they weren't here already, they would be soon, the doctor and his friends, banging on doors, demanding to inspect the premises, constables for reinforcement. I would have to hurry.

When I had the chance, I made my way north a few blocks to Cable Street. "Cable Street, Knock Fergus, New Road and Back Lane," I sang to the baby, or perhaps to myself. "Blue Gate Fields, Sun Tavern, then onto Brook Street, we're off to the Tower of London." None of those names were here now, though from time to time I'd spy one on the side of a shop or in the name of an inn or a tavern. Sweet smoke wafted out of shuttered windows to tickle my nose. Opium dens, I surmised, as the doorways were cluttered with dissolute men, collapsed, addled and adrift.

Once I passed the Tower Hill, I pushed on towards St. Paul's Cathedral and then along the edge of Covent Garden. I'd snatched the cloak but not the gloves, and now my hands were freezing. As the sun drooped in the sky and the shadows grew long, an eerie feeling crept over me that I was being followed. I dared not look back behind me, but instead stepped up my pace, turned up Drury Lane and rushed into a jolly mob on the left, which was amassing to enter a ratty little playhouse. I stood still as if to find my ticket, and let the hubbub swirl around me as I turned to look for my pursuer. I saw no one of note. If someone had been stalking me, I had lost them or they had moved along.

I excused myself through to the other side of the crowd and ducked round the corner into the alley that led to the backstage door. My feet were sore, my legs were sore. I was hungry, hungry for two. I leaned my back against the bricks and sighed, once again near tears. Despite the chaos on the street, my ear was tugged by a sound further down the alley, a rustling, a whimpering, a scuffle. I left my perch on the playhouse wall and crept down deeper into the shadows, where I saw a portly balding man and a much younger, prettier girl grappling in what appeared to be the throes of passion. At first, I was abashed and moved to leave them, but then realised that what I mistook for passion was an attempt at ravishment: the man was drunkenly trying to have his way with the poor young thing, and she was trying to push him off to no avail. He had seized her wrists with one hand and fumbled at himself with the other. But what could I do to stop him? I had nothing with which I could stick or slice him, not even a hatpin. And yet, as I felt around inside my pockets, I heard a voice in my head as clear and true as the Bow Bells that sang every Sunday.

"Make good use of it. It opens every door."

I pulled out the brass key from her lady's bedside table, placed the bit in my mouth to moisten it, then swooped over to the pair and held the sharp edge of the wards against the drunken man's throat. He froze. I knew the chilly wetness on his neck would fool him into thinking I'd drawn blood.

I lowered my voice and gruffly said: "Back away and leave her, or I'll rip your gullet open."

The young lady gasped, wide-eyed, and saw her moment. "Leave off, pie man, or we'll both give you a hiding. One you won't enjoy!" She raised her now-freed hands and shoved him backward, past me and into the muck along the alley's edge. He slipped and fell, and scrambled in the slops to get back to his feet. I bounded over and kicked his arse and sent him sprawling again.

"You dirty bitches," the pie man shouted as he crawled and stumbled and staggered away from us. "I'll be back for both of you!"

"Limp-pricked old bugger, you can barely handle yourself!" the lass shouted back. For some reason, this struck us both as terribly funny, and we stood there laughing in the dark till we were breathless.

"Well, thank you for coming to my rescue," she said as we dusted ourselves off. "Oh my!" She caught sight of my figure in the fading light and realised my situation. "I'm even more grateful now; you put yourself at such a risk. My name is Francesca, but nearly everyone calls me Fanny."

"Francesca is a pretty name. Mine is Margaret—not so special, but if you like, you can call me Peggy," I replied. A new name would give me a fresh start, and throw any pursuers off the scent. "And I'm glad that I could help." Even in the approaching darkness, I could see that she was finely and fashionably dressed in silks of brilliant blue and deep maroon. "I think we should walk together for a while," I proposed, "in case he decides to come back. Which way are you going?"

Fanny pointed to the other end of the alley. "Just through there and then up through Piccadilly. I'm heading home to Mayfair. I was to go to the theatre, but that's all ruined now. Will you be too cold? Please, take my gloves. It will be nice to have the company." I shook my head no, and tucked my hands into my pockets. It was just then that I realised I no longer had the doctor's card. Where had it fallen? Back when I pulled out the key in the alley?

"What's wrong?" Fanny asked. She could see the consternation on my face. I shrugged, shook my head. "You've had as much of a fright as me. Come closer, it's getting chilly." She wrapped her arm in mine and pulled me tight till we were shoulder to shoulder. I willed myself to forget about the scrap of paper that had rescued me, and within a few short blocks I succeeded.

We began to walk together, and more than once I glanced back to make sure that we were alone. She limped slightly, and was quiet, still recovering from the audacity of her assault. I peeked under her cloak and saw her silk gown was torn at the sleeve and near the waistline, and her pretty gloves stained.

She looked at them and wrinkled her nose. Then, to my astonishment, she peeled them off and dropped them in the gutter. "There," she said. "Now we'll be cold together."

"You called him the pie man," I asked. "What did you mean?"

"Exactly that," she replied. "He has a shop by St. Dunstan's where he bakes pies and tarts, but a meaner, more miserable baker there has never been. He was once quite well-to-do, but times change and tastes change and now the fancy folk treat themselves to cakes and sponges and puddings, and the workers buy their handpies from the carts outside the factories and taverns. He's yesterday's man, our bitter baker, and he drinks like there's no tomorrow."

I was going to ask how she knew all this, and how she came to be in an alley with him, but I thought better of it. Instead, I pulled her close like an old friend, and matched my stride with hers.

She told me of how her father died of a heart infection, and how her mother remarried soon after to a much older man, wealthy but cruel and given to drink. She fled her family before she could marry, and now lived the bohemian life of an artist, a student of beauty and grace. I, in turn, told her of my childhood on the Row, my abrupt entry into adulthood, and my brief tenure as a maid-of-all-work. I spared her the horrible details, but from my delicate state, she surmised that I had been mistreated. The tears I had been holding back all day poured out in a flood and she took me in her arms, an embrace I had not felt since that of my mother. "Who was this monster?" she asked. "Please, you must tell me." I shook my head and told her I had already said too much. She sensed not to push further, gave me a tender squeeze and allowed a soft silence to fall over us. Finally we reached the edge of Piccadilly, the crossroads where she would continue west while I made my way north. I could see ahead into Mayfair where the streets were dotted with gas posts and lanterns, while the northward turn was thick with gloom.

"And where will you go now?" she asked. "Do you have family? Do you have friends?"

I shook my head and said the word I'd been afraid to say to anyone. "Marylebone."

"Oh no!" she cried, and clutched my hands in hers. "You mustn't! We can't have that, I won't allow it. Please, come with me. We will find room for you in our house. We'll put a meal down in front of you and get you a bed of your own to sleep in." I started to protest, but she dismissed my words with a wave. "I won't hear of it. I will introduce you to my sisters and explain your plight. I am certain we can come to some arrangement, if only for tonight."

Resigned and relieved, I let her lead our way through the tangle of streets in Mayfair. The farther we walked, the larger and more extravagant the townhouses and mansions became. I realised quickly that we were only a few steps away from the house where the tumorous old woman had died. A shiver wriggled up my spine right to the top of my head. But at the last moment we veered away and found ourselves on Park Street, a stone's throw from Grosvenor Square, in front of an elegant construction of black brick and white stone, scrubbed spotless, each slender window framed in white trim and crowned with a red brick brow. A flickering golden glow emanated from the lowermost windows. An unusual cluster of letters were gilded above the front door. I later learned they spelled the name of the ancient Greek goddess Athena.

I watched as she tapped on the door: two knocks, three knocks, and then two. The door swung open, revealing a comely young man with a sly feminine cast to his face, dressed in a rose-coloured blouse and well-fitted, wine-dark trousers. His lush black hair was parted in the middle and shaped in the style of a page. Behind him, the vestibule was a rich, deep red, as if the walls had been painted with satin. "It's late, and you're early," he said to Fanny, and then looked over her shoulder at me. "Who's this?"

"Peggy, this is Florian. We all call him Fab. Fab, this is my new friend, Peggy," Fanny answered with a wink. "She needs our help. We can explain everything." Fab looked at us from each to the other, and then glanced at the heaviness I carried. As he did so, I felt a sudden pang of shame.

"Aphra won't like it. She'll say it's bad luck." Just then, the young man froze. He was looking at something behind us, and gestured to us with a glance. Both Fanny and I turned around to see a figure across the street, lurking in the passage between the houses. As we watched, the shadow stepped back out of sight.

"Come inside," Fab said, keeping his eye on the shadows. Fanny entered, and I followed close behind. The youth reached out and rested his hand on my shoulder. "Welcome to the Symposia Heliconia. You're in for a treat." He leaned in close and purred in my ear: "Ancient Roman architecture." Before I could ask what he meant, he pulled me inside and locked the door behind us.

M.E.

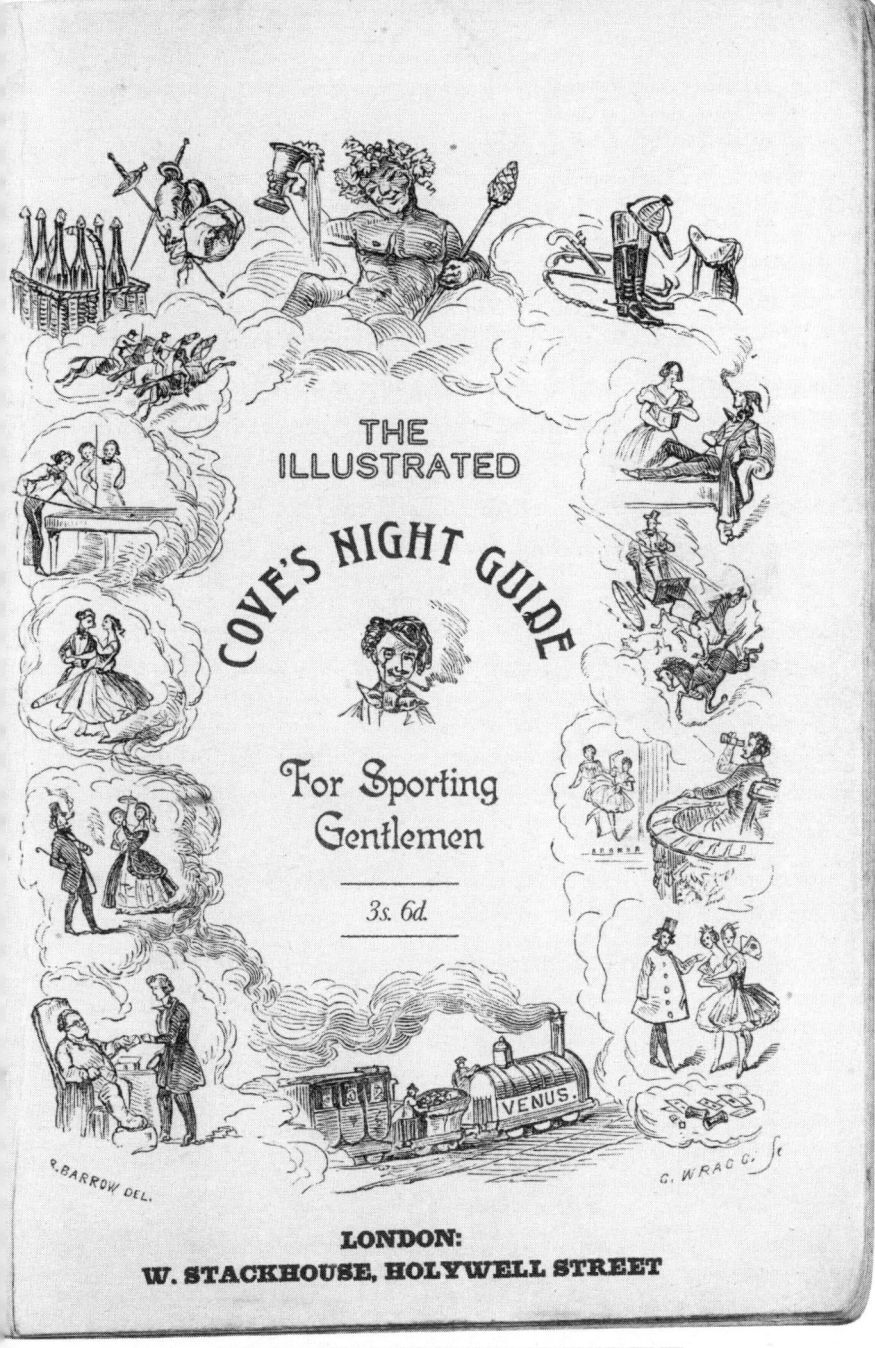

ST. ANNE'S PRIORY
Hampstead, London

JULY THE 28TH, 1887

Miss Gibson,

I am very glad to have heard from you at last, and relieved to know that your father is making a rapid recovery. I imagine it has been a terrible ordeal for your family. We at the Priory will keep him in our prayers.

Even as I fear that I will drive poor Sister Catherine from my side, I feel compelled to tell you all I can about the Symposia Heliconia, the house in Mayfair where my new friend Fanny brought me for refuge.

It was magnificent.

Young Florian swept me from the crimson vestibule through a tasselled velvet curtain into an enormous entrance hall, the grandest I had ever seen, even to this day, with soft blue walls trimmed with frothing white plaster friezes, lined with gilt-framed portraits of the gentry and lushly rendered studies of lithe young ladies in gauzy gowns posed among the trees and by the riverside. Gold wall sconces held half a dozen candles, crafted from the finest beeswax, and tall mirrors set at intervals allowed me to watch myself trailing behind Fanny. Even in her state of injury, she glided with her chin in the air, while I lumbered behind with my hand under my belly, my hair and dress and cloak decidedly shabby in comparison. We passed beneath three chandeliers dripping with crystals, and trod upon a marble floor with diamond-shaped tiles in petal pink lightly veined with green. The whole house, it turned out, was decorated like a delicate plate of fancies as Her Majesty might have for tea, and all wrapped up in glittering gold.

Fanny took me to the last room on the left and knocked gently on the door. She put her hand against the polished oak and spoke through it. "Madame Quince. May I speak with you for a moment? I have brought a visitor."

There was some murmuring inside, then a plain-faced young woman, in a soft blue dress topped with a crisp white apron, opened the door and stepped aside, bobbing her head so sharply to both of us that her frilled cap nearly flew off. Fanny took my hand and hurried into the room with me at her heels. It was a richly appointed private study, lined with framed maps, engravings of picturesque vistas and countless shelves of books. Where I would expect to see evidence of a masculine hand, I instead received the impression of the offices of a duchess. Lamplight slanted through tall windows framed by gentle blue curtains and fell in squares across a lush claret carpet strewn with roses. A pair of fruitwood chairs with elegant, curving legs and brocade cushions were set by a cheerful fire, and sitting behind a desk embellished with golden marquetry was a middle-aged woman with a soft, round face, rouged cheeks and squinting eyes; her mouth was a straight line with a ruby-red bow painted over it, and her hair which curled neatly around her face was a rich russet brown with a shock of white spiralling out from above her brow. No doubt she had been attractive when she was younger, though perhaps not as handsome as Fanny. As she looked up from a sheet of correspondence with a quill in her hand, it was difficult to read her expression, until her gaze flicked towards me briefly, then her features arranged themselves into a scowl of disapproval.

"Fanny, what time is it? You're supposed to be at the theatre," she scolded. "The Baron is attending our salon on Friday. Whatever will we talk about, if not this latest production of his precious Lady of Lyons?" Her eyes returned to me and took me in from top to toe. She opened her mouth to say something else, but Fanny interrupted her.

"Oh, Madame Quince, I was accosted in the street!" The young girl held up her arm to show where her sleeve was torn, where her silk dress was soiled with muck, and where her fine shoes were ruined.

"Accosted?" Madame shot up out of her chair and came quickly around the desk. "Are you injured? Are you marked?" She turned Fanny's face from left to right, and gasped at the sight of a darkening bruise on her pale cheek. "What bastard has mistreated you?" Fanny winced as Madame grasped her chin. She turned her head towards the light, examining the flesh for imperfections. "What about your body? Did he . . . violate you?"

"No, no, thank God," she replied. "The dress got the worst of it, really. He was intoxicated and inept, but he was still too strong for me to make my escape."

"You told me you knew him," I said. "Are you going to say

who it was?" Fanny shot a glare at me, then let out a sigh.

"It was the pie man, Lovett," she replied. "He was drunk. He pulled me out of the theatre line and dragged me into the alley. Peggy here heard my cries and came to my aid. Put her life on the line for me, she did, and that of her baby as well."

I've never seen a face turn livid so quickly as Madame's did in that moment. "Lovett! That reprobate. How dare he lay a hand on you. That will be the last of him in this house, make no mistake." She turned to the maid who was standing nearby. "Louisa, have Florian fetch some ice for the swelling, and bring a pitcher of warm water up to the dressing room so Fanny can wash herself properly and change." The maid curtsied and slipped out.

Madame Quince turned to me. "We are very grateful to you for intervening in this most heinous crime, and for preventing it from escalating further. I should be able to give you some small token of our appreciation." She went back to the desk and opened a drawer, started rummaging through its contents. I couldn't help but notice a card on a stack of papers inside the drawer, once again inscribed with the mysterious symbol of the eye inside the triangle, similar to what had been drawn on the back of the doctor's card.

"Madame," Fanny said. "However else you may wish to reward her, young Peggy has been cast out of her job as a housemaid and has no family left to rejoin. I brought her back here to speak to you. Would it be possible for her to stay here with us? Until the baby is born?"

Madame looked up from her desk and let out a little sigh. "Oh, Fanny, what a kind heart you have," she said. "I'm afraid it's out of the question. We do not take in guests here at the house; everyone who lives here must work, either in the front rooms or belowstairs. Peggy is in no condition to put in a full day of cleaning or cooking or toiling in the scullery. We don't want her to endanger her child any more than she already has. Even if she could somehow summon the strength, think of our clients. What would they make of her presence here?"

Fanny looked crestfallen, but then her eyes brightened, and a smile curled the corners of her lips. "What about Aphra? She desperately needs a lady's maid, one who will help to dress her, maintain her appointments and heed our bells and calls." Fanny turned to me, lowering her voice slightly. "Aphra's deaf, you see, and cannot speak as we do; but she is quick and clever, and communicates in other ways."

"She is also tremendously superstitious," Madame Quince added. "She recoils at the thought of a pregnant cat in the house, never mind a pregnant woman. However, you are welcome to persuade her. If she agrees, and only then, return to me and I will provide you with a contract for the next three months." She looked down at my belly again, her eyes narrowing. "What of the child's father? I don't want any more odious individuals skulking about, mishandling my girls and meddling in our affairs."

I knew I had to be careful about what I told her. Too much information could send me back to the house in Highgate. "He has no interest in the baby, nor in me," I replied, my voice sharp as a blade. "Not now that his wife knows everything. He'll just hire another girl, and turn his attentions to her."

"What we women endure," Madame Quince sighed. The clock let out a little chime as if to agree. She glanced over at it, her expression souring slightly at what she saw there. "We have just half an hour before I convene our evening lecture. Both of you, go speak to Aphra. Secure her approval before commencement, or else our young Peggy must depart with all due gratitude and a small reward. And Fanny, we will release you from your duties tomorrow night to return to the theatre to see the Baron's production. I will accompany you in case that scoundrel Lovett attempts to attack you again. Tonight, once you have refreshed yourself, I enjoin you to meet us in the parlour. I will be speaking on the key structural elements of Ancient Rome: the dome, the vault and the arch."

Fanny gave a quick curtsy. "Thank you, Madame. Come, Peggy, let's go see Aphra." She took my hand and tugged me back out the door and led me down to the other end of the hallway to the servants' stairs. They were much less steep and treacherous than those in the physician's house, wide enough for two to climb, and illuminated with pert little windows through which you could see the trees and houses of Mayfair and the towers of London beyond.

"I've never seen such a place as this," I said as we ascended. "Is this a school for ladies?"

"That's certainly how Madame Quince sees it." As we reached the first floor, Fanny pulled aside a lush green velvet curtain and pointed to a room on the left; its door was partly open, and the golden glow of candlelight scattered shadows on the walls ahead of us. "Wait here, I will go first and announce us. I don't want us to give her a start." She stepped through into Aphra's room while I settled myself on a pearl-pink velvet slipper chair with ornately turned rosewood legs, next to a narrow hallway table which held a vase full of exotic feathers and a few tiny watercolours framed in brass. Ladies' faces, delicately portrayed.

As I sat and waited, I saw the shadows in the hallway flicker at a greater speed. I was reminded of the creatures my mother made on the wall when I was a child. No sooner did I try to make sense of them than they abruptly stopped. The light was calm and clear once again. Then a larger shadow as Fanny appeared. She opened the door wider for me, reached down to help me out of the soft low chair, and welcomed me inside. Aphra's room was done up in creams and gentle yellows, with ribbons of gold striping the walls, the curtains, the chairs and the linens on her bed. The Queen herself could not have so beautiful a room, I thought. The marble of the fireplace, too, was like ivory veined with gold, a stone I'd never seen before, and seated in its circle of warmth was Aphra, who could have been carved from the very same stone. Wide-eyed and wary, she watched me enter, gestured for me to take a seat on one of her elaborately carved parlour chairs. It looked like it would buckle under the weight of a mouse. I looked at Fanny, who nodded. I gave Aphra a tiny curtsy, then seated myself before her. Mercifully, it was much sturdier than it looked.

Fanny made a gesture with several of her fingers, and Aphra watched her as she softly spoke. "Aphra cannot hear you, but she can read your lips. Do not raise your voice to speak to her; in fact, she will understand you best if you speak quietly and slowly. She can also make words with her hands, signs, as I am doing now." Fanny was turning her fingers this way and that as she spoke. I could see them change with what she said, and watched Aphra nod as she followed. "These are not difficult to learn. You will pick them up quickly. You will understand each other much more if you use both."

Fanny turned her attention to me entirely but continued to speak and gesture for Aphra's benefit. "As Madame mentioned, Aphra has certain beliefs about women in your condition in a house such as ours. However, she appreciates your plight, and is grateful for how you helped me so selflessly. She has agreed to take you on as her lady's maid. Do you agree, Aphra?" Aphra watched her mouth and hands carefully, then nodded solemnly. I gasped, tears springing to my eyes. Fanny smiled, but continued her recitation. "For your first task, she wants you to accompany her to this evening's lecture downstairs. For that, you will need to tidy yourself and change into something appropriate. We will have some dresses made for you; until then, Aphra will lend you a grey and blue morning gown. You'll find it in her wardrobe. There is a washstand in the corner that you may use. I'm off to see Louisa and Florian, but I'll meet you downstairs later."

I gave Fanny a quick bob, wiping at my eyes with the heel of my hand. "Thank you, Fanny. Thank you so much for everything." She stepped over to me, clasped her hand in mine, then turned and left the room, keeping the door ajar. I looked back at Aphra and was startled to see she was up out of her seat and standing at the wardrobe. She tugged the door open, peered about inside, then pulled out the grey and blue quilted robe that Fanny had mentioned, trimmed with lace and ribbons. Aphra's least attractive, most utilitarian garment was ten times finer than anything I had ever worn. She pulled the laces loose across the bodice, then helped me out of my cloak and dress and into the morning gown. It was a bit snug and perhaps a half-inch too short but otherwise it was lovely. She frowned over my soiled little boots and had me switch them for some blue satin slippers. I blushed, as it was all so irregular, a lady helping her maid to dress! Aphra showed tremendous kindness to me, fixing my hair, wiping my face, even though her unease with my situation was apparent. I wondered what the nature of the superstition was. I knew that many people wished to conceal childbearing women from public view until after the babe was born, but I had never experienced such an aversion as this.

She beckoned me to a delicately carved writing desk across from her bed, picked up a dip pen, touched it into a pot of ink and wrote on a page she had waiting there: "Can you read?" She looked up at my face expectantly.

"Yes. Yes, I can," I replied, quietly and slowly as I'd been told.

"Good," she wrote. "This will help us as you learn my signs. Now we must go." She set down the pen and took me by the hand, snuffed out the candles on her desk and her bed-table, and then led me down the back stairs to the parlour, where several other young women awaited. Florian was there too, affecting an air of boredom. Madame Quince was at an oaken lectern, arranging a sheaf of pages. Fanny was nowhere to be seen. As soon as I stepped into the room, I could hear the murmurs and feel the stares of the others set upon me. Madame Quince looked at Aphra, and Aphra nodded in return. Madame turned her eye to me and gestured for the two of us to sit at the front, presumably where Aphra could watch Madame speak without hindrance.

"Good evening, one and all," Madame Quince began. "We welcome a new member to the Heliconian family. This is

Peggy, lady's maid to our sister Aphra. Everyone please give her your fondest greeting." Unable to conceal their surprise, the gathering offered up uncertain replies of "Welcome, Peggy" and "Greetings, Peggy." Madame Quince continued: "Peggy came to the aid of our sister Fanny earlier this evening when she was accosted by a miscreant familiar to our household, the loathsome Mr. Lovett."

Aphra shifted in her seat at this. I placed my hand on hers. I couldn't tell what about this discomfited her.

"You are all advised that he is banned from this moment forward, and good riddance. As a gesture of our gratitude, Aphra has agreed to take Peggy on until Peggy's child is born, which looks to be two or three months hence. While she is with us, she is as dear to us as any other in our circle. As a measure of discretion, however, Peggy will use the back stairs when travelling through the house, and will take care to stay out of sight when we have visitors. I will brief her on all other requirements when I arrange her contract. Any questions?"

Silence. Aphra gave my hand a gentle squeeze.

"Thank you all. In your grace, I begin our prayer: I sing of Pallas Athena, the Protectress of our Symposia; sister of Apollo, and of the Muses nine; Goddess of Courage, Wisdom, the Arts. It is She who protects the people, wherever they might come or go. Hail, Goddess, may you keep us, watch over us, and give us good spirits and blessed favour." The others responded full-throatedly and as one: "Hail, Goddess!" Madame Quince nodded, consulted the first of several pages on the lectern, raised her head and glared at all of us.

"Ancient Roman Architecture!" she declared. I glanced over

at Florian and he smiled back at me. "The arch, the vault, the dome! The tools by which the unnamed Roman architects harnessed in earthly form the grandeur of the universal cosmos!" I pulled my gaze back to Madame Quince and settled in for what I sensed would be a long and enervating evening.

After three hours passed in only ninety minutes, Madame Quince released us from our lesson and bade us good night. I had hoped to make my introductions to the others but they fled up the stairs before I could even turn around. I shrugged and smiled at Aphra, who kindly led me back up to our rooms, by the front stairs this time. A tasty meal awaited each of us, under a silver dome. By the end of that evening I had learned the hand-words for "hair" and "face" and "dress" and "shoes" and "soup" and "bread" and "happy" and "sad." What we could not say with our hands, we wrote in notes to each other as best we could.

At one moment, I saw a curious look cross her face. She wrote out the word "Father?" and touched her hand on my belly inquisitively. I shook my head and said, "My former master. I ran away. It was a nightmare."

She wrote another word: "Rich?"

"I think so, yes," I replied. "Not as wealthy as Madame Quince, I'd say. Looking back, I think it may all have belonged to his wife, poor creature." A clamour of horrible memories rose up in my mind. I shuddered and shook my head to clear them. "It's all in the past now. I'm safe here, thanks to you."

With a stretch and a yawn, she declared it was past our bedtime. She gave me my own beeswax candle and my own pack of lucifers, and a loose white shift to slip into for nightclothes.

She then showed me to the little room adjacent to hers, and I daresay it was as fine as the one that the doctor gave to his wife, if not near as large. The walls were a soft coral colour and dotted with posies, the window was netted with fine lace curtains from Ireland, the washstand in the corner had a crystal vial of rosewater perched upon it, and the bed was dressed with French linens and Witney blankets under a white cotton counterpane. I did not yet understand the Symposia Helliconia and its purpose, but I was grateful to be accepted by its residents and to be offered such exquisite sanctuary. I was very fond of Fanny and Aphra and felt safe in their company; I hoped they would come to see me as a friend.

As I lay in my bed that night, I rested my hand on my swollen belly and thought of the creatures in the jars on the doctor's shelves. One of those was growing within me, and soon would push its way out. The midwives claimed that our children are born with the same gifts as we are, and the same inescapable curses. I had always felt disconnected from the world. If not unloved, then unloving. My mother sometimes complained that I lived in my head and not in my heart. Cold as a fish, she once called me. Would my child be the same? Would he be graced with a gentle hand, or a fist like a cudgel? Would he be sharp with money and numbers like my mother, or sharp with a blade instead, marked as a letter of blood, as a carver of meat, like my father, or the doctor or me? What did it matter? I could not keep the child. And how could I want him with such an unholy provenance? He was the product of a vile act and no doubt vile himself. And yet I yearned for him, I ached to see him and hold him, and to love him in a way I had never loved anyone before.

And surely my love would redeem him, and in time transform us both. These thoughts haunted me from time to time, and as the date of his birth grew closer it became more difficult to banish them. I felt his little body under my hand shift and stretch and settle, and I settled along with him. That night was the first in many years when I enjoyed a long, sound sleep, free of the burden of dreams.

I must sign off for now, my candle here having shrunk to a button, and poor Sister Catherine and I on the verge of being plunged into darkness. There is much more to tell you about my time at the mansion in Mayfair, including the re-emergence of ghosts from my past, and of my future. Have a little more patience for me, Miss Gibson, and I will unravel it all for you.

Ever in your heart,

M.E.

July the 30th, 1887

Dear Miss Gibson,

What a delightful surprise to hear from you once again. Thank you so much for your kind thoughts for my mother. She has rallied somewhat since your last letter and is in better spirits. She has her good and bad days, as do we all, but has had a particularly fine run of late.

As you requested, I have asked her about whether Dr. Desmond might have had any children. She does recall a daughter, adopted from one of the orphan asylums, and she thinks the child might well have been named Marie. This would have been after the death of Mrs. Desmond, who had been confined to her bed for most of their marriage and ultimately succumbed to whatever illness had debilitated her. My mother recalls the child being poorly as well. She was not long in that house when her leg was amputated, by the good doctor himself. She had apparently fallen down the servants' staircase and the resulting injuries became gangrenous. A horrific thing for a child to experience, I'm not sure she ever recovered. She was only ever a shadow in a chair at the upstairs window after that, and died in the house when she was still quite young. Mother does not know of any other children, though it seems there was some talk of a boy.

She did set her mind again to the question of the household. She could recall nothing more about Dawson, the hall boy, or a maid named Margaret. If something should occur to her, I will be sure to contact you immediately.

My very best wishes to you,

Mr. Henry Boulton

Bell House,
Norfolk Street,
Mayfair

ST. ANNE'S PRIORY
Hampstead, London

AUGUST THE 10TH, 1887

Miss Gibson,

Someone came to the Priory today, an old woman—even older than I, it seems. She asked for me by name, by my given name, which few would know even within the Priory. She would not identify herself. Plainly dressed in brown and green, sharply spoken, stern and evasive. Sister Augustine dismissed her enquiries, and bade her to leave at once. This set the woman to shouting, a grotesque stream of obscenities and accusations. She demanded that I be brought to her. Augustine would have none of it, she sent word to the kitchen maids to fetch the bobbies. Three of them came in with clubs raised, dragged the woman out into the street and drove her off. It was an ugly scene. I was down in the scullery doing my chores, and knew nothing of what was happening. When I came up from my duties, I was treated to a slew of ashen faces. Augustine shut herself in her office and refused to discuss the incident. Sister Catherine trembles at the merest mention of it.

Have you told anyone of our correspondence, of your investigations? I've entrusted all my most private thoughts to you, I hope not in vain. Sister Catherine believes someone passing by the Priory has seen me, or overheard me, and has set some tongues to wagging. It may be someone close to one of the Sisters or the kitchen maids, or even one of the merchants who makes deliveries. For all I know, it is Augustine herself who is the cause of this attention.

It is a sin to tell a lie, even if told to protect the Church and its agents. Not for the first time, I feel the walls closing in all around me, stones shifting slowly, sliding towards me as if to crush me. Wealth has put me in this place, has kept me here, and only wealth can take me out. That may surprise you. I assure you, there are powerful men, and women too, who can only maintain their power through the silence and complicity of their lessers. They fear me. It is a fear they cannot abide.

Do nothing, say nothing, not about anything that I've shared with you, not even to your father. Sister Catherine is sworn to uphold my confidence, and you must swear it too. It may be that our correspondence will come to a sudden end before I can even touch on the meat of the matter. Yet I dare not violate my chronology, nor spill my secrets too freely. I will continue to tell you of my brief time at the Symposia, of the birth of my beloved child, and then of my incalculable loss. And this story I shall tell in my own time.

My first morning in the Symposia was spent in Aphra's rooms, where we received our breakfast together and I learned a few more words, like "ham" and "cheese" and "egg" and "fork" and "knife" and "plate" and "spoon." Aphra wrote a little note to tell me that her last lady's maid was not near as quick a student as I was, nor did she care to be. This made me very proud indeed, as I rarely received such praise even from my mother and father when working in the shop. I was skilled with my hands, at learning and repeating short sharp clear movements, and for the first time could see how useful these skills could be. I also learned the word "Wednesday," which was that very day, and that Wednesdays were when the young women and Florian would present a theatrical in the parlour for invited guests under Madame Quince's direction. Thursdays were concert nights, Fridays were salons, Saturdays were dedicated to the fine arts, Sundays to literature, and Tuesdays, as I had discovered, were reserved for the classical arts of Athens and Rome. Monday nights were for private study. Once a month, the Symposia would host a party for its patrons, the planning of which would occupy Madame Quince for fully a week beforehand. So it is a school, I thought to myself as Aphra wrote out the list for me. A school for ladies. But what was the purpose, if not to prepare them to become better wives for their eventual husbands? And why was Fab among their number? I barely had time to contemplate the implications, as I was immediately swept up in Aphra's preparations for the evening.

The evening theatrical was to be a tableau vivant, somewhat like the game of statues that we used to play as children. The tableau would recreate a scene out of Greek mythology and present it to an audience of patrons as if they were watching a living painting or a sculpture garden. On this occasion, each of the five women was to pose as one of the Greek muses responsible for the creation of the five senses. I knew very little about Greek mythology, so Fanny was tasked with explaining the scene to me while Aphra stood at the side and practiced her various postures, watching us as we talked. Aphra was to play Urania, the muse who invented sight in all creatures large and small, including man. Sight made it possible for us to appreciate the beauty all around us, so Urania was equipped with an elaborate gilded frame that would normally hold a portrait or a landscape but in this instance was empty. Aphra, as Urania, was to hold the frame in front of her and admire whatever she saw within it, and the patrons in turn were to admire her. For this role she had a long white gown made of sheer silk, gathered and belted at the waist with a golden satin rope. Fanny was to play the muse Thalia, the inventor of the sense of smell; she was to wear a similar gown, in limpid blue, and to carry a posy of fragrant flowers, their delicate scents permeating the room. The design and construction of their garments was confusing to me; I was unsure how anyone could wear them without revealing their bodies in their entirety, every wrinkle and dimple and mole as if they were utterly unclothed. Aphra and Fanny seemed unconcerned, their attention occupied with the weight and size of the wooden frame, and the way that the flowers were arranged within their bouquet. They stood before me and rehearsed their selection of poses, turning this way and that while I struggled to keep from staring at the ceiling. As the morning wore on, I calmed myself and concluded that these costumes must have been authentic for their time and place, and that the patrons had without doubt seen many fine masterpieces that revealed the glory and the delicacy of the human form.

We took our midday meal downstairs in the garden room, so named because of the large bright windows and the many potted palms and ferns that filled the room with greenery. It was there that I saw the costumes for the other young women, and for Fab, and felt a rush of embarrassment scald my face at the sight of their immodesty. Though the costume for each muse was slightly different from the others, all were equally exposed: clefts and bosoms and buttocks fully on display for everyone to see. Fab's garment was the most startling. Instead of the long white linen tunic that one might expect, he instead had a gossamer loincloth wrapped about his hips, presenting his generously proportioned sex to anyone who glanced his way. I had never before seen a man's most intimate parts, and my mortification was so profound that I was speechless. I averted my eyes from everyone and kept them trained on my food, such that Aphra passed me a note asking if I was unwell. I shook my head but remained silent. Fab took note of my demeanour and set his mind to teasing me.

"Are you from Mother Trapp's?" he asked, glancing at my belly.

"No," Fanny said sharply. "She was a maid mistreated by her wealthy employer. She barely escaped with her life."

The young man tilted his head in amusement. "She doesn't look much worse for wear. Is Madame Quince to open a nursery?"

"I'm to give the baby up to an orphan house," I replied. "Not that it's any business of yours."

"But it is our business," he stated. "We're all one happy family here, and we'd like to keep it that way." He saw that he'd struck a sour note and not just with me, so he took a more conciliatory tone. "I'm sorry, I've forgotten your name."

"Everyone calls me Peggy."

"Peggy," he repeated. He sucked on his bottom lip, and I was struck by how handsome he was, and effortlessly sensual, yet there was something oddly feminine in the way he moved his hands and looked up through his eyelashes. "Will you stay with us after the child is born? I see that Aphra has taken to you, and she barely likes anyone, least of all me."

"Never mind him, he thinks he's being clever," Fanny said to me. "He's our little rooster, aren't you, Fab?"

"Why didn't you just get rid of it?" someone asked, not in a malicious or mocking tone, but there was an archness all the same. I turned to find a handsome woman with long, lustrous brown hair staring at me intently. She had fine, delicate features like those of the young ladies who had visited the doctor's house under cover of night. I wondered if she had been one of them.

"My employer forced me to keep it," I replied. It was the simple truth. "And now I'm seven months along at the least, and it's too late for both of us. And his poor wife . . ." I let the sentence trail off. Any small detail could identify the doctor, and then all the fires of Hell would rain down upon me.

"Poor wife, my arse," the woman said darkly. I flinched as if I'd been slapped. "I'm sure she was thrilled, not to have to suffer under him night after night. All these wives who snap shut like oysters once the ring is on their finger, and then who bears the brunt of it? We do." Aphra slipped a note in front of me. "Victoria," it said. "Like the Queen, and she thinks she is one." I picked up the note and crumpled it into the pocket of my robe before anyone else could see it.

"At least we get the toffs," said Fanny. "Or the ones who spend like they are, not that we get to see too much of it ourselves. But

Madame Quince is good to us; we have no cause for complaint."

"You've not been here as long as I," said Victoria. "I've had my insides scraped out four times now, bleeding like a stuck pig and feverish till I thought I'd die. Gowns and jewels and French lessons are useless in the grave. And not a one of these men will wear a capote, no matter what Quince tells them. They just spit in it and toss it in the corner and hand you an extra quid."

"Really, Vickie, you should do what I do," Fab said drily, reaching for a cluster of grapes. "Everyone knows bum babies don't live."

Fanny gasped, scandalised, and then all the girls burst out laughing, even the servants who hovered over them. Even Vickie herself cracked a smile. Florian popped the grapes into his mouth, one right after the other. He looked over at me and grinned even more broadly. "Poor Peggy," he said. "She has no idea what she's wandered into."

"Oh my God," Vickie said, taking in my expression. "She doesn't. She really doesn't. Fanny, what did you tell her?"

Now it was Fanny's turn to blush. "I didn't tell her anything," she stammered, her eyes trained away from me. "How could I? She was so kind to me, like a friend would be. She saved my life. I didn't want to frighten her away."

I took her hand and held it tight. I had a growing sense of what had not been said, but I didn't want it to be true. "Fanny, please tell me. I don't understand." She kept her face forward and shook her head. I could see she was filled with sadness and shame.

Vickie reached over and touched my chin, turned my face so that our eyes met in a level gaze. "Peggy," she said gently. "We're whores."

I pulled my head back like a startled horse. I looked over at Fab, I suppose with some need for confirmation in my eyes. Whatever he saw in my expression, he nodded in response. "Yes," he said. "All of us. Even Aphra, even me. Especially me, truth be told."

Vickie laughed. "He's the most expensive of all of us."

Fab arched an eyebrow. "Thanks to my many talents."

"Our little Fab can take two or three in a night," Vickie continued, tugging one of the grapes from its stem and popping it into her mouth. "Four if he gets his game on. You'd be surprised how many will pay him a visit if the girls are otherwise occupied."

I was flabbergasted. All I knew were the ragged poxy street walkers who strolled at either end of the Row. I never imagined whores with fine clothes in grand houses, attended to by servants. With all that I had gone through, I still knew so little about the world. I felt like such a child, and a foolish one at that. "But what about Madame's guests, the ones coming here tonight?" I wasn't sure what I was asking, but I was answered all the same.

"They are our clients, with particular exceptions," said the dark-skinned girl whose shoulders were wreathed in lavender. I later learned that she was Dominique, who had come to London as a child from West Africa. She had her arms around another girl, Rose, pale and freckled with ringlets of flame-red hair, her gauzy bodice dotted with tiny red rosebuds. They held each other close as Dominique toyed with Rose's hair. Something in me quivered at their easy unguarded affection. "They come and watch our little entertainments, they feast on our hens and sip our whiskey and applaud our antics, pinch our bums and squeeze our tits, do their little deals and pat each other on their backs. Then they pay Madame Quince, ever so discreetly of course, and take one or another of us up to the circle of boudoirs on the first floor, where they complete their business." I remembered passing these rooms on our way up to the bedrooms, and had been curious about the wooden plaques affixed to the doors: the Bridal Suite, the Safari Lodge, the Royal Chamber, the Misericord. I had wondered what they meant and now I had an inkling.

"Nicky," Rose said quietly, "leave the poor child be." She turned to face the others. "All of you. You're frightening her."

"Excuse me," I said as I stood from my chair. "I must apologise, I'm afraid I'm not feeling well after all. If I may, I'd like to go to my room and rest. All this excitement from the past few days . . . I think the baby is somewhat unsettled."

"Yes, of course, the baby," Florian murmured. Fanny raised her eyes at last, with a glare vicious enough to tear a strip from him.

Aphra looked up at me, watching my mouth in confusion. She turned to Fanny, tugged on her arm, but Fanny refused to meet her pleading gaze. I stepped out of the room into the hallway and ascended the back staircase until I reached the second floor, then turned out into the passage that led to Aphra's room. Once inside, I tore off the morning gown and left it in a heap on the floor, threw myself onto my bed and sobbed, great heaving sobs that shook my body. How could I be so foolish? The baby protested, kicked and punched at me until I longed to punch it back, to beat it with my fists until it fell out of me. But, of course, I did not. I tried to soothe it, I stroked my belly and through my sobs I tried to sing.

> My young love said to me, "My brothers won't mind,
> And my father won't slight you for your lack of kine."
> Then she turned her head to me, and this she did say:
> "It will not be long, love, till our wedding day."
>
> She turned away from me and she went through the fair,
> And fondly I watched her move here and move there.
> Then she turned away homeward with one star awake
> Like a swan in the evening moves over the lake.

After a time, I felt the air stir behind me as someone entered, knelt behind me and put their arm around me. I imagined it would be Aphra, but when I turned I saw that it was Fanny, as distraught and tear-soaked as I. "I'm sorry," she hushed into my ear, her voice broken. "I should have told you."

"You were right not to," I sighed. "It's true, I would never have come with you. I'd be in Marylebone now or abducted back to Highgate. Dead for all I know."

"Please stay," she said, clutching me tight. "Please don't run away from us. Aphra needs you, and so do I." I couldn't say anything; my mind was awhirl. Apart from the workhouses and the dormitories, I had nowhere else to go. I had no idea where my mother was. I would never be welcomed back to the Row. I had no choice but to stay in Mayfair, at least until the baby was born and given over to the orphanage. Even then, I would find myself lost as if in a dense, dark forest, disguised as a city, with few paths open to me and countless dangers lurking and watching from the shadows. I recalled the dark figure on the street outside the brothel and shivered. Was it Lovett, or Jonas, or the doctor himself? Why had they been there? What had they wanted? "Oh no," Fanny said from behind me. "You've turned to ice. Let's get you in front of the fire."

Just then, Aphra appeared at the door, her face tight with worry. Fanny made a few quick signs with her hands and Aphra helped her lift me up from the bed and into the main room, where the fire still licked at the logs placed there at the break of day. They had me sit near the flames and warm myself, Aphra fussing over me as a child would a pet, wrapping me in her coverlet and thrusting a hot cup of chamomile into my hand. After a few sips I felt calmer. I was safe; I had a place to stay; I was among friends; I would be cared for, at least until the baby was born. I resolved to be grateful. I resolved to be happy, for all our sakes.

"What's all this then?" Louisa, the housemaid, was peering in from the hallway. A few strands of chestnut hair snuck out from under her cap, curling down onto her forehead. She had a basket of linens and towels tucked under her arm that seemed to be destined for the scullery. "Aphra, Fanny, you're to join the others downstairs, Madame is delivering instructions for tonight's pageant. Peggy, if you're feeling poorly, you can stay up here. No one will think the worse of you for it. I can make you a nice tray to go with your tea."

I glanced over at Fanny and Aphra. "I'm much better now, thank you. I don't know what came over me. Nerves, I suppose. If Aphra would find it helpful, I'd like to stay near her, and help with whatever she needs." Louisa nodded, and Fanny and Aphra smiled. They helped me back into the morning gown, holding my tea as I pulled the slippers back onto my feet. We made our way down the stairs together, and into the entrance hall, where Florian was arranging chairs and Madame Quince was directing two of the servants on the placement of urns, columns and ivy on a tiny velvet-draped stage that had been set up in a shallow alcove.

I slipped into a seat near the front and watched as the young women stepped up onto the stage for their rehearsal. Aphra and Fanny were Urania and Thalia as I've already mentioned, the inventors of sight and smell. Dominique and Rose were to play Euterpe and Polymnia, the creators of hearing and taste, respectively. Dominique wore a necklace of tiny silver bells, and Rose held a wooden plank piled with sugared peel, boiled sweets, chocolate bonbons and marzipan. Vickie was to play Terpsichore, the inventor of touch. She held an impossibly large white ostrich plume. Florian sat on the floor of the stage with his legs dangling off the edge, as Orpheus with his lyre.

Shortly after their arrival, Madame Quince began to place the women on the stage, instructing them in their poses, how to hold their arms, where to place their legs, how to display their inventions and creations, and themselves, to the audience. Dominique and Vickie showed the most grace in the way they held their figures; Fanny and Rose presented their elements with intense concentration; but Aphra outshone all the others with her poise and stillness and luminous beauty. Without words, and with few gestures, she was able to convey a tenderness and sly humour that set her apart from the others. I grew so proud of her as I watched, and then slowly something more. I felt a stirring in my breast, an ache for which I had no name, no precedent. I thought of Dominique and Rose and their languid embrace, and I imagined Aphra and I in a similar pose, soothing each other with soft caresses, entwined like myrtle flowers on the vine. What were these strange emotions awakening within me? What peculiar loneliness unleashed these curious yearnings that prickled at my privacy?

Two sharp claps from Madame Quince startled me out of my reverie. She was a stern taskmaster, and it was a gruelling rehearsal, particularly for those of the ladies who had never been still for a moment in their lives. Their greatest difficulty was to remain absolutely frozen for thirty seconds, the subjects in a living painting, before changing in unison to the next required position. Ten positions each, ten tableaux overall, each tableau telling a different chapter of the unfolding story and revealing different physical aspects of the muses depicted: a breast here, a cheek there, a glimpse of fleece as the veils swayed and parted. Florian remained on the floor of the stage throughout, strumming his lyre, untouched by the constraints imposed on the others, his legs slightly spread, his ample manhood casually displayed. It was as if he existed outside of time, even as he sat at their very feet.

After an hour or so of work, Madame Quince gave two more sharp claps and concluded the preparations. Orpheus and the Muses would have an hour to change out of their costumes and refresh themselves, after which they were to assemble in the drawing room for afternoon tea. Before I could even stand, Aphra seized my hand and pulled me out of the chair, across the room and up the stairs. Once we were in her rooms, she threw her arms around me with great excitement and scribbled a note asking if she had done well, if the others had done better, and if Madame Quince was happy with her work. I assured her that she had performed wonderfully, and that everyone would be impressed. So delighted was she with these few small compliments that she positively glowed, and I could not stop myself from blushing like a silly schoolgirl. I struggled to compose myself and carefully helped her out of her gauzy garment, averting my eyes as best I could from her lissome figure. I quickly searched through the clothes press and found a pretty day-dress in gold and green embroidered with floral garlands across the bodice and around the wrists and hem. I held it up by the shoulders and Aphra nodded, so we changed her into that for the afternoon. As I was fastening the last of the buttons, I had a sudden thought. I gestured for her to come to my room and showed her the earrings that I had found on my bedside table at the doctor's house. Wide-eyed, she pointed and asked, "Where?" I told her they were a gift from my mistress at my previous position, then offered them to her, saying that she would have more use for them than I ever would. She tried to refuse, but I insisted. "They carry sad memories for me," I explained. She held them up against her ears, and I helped her slip them into her lobes. It was obvious that she loved them as much as I had. She threw her arms around me and gave me kiss on the cheek, pulled away and then, with a saucy impetuousness, kissed me on the lips as well. However much I had blushed before, I was positively crimson now. She laughed, a glittering bell-like sound, and then lightly touched my throat as I laughed as well. A sharp knock at the door interrupted us. It was Louisa, calling us down to afternoon tea.

Madame Quince joined us in the drawing room, so we had none of the bawdy talk or probing questions of our previous meal. We ate our French fancies and tiny sandwiches in quiet while Madame spoke at length about the history of tableaux over the centuries, in religious presentations and in art. Her tea sat cooling until it was chilled; her food congealed on the plate, untouched. On occasion she would pause and cast her gaze among us but then she would embark on another topic before anyone could utter a word. As the servants gathered the plates and cups, and the others rose to prepare for the evening, Madame Quince kept me back and took me aside where none of the others could hear.

"I am pleased to see that you have already formed such a close bond with Aphra," she began. "However, you will not be needed downstairs for our evening activities. She will have Fanny and Florian and me to rely on while she is there. Your task is to remain among the evening rooms. Tonight, Aphra will entertain her visitors in the Parisian Room." Madame Quince reached over and took my hand in hers. "You must understand: Aphra is strong, intelligent and resourceful; yet she is uniquely vulnerable because of her condition. There have been incidents of physical abuse, the details of which are too upsetting to share. While we do our best to ensure the quality of our clientele, I'm afraid I cannot permit her to be in her room alone. As her lady's maid, I ask that you stay there with her, watching over her, concealed from view."

To say I was shocked would be a grave understatement.

"While she is meeting with these men? But how?" I asked. "Where will I be? What do I do?"

"It's quite simple," she explained. "Each boudoir has a large folding screen, ostensibly for washing and dressing. Behind each screen is a chair, a small table, a washbasin and a bell. The screen is designed so that you can see through it without being seen. Sit silently, watch and listen. Draw no attention to yourself. If anything untoward should occur, ring to call for help."

The arrangement did sound simple, and I could not deny its necessity given Aphra's plight, but I felt intensely uncomfortable at the thought of watching someone who was so dear to me engaging in relations with a succession of strangers. If Madame Quince observed my unease, she chose to continue to talk right past it. She held up a small lined card laced with a gold ribbon, and consulted the list of names inscribed upon it.

"We can expect a Mr. Smith and a Mr. Johnson, both of whom are fond of Aphra and have enjoyed her company in the past. They are pleasant but tedious, so her inability to hear them is an unexpected asset. We may see a third gentleman this evening, a Mr. Brown, a friend of a friend who is visiting from the continent; he is unfamiliar to us and as such will require close attention. Between visitors, Aphra will require your assistance with her toilet and with changing the bedclothes. She will show you what needs to be done. Do you understand?"

"Yes, Madame," I replied with a nod and a bend of my knee. She took note of the uncertainty in my expression, and placed her hand upon mine.

"These aspects of your position can be unpleasant," she stated. "However, they are vital to ensure Aphra's safety and indeed the safety of everyone at our Symposia. They thank you, I thank you, and Pallas Athena thanks you. Now, please help Aphra back into her costume, and she will take you to the evening rooms on the first floor. I hope you enjoy your first taste of Paris."

I curtsied again, excused myself and then hurried up to where Aphra was waiting. The earrings dangled prettily in the late afternoon light. I held the silken robes up for her so that she could slip into them with ease, then knelt to lace her sandals. She nearly forgot the picture frame; I had to wave at her to remind her. She then led me to the Parisian Room, a large cream-coloured bed chamber with narrow stripes of gold and green painted from floor to ceiling. She pointed to an exquisitely carved wooden screen that might have come from the Orient, and then showed me the balloon-backed chair behind it, shapely with a pink-striped seat, and the brass handbell that I was to ring if we needed assistance. I was nervous about who Aphra's visitors might be. I had not forgotten that brief flash of the symbol among the cards and papers in Madame's desk, the same symbol used by the physician and his chums. Any one of them could be a patron of the Symposia, "a friend of a friend."

I need not have worried, at least not on this night. The performance and reception were only to last an hour but the wait felt much longer. I was overtired and had to pinch myself to keep from falling asleep. The seat of the chair was firm and unyielding, and caused my legs and back to ache. I wondered how I would get through the rest of the night.

As I was about to drift off again, the knob rattled and the door swung open. I could see through the small openings in the screen that Aphra had brought the first of her suitors into the room, presumably Mr. Smith. I turned my gaze away from them and listened. As Madame Quince had warned, he spoke at length about his employer, his position, his wife, his children, his mistress, his various ailments, until Aphra's vigorous attentions caused him to drift into a reverie. Soon after, he let out a gasp, cleared his throat and begged Aphra's pardon. I peered through the screen and saw that his visit had reached its natural conclusion and that he was refastening his trousers and shirt.

Once Mr. Smith was out the door, I emerged from behind the screen and helped Aphra clean her pessary and refresh her womanly regions, then replaced the half-sheet that lay across the centre of her bed. Then, a knock at the door and I returned once again to the chair behind the screen. Aphra admitted the next guest, likely Mr. Johnson, with yet another dull recitation of his personal history, punctuated with a few grunts and sighs and an amusing bout of hiccups. He and Aphra had frigged each other, near as I could tell, or perhaps he frigged himself while Aphra watched. In any event, he finished quickly enough. Once he had departed, I rejoined Aphra and helped her tidy herself and the room, and then sat behind the screen in anticipation of the third visitor.

Mr. Brown, if it were he, was a quiet man, much older, with a large white moustache and a grey tweed jacket and vest. No sooner were his pants off than he was flat on his back asleep and snoring like a fox in a snare. Aphra used a few dabs of pomatum to create some artful stains on his shirt and pants, then gave him a poke to wake him. He let out a little yelp, then saw the mess on his clothes. He stammered his apologies as he redressed himself, and then threw himself out into the hallway with a slam. Aphra barely needed to rinse herself after Brown's appointment, so we whiled away an hour with more lessons in hand-words: "mother" and "father" and "sister" and "brother" and "baby" and "friend" and "love"; "enter" and "leave" and "wait" and "hide"; "help" and "hurry" and "rest" and "sleep." I did confuse words from time to time, and accidentally invented words that no one had ever known before. I asked at one point if she wanted something to "eat," and then mangled it terribly, performing instead the word for "goose."

"Do I want a goose?" she asked, laughing. "A little goose?" And I shook my head no, and tried again, and she laughed even harder, and so did I.

"You are a little goose, you!" I said, pointing to her. We laughed again and from that moment my name for her was "little goose."

"Love—you—friend," she gestured, and I signed the same in return. "Please—no—leave," she replied. I shook my head and responded: "I—no—leave—you—little—goose." She gave me another kiss on the lips, then pulled me close with a smile. We cozied on the chaise until the darkness enveloped us. Was this what love was like? I was not one for reading books, but when I heard about such stories, they always seemed to be filled with swooning and pining and passionate declarations of everlasting affection. None of that interested me. What I wanted, all that I ever wanted, was what I had there, right there and then, in that moment.

Just then, I heard three gentle taps at the door. I gestured to Aphra to wait, then stood up from the chaise and answered. Louisa was there with Madame Quince.

"You've done very well," Madame Quince said. "All three of

this evening's visitors left quite satisfied, though Mr. Brown was in a bit of a fluster. No matter, he gave very generously to the Symposia, and has vowed to return at his earliest convenience. Now, Aphra may retire to her room while you and Louisa tidy up in here. Tomorrow, you may join the household staff in the kitchen for a light breakfast at seven, and then meet Aphra in her room to help her prepare for the day. Aphra receives her morning tray upstairs at eight o'clock, and then full breakfast will be served at half past nine in the dining room. You are welcome to join us, of course." I nodded, then beckoned to Aphra to make her way upstairs, then Louisa and I set about returning the Parisian Room to its original state.

We have gone too long, poor Catherine and I, our eyes are wet and heavy. We must put this to rest and pray. You too must watch for tares among the wheat. Do not lose sight of me, Miss Gibson. Our tribulation is at hand.

M.E.

Miss Gibson—You should have seen her, that horrible woman screaming "Murderer, murderer!" out at the gate. She was so loud, I'm sure they heard her at the village square. What are they saying outside the Priory? Have the rumours about the Reverend Mother reached the streets? Margaret did say something, she whispered a name: "Johanna?" Is this someone you've spoken to? Why did she come here? I fear for us all. —Sr. C.

Oranges and lemons
Say the bells of St. Clement's

Halfpence and farthings
Say the bells of St. Martin's

Eve ate the apple
Say the bells at Whitechapel

Kettles and pans
Say the bells at St. Ann's

When will you pay me?
Say the bells at Old Bailey

When I grow rich
Say the bells at Shoreditch

When will that be?
Say the bells of Stepney

I do not know
Says the great bell at Bow

Here comes a candle to light you to bed
Here comes a chopper to chop off your head

Chip chop chip chop

The last one is dead

REPORT NO. 435

**CHARING CROSS STATION,
COVENT GARDEN DIVISION**

16th day of August 1887

Sir,

At 5:30 p.m. 14 August, Miss. E. Gibson returned from afternoon tea with her companion, Miss J. Blackwell, to find the door ajar at her rooms at 22 Cecil Court, and her possessions in a state of disarray. A journalist, Miss Gibson is the daughter of Sir H. Gibson. She is unmarried, lives alone, receives an allowance from her father. Upon examination, the door appears to have been forced with a sharp object, possibly an awl or a chisel. Miss Gibson's valuables were undisturbed, but her books, notebooks and personal papers were strewn about by someone in a state of aggravation. Nothing of significance was destroyed or damaged. Nothing appears to be missing. Miss Gibson noted that she does hold numerous documents of importance, in accordance with her profession, but they are kept safely off the premises. This may have been an attempted theft of these documents, or an intrusion designed to intimidate Miss Gibson into abandoning a line of enquiry. I have assigned a member of the constabulary to inspect her apartments once per day. Meantime, she has arranged for alternate lodgings in St. Martin's Lane. She will return thrice weekly to retrieve her correspondence, and has arranged for a chaperone to and from her office at the Post. Trusting this meets with your approval.

J. Smith, Insp.
HON. SIR CHARLES WARREN
G.C.M.G., K.C.B., F.R.S.

ST. ANNE'S PRIORY
Hampstead, London

AUGUST THE 19TH, 1887

Miss Gibson,

As I write this, a thick yellow fog has crept up from London and enveloped the Priory in its malodorous embrace. The fogs these days are dense with factory smoke, so different from those that we suffered on the Row when I was small, the ones that scalded our eyes with the noxious fumes from the dirty Thames. Mother used to hang sheets across the windows, sheets soaked with lime, in the hope that they would close out the poisonous stench. These were the days and nights when you couldn't go outside, when you would seal yourself in one room and wait for the fog to pass. Of course, it crept in through the cracks in the walls, underneath doors, up through the floorboards. No escape. It was worst in the dead heat of summer. We would hold wet rags over our faces, put chips of ice on our eyes and our tongues. We would pray for a change in the air, a fierce wind, a vicious storm, but sometimes days would pass without respite. We would lie in our beds and listen as the fog stretched and distorted the sounds from the street, from the docks, from the river itself, so that it seemed like monstrous creatures were scrabbling across the cobblestones and up the very walls. As I say, though, the fogs are different now. The mist is sulfurous, gritty with dust and flakes of soot, wet and clammy and foul, like a cold dead hand on the back of your neck. What hides in the fog is different as well. That cold dead hand can as easily cover your mouth, catch you by the throat, it can pull you back into the darkness and squeeze your last breath out of you. One thing hasn't changed: when I was at Madame Quince's, I took care to stay away from the windows lest I be seen and recognised, but I knew that out there in the fog, across the street or around the corner, someone was waiting. Watching for me. Wanting my baby. They would take it and, if they had no choice, they would take me. And somehow, the same is still true today. Just a few hours ago I looked out past the Priory wall and saw figures in the fog, five or six of them, standing and watching across from the gate, unnatural in their stillness. Sister Catherine saw them too. At the front was the woman from last week, or so we believe. Even though I could not see her clearly, I felt her gaze upon me. I felt it penetrate my soul.

Sister Catherine and I have barely slept. The shrouded air outside is indistinguishable from that within the Priory, dark and unsettled as if we are in the path of a gathering storm. I fear this letter to you will be my last, that I will be forced to leave this place, to hide myself, an anchorite imprisoned behind the stones, silenced, immured, yearning for deliverance. Augustine has withdrawn to her offices, and the others are now shying away from us, brandishing rosaries, hushing into whispers whenever we enter the room. I know that Catherine's ears will blaze with the licentious nature of the events I am about to relate, but she will find strength in Our Lord as she takes down these words. So much of my time at the Symposia was filled with warmth and friendship and kindness and joy. But I must acknowledge that there was sadness and sorrow there as well, and a subtle degradation that numbed and eroded the soul, for which no amount of finery could compensate. And, always, the figure in the fog that, even if unseen, was never entirely absent from my thoughts.

As those first few days at the brothel stretched into weeks, Aphra and I became boon companions, with Fanny as our ally and confidante. My discomfort with the activities in the evening rooms soon faded and as I observed Aphra and her visitors from behind the screen I became increasingly curious about the games of pleasure that she played with them. In our time together, I learned more and more of her hand-words until she and I could communicate with our own secret code, one that even Fanny struggled to untangle. Dominique and Rose and Victoria were pleasant enough to us, but had formed their own passionate sisterhood well before I arrived, and seemed none too keen to admit us into their circle. As for Fab, well, he could be a doting mother at one moment and a spoiled child at the next. He maintained a studious distance from the girls, yet he could also be as close to any of us as he wished, almost in an instant. He had an air of loneliness about him, a melancholy that I felt pierce my heart whenever I observed it. Mischievous as he could be, I loved him, and I expect he loved a few of us back, much as one might be loved by a cat who only came to one's knee for meals and affection and otherwise remained aloof. He was indeed the most popular of all the whores, with a succession of gentlemen from the highest levels of society seeking out his company. Every second Sunday, Fab would engage in a play-acting ritual, where he would play a blushing debutante, cheeks rouged and curls beribboned, his slender frame fetchingly wrapped in white lace and satin, lounging on a chaise while his gathered suitors vied for his hand in what would be a temporary marriage. I soon perceived that some of them could only allow themselves to be attracted to him if he was presented in a more feminine form. Fab would make a great show of accepting one of the many proposals offered, and then a mock wedding would be conducted in the early afternoon, officiated by Madame Quince. The consummation would follow promptly, and often noisily, in one of the upstairs rooms, and then the whole charade would conclude with a joyous divorce founded on one amusing pretence or another, just in time for a bounteous feast for everyone in attendance, paid for of course by the bride's newly liberated husband. As always, I kept my distance from these events, and either confined myself to Aphra's room or lurked on the stairs in case she needed me.

But I no longer found them shocking, and in time came to see them as full-grown versions of the dress-up and pretend parties we sometimes had as children on the Row. Perhaps this was the province of the privileged, a sumptuous indulgence for those who could pay the price.

With the pageants and concerts and theatricals, each of the Symposia's coterie had their turn in the spotlight, including Aphra who was revealed to be an exceptional painter and poet. The evenings that created the greatest sensations were those that shone a light on the higher pleasures, of the mind and heart and soul: Madame Quince's weekly salons, which attracted artists and sculptors, writers, actors, critics, philosophers, professors, lawyers and judges, financiers, politicians and even members of the clergy. I found the subjects interesting and the speakers enticing. When I could, I sat on one of the lower steps in the servant's stairwell, and kept myself very still, so that I could remain concealed but still hear quite clearly the presentation by the honoured guest and then the ensuing debate among the invitees.

Early on in my stay, Madame Quince hosted a lecture by an author visiting from France by the name of Dumas. He had just published a novel in Paris titled Captain Paul and had left his wife and son behind to come to London, and to the brothel, to celebrate with several of his writer friends. They arrived at the house quite intoxicated, and Madame came to realise that Dumas knew not one word of English, had no remarks prepared, and had firmly set his rather blurry sights on Vickie. No matter, Madame exclaimed, he could address the room in his native French and she would translate for those in attendance. I sat hidden on my step and listened as Dumas took the lectern and then lurched and staggered his way through a rambling ruin of a speech. Every few sentences he would pause, and Madame would leap in with her interpretation of what he had said. Just a few minutes in, I heard a small disturbance and Dominique suddenly appeared in front of me, a handkerchief held in front of her face. I had thought she was weeping, but she was fighting back tears of laughter. "It's Madame," she whispered, dabbing at her eyes. "She cannot know any French at all! She has no idea what Dumas is saying. He is describing all of the whores he's had, all sorts of filthy stories, and she's just telling us nonsense about the artists of Montmartre. I'm heading upstairs before I piss myself!" With that she squeezed past me and tiptoed up to the boudoirs.

A moment later, a gentleman appeared before me, one of the invited guests, tidy in his proper evening dress, silk hat in hand, a lock of his thick black hair drooping onto his brow. In a moment I realised who it was: Dr. C's friend, Jonas. He stood there startled as he saw my abundant figure. "I'm so sorry," he said. "Have I seen you here before?" I was certain he hadn't recognised me, and I couldn't have been more grateful.

I hauled myself up and gave a quick curtsy, keeping my eyes trained downward. "Peggy, sir. I'm a maid to one of the ladies."

"Oh, I shouldn't think so, then." He pointed up the stairs behind me. "The young woman who just went up, is she quite all right? She left in rather a hurry."

"Yes, sir. Dominique. She was feeling unwell, you see, and has gone to her rooms for some rest. I could pass a message to her if you like." He shook his head and mumbled something, his eyes firmly fixed on my belly, then quietly returned to his seat. I peered around the corner into the room and saw that Madame Quince was looking back at me, her eyes narrowed, her lips pursed into a tight, bloodless bow. I pulled my head back and then snuck up to the Parisian Room and concealed myself behind the screen, in case Aphra was to entertain a visitor. Jonas seemed not to recognise me, but had he? Would he? Would he wake up in the night with my face fresh from his dreams and tell the doctor of my whereabouts? My worries overwhelmed me to such a degree that they exhausted me; I felt like I had weights of lead shackled to my every limb. No sooner did I lower myself onto the chair than I closed my eyes and sank into a dark dreamless slumber. I awoke to find Madame Quince and Aphra standing over me, still in their gowns from the salon, Aphra shaking my shoulder gently. I placed my hand on hers and she stopped. Her face was fraught with concern.

"Peggy, poor Aphra found you here, tossing and turning and crying in your sleep," said Madame Quince. "She is quite distressed. We all are. I have brought you a soothing Egyptian chamomile, and I am going to sit with you until you drink it all down." In her hand was a gilt-edged porcelain cup and saucer painted with tea roses, one from the set that we reserved for our visitors. Trembling, I reached for the cup and brought it to my lips. The tea was sweet and mild and tasted faintly of apples. The warmth that it brought to my throat and my chest soothed me instantly.

Madame Quince gestured to Aphra, who looked up and watched her speak. "Aphra, could you please leave us for a moment? I'd like to have a word," she said. Aphra nodded and retreated from sight. I knew I was in trouble; I had no choice but to face it.

"Now, Peggy," she began, "I appreciate your concern for Aphra and your curiosity about the events we hold in the downstairs rooms. But you are making it harder for us to keep you on here." She placed her hand on mine to steady it, and helped me raise the teacup to my mouth once more. I glimpsed for a moment the difference in age between us, her hand creased and veined and spotted, with pretty polished nails, and mine smooth and firm, toughened from tending fires, mending clothes, working in kitchens and sculleries. She was as much a mother to me in this moment as my own had ever been.

"You must understand," she continued. "The men who come here, they come to experience a fantasy of womanhood, and the young women here are engaged to fulfill that fantasy. Part of that fantasy is an intimacy that is consequence-free, offered lightly from a place of mutual desire; the reality that we are providing is that any consequences that do arise from these assignations are borne by women alone, and women alone must resolve them invisibly and without complaint. When one of our visitors sees you in your parturient state, it pierces the fantasy and unsettles him. He becomes wary and fearful and a potential danger to our enterprise. This, I believe, is the root of the superstition that you have heard us mention: that a pregnant woman brings trouble to houses like ours if she is permitted to cross the threshold. It's nonsense of course, but even the most powerful people in our realm are enslaved by superstition."

"The gentleman who saw me, did he complain?" I asked. "I was very polite to him. I tried to be helpful."

"I wouldn't say that he complained," she replied, "but he was surprised, and he came to me directly to ask about you. I was able to assuage him without revealing too much of your plight. However, I must implore you to conduct yourself discreetly, and to confine yourself to the servants' quarters and passages when we are open to guests. Even when we restrict our events to our closest circle, there are those we dare not trust. This could all go away in a moment if we are not exceedingly careful."

"Are you angry at me?" I asked.

"No, my child," she sighed. "Not at you. I am angry at the

world. Now, finish your tea and let's get you up to bed." She gave my hand a squeeze and I nodded in agreement.

I could no longer take such risks, not with so little time left before the baby's arrival. I raised the cup and emptied it, letting the quietude that it imparted extend throughout my being. She took the cup from me, smiled, and set it back on its rose-wreathed saucer.

"Madame Quince, this will seem odd, but I have a question about something I've seen. It may be unimportant. I just can't be certain." Having said the words, I felt a flutter near my heart. But I had formed the query in my mind and I was determined to follow through.

She cocked an eyebrow in my direction. "Yes, my dear, ask away and I will answer if I can."

"I have seen something, a drawing, that is unfamiliar to me: a triangle with an eye in the centre. I was wondering if you knew what it meant." I affected a certain shyness as I asked, turning my face away from her slightly but training my eyes on hers so that I could see her reaction. A shadow crossed her face, lingering on her brow, but it vanished quickly enough.

"An eye, you say? That does sound peculiar. I'm not sure what I can tell you. Where did you see it?" She had a curious look about her, fearful but also expectant.

"When I was at the master's house," I replied, "he had friends who would come and go at all hours, toffs with top hats in carriages and cabs, they would present their cards to each other and to their drivers, and some of the cards had the drawing upon them."

"Oh Peggy, we mustn't call them toffs, it is such a vulgar

term. Even if we do not care for someone, we should speak of them with respect." She paused for a moment as if considering how to respond. "I believe I know the symbol you describe," she said finally. "An eye within a triangle. I have seen it myself from time to time. It indicates that the bearer is a member of some distinction, that he holds a certain level of wealth and authority. The card functions as a promise of payment for a service, or a request for a favour. Much of what we wish to do in this world cannot be done alone. One needs a cohort of friends and like-minded associates who can assist each other to achieve their common goals. Oh, good, here is Louisa, come to check on us." Madame Quince gave my hand another squeeze, then called to Louisa, who set her fresh linens and towels at the foot of the bed and found us behind the screen. Together they helped me out of the chair, and Louisa led me upstairs to my maid's room and into my bed. The baby was awake now, twisting and pushing against my insides, but still I could barely keep my eyes open. Louisa kindly pulled the covers over me, tugged at the curtains and left me to rest.

The fortnight that followed passed with increasing slowness as I grew larger and heavier and faced greater difficulty dealing with the Symposia's abundance of tall shelves, waist-high furniture, and its narrow passages, doors and stairs. Eventually my world shrank to my maid's room, Aphra's room, the first-floor boudoirs and the halls and stairs between, and then finally just to my own bed, where I spent more time asleep than awake. Aphra, Fanny and Louisa would each sit with me in turn, but there were many hours, especially at night, when I was alone in various kinds of discomfort wondering what would become of me once the baby was born. My attachment to it was ever more fierce, as was my furious desire to be rid of it, and my horror at what it had done to me.

Then came the night, a Friday night early in March. I awoke as if I'd been struck. The room was dim and strange in the moonlight, I only knew it was mine from the smell and feel of my bedclothes. The clocks were ticking throughout the house like insects; the flickering gaslight cast an eerie glow across the fine silk rug just outside my door. I felt a burst of fluid rush from between my legs. A few moments passed, then sharp, searing pain tore through me, shocking me out of my stupor. I began to shiver all over, violently, as if at the start of a terrible fever. Was this how it began? Was this the baby? But it was too early! I tried to sit up but I couldn't. My arms, my legs, they were stiff and heavy and unable to move. It was as if my head had been chopped from the rest of my body. I knew in that moment that something was terribly wrong. I went to call out, but where my voice had been, there was only a whisper. Aphra couldn't hear me, no one could hear me. I heard the rustle of sheets in the next room, the sound of bare feet walking across the wooden floor. Aphra was awake, she was going to use the chamber pot, she would pass right outside my door. It took all my strength and effort, I was sweating and gasping, but I was able to push the bedclothes off myself and onto the floor. Aphra appeared in the doorway, clutching a candle. She looked at the linens on the floor, then at me. She stepped into the room, holding the flame aloft, and then gasped. She turned and ran out of the room, out into the hallway. The bell for the servants rang and rang and rang until the whole of the house had clambered up the stairs to

Aphra's door. Fanny rushed in first. She and Aphra lifted me off the bed and carried me out near the hearth fire.

It was then and only then that I saw the blood on my nightclothes, gouts of it, thick and black and clotted. Insensible, I was taken back to my days on the Row as a child, where I had joined my father in the rigours of butchery, but now the sight confused me. Whose blood was it? Where did it come from? Why was it all over me? My nightgown was ruined. Mother would be so upset. Madame Quince knelt down, hovered over me, pulling her wrapper tight around her waist. "Vickie, go round the corner and wake Mrs. Price!" Mrs. Price was a midwife, a friend of Madame Quince's, a burly little Irish woman with wiry hair and heavy black brows who always looked ready to wrestle down the devil. She often came to the salons, and looked in on the girls from time to time. She was as good as any doctor, at least in times like these.

Vickie leapt up from my side and hurried out the door in just her dressing gown. A few moments later I heard the door downstairs squeal open, and slam shut. Madame Quince called out across the room. "Rose, get Louisa to bring us some hot water and clean towels. Hurry!" I felt Madame's hand turn my face towards hers. "Peggy, look at me. You must listen. Mrs. Price is on her way. She'll be here at any moment. Close your eyes and count to ten, then count backwards down to one. Do that over and over until she arrives."

"One two three four," I whispered, "five six seven eight nine ten." Another gash of pain across my belly, as if I was being split open. I felt my face clench, my teeth grind against each other. "Ten nine eight seven six five four three two one." Even though my eyes were closed, I could see the thick black fog creeping up through the streets of Mayfair, erasing everything in its path, encroaching on the house, surrounding it, slipping under the front door and crawling up the stairs, and within the fog I could see the dark figure, the watcher, drawing ever closer, step by step, until he crossed the threshold into Aphra's room, standing over all of us, looking down at my swollen belly, my bloodied nightgown, I could see him, even though my eyes were closed. "One two three four five six seven"—and then I watched as he leaned over Madame's shoulder and he reached for me, as the burnt black fog enveloped me, glowing red cinders dancing within it, and then I sank into it like a stone until it swallowed me. "Six—seven—eight—nine—ten."

When I opened my eyes, I was back in my bed, alone. I felt like I had been whipped and flayed. The sheets were fresh, my nightgown was unsoiled, my breasts swollen and sore, my belly soft and sagging. The baby. Where was the baby? I looked around my little room, then out the door into Aphra's suite. Madame Quince was seated on Aphra's hearthside chair, drawing a needle back and forth through a cloth on a hoop. The golden thread gleamed in the firelight. "The baby," I croaked. Madame's eyes shifted towards me. She set aside her needlework and came to the doorway. "The baby," I said again, my throat clearing, my voice returning. "Where is it? Where is the baby?"

"Oh, my child," Madame Quince said, her wizened hand grasping the side of the door frame. "How wonderful to have you back with us! You have been through a perilous time. I am so sorry to be the one to tell you this. Your child did not survive."

The orange light of the fire flickered behind her, illuminating the tears on her face. "We all share your grief, Peggy. It is such a terrible loss. He was a beautiful boy, perfect in every way. It was just too soon. He never even drew a breath. Mrs. Price did everything she could."

I was struck blind for a moment, my eyes shimmering with pain. "Where? Where is he?" I cried. "I want to see my baby."

"Peggy, my dear," she replied evenly, as if she had been preparing for this. "It has been two days. We nearly lost you as well. Mrs. Price took the baby to be buried at Cross Bones, across the river in Southwark. She did say that she thinks you could have another child someday, with a proper father in a proper home. So perhaps things are as they should be."

"What are you saying? Where is Aphra?" I cried. I couldn't understand. "Why isn't she here with me? I want to see her, I don't want to see you!"

She flinched as I spat the words at her, and a part of me was pleased, that in my time of gravest injury I could still deal a blow to others. "She is downstairs with the others. We have a party this evening, a Games Night, she has a full card. I didn't want you to be alone, not after all that you have been through. I will send her up to you if you wish, as soon as she's free."

"I want to see her," I replied deliberately, barely repressing my rage. If I'd had the breath within me, I would have screamed and screamed and screamed. I knew it was childish, but I didn't care. I had never wanted the baby so much as when I was told I could not have it. Madame gave me a pained look and then departed from my sight. Some time later, Aphra appeared at the door, then came in and sat on the bedside chair. She had brought a pen and paper, ready for what she knew would be an onslaught.

"Peggy—I am so very sorry," she said, her hands quivering as she gestured. "Your baby. Everyone is so sad." I could see her eyes were red and swollen.

"She said the baby is dead," I said. "That the baby was born dead." She nodded, looking down at the blank page in front of her. Tears dripped down and stained the paper.

"Yes, dead," she wrote. "He never breathed. He was taken away by Mrs. Price."

"To Cross Bones, across the river," I said. "I want to go there. I want to see him."

"There is nothing to see," she wrote. "The graves are unmarked."

It was then that the full flood came. I sobbed and sobbed and tore at myself, and Aphra threw down the pen and clasped her arms around me. Even though I loved her, it was like being held by a ghost. And the pain, the pain was like iron, red and hot and heavy, thrashing my insides, but I didn't care. Why hadn't I died? Why hadn't he lived? If I killed myself, the pain would be gone, and we would be reunited, even if only in Hell.

After a time I composed myself, and pointed at the paper. Aphra dried her cheeks and picked it up from the floor. "What happens now?" I asked. "What's to become of me?"

"Upstairs for a fortnight, then away," she wrote. "She wants to keep us apart."

Up with the other servants, away from everyone else. "Why? Why can't I stay here with you?" I asked, but I already knew the answer.

"You are unwell, and I must work," she wrote. "She will write a letter for you, if you wish." I knew already what this would mean. I could only ever work for one of Madame's guests or associates. No one else would hire me. A housemaid who worked at a brothel, even one as refined as the Symposia, may as well be a whore herself.

Louisa appeared at the door, ready to move my things. Aphra put her arm around me and half-carried me up the servants' stairs to the top floor where an empty room awaited, smaller and plainer than the one below, with an engraving of Old London Bridge on the wall above the bed, simply framed in cherrywood. Louisa followed with my clothes and shoes, which she arranged in the old oak cupboard on the far wall. Aphra turned down my bedclothes for me, and placed a white woolen blanket at the foot of the bed. "I will send up some food for you," she gestured, then gave me a light hug. Louisa curtsied and excused herself and then the two of them made their slow descent down the back staircase.

I spent the next five days in bed, exhausted and wracked with fever. In all that time I never saw Aphra, though she may have looked in on me while I slept. Twice a day one of the kitchen girls would come up to feed me and clean me and change my chamber pot, and then help me express my breast milk into jars to give to Mrs. Price to sell. There was always a demand for milk for newborns among the women in the upper classes, women like the wives of our clients at the brothel. They believed that nursing babies was crude and vulgar, and best left to nannies, wet nurses or servants. In the evenings, I was gently bathed and given a fresh nightgown, and tucked back under the covers. That fifth night, when I lay down to rest, I slipped my hand under the pillow and found the thing that would change my destiny.

It was a piece of paper, folded in quarters, a handwritten note. How it arrived there, who placed it there, whether they knew what was written within it, I still do not know. It said:

> I know who you are, and I know who you were
> and I know one more thing too.
> Your baby is alive.
> Meet me tonight at St. Dunstan's as the clock strikes three.
> Come alone. Say nothing. If you want your friends to live.

The gate. The door. I am to be vanished. I have one last gift for you, Miss Gibson—you will have it soon enough, but I will tell you this: I have nothing left in this world, and nothing to hide. There is no one left for me but you. Sister Catherine, who has prayed for my redemption and has yearned for my salvation, she can do nothing against the forces that have aligned themselves against us. These three words I leave you with will tell you all you need to know.

<u>I AM SHE.</u>

AUGUST THE 20TH, 1887

Miss Gibson,

She is gone. She has been taken. May the Lord have mercy upon her.

I was instructed to pass this package to you. I am shocked to learn that she has been writing privately these past weeks in a register that she had taken from the Reverend Mother's rooms, in the guise of scriptural contemplations, and has kept it hidden, even from me, until just moments before her departure.

Sin upon sin upon sin!

I have peered into its pages, and a single glance was enough to repel me from reading further. Margaret is a troubled woman, dangerously disturbed and prone to dark fancies and unanchored fears. She has been faced with terrible choices and has committed heinous crimes. She has lived many lives to survive just one. Please, do not show this to anyone lest her situation grow even more precarious. She is in grave danger, I know it, but there is little we can do to help her now. We can only pray.

I must caution you that, unlike the letters that she dictated to me, this is unadorned and unmitigated by my hand. I cannot speak to its contents. I can only imagine the ghastliness of the recollections within. I should like to burn this book, but I must not. I have given my word, and now these words I give to you. Whatever else you may find in these pages, I hope they give you the answers that you seek.

Perhaps Margaret's mother knew something that we do not, to have abandoned her so easily, and so coldly. Did you kill your father, Margaret? Did you kill the child maimed by the carriage? What is the truth behind the truth you tell?

Merciful God, forgive us all.

Sister Catherine

St. Anne's Priory
Common Accounts
1887

JULY 24

Psalms 31:10
For my life is spent with grief, and my years with sighing: my strength faileth because of mine iniquity, and my bones are consumed.

I swear what I write upon these pages is the truth, the whole of it, as best as I recall these fifty years hence, so help me God.

You want to know the true tale of the wicked woman, the murdering monster? The one who baked pies stuffed with bits of her victims? The talk of London Town? I suppose I can't fault you for it. We're all rats scrabbling for crumbs. Dogs fighting dogs for bones behind the dung heap. Every one of us wants to put themselves above every other. Why should you be any different?

I wonder sometimes about what you've lived, what you've seen. Have you ever loved someone you could not have? A love that set the whole world against you? Have you ever had a child? A child you couldn't keep, that was taken from your breast and handed to strangers? It may be that you have. Catherine read me things you wrote in the papers. It may be that my story is more yours than you have let on.

Have you ever killed a man? Maybe not, but did you ever want to?

I'll tell you what you want to know. Though it may well be

the last thing I tell. But know this. I would not have done all that I did if Lovett had not written those four terrible words that cut me to my very soul.

"Your baby is alive."

That awful day I roused myself from bed just past the hour of two. The message said to meet at St. Dunstan's at three, the night's darkest hour. I was still torn up from the birth, my dugs still sore, my belly still swollen. I ached everywhere. I crept down the stairs to the second floor, found Aphra's room and slipped inside, then hurried across to the maid's room where all of my things were still gathered. I moved around the room in the dark, pulling a heavy grey cloak over a brown plaid dress with pretty flowers that Madame Quince had ordered special for me. I took out an old leather case that had been tucked behind the cupboard, squeezed in another dress, blue, some gloves and stockings and underthings. I strapped the case shut and I stepped back into Aphra's room. The air was filled with sweetness. She had snuck an orange from the kitchen and left it on the table near her bed. Next to it was a long slender knife with a clever little hook at the end. As I tucked it into my pocket, she stirred and blinked then stared at me. I took her hand and pressed it to my cheek, then to my mouth. "I must go, little goose," I whispered.

She sat up with the weight of sleep still clinging to her. She didn't reply, but shook her head no as her eyes filled with tears, as did mine. High in the sky, a cloud moved away from the moon letting its cold clear light shine down on us.

"Don't look for me. I will find you one day." I kissed her fingers, then touched them to her lips. Tears spilled down her cheeks. My throat was tight. If I thought about those tears too much I might change my mind, and not leave her. So, I swept out of the room, down the back stairs and into the servants' lane. Aphra was wise not to follow.

I walked fast, my hand tight around the knife in my pocket. I stayed in the light, watching my step, my heart jumping in my chest, until I saw St. Dunstan's towering before me. I ducked into a laneway and hid my case where no one would find it, then walked to the iron gate leading into the burial ground. A figure stood there, a shadow among the shadows. A cloud drew back from the moon, lighting the figure's face like a lamp, and I gasped from a shock that ran through me into my bones.

Lovett.

He heard me and turned and smiled, a wicked dirty grin, and gestured for me to come to him. Even now, in this place, he stank of gin and wobbled like a jelly pudding. Off in the distance, a clock chimed three. My hidden hand clutched the knife. I could feel a blind rage building inside me. Why was he here? What did he know? Did he have my son? He stepped towards me, stumbled, righted himself. The gin gave him a few moments of courage, but neither strength nor sense.

"Good girl," he said. "You be the doctor's maid. Maggie or Meggie or Peggy. You weren't expecting the likes of me, were you?" He reached into his pocket, pulled out the doctor's card with the strange symbol, the one I'd lost in the alley when I was with Fanny. My heart sank to see it in his clutches. I reached for it and he snatched it away, slipped it back into his shirt pocket. "Naughty girl," he leered. "He'll want you back, you know. A wee lad needs his mother, at least at the start. I reckon he'll pay a quid or three for you, and even more for me to fetch your boy from wherever the orphan house has put him."

"What makes you think I'll go anywhere with you?" I looked behind him and all around the graves. Were we truly alone? "Where's the doctor? Where's my son?"

"The good doctor is back in Highgate. Oh, he'll have nowt to do with the likes of me, least not till I drag you to his doorstep. Then he'll change his tune about Old Lovett. They all will. You will too. Once he's got you, he'll fix you up so you can't run off again. Just like his poor wifey."

I thought about the wretched woman crisscrossed with scars, and of everything the doctor had done to her and to me. "What about my son?" I asked, barely holding in my fury.

Lovett pulled back his coat, unbuttoned his trousers, and reached in to touch himself. "He's where all of Quince's bastards end up, out on one of the farms where they'll put him to work as soon as he can walk. I'll have a little chat with her to set things straight. My money's as good as anyone's. She'll sell the wee one to me if the price is right. But don't you worry about that. You want to see your baby boy, you'll need to take care of me first."

"Oh, I'll take care of you, all right," I said as I stepped closer, squeezing the knife till my hand was numb. "You've been needing a woman to take care of you for a long time." I couldn't help myself, I couldn't stop myself. In my mind it was all I could see: Lovett forcing himself on Fanny, Lovett lurking outside the brothel, Lovett holding the doctor's card with his face twisted in triumph. He would not win. I would not let him win. I reached up with one hand to cradle his chin, then brought the other swift across his neck with the clever hook on the knife slicing through his flesh like tallow. He squeaked like a cornered mouse and grabbed at his throat with both hands, trying to hold in all the blood spraying between his fingers. A great rush raced through me, making my own blood sing. I stepped to the side, mindful of the mess. And I couldn't help but smile as I grabbed the collar of his coat and pulled it up across the gash. I reached into his coat pockets, pulled out his coin purse and keys. His eyes were wide with panic. "Oh no, you're hurt," I said, with great sympathy. "I know how to help you. Quick, where is your shop?" Pale and weak, he lifted his arm up and gestured out past the front of the church into Fleet Street. My case was just around the side. "Very good. Put your arm around me. That's it." I led him out of the churchyard and onto the street looking like an old alley whore clinging to a drunken customer, or a long-suffering wife with a sot for a husband.

Husband.

I found the pie shop easy enough. A squat grey box near Fetter Lane. Mean and grim, overshadowed by the church tower. Quince had stolen my baby and hidden him somewhere. The doctor didn't know but could find out soon enough, if he or someone in his circle made their way to the house in Mayfair. There was no going back to either of them, not as I was. Not if I wanted to live.

When I saw the Lovett's Pie Shop sign hanging over the door, a sly smile stretched across my face. Margery Lovett, I was, or would be. The pie man's widow. And who was to say I wasn't? This was my pie shop now. His keys and purse were in my pocket. If Lovett's money was as good as anyone's, then so was mine. If I could become a woman of means, if I could climb the shit-covered ladder that stretched up between me and them, maybe somehow I would see my baby again.

I kicked open the back gate and pushed the old bastard into the yard, then slammed the gate shut behind us. I went round and unlocked the front door with the big key I took from his pocket. He stayed put, gasping and squirming. He wasn't going anywhere, except maybe to Hell.

The door squealed as it swung wide, and a rusty old bell jangled. The whole place stank of rotten meat, and was thick with dirt and dust and grit. The floor wasn't swept and the lamps were grimy. The windows, black with soot, had cobwebs for curtains. Sticky papers hanging from the ceiling were stuck with old flies and even a few little birds, tiny brown wrens, long dead. The pie oven was lined with ash and grease. There were bellows and shovels for the coal fire, and a long paddle for putting pies into the oven. Rusty cleavers, knives and dirty mixing bowls sat on a big table. Pie pans and tools were all crusty and oily. The tables were smudged with old gravy, and beetles raced over the counter. A rat ran over my toes. I kicked at it but it was too fast.

Then at last I saw what stunk. It was a giant meat grinder, its funnel and screw clogged with green meat. Piles more had dropped on the floor. Heaps of suet were bursting with maggots. I gagged at the smell, wishing I had a boy like Tom to help me clean it.

It was like the place had been shut up for weeks. I couldn't keep a shop as foul as that and expect customers. How did

Lovett do any trade at all? No wonder he couldn't pay for a clicket with Fanny. No wonder his clothes were so shabby. He didn't care about nothing, least not himself. I reckon I'd done him a favour by ending it all.

Even worse than the shop were Lovett's own rooms. A straw pallet crawling with bedbugs and a chamber pot full of piss. The fireplace was heaped with ashes, the stained carpet had a patch gone, eaten by moths, and he'd left a bowl of grey water with whiskers floating in it. Mrs. Dawson would have had fits at the sight of it all.

I took down a sketch of him tacked to the wall. He was standing in front of the shop when it looked worth a visit. The frame would go to the pawnshop. His stinking, sweat-stained shirts, his shabby boots, his comb and worn-out coat would go into the rubbish.

Next I found the back larder. Bugs and mice scurried into the corners as I opened the door. Two tables were set up for baking and butchery, scattered with bits of meat and fat and hardened dough, and swarming with bluebottles. Dirty sawdust covered the floor like our shop on the Row. At the back of the room a tar-black door opened onto some dark stone steps. I wondered if they led down to the tunnels under St. Dunstan's. I had heard tales of the tunnels since I was a little girl. I wondered what they were like and if there were coffins stacked along their walls. In the ceiling of the larder, I noticed a sprung trapdoor with a rope hanging down from it. What on earth could that be for?

I spotted boxes of flour dotted with fleas stacked next to sacks of wrinkled potatoes with wormy roots growing out of their eyes. Tiny white larder moths fluttered like fairies around my head. There were soft onions with black spots and old filthy pie tins and patty pans that would turn your stomach. Oily pots, chipped crockery and moldy bread. And me, having just come from a brothel where pies and pastries were baked with gobs of butter in shining copper pans and served on China plates with twigs of rosemary. There was none of that at Lovett's. A disgrace, it was. Eat a pie from here, you just chuck it all up round the corner.

Outside I found Lovett still coughing and heaving with gobs of black blood foaming out of his mouth. How was he still alive when he'd already been half-dead to start with? Gin was a greater medicine than I thought. I looked around the yard. A table, a bench, a slops bucket. An ice house of sorts, slapped together out of old grey boards. And in the ground next to it, a square wooden door. I went over and pulled it up and open. An unholy stench nearly knocked me backward. A pit for scraps and rubbish. That would do nicely. I took Lovett by his scabby hands and pulled him to the edge of the pit bleeding and gurgling. I lifted his legs up and pushed him in. He fell with a crack and a thud. I pictured his brains spilling out across the floor, the rats ripping at his face. Good night to you, sweet husband. Take all our secrets with you.

As I dropped the pit door down with a slam a little light caught my eye. A candle flickered in the window above my head. A shadow hovered there. Someone lived above the shop, above my shop, but who? Had they seen my dirty deed? The light flickered again, and a slash of red snagged my attention. A painted red-and-white pole stuck out into the street from a doorway near the back of the pie shop. Underneath was a sign that said "Sweeney Todd, Barber." I looked up at the window again. All was dark and still. A nosy tenant. I would have to ready a tale for Mr. Todd, lest he get any ideas of taking the shop for himself. I'd work up some tears for my beloved husband if I had to punch myself to make them. I scuttled out the back gate, grabbed my leather case from around the corner, and brought it back inside. I found myself a tolerably clean towel and laid it across the only good chair, then had myself a short nap as a reward for all my labours.

Does it shock you, how quickly I rid myself of the devil Lovett and set about taking over his shop and his home? It shouldn't. I have been cleaning messes all my life, and precious few of them my own. Lovett had been living in squalor for years, hoping he could lure some poor girl to come in and change his life. I changed it, all right, by ending it. True, I didn't yet know where my baby was, but I believed him when he said that Quince had taken him. Only a fool would head back to the brothel and start a row, making demands that wouldn't be met. A good way to end up in prison or the madhouse. I needed to keep my wits about me. I wonder what you would have done in my place.

Once I awoke, I bundled up Lovett's bedclothes and other belongings and tossed them down the rubbish pit. I chucked the piss pot in the yard and scraped all the filth off the pie pans. I washed the windows and floors, and every chair and table. It took hours but by the end I'd got rid of every trace of Mr. Lovett. I sent a boy round the corner to get a cart from the pawnshop, got myself two pounds ten shillings once the cart was filled. The profit would pay for a new mattress and kettle, tea, firewood, coal, candles, and lamp oil, plus two plain frocks and two striped aprons to wear when serving pies.

That night, I went through papers Lovett had stuffed into a drawer. There was a half crown in that coin purse of his, but nothing else that I could find. He'd died owing money to every shopkeeper from Cheapside to Covent Garden. If I used the name Lovett with any of them I'd never get any credit. I'd have to pay cash till I could square his debts away. I tried to remember what my mother showed me in our shop, and what Mrs. Dawson showed me of the doctor's accounts, but I couldn't make much sense of the numbers so I practiced signing my new name instead.

Mrs. Lovett. Mrs. Margery Lovett. Mrs. M. Lovett. Margery Lovett (Mrs.)

It looked good on paper, as though I'd had that name all my life. Next I wrote a list of ingredients for the pies. Flour, eggs, lard, onions, meat. That would cost a pretty penny. Maybe organ and tongue would do. Or maybe the cats' meat man was about, and I'd get some scraps for a bargain. I swore I'd bring the old customers back to Lovett's Pie Shop and more besides. I knew a few tricks from watching Dawson. I'd make the best pies from Temple Bar to St. Paul's Cathedral, maybe in all of London. I could never go back to Quince's, not with the doctor looking for me. I was safer there than anywhere, at least for the moment. And if that filthy pie man had told the truth for the first time in his life, then my little boy was alive. I would need to plot and plan for a way to get him back.

Just then, I heard him. The tenant above me, curious Mr. Todd. From one end of the room to the other, he walked, creak by creak across the old wooden floorboards. Slowly at first, and then faster and harder, until he was stomping like a soldier. Faint wisps of plaster dust sprinkled down onto me. I was just about to bang on the ceiling with the end of my broom when he stopped, just stopped, right above where I sat. And he stood there, still as a statue. As far as I could tell, that's where he stayed until I set my pen aside and went off to bed.

Speaking of, it's time to tuck this away for the night. I was looking for you earlier. I was at the window just before Compline, hoping to see you at the gate. There was a rabble of magpies in the linden tree outside the wall. I could barely count them all before they flew off.

One for sorrow,
Two for joy,
Three for a girl,
Four for a boy,
Five for silver,
Six for gold,
Seven for a secret that's never been told.

JULY 26

Jeremiah 15:15
O Lord, thou knowest: remember me, and visit me, and revenge me of my persecutors; take me not away in thy longsuffering: know that for thy sake I have suffered rebuke.

I am rarely alone for long. I can count the hours on a single hand. Mostly a moment here or there, barely long enough to bring out this book. Putting these words down is tiring work, as much as anything I ever did at the shop, but I couldn't stop now even if I wanted to. Tonight I nipped a candle from the altar and brought it to my room, and will stave off sleep so that I may add to my account. A Great Silence falls over the Priory every night from Compline till the morning's first prayer. I can scratch away in this little book with no one catching on.

I was telling you about fixing up the shop and getting everything straight. So I will continue with the next day when someone hammered at the door like a maniac, shouting for Lovett as if to wake the dead. The morning light was barely creeping into the sky. How many of these men would come calling before the day was out?

I rushed to the door to open it before its hinges broke. A rough red-faced bully pushed his way in nearly knocking me off my feet. He had a bloody butcher's apron on and carried an empty meat tray. His buggy eyes searched the room before he looked at me. "Where's Lovett?" He growled. "He owes me nine quid for pork and lard and I mean to get it."

"He ain't here," I told him. "I don't know where he is. He's legged it and left me alone. How'd he run up nine quid on pork and lard? Seems like you're more the fool than me."

The butcher swore a streak that would make a sailor blush. "Are you his missus?"

"Might be," I replied, leaning on the counter.

"You owe me nine quid then, and I won't leave till I collect it."

"You think I've got that kind of money laying about?" I asked, reaching for a rolling pin. "And do you think I'd give it to you if I did? Go beat on somebody else's door."

Another spray of curses erupted from the butcher's mouth. He said he'd ruin me and the pie shop. "You can't make pies without meat, and I'll tell every butcher in London that the Lovetts don't pay their bills."

"I'll make 'em with fish if I have to. You've never had a fish pie like mine in your mouth," I laughed, "and I reckon you never will." I gripped the rolling pin in my hand thinking about bashing him in the head when I heard a low chuckle from behind me. Made the little hairs prickle on the back of my neck. I spun around with my heart pounding. Who had snuck into the shop without me knowing? At first I saw no one, and wondered if Lovett's ghost had crept up through the floorboards, come back to torment me.

"Who is this raving fool," said the bodiless voice, "and what will it take to shut him up?"

"Lovett?" the butcher shouted. "Come out here and face me like a man."

Out of the shadows, back near the larder, a giant of a man stepped forward with a jaw like a box and hands as big as spades. "I'm not Lovett," the giant said. "And you don't have the cods to face a man like me."

It could only have been the barber from upstairs, who somehow had a passage into the shop's back rooms. He smelled of shaving soap and sweat, and his black hair was so thick and tall he could have hidden his razors in it. Dressed like a gentleman in fine trousers and a waistcoat, he had an apron tied around his waist that hung down past his knees. As he came closer, I saw a smear of dried blood upon it. He'd nicked someone I suppose.

"Mr. Todd, sir," the butcher stammered as the giant drew near. "Begging your pardon. I have no quarrel with you." Todd was eerie calm, and the butcher had gone meek as a lamb. A more sudden change come over a man, I had never seen.

"I'd rather you had no quarrel at all, so I could do my work in peace." Mr. Todd reached into his waistcoat and pulled out a fat bag of coins. "Nine quid, was it? Is that what you were squabbling about?"

The butcher nodded, his knuckles going white as he clutched his meat tray. There was something about that barber. You got the feeling of it right away.

Mr. Todd pulled open the neck of his bag and counted out ten shiny sovereigns right there on the counter. "This clears the debt, and pays for her next order. Give the woman what she needs."

I don't know who was more shocked, me or the butcher. I wondered how many shaves it took to make ten quid. I reckoned Mr. Todd was a dab hand with a blade.

Mr. Todd told the butcher to take the money and clear out. "I trust you won't ruin the good name of Lovett now your bill's been paid."

The butcher nodded quickly, muttered his thanks, swept the money into his palm and rushed out.

Mr. Todd cast a dark eye around the pie shop and landed it on me. "We've not met," he said tartly.

"I'm Mrs. Lovett," I said. "Mrs. Margery Lovett." I put my chin in the air to look confident and told him the pie man and I had married not six weeks before, that he'd taken my coins and jewels and bolted on me. Who knew if he was ever coming back?

Mr. Todd cocked a woolly eyebrow. "I've never seen you here. And Lovett never mentioned a wife."

"I'm not surprised," I replied. "He was a bloody scoundrel. He got what was coming to him. The way he treated me was shameful." The admission of my crime had slipped out before I could stop it.

"Did he now?" Mr. Todd laughed. The sound of it gave me a start, it was so deep and wicked, it rumbled through me like thunder. "I never thought much of him and it's no affair of mine what happened with the two of you. Everyone has their secrets. Especially those that are married. I would never tell yours, and I expect you'll never tell mine. We'll know all about each other in due time."

"I won't let a strange man pay my debts," I said. "I don't

want to be owing nothing to nobody." Something about him made my stomach tight and hard as a fist.

"Few are the men I met that were stranger than your husband," he laughed. "Besides, we're old friends now, aren't we. We've got to look out for one another. Custom for the pie shop means custom for me. You feed 'em and send them up to me. I'll shave 'em and send them down to you."

I looked down at that smear of blood on his apron, then right back up to his face. It all sounded reasonable enough, but I could already tell that Mr. Todd was a sly one. I didn't trust him then, nor any day that came after. All men were villains, leastways all the men in London. Damn the lot of them.

"Mind my asking," I said, "what arrangement you had with my husband? How much rent are you in for?"

"Half crown every fortnight, paid just three days ago. It's a half crown too much, seeing as my rooms have got cracks in the walls and holes in the floor and rats as big as your arm. Your husband spent all his money on cheap gin and harlots, nothing where it was needed. I hope you'll run things differently.

"I've got no taste for gin or harlots, if that's what you be wondering." He laughed loud enough to make the mice bolt out from under the cupboards. I looked him over once more and thought that maybe we could help each other, Mr. Todd and me, maybe even be friends in time. It's foolish, I know, but I did wonder sometimes if the world put people in your path to set you on your way. Mind you, he knew I'd done away with Mr. Lovett, or at least he had his suspicions. That put me under his thumb, and that was my mistake. I'd swing for it if the slops found out. But half a crown a fortnight would come in handy, and a big brute of a man like him would keep my troubles away.

"When are you opening the shop again?" he asked.

I narrowed my eyes as I looked at him. "Soon as I've got meat."

JULY 28

John 6:35
And Jesus said unto them, I am the bread of life: he that cometh to me shall never hunger; and he that believeth on me shall never thirst.

It's the Great Silence once again. My candle's burned to the quick, but I dare not pilfer another. I think it will snuff itself out very soon, plunging me into a deep darkness even with my little window. I will have to write quickly.

Early the next morning, I made a visit to the butcher Mr. Todd paid off. He seemed more the devil than he was before he was paid, but he served me all the same. We struck off the quid I had as credit, and he wrapped me up a side of pork, though it was starting to go off, and a pound of lard, plus a bag of potatoes, a quartern of flour, onions, and salt and pepper for seasoning. I'd made enough pies with Mrs. Dawson I didn't need a recipe. It was all in my head. She'd had the best ingredients in her kitchen and her pies came out crisp and golden. But I'd have to make do with what I'd got. I offered up a shilling for a boy to help carry, and the butcher brought out his oldest son, a strapping young lad who reminded me a bit of Ned. He was quiet but agreeable and made the walk home easier.

Once I was back inside, I set out my knives and carved up the half-pig as best I could remember. All I'd learned came back into my hands quicker than I could believe. Father taught me how to do it with no waste. It's an art, he used to say. How you use the knife, how you get the best cuts and leave nothing behind. Bits of the meat were green and greasy so I shaved them off, then sliced the flank and pulled the kidney out. I cut between the ribs and broke the shoulder with a crack, stripped off the belly and sawed along the spine. The bone was hard, but I was strong. I chopped off the trotters and chunks of fat, then flayed the carcass from snout to tail. The Dutch artists painted butchers in their shops with pigs and cows hanging about them like curtains. Shame no one ever painted me.

The skull and bones I set aside for boiling, and the flesh went through the meat grinder, which I'd cleaned until it shone. It was a beast of a thing, easily mashing up whatever I put in the funnel. Turning the crank was nothing to me. Sawing through bone was harder.

The first pies that came out were coarse and pale. The oven I'd need getting used to. The pork was tough, not like at the doctor's house. I hadn't learned my lessons well enough. Even though they weren't perfect, I baked up two dozen pies and put a sign in my window. Fresh meat pies, a penny apiece.

It was late in the day but a few sailors wandered in, and a labourer or two. They handed over their pennies and took a few greedy bites. "Not the worst," one of them said. "A bit gummy," said the other. "Good thing they're cheap."

Two days of that and my pie shop went quiet as a church. My second and third batches were better but still not the best. Dawson would have flung them at me if she'd seen them. With more meat and more flour, I'd be able to fidget with the oven, try a few things, but I was afraid to ruin what little stuffs I had. By the end of the week I'd made eight shillings, eaten three of my own pies and tossed the rest to the dogs. I ventured up the block to the baker's at the other end, Fiddler's Pies. His were a mix of pork and veal, golden brown and shiny on top, two pennies each and a line around the corner. Fiddler saw me, knew me, gave a smug little wave, then sent a boy out with a pie for me free of charge. "Me dad wants to know what happened to your man Lovett," the boy said.

"He fell down a well and broke his neck," I said back. A little too close to the truth but I didn't care. My tone gave the boy a bit of a fright and he ran back to tell his dad. Good. I bit into the pie and felt the creamy juice running down my chin. It was a good pie, no mistake. A bit of rosemary in there, a bit of thyme, some onion, some chopped potato. Mine would have to be better if I was to make a go of it. And I would need to make a go of it, I would need the shop and the money if I was to get my baby back from Quince. How much would a baby sell for, and who would want to buy it? I kept hearing Lovett whisper in my ear, "Your baby is alive, your baby is alive." I had thought of going back to Mayfair to see if I could find Fanny or Aphra, but it had only been a few weeks since I'd left and I'd be putting myself into danger. I could go to Mrs. Price, she'd know something, but she'd turn me in to Quince real quick, they were thick as thieves.

It was on the Sunday evening, while I was scrubbing down the grates and bucketing the ashes, I heard a bang and thump in my back room. The floorboards jumped under my feet. I thought the ceiling had come in. When I rushed through, I saw a man gasping and bucking about on the floor, blood gushing from his gullet where he'd been slashed from ear to ear. A pool of blood spread fast across the boards. He was wearing a merchant sailor's jacket and a white shirt and waistcoat, now soaked red and stinking like pluck. He stared at the ceiling twisting and shuddering with his mouth gaping, his tongue lolling, his neck flapping like a wattle. He reached out and grabbed my ankle. I let out a little shriek and shook him off just as quick. Soon enough, he was still. I looked up at the trapdoor in the ceiling with the rope hanging off, swaying, its end tied like a little noose. Somewhere up there was the barber's chair. So that's what it's for, I thought.

Mr. Todd slipped into the shop and found me with the sailor. "What's all this?" I cried. "What have you done?" He gazed past me at the dead man, cool as an eel on ice. Without a word, he stepped past me, leaned over the body, and plucked a string of pearls from the fellow's coat as if from a box of jewels. He held the string up so the pearls glowed in the light. Fancy, they were, like none I'd ever seen, even at the Symposia.

"I do believe they're real," he said, and slipped them into his pocket. "Better than I would have guessed."

I could scarce think what to say. What had I gotten myself into? And had Lovett known the truth about Todd? I stood up on wobbly legs and blurted out in a fury, "What are you about, killing a man and dropping him into my shop? Just look at my clean floor!"

"Get his feet," Mr. Todd grunted. "And you aren't in a position to say nothing to me about killing a man." He dragged the sailor towards the back door. "We'll tip him down the pit in the yard after dark, unless you can think of something better to do with him."

Something better, I said to myself. Then, shocked at my own wickedness, I pushed the thought away. Maybe not far enough. It sat there in the darkness taunting me. Something better.

Even with that I was still in a rage. "Down the pit and then what? We'll hang for murder if anyone finds him. His head bashed in and his throat cut like some kind of animal."

"Your Lovett didn't have any problems with it," he answered. "He brought me plenty of necks. There's lots down that pit that's never been found. None's ever cared to find them, neither."

Now I knew the whole story, or so I thought. And if I was to keep the shop and stay alive, I would have to play along. I looked back down at the poor sod on the floor. He was a fine one, a few years older than me. He'd probably never done nothing to nobody in his whole little life. And surely there was someone who'd cared for him, or else why did he have those pearls?

"We can't leave him like this," I said. "Anyone can tell who he is. We'll have to get rid of his clothes. We'll have to chop him up." I glimpsed the grinder on the counter, and I felt the devil's hot breath whisper in my ear:

Meat is meat.

A whole fresh carcass on the floor of my shop for free. And who would care what kind of meat it was, long as it wasn't cat? It would be easy enough to take the flesh and grind it through, the arms and shoulders, the legs and thighs, the face. The bits people might recognise. Then the cuts I could never afford to buy, the chops, loin, ribs and belly. I poked the sailor and pulled off his waistcoat, then his shirt, just to see. He had a tattoo on his shoulder, big as your hand, an anchor with a letter J on it. That would have to go. Any kind of moles or marks that would make him known to his people.

"What are you doing?" Mr. Todd asked.

"Solving both our problems." I knelt down, stripped the lad naked and bundled his clothes in the corner. I lashed a rope around his ankles, and pointed at the hooks hanging along the far wall. "Hoist him up and let's get to work." Todd made an ugly face, but he did not object. He picked up the body and turned it around, then hung the lad upside down on the hook. His arms swung back and forth as he swayed. The last of the blood spilled out of him onto the floor, thick now, nearly black. When it had slowed to a trickle, I scattered sawdust over it and swept it aside, then set a bucket by my feet and lined it with a clean white rag. It wouldn't be white for long.

I started slicing through the skin and peeling it away, exposing the flesh underneath. No organ meats, no cutting into the cavity. The innards of a man weren't like those of a pig or a calf. I wanted to make quick, neat work of it. I cleaned the meat off the arms and legs, the shoulders, ribs, and buttocks, and I scraped the face off, down to the bone. Into the bucket it all went. It was messy, filthy work, but it went quickly enough. It was fairly easy, to my surprise. It might have been different if I'd known the boy. That might have held me back.

When I was done, I motioned for Todd to pull the body down and lay it on the worktable. A few sharp chops of the cleaver and the corpse was in pieces. Those went into an empty potato sack along with the bloody sawdust. I'd burn the clothes in the oven once I was done, save for the brass which could go to the pawnshop. They were never too picky about where things came from, or where they went.

"There," I said. "No one will know who he was. The rats and worms will get into him fast enough."

"And what will you do with all this?" Todd waved his hand at the meat I had scraped and saved. We had ten, maybe twelve good pounds, fresh as you could hope for.

"I'll salt half and set it aside, then grind the rest with what's left of the pork, bake up a few pies and run them over to the men in the morning line at Fiddler's. If they go over well, I'll make up the rest and sell them off, then start on some more for Tuesday. They'll be two pennies each, maybe even three."

Todd looked at me, his eyes wide with a kind of awe. "Mrs. Lovett, I have met many a woman in my life, but none the likes of you. Your husband met his match, no doubt about it."

He reached out his blood-soaked hand and, after a moment's thought, I shook it. Partners.

He dragged the sack out the door and dropped it into the pit while I mopped the last of the blood and readied a stew pot on the stove. Potatoes, onion, herbs, the last ones in the shop. I'd need to make the most of them. Cube the potatoes, chop the onions, fry them up in some pork fat, get them brown and tasty, set them aside, mix up the pastry, then grind the meat and brown it. I would be up for hours but I didn't care. Once Fiddler got a whiff of my pies, the look on his face would be worth it.

JULY 30

Hebrews 9:22
The law requires that nearly everything be cleansed with blood, and without the shedding of blood there is no forgiveness.

I wonder if little sins add up into big ones, like farthings into pence into shillings into sovereigns, or if each is separate from the other. I've a little Bible in my cell, old as the hills. Pages so thin you can almost see through them, the ink worn away by countless God-fearing thumbs. I took it from the Reverend Mother's room when she was in hospital, someone left the door unlocked. I've been making good use of it. Studying it, thinking on it. Sister Catherine thinks I pray with it, that it purifies the heart. My heart could use it, I suppose. She's a kind soul, and I'll let her think what she likes. But for now, I'll keep on with my tale.

That night I stayed up until the pink morning light touched the sky, grinding meat and making pies. I tried hard to remember what I'd learned from my mother and from Mrs. Dawson, and what I remembered from tasting that pie of Fiddler's. I mixed the flour with lard and water then rolled it all out, thin but not so thin as they'd crack and crumble. I pushed each circle of dough into the tins I'd scrubbed clean. I mixed the meat with the potato and onion, and spooned it into the crusts, then brushed them with egg wash. Pig skin and bones boiled over the fire made a nice, thick gravy. By the time the lamplighter whistled past my door to put out the lanterns, I had two dozen pies baked and two dozen more ready to go. I was tempted to try one myself, but the thought of that poor boy in the pit set me off that idea quick enough. Besides, they were for the customers.

Round about eight o'clock, I put six of the still-warm pies into a cloth-lined basket, locked up the shop and wandered down to Fiddler's. The men were just starting to gather. Barristers, clerks, labourers, dockworkers, sweepers and toshers, men who would never stand next to each other otherwise. They all had their pennies out waiting to pay for their pies. I sauntered past Fiddler's front door, made sure he got a good glimpse of me, then went halfway down the line to flash my wares at a trio of law clerks done up for the courts.

"No need to wait in this long line," I said. "How about one of my pies? Just as good as Fiddler's, maybe even better, and priced just the same." I fanned the cloth so the smell of the meat wafted up into their faces. All three looked at each other, then at the pies, then they eagerly handed me their pennies. By now the fellows standing in front and behind were watching and listening, curious to see what was happening.

The first clerk bit into his pie and a smile burst across his face. "It's really good!" he cried, his mouth half-full of meat and potato. "Better than Fiddler's so they are!" The second and third bit into their pies and agreed that they were a good bit tastier than what they were used to. I sold two more to a pair of tradesmen working on a row of houses round the corner, then kept back one last pie for someone special. Sure enough, I turned around and saw Fiddler's boy come running up to me, and Fiddler himself standing outside his door with his fists on his hips, watching the two of us, a surly look on his face.

"My da says you got to go or he'll call the slops on you. He says you got your own shop and you should keep your muff where it belongs, behind the counter."

"What a charming man your father is," I replied. "Tell you what: here's a nice hot pie for you to share with him. It's my last one! You take a nice big bite and tell me what you think." I handed the boy the most beautifully golden and perfect pie, the best pie truly, and he grabbed it as greedy as any pig that ever swung from a butcher's hook. He bit into it, took a mouthful so big his cheeks were stuffed with it. His face lit up as he chewed. He could scarcely speak.

"That's better than any we got in our shop!" he shouted after swallowing, then spun round, and ran back to his father. I turned to the rest of the men in the line and gave them a little nod and a wink.

"I have a few more back at my establishment, you can come with me if you like. Otherwise, I'll have another batch ready round this time tomorrow." A group of barristers and labourers peeled themselves away from the line and followed me up the street with Fiddler looking on in a fury. I couldn't help myself; I gave him a cheeky little wave. His boy stood in front of him, holding my half-eaten pie up to his mouth. Fiddler smacked it out of the lad's hand and it splattered across his front window.

Over the next twenty minutes, more and more men from Fiddler's came to my shop to buy my pies. I finished the morning with six shillings and nine pence, on account of one of the young ones only had a penny to his name. Even so, it was enough to buy more pork from the bully butcher and other goods besides, but still not enough to make a morning batch without dipping into the special stuff provided by Mr. Todd. I still had the salted sailor's meat I had held back. But I would need more, and soon.

As I put my coins away and began to stack the tins for washing, I spotted someone out of the corner of my eye, standing across the street. It was Fiddler. He was none too happy, and he made a point of showing it. I let a smile stretch across my lips, stepped up to the front door, and turned the lock over with a snap. Just then, something caught his eye above me, a face in the upstairs window perhaps, and he scuttled off back up the street.

I turned on my heel, picked up my pans, and got to cleaning. Mrs. Lovett's pies would be famous all over London. And I would see my son again. I would make sure of it.

JULY 31

Ezekiel 24:10
Heap on wood, kindle the fire, consume the flesh, and spice it well, and let the bones be burned.

Sundays are good days for writing, as the Sisters are kept busy with their devotions. My mother used to tell me stories on Sundays, a special treat to send me off to sleep. Sundays are for prayers, and stories, and secrets. And here I am telling you all my stories, all my secrets, things not even Sister Catherine knows.

Whatever anyone else has said to you, I did no harm to Mother Mary Angelica. I have heard the lies being told and I fear that they have made their way to you. When I write to you here, it is as if you are in the room with me peering over my shoulder, you and the Lord and no one else. Not even Sister Catherine, whose love of God blinds her to how ugly life can be. These are my truest words, here in this book. When I go to sleep at night I tuck it under the mattress. And none but you and I shall read it.

So many have thought me weak because I am a woman. My father. The doctor. Mrs. Dawson. Ned. Madame Quince. And now Fiddler. Here I was, a young widow alone. Easy to crush under his heel. I saw it in his face. Well, I wouldn't have it. The dark thoughts I had lit a fire under me, and in that fire I could see the whole world burn.

All was quiet and dark at Mr. Todd's through the evening. So I mixed up the next day's pastry, my mind filled with plots and plans of putting Fiddler in his place. I left the bowl in the back to chill while I stole a few winks of sleep. I roused myself when the clock struck four. Yawning, I went back into the kitchen and got on with my work. Six dozen pies this time, with a few handfuls of chopped carrots and peas added, the egg for the wash mixed with a spoonful of butter and a sprinkle of salt tossed over them for good measure. Into the oven they went, then onto racks I'd set out on the counter, the better for passersby to catch a glimpse. How surprised was I to see one of the barristers from the morning before, a tall round fellow with wisps of hair combed over his shiny head, standing outside patiently, though I wasn't to open for nearly an hour. I unlocked the door and peeped out at him.

"You're very early," I said. "I won't be ready for ages yet. Come back around seven. I can put one aside for you, you needn't worry they'll all be gone."

"Oh, I'll be hard at work before seven, and won't be able to come back till noon. Could I slip inside and wait till you're ready to part with one?"

He seemed an amiable enough gentleman, and the air was sharp with frost, so I took pity on him and let him sit on a stool while I finished laying out the pies and setting aside the pans for washing up. I tore off a square of brown paper and folded it round the nicest and sturdiest of the pies, then handed it to him. He dug round the inside of his pocket and pulled out three pence, insisting I take it all.

"It's a fine pie and worth five pence if you ask me. I'll come and get one daily if I can. I'm set to become your most loyal customer." He extended his hand to me, plump and lightly lined, not rough and raw like mine. I shook it all the same. "Jennings is my name, Theodore Jennings, Esquire."

"A pleasure, Mr. Jennings. I'm Margery Lovett. The Widow Lovett, or so it seems, left here to fend for myself. I appreciate the company." Just then I heard footfalls above that told me Mr. Todd was awake. Who knew what mood he'd be in today.

"What's he like, your man upstairs? The barber? I've seen him about on the street, a handsome chap, but very broody." It's funny the little things a woman picks up on. Just in that moment I saw that Jennings was much like the molly men who mooned after Fab back at the Symposia, though perhaps he was shyer about his interests than they had been.

"Broody is a good word," I said. "Mr. Todd is a quiet man, and a good tenant. He pays what he owes and keeps to himself. He does have a temper though, and I wouldn't want to be on the wrong side of it."

"He does have a bit of a reputation," Jennings said quietly, looking up at the ceiling as he spoke, imagining Todd listening from above I expect. "They say he was a sailor, a convict, a violent man with a violent past."

"Oh, I don't know about any of that," I replied. "And he's not caused me any harm. I expect those are stories told by folk who envy his success. He has done quite well for himself, has our Mr. Todd." I glanced past Mr. Jennings out the front window and saw that a crowd of men had gathered, some I recalled from the day before, others who were new to me. I checked the clock and saw that I still had fifteen minutes before opening.

Word had gotten round it seemed. Good pies for good prices at Mrs. Lovett's, one taste and you'll see. "I should finish getting ready for the morning rush," I told him. "This crowd doesn't look too patient. You pop round whenever you like. I'll be sure to set aside something special for you."

"Very much obliged, Mrs. Lovett," he replied as I let him out into the throng. "Just ten more minutes," I shouted to the other men, who scowled and muttered their displeasure. Then I locked the door again.

"Who was that?" Todd asked sharply. He was practically at my neck. How he appeared so quickly and silently I'll never know, but it was one of his many unnatural talents. There were times I wondered if I had fallen in with a demon.

"That was one of my new customers, a barrister," I replied. "He was in the line at Fiddler's yesterday, and he's shown up here today. He's not the only one." I gestured out the window at the crowd that was growing bigger and more restless.

"See anyone you'd like to send up for a shave?" he asked slyly, leaning towards the window as he sized up the men in line. My nose wrinkled when I got a cloud of his hot foul breath in my face. "I have this little itch that only my razor can scratch," he said.

"None that wouldn't be missed," I replied. "Now, you head back upstairs while I let them in. I don't want you scaring them off. If I see someone who needs an extra bit of grooming, I'll be sure he pays you a visit." That was the first time I felt a bit of fear around Mr. Todd. When I felt that every neck was the same to him, including mine. I realised then that I was to be the Judas Goat, leading the sheep to slaughter to save myself. And

I'd best choose our victims wisely so as not to raise suspicion.

Mr. Todd threw me a nasty look, then stormed out the back stairs and up to his shop. He had wanted to leer at and pick out his prey, and I had spoiled his fun. Too bad, his glowering was bad for business and would give the customers sour stomachs. I hurried to the door, flipped the sign from Closed to Open, undid the lock, and let the first few men into the shop. I told the others to keep an orderly line, there were pies enough for everyone, and to scrape their boots at the door. I didn't need any street muck tracked onto my floors. I took my chance to peer down the block, and saw that Fiddler's line was half as long as mine. Good.

The men and boys filed in and out of the shop, one by one and sometimes two and three at a time, picking their pies from the rack and pushing their pennies across the counter. It was then it dawned on me that they were mostly unmarried and living alone or in rooming houses. They didn't have wives to cook for them, no mothers or sisters to care for them. Some were travelling workers, some had come in from the country to make the city their home, some were Londoners born and raised but for whatever reason they were alone.

Men like Jennings had done well enough and likely had a maid for cleaning. The builders and labourers and dockers had no one except maybe the widows that ran their kip-houses and tossed them a bun for breakfast. It was a sad life when you came in with nothing, left with nothing, and had no one to leave it to. If a pie and a pint could give a man a bit of pleasure, that might be enough to make him want to keep living. And yet here I was, the Grim Reaper herself, looking each one of them over as they came in, with an eye to sending one to the pit. I had the power of life and death, and yet no power at all. I was a monster as much as Mr. Todd, with no choice but to be one.

Finally, after an hour, the line had shrunk to just four men and three pies. Three were builders, brothers they seemed, all jolly and happy and eager to eat. The fourth was a lad from the day before, a dockworker from Genoa I'd heard his mates say. He was the one who'd only had a penny yesterday, and today only had one more. He barely knew a word of English, but his sorrowful eyes told stories of their own. I gave the three builders their pies and sent them on their way. The lad pushed his penny at me. I had some scraps and leavings from the oven, some burnt bits scraped into a heap in the tin, but truly I would not have fed them to a mouse.

"Mrs. Lovett!" shouted a rough voice from behind me. "I've not given a single shave this morning, my razor is crying for company."

My heart sank like a stone in my chest. I pushed the penny back at the boy, and whispered: "Go. Go." But he didn't understand. He pushed the penny at me again, and then Mr. Todd was upon us.

"What's this?" he asked. "A young man with a penny, and a face and neck as rough as a bramble. Are you all out of pies, Mrs. Lovett? Does the young man not speak?"

"He's a docker from Genoa, in Italy," I answered. I could not keep the sadness out of my voice. "He was in the line at Fiddler's yesterday with the other dockers, but he's all alone today."

"I know all about Genoa. I hear they make a good sausage."

Mr. Todd laughed. "We could use some Genoa sausage round here. Come upstairs to my chair, young lad. I'll give you the closest shave of your life! Then Mrs. Lovett here will fix up a meal fit for the Pope himself. Isn't that right, Mrs. Lovett?" It wasn't a question, but I gave it an answer.

"Yes, Mr. Todd. A meal fit for the Pope himself."

Todd led the unsuspecting lad around the side of the counter, out the back, and up the stairs. I went to the door, flipped the sign from Open to Closed, clicked the lock shut, and waited at the back of my shop. I didn't have to wait long.

Matteo. His name was Matteo.

Are these the stories you wanted to hear, Miss Gibson? Do they thrill you, excite you, make you giggle and shiver? I do hope I haven't ruined your appetite. At Mrs. Lovett's, every pie has a tale to tell.

AUGUST 3

Job 3:20
For my sighing cometh before I eat, And my roarings are poured out like the waters. For the thing which I greatly feared is come upon me, And that which I was afraid of is come unto me. I was not in safety, neither had I rest, neither was I quiet; Yet trouble came.

It's nights like tonight, when the moon is hidden and the whole of the Priory feels like it's holding its breath, that's when it all comes back to me in a flood, filling my mind with horrors till I lose all hope of sleep. I remember back to what Mrs. Dawson said about unpleasant thoughts. I'm not one to credit her with much but she was right in this: the devil warms himself in the fires of idle minds and aching hearts.

Something changed in Mr. Todd after Matteo was killed. I thought it would calm his urges, but instead they seemed to grow. He was a murderous fiend and worse every day, and there weren't nothing I could do to stop him. I could hear him above me stomping and raging, and I dreaded the moment when he would appear in my back rooms demanding more men, more necks, more blood.

But what could I do? I dared not refuse. If I'd gone to the coppers, I'd be as good as dead myself. It was my own neck I was saving, I will not deny that, but I might as well have gone to the gallows for all the good it did me. It was a horrible task choosing men to visit the barber chair and then stripping and butchering their bodies, sometimes still half-alive, removing and grinding the meat, ever mindful that we not be caught. At first I tried to send up thugs and brutes, ones that would not be a great loss to the world, but Mr. Todd's tastes were more refined. He liked them younger, softer, more sensitive, less likely to fight. It made my skin crawl, and still does to this day. He made a show of being my friend and telling me he'd protect me, but his eyes grew wilder, his needs came quicker and more difficult to satisfy. Every corpse that ended up in my larder, hung from the hook and bled and stripped, I always thought that I'd be next, that he'd leave me on the shop floor gasping and gurgling. He'd nick all my money what I was saving to claim my boy, grab his things and hop a carriage to some seaside town, never to be heard of again.

I slept less and less, and worked more and more. Trapped, I was, in a tangle of dreadful dreams, ghastly horrors where the dead crawled out of the rotten pit and dragged me from my bed. They'd chop me up alive and grind up my guts while I watched and screamed, then they'd roast me in the oven.

But there were other visions, even more terrible, where my baby cried and called out for me all alone in the dark, and I'd be unable to find him and reach him and hold him and save him. Rotted rat-eaten corpses would rise from the shadowy tunnels under the city and my child's screams of terror would climb higher with the smell of death all around him.

It was in one of those horrible dreams in the small dark hours, not more than a fortnight after I opened the pie shop, that a sound from the back room woke me. I was sure it was Mr. Todd come to collect me at last. I froze in my narrow bed in terror as I watched a shadow creep across the floor. Finally, a figure appeared in the doorway, so close my body trembled. I could tell from the shape of the man, shorter and stouter, that it was not Mr. Todd. No. It was Fiddler in a drunken fury, unsteady on his feet, stinking of gin, holding a poleaxe used to stun a pig or a calf before the beast is bled.

"I know what you're up to, you filthy bitch," he whispered. "You and your barber friend. I been watching you lure away my business, pushing your dirty pies on my best customers, taking them for your own." He leaned in closer. I could feel his hot breath upon me. "What's in those pies? Where do you get your meat from? Your husband spent this shop into the ground. How do you have any money?" His face squeezed up like a baby's as tears started streaming from his eyes. "Someone sent you here, someone who wants to ruin me. Where's your husband at? Is he behind all this? Your barber friend is skint, he can't make much shaving faces. You two ain't in this alone."

I let him babble. I didn't move, I didn't breathe. I kept my eyes on the poleaxe, dreading the moment he would swing it back and strike me in the skull, its spike slicing into my brain. Those animals didn't always die right away—sometimes you struck them two or three times before they fell to the floor twitching and squealing. Is that what would happen to me?

Fiddler leaned in even closer. I realised he was afraid, perhaps more than I was. "It's them Freemasons, innit?" he whispered, as if they were in the room with us. "I wouldn't play along with them, right? And now I'm paying the price. Is that it? Tell me. You got to tell me!"

I was so shocked, I spoke before I could think. "Freemasons?" I shouted. "What in God's name are you on about?" Truly, it was the last thing I expected to hear out of his mouth. It was like a cold knife in my chest.

"Don't you lie to me!" he shouted. He raised the poleaxe above his head. He had murder in his eye. Just then, another shadow slipped across the floor. Two hands reached in from beyond the door frame, holding one of the empty flour sacks. They pulled it down hard over Fiddler's head and wrenched tight around his neck. Fiddler dropped the poleaxe and grabbed at the sack, trying to pull it loose from his throat, but he couldn't. He was too drunk, or else his hands were too sweaty, or he just wasn't strong enough. He fell to his knees and then onto the floor. The hands kept pulling tighter and tighter until I could hear a crack, and then they suddenly let go. They yanked the sack off Fiddler's head. His face was blue and his neck was bruised. His eyes bulged, his tongue stuck out. Mr. Todd poked his face into the room, looked down at the body, then at me. "Was this man bothering you?" he asked. Then he laughed his dark, devilish laugh that shivered me more than the sight of Fiddler's pig hammer.

"What have you done?" I cried. "What in God's name have you done?"

"I've saved your life, that's what I've done, you ungrateful cow," he growled. "Should I have let him crush your head like a cabbage?"

"I'm not ungrateful!" I rushed to say. "He was fit to kill me, sure enough, and I couldn't make a sound. But what are we going to do with him now? He has a wife, he has a child! They might know he came to my shop. We can't make him into pies or throw him in the pit."

"Shut up, woman. Let me think." He stared down at Fiddler's body, at Fiddler's face, then smiled. "I know what to do, but we have to be quick. I'll toss that axe into the pit. Find me a long piece of rope, like you use to string up a pig, and two or three more of those sacks if you have 'em. We're going to wrap his head in the sacks, haul him down to the tunnels and then up behind St. Dunstan's. You're going to come back here and bake your pies. Leave the rest to me."

I had no choice. I did what he said. He tossed away the poleaxe, then wrapped the sacks around Fiddler's head. He tied the rope tight around the pie man's arms and waist, and together we dragged him to the stairs and pulled him down to the tunnels, down through the dung, dead dogs and offal. Rats squealed all around us. I held a lamp out to frighten them off while creeping along the dirty dripping walls, feeling our way along until at last we were under the back of St. Dunstan's. It couldn't have taken ten minutes, but it felt like an hour. I could see a ladder set in the stone along the north wall that led up to a grate above our heads. A few wisps of fog floated down through the gaps, glowing by the light of the moon.

Mr. Todd wrapped the end of the rope around his shoulder and climbed to the top of the ladder. He shoved the grate aside and hopped up out of sight. After a minute, he began to pull the rope, hauling Fiddler up and up, inch by inch, as the fog drifted down towards me. A few feet from the top, Fiddler got stuck, hung up on the rungs, and I had to climb up under his arse and push him with my shoulder until he swung free again.

Once the body was all the way up through the hole, Mr. Todd leaned over and said, "I hope you weren't too fond of that rope. You won't be getting it back."

"What are you going to do?" I asked,

"The less you know, the better," he answered, then pushed the grate back into place. "Go home," he said as he stood, and then stepped away into darkness. So home I went, careful to follow the path we'd walked to get there. I came back up the steps into the shop and saw out the window how thick the fog was. Whatever Mr. Todd's plan was behind St. Dunstan's, no one would see him. I pulled out the dough I'd chilled, slid the pans off the shelf, and started greasing them. The men would be lining up soon enough. I couldn't help but smile knowing there would be no line at Fiddler's.

Near an hour later, as I was setting the first racks of pies into the oven, Mr. Todd threw open the door leading up from the steps, giving me such a scare he nearly put me in my grave. "It's done," he said. "The blues will come round, I'm sure of it, but don't you say nothing. Not to them, not to the wife or the boy. We've had a quiet night here with no complaints. If there's talking to be done, leave it to me. Understood?" I nodded. "Good. I'll be down when I'm needed." He went to the back and pulled the door open. Splinters and chips of wood were all over the floor beneath it. "You'll need a new lock for this. Bastard prised it right off." He slammed the door behind him and trudged up the steps to his parlour.

I started working on the next trays, wondering what Mr.

Todd was keeping from me. What had he done with Fiddler? What would be bringing the slops to my door? I greased more pans, then pulled out the first two and set them to cool. I was glad to have busywork, or I would have gone sick with worry.

As I got ready to let in the day's first customers, I heard whistles then screams from across the way. The fog had thinned to a faint yellow mist with the rotten taste of the Thames in it. A great racket soon began, with onlookers craning their heads and murmuring. The men in line at the door stepped aside for two stern-looking coppers and a sobbing woman in blue who I took to be Mrs. Fiddler. The boy was there too, clutching his mother's skirts. His face was pale and slack like he'd just seen a ghost, and not just one, but ghost upon ghost no matter where he looked. The slops banged on the door sharply, loud enough that Mr. Todd would surely have heard it. I dusted my hands on my apron, unlocked the door, and opened it a crack. "We're closed," I said. "Back of the line." As I went to slam it in their faces, the first one put his hand against it and pushed his way in. Rude.

"Where's Lovett?" The tall one with the round face asked. "And who are you?"

"He's gone and I'm his wife. What's it to you?" I demanded. "And who's this weepy wailer?"

"This is Mrs. Fiddler from the bakery up the street."

"Ah, right. Fiddler's wife. He's gone and chucked you out, has he? Well, it's for the best, I tell you. The man's a pig in pants what can't keep his hands to himself. He'd stick it in any old thing that had a hole or two. You're best off without him." With this, his missus cried even louder. "I'm sorry, love. It's desperate times, but you can't stay here, all my rooms are full. There's a doss-house up the street might take you, but you'd have to earn your keep I reckon."

"You slut!" she screamed. "You beast!" She lunged at me to grab my hair. It took the boy and the shorter of the two officers to hold her back. "What did you do to my husband?"

"Me? He was all over my tits, out in public as all these gents saw, when I was just walking along the street showing off my pretty pie basket!" I glared at the men on the stoop, daring any of them to argue with me. Then I turned my black look on her. "You need to keep that man of yours on the end of a rope, don't mind me saying."

With this she went quite mad, pushing down the smaller bobby, and lunged at me again. "Mum, Mum!" the boy shouted, poor thing. Three of the men in line pulled her back and held her outside the door. By then a great crowd had gathered, all wanting to see what the racket was, and me just wanting to get on with my morning.

The tall one spoke gravely. "Mrs. Lovett, or whoever you are. Mr. Fiddler is dead."

"Oh, well, why didn't you say so!" I took three of the best pies from the rack and tied them into a linen cloth. "She'll be wanting a party then, and who can blame her? Good riddance to bad rubbish. Have a few pies on the house." I handed them to the short bobby. "She can come back and give us an order, just let me know the number of guests. I'll bake up something nice and special."

"What's all this then!" a voice thundered from behind me. Mr. Todd had made his entrance. "Can't a man get any sleep around here?"

"Who might you be, then?" asked the taller officer. "Are you Lovett?"

"I bloody well am not," Todd answered. He appeared beside me, shirttails out and one of his braces hanging down. "Lovett's been gone for weeks. I've not seen hide nor hair of him, and we're all the better for it. Now, what's all this caterwauling?" He set his gaze on Fiddler's wife. She shuddered all over and shut her mouth, hushing herself to a few snivels.

"That's the wife of Mr. Fiddler," I told him. "The pie man up the street. Husband's dead they say."

"I'm not surprised," Todd answered. "All this shrieking and carrying on would put any sane man in the grave."

"Fiddler was found hanging from a tree at the back of St. Dunstan's," the shorter one said. "Wife here says she thought he was coming to see you."

"That dirty man and his dirty hands, over here? Never," I said. "I was snug in my bed till four, then up and baking like usual. Did you hear anything, Mr. Todd?" I kept my voice steady.

"Nothing at all," he answered. "Why was Fiddler coming here in the dead of night? Certainly not for a pie!"

All eyes turned to Fiddler's wife. "I don't know," she stammered, her face red as a beet. The weeping boy tugged on his mother's skirt. She put her arm around his shoulder to shush him.

"Well, whatever he had in mind," I said, "he didn't get too far before he thought better of it. Now you'll excuse me. It's past my opening time and I got a business to run. Unlike some people." I waved the men up to the counter, taking pennies and handing out pies till the blues and the Fiddlers were bustled out into the street. They stood there for a minute or so, and the wife started sobbing again. Last I saw, the bobbies were walking her up the street, one on each arm, the boy clutching her skirts and looking back at me the whole way. He put me in mind of my own son, and I shed a tender tear as I carried on with my work.

Sir—

The attached letter was inserted between these pages. I have left it here for you to examine "in situ" rather than remove and append it to the back of the dossier. There are a few other items tucked in later on as well. No receipt for the orphan house, though, and no sign of an emerald earring.

—Dew

SEPTEMBER THE 7TH, 1887

My dear Miss Gibson,

I know where she is. I know where they have taken her. I found an address among the papers in Reverend Mother's office, under a false floor in one of the drawers. If I am right, she is not far from us. I will slip out under cover of night to where she is being held. Oh God please forgive me the depths that I have fallen. I thought I was saving a soul in peril but instead I was sacrificing my own.

You see, Miss Gibson, she did not write that note, the one that was found with Mother Mary Angelica. She could not write that note. I know she did not, and could not, because the person who wrote it was me.

I knew Margaret would become the target of their suspicions, I knew they would never accept that the Reverend Mother had poisoned herself. For it wasn't true. I am the one who put the poison in her tea. I pushed the washrag into her mouth while she was writhing on the floor so that she couldn't spew it back up. I wrote the suicide note that Augustine found. I did it because I had seen your letters that the Reverend Mother was holding back from her. I wanted your words to reach her, I wanted you to help her find her son. How she has longed for him! How she has suffered! You were her only hope. What kind of madness has infected me that I would commit such crimes to achieve such ends!

I cannot be sure my messages are reaching you untouched. I can only say that the eye of providence sees all. If I should succeed in freeing Margaret from her captors, I will ask her to kneel and pray and repent with me, to cast her sins behind her and begin her life anew. It's not too late, I know it's not too late. You will hear more soon. Please Miss Gibson, forgive me my many deceptions. I was so afraid for her, as I am even now, even more than I am for myself.

Oh Lord, I will fear no evil: for thou art with me; thy rod and thy staff, they comfort me.

Sister Catherine

AUGUST 5

Psalms 52:2
Thy tongue deviseth mischiefs; like a sharp razor, working deceitfully.

I hadn't expected Fiddler to end up dead, I was trying to take some of his custom was all. He had more than enough to carry two shops, and the men would choose whichever they liked. All that Freemasons talk got under my skin. I didn't want nothing to do with them and I didn't want them near my shop. They'd bring the doctor right to my doorstep.

The next few weeks, my days were spent chopping and mixing, baking and serving. I was run off my feet but I was my own woman and whatever mistakes I made, I learned from them. All the men from Fiddler's shop ended up at my counter, and I'm sad to say more than a few ended up in Mr. Todd's chair. I was careful about who I sent upstairs. Lonely labourers, toshers, clerks, sweeps and street peddlers. I slyly asked about wives, children, and mothers. I didn't need a whole troop of them tramping in, crying over their missing boys.

One bloke had a loyal dog that nearly got us in a pickle. It sat outside the shop for two days. Now, it turns out Mr. Todd didn't like dogs. It was the only thing I ever saw him nervous about. He threatened to cut the creature's throat like he did its master, as he feared it was making folk suspicious. But I wouldn't go along with it. I'd rather polish off a hundred men than such a devoted creature. When the dog finally vanished, I didn't know whether Mr. Todd had gotten to it or if it had wandered off hungry. I hoped a new owner took it in and gave it a capital life.

I knew in my heart that every pie I sold, and every coin I pocketed would bring my baby boy closer to my waiting arms. I kept the coins in a little tea tin on a shelf over the stove and as each penny and shilling clinked against the metal, I thought about what a good mother I'd be, and all the things I'd spoil my child with. Sweeties, toy soldiers, soft leather boots and a feather pillow to lay his head upon. Maybe even a canary in a cage to sing for him. I wanted nothing more than to have him back with me, and to be the mother he deserved. And for that, I'd chop, stuff, bake and sell every pie in London.

I will say, I learned a thing or two about customers from the ladies at the Mayfair brothel. They knew how to make men weak and greedy, and it had as much to do with nods and nudges and winks as taking off their clothes. I copied what I'd seen them do, flattering the men, leaning over the tables, giving them a peek at something they never got at Fiddler's. They smiled when I smiled, laughed when I laughed. A well-placed hand on a shoulder or a squeeze on the arm sold two pies to a man who'd otherwise only buy one. And any man who thought to give me trouble needed only to look behind me to see Mr. Todd, big as a bull and twice as mad, his razor clutched in his hand.

Most days passed like the others till the morning a pretty little pullet came through the door, all fussed about something, I couldn't tell what at first. I remember how light and fine she was, with shiny dark locks pinned at the nape of her neck and blue eyes wide with worry. Her face was small and white like a doll's, her waist tied so tight you gasped to look at it, and her fingers were as fine and soft as velvet. She wore a straw bonnet with silk flowers around the brim, and a day dress dotted with roses. Usually, the shop brimmed over with blokes in drab suits and muddy overcoats. She drew the eye of everyone in that place, me and Mr. Todd included.

She peered about the room, up and down, back to front, quite desperate for something, though I knew it wasn't for a pie. All the men puffed up when her gaze touched upon their weathered faces. She pushed up to the counter and leaned in to speak to me, her voice clear and sharp and sweet all at once. Johanna Oakley, her name was, daughter of a spectacle maker on Fore Street. I knew the shop straightaway as it had a huge pair of pinch-noses hung out front, each lens as big as a cart wheel.

The girl fixed her bright blue eyes upon me and asked if I'd seen a young sailor man, a Lieutenant Arthur Thornhill. They were engaged to be married. I kept my face straight when I guessed it was the first chap Mr. Todd had dumped into my larder. She listed off the blue jacket with brass buttons and the waistcoat he'd worn, the hat with an H.M.S Star on the front in gold letters, and she said that his hair was fair, the colour of African sand. I could hardly keep from shivering as visions of his bloody throat, blank eyes and butchered innards spun through my head like pictures in a lantern show.

I placed my hand on her sleeve. "I've never seen such a gent around here. You see the lot I have to deal with. I'd have remembered a chap as handsome as that."

She stepped closer to me, a sour smell beneath her orange water and rose oil, as if she had walked the city since dawn. Had she been up and down the street, in and out of the shops? Had someone spotted her coming in to see Mr. Todd? She took my hands in hers and stared hard at my face. My heart thumped in my chest. She reminded me of sweet young Fanny, and a little of Aphra too, but this girl was pure and unspoiled. Her eyes, glittering like jewels, filled with tears, and mine nearly did too as she looked at me with such suffering. She was so beautiful and so filled with sorrow I nearly confessed to everything. She told me to think very hard and asked again if I was sure I'd never seen such a young man. Her heart would break if she never saw his face again. I thought of all I'd done, and all I'd lost, and felt ashamed. That boy hadn't been anything to Mr. Todd but the pearls in his pocket. And as though she'd opened a window into my thoughts, she said, "He had a strand of pearls from Hyderabad he brought as a gift to me. We were apart for two full years."

I tried to remember what Mr. Todd had done with the pearls. I hoped he'd sold them off because if the coppers found them on him he'd dance a jig at the end of a noose, and I'd be right there with him. I brought my voice low and told her that if anyone knew a sailor to have some pearls in his pocket he'd have got robbed in the street. Perhaps he'd been careless and flashed them around, I said, and gotten himself knocked about. She put her hand over her quivering mouth as if she might be sick.

But then she said something else. There were witnesses who had seen her sailor on this very street, on his way to see a barber, and there couldn't be too many of those, could there? Two, three? Her eyes darted over at Mr. Todd's sign, then back to me. My mouth went dry as cotton wool, I didn't know where to look. She saw something in my face. "You've seen him, haven't you?" she asked, her tiny hand gripping my arm. "Please," she cried. The men stood all around us, waiting for their pies, and here was this poor creature carrying on. Much more of it and His Nibs would be down those stairs, though Todd had never killed a woman, as far as I knew.

"We're to be married," she sobbed. "He would never leave me! You don't understand!" She thought I was a poor lonely widow, no money, no prospects, hard at work day and night with no one to love me. I thought of my lost baby, and my dearest Aphra, and I felt a darkness come over me. She thought she had something I could never have. Here she was, putting on airs, thinking she was better than me.

"I understand more than you think," I said. I pushed her hand off and stepped back. "He's run off on you, you silly bitch. You'll never see him again. So stop your sniveling and pull yourself together." She gasped as though I'd struck her, but I had my back up and couldn't stop myself. "You think you're the only girl who ever had a lover, a sailor, a string of ruddy pearls, and left without a pot to piss in. And you come into my shop asking me to help you."

My face was hot as coals, everyone in the shop drew back. I saw Johanna's eyes widen as the tears streamed down her face. Something wicked inside me took pleasure at the hurt I'd caused her.

"Take my advice," I said, "as I'm giving it for free. No man is worth such pretty tears. They're all rotten at heart and want nothing but for a young tart to spread her legs for them. That's where your precious pearls are, around some harlot's neck." I turned and glared at the men. "Am I right?" A few of them nodded nervously. "That's right. If not you, there will be some other poor slut, then they're away like the wind." I pointed at the door. "Go on and find yourself another sailor. They're ten a penny down at Victoria Docks."

Johanna looked at all of us staring at her, then turned on her heel and fled the shop weeping. I turned back to the men crowded around the counter, speechless to a soul.

"That's enough of that," I said. "Let's get back to business. Now, who here wants a pie?"

The hours passed quickly after that as I recall, and the morning's pies sold quickly too. Not for the first time, I wondered if I would ever have a helper the way my father had Ned, my mother and me. Should I spend some of my earnings on a lad to stoke the oven and move the pies in and out? But perhaps he'd end up under Mr. Todd's razor in his tricky barber's chair. I decided it would be safer to go it alone, at least for the moment, and to ask dear Mr. Jennings if he might help me find my child. Though I would need to be careful as I didn't know yet if I could trust him.

I was just finishing with my last few customers when I saw Mr. Todd storming around the corner dragging someone by the arm, and that someone was Miss Johanna, the mewling sailor's girl. Her face was nearly purple, and she was pulling herself this way and that, trying to escape his grip. I jumped back as he threw the door open and pitched her inside, demanding to know why I'd sent her poking around his shop.

"Why the devil would I do such a thing?" I asked. "I may be daft but I'm not as daft as all that." Near as I could tell from Mr. Todd's bluster, Miss Johanna had slipped into his rooms and went through his things when he nipped out to the pub. And when he'd come back he caught her in the cupboard where he kept all the toppers, walking sticks and boots he'd pinched from his victims.

Miss Johanna wasn't crying anymore. She pushed herself away from me and stood toe to toe with Mr. Todd, accusing him of being a thief and a blackguard. She had the foolish courage of a dog that had never seen the outside of its master's house. I looked over at Mr. Todd's face, saw his eyes had darkened to coal, and his mouth flattened into a thin white line. She'd pushed him into a corner, and if she weren't careful we'd all regret it. He was already breathing as hard as a pair of old bellows. It wouldn't take much to push him past his senses.

I softened my face and voice to be gentle with her, begging her pardon for being so rude before, when the shop was full and I was at my wit's end. I told her she was letting her fancies run away with her, and she shouldn't go snooping where she didn't belong. I said in fact Mr. Todd was a charitable man, that he collected those fine hats and things from gentlemen customers that they no longer needed, then sold them to raise money for the almshouse. Mr. Todd wasn't a thief, not with some of the finest customers in all of London at his door. The whole time I kept glancing over at him, watching him glower and seethe.

"I'll fetch a magistrate and you can tell your lies to him," she threatened, all saucy. The customers went quiet and stared at us wide-eyed. They didn't know whether to stay or leave. Mr. Todd leaned close and whispered in my ear.

"If you don't shut her up," he said, "I'll take her to visit her lover in the pit." His steaming breath on my neck made me shiver.

Thank the Lord, Mr. Jennings the barrister stepped in the door, saw my distress and asked what was the matter. I explained Miss Johanna's plight, that she was searching for her lost love, that she thought Mr. Todd had taken some things that weren't his. But it was all a misunderstanding. She'd found some old hats and boots in a cupboard was all. Our Mr. Todd had a heart of gold, I said, though I had to bite my cheek after I said it.

"A heart of gold?" Miss Johanna cried, overhearing me. "He's a liar and a scoundrel and a beast and he deserves to hang."

Mr. Jennings turned to the last of the customers and asked them to leave so that we could speak in private. He took the girl aside and quieted her with his soft voice and soothing manner. He told her I was an honest person, and he was sure I wouldn't rub along with any criminal. It was the first time someone had ever taken my part like that. He told Miss Johanna he was a barrister and knew plenty of magistrates. He said he'd send for one personally if it would make her feel better. She would get a report of his findings on the condition she would accept them, and never return to the pie shop again.

I heard the hiss of air between Mr. Todd's teeth, felt his whole self tighten next to me. I clutched his arm to hold him still. "Wait," I whispered.

Miss Johanna agreed to what Mr. Jennings proposed and asked him to send word to her father's shop on Fore Street. She gave me a sharp look and ignored Mr. Todd entirely, then out she toddled with her nose in the air. I was glad to see the back of her and shut the door loudly after she left, rattling it in its frame. I turned and told Mr. Jennings there was no need to send for a beak. I said everything in my shop was on the up and up. To his credit, Mr. Todd stayed quiet, but kept his eyes on me like a cat crouched behind a nest of starlings.

"Oh no, fear not, I have no intention of bringing in a magistrate," Mr. Jennings said. "No doubt the young lady's fiancé came to his senses and ran off, and not a moment too soon. Any man would find his patience tested by such a creature. I will send word tomorrow that an investigation of Mr. Todd's shop found everything in order, and strongly suggest that she shouldn't have entered while it was unattended. She'll leave you in peace after that."

Mr. Todd didn't say a peep, though he did give a nod in agreement. I never heard him thank a man, I don't think it was in his nature. So I thanked Mr. Jennings for the both of us, gave him a peck on the cheek that made him blush and sent him off with a lovely lamb and carrot pie on the house.

Still, I was worried about Miss Johanna and her sailor man. A chill ran through me when I thought how close she had brought us to the edge of our graves. Mr. Jennings stayed true to his word and sent a message to the Oakleys at the spectacle shop on Fore Street. But I knew it wouldn't keep the girl quiet for long. And not two days later, I was behind the counter once again when I saw a fluttering across the street, through my window. And there she was, Miss Johanna, standing as if frozen to the spot, glaring at me, her rose-specked skirts billowing in the dusty wind, her pretty face twisted into a knot of hate. Then a rattling black carriage passed between us and, quick as a blink, she was gone.

AUGUST 8

Psalm 73:2
I was envious at the foolish, when I saw the prosperity of the wicked; for there are no bands in their death: but their strength is firm; they are not in trouble as other men; neither are they plagued like other men; therefore pride compasseth them about as a chain; violence covereth them as a garment.

A horrible dream or a vision, I know not which. Somehow, I was both my mother and myself while she, or I, was giving birth, and we gave birth to a boy, who was my son but also me. We were in the bedroom above the shop. It was winter, the fire was banked high, the windows sealed shut, the curtains drawn, and every crack between the wall and floor stuffed up with rags. Even the keyhole was blocked lest a tiny draft cause my mother to catch cold. The room, as my mother told me, was insufferably dark and hot.

A midwife was there, very much like Mrs. Price, and she had my mother squat over a birthing chair. My mother pushed and pushed, as she had told me, for hour upon hour. She screamed and screamed as I was stuck in her like an oyster in its shell that doesn't want to be shucked. My father was there, and was pressed into service, as strength was needed to pry me from my sticking spot.

My father took up his place behind my mother to hold her

steady. The midwife held my mother's legs as the pains of Hell rained down upon her. Then, as my mother was gasping and panting, the midwife put pig lard on her hands and stuck them up inside my mother's privates. She grabbed my head and pulled with all her strength till I gave up my hold upon my mother's innards and sprang forth—but instead of myself, I was a boy, and instead of a boy, I was a demon, and I looked down at what had emerged from me, bloodied and black-haired, and grinning, his cord between his teeth, and I screamed myself awake to find myself in another Hell. What else to do other than pick up the pen and tell you of my next unexpected visitor.

After Miss Johanna's departure, Mr. Todd and I had a few quiet days where we kept to ourselves and didn't speak. But barely a fortnight passed when he struck again. I'd closed up shop and was in the back part of the kitchen rolling and scraping and chopping pastry when a flash out of the corner of my eye made me jump and put my hand to my chest. Mr. Todd had slipped through the back door, creeping around like a cat, scaring me out of my wits for his own amusement. In my fluster I dropped my rolling pin on my foot and cursed him as I picked it up. He laughed and told me to mind my language. He was a fine sight, I must admit, didn't look like his usual self, dressed in a flash waistcoat with his hair oiled and standing tall on his head. A gold watch chain peeped out of his pocket, and he smelled of Macassar oil, bergamot and Bay Rum. He told me he was expecting a guest to the pie shop who'd knock three times so we'd know it was him. Mr. Todd said I should open the door to his guest and make him welcome.

"Why are you meeting him here?" I asked. "You think I'll

feed you for free?" I had a mind to tell him to sod off back to his own shop, but he said he'd make it worth my while. It was a jeweller coming to see him, he told me, and Mr. Todd had to be above suspicion. The jeweller had to think that Mr. Todd was a man of means and purpose, and that he had something of value to sell. I gasped in shock as he pulled the accursed string of pearls from his pocket and asked if I remembered them. "Of course I do!" I said, and told him to put them away. "I thought you'd gotten rid of the blasted things. Why do you still have them?"

"I have been waiting for the right buyer, and at last I've found him."

"Well, keep them out of sight till he gets here," I said. "I've not forgotten that gibbering Oakley girl. I expect she's been sneaking about, peering into our business. We don't need any more trouble from her."

He squinted towards the front windows. The street outside was thick with fog and shadows. Anyone could have been out there. He frowned and slipped the strand back into his pocket.

"You should have met him at a counting house, not a pie shop," I said.

"The meeting must be private," Mr. Todd answered. "We can't have any witnesses other than you. And, as I've said, I'll make it worth your while."

That's when I knew Mr. Todd trusted me, as much as he could trust anyone. Our fates were in each other's hands. Perhaps if he finally sold his precious pearls, he could close up his grim little parlour and set off for sunnier shores. They would fetch a fine sum, of that there was no doubt.

When we heard the three knocks, Mr. Todd shooed me towards the door and took his seat at a table near the back. With a lamp in my hand, I unlatched the door and opened it to find an old man on the stoop. He had very white hair waving out from under a plush silk topper, and he wore a black frock coat, satin tie and small round spectacles on the end of his nose. He introduced himself as Beacham the jeweller and asked if I was Mrs. Todd. I near laughed in his face at the idea of it, then told him I was the widow Lovett, who owned the very shop he stood in. I held the door open as he stepped inside and peered about in dismay. Mr. Todd beckoned from the shadows and asked that I bring his guest closer, and serve them each a nip of gin while I was about. He was only a voice in the dark. The old man squinted to see him. As I closed the door I thought I saw someone between the buildings across the way, but after a second look there was no one. I shivered and closed the door and turned the lock over hard.

I took the lamp to the back table and set it by Mr. Todd's elbow. He leaned forward towards Beacham, his dark eyes and narrow chin catching the light. The old jeweller sat down and wondered aloud why he and Todd were meeting in a place such as this. But he tilted his head curiously and pushed his spectacles up his nose, eager to see what Mr. Todd was up to.

"I have something to show you that would get me robbed in the street if it were spotted," Mr. Todd said. "Something you'll want as soon as you see it."

I rattled about for some cups, peeking out into the darkened street for any sign of the girl, then poured Mr. Todd and his guest a finger of gin each, and one for myself. After setting the cups on the table I stepped away, but not so far as to be out of reach were I needed.

The jeweller said he had just come from seeing a necklace crafted from emeralds and amethysts, made to look like bunches of grapes. Very pretty it was, such things were all the fashion. Was it sapphires we had, rubies, or garnets? "Pearls," Mr. Todd said, "as fine a strand as any you've seen."

The old man looked skeptical. "Seed pearls, I suppose. They don't fetch much, you know." Mr. Todd lifted the string of pearls from his pocket and lay it on the table between them. He pushed the lamp close. "Just take a look at these," he said. The pearls shone like little moons on a cold clear night. He held them up from the table, turned them over and back to show them at their best. The jeweller took hold of the string, looked at one pearl closely, rubbed it between his thumb and finger. Then he reached into his coat pocket, pulled out a special eyeglass and held it up so the pearls looked as big as fists.

"How did you get these?" the jeweller asked. "Where is the owner? Where are the papers?"

Even in the darkness at the back of the room, I could see Todd's face sour. "What does it matter? I am the owner now. What papers do I need?"

The jeweller explained that pearls such as these, if they were real, would have come from abroad and required documents of importation. A string of pearls with proper papers would be worth much more than those without. The purchaser could be sure they weren't lost or stolen or fake.

"Fake?" Mr. Todd shouted. I waved for him to be quiet. "You suggest my pearls are fake?"

Again, the jeweller explained that there were those who had the skills and the means to make strings of sham pearls, some made of paste, some of glass, and that the best were fiendishly hard to detect. "I'm not saying you're dishonest, Mr. Todd, but perhaps the person who sold them to you was less than honourable."

For the first time, I saw a flicker of doubt cross Mr. Todd's face. How could he know if the pearls were real? Perhaps the sailor had been duped and then murdered for nothing. A string of beads made of paste. The thought chilled me to my bones.

"Those are real pearls," Mr. Todd said flatly. "Don't play games with me."

"I assure you I am playing no game," Beacham replied. "What do you know about them? Where are they from?"

Mr. Todd explained that he had acquired the pearls from a gentleman who had visited the Orient. They were to be a gift for Mr. Todd's wife but she had recently died and now they were useless to him, an unhappy reminder of happier times.

The jeweller nodded, looked back into the eyeglass. "I have seen pearls similar to these from India. They have a rosy hue. Mind you, all the best shams are from overseas." Suddenly, and strangely, he held the strand to his mouth and rubbed one of the pearls on his front tooth.

"Hey there!" Mr. Todd roared. "What the bloody hell are you playing at?"

"It is a test," the jeweller replied. "A crude one but largely accurate. Pearls are not perfectly smooth like glass, they have a roughness to them." He took two pearls from different ends of the strand and rubbed them together. In the light of the lamp, the dust danced off them into the air. "If they are fakes, they are very clever ones. But that doesn't make them any more valuable."

Todd was as mad as I'd ever seen him. I thought he'd reach across and catch the old man by the throat. He called the jeweller a fraud and said he didn't know pearls from onions. The old man said he'd been in the trade forty years and knew pearls better than any man in London. He tossed back the gin, to fortify himself I reckon, then said, "There may be a real pearl or two somewhere on the string. If so, it may be worth a hundred pounds."

Mr. Todd scoffed and leaned across the table. "They're worth twelve hundred if they're worth a penny. But I'll take one thousand to be fair, given the lack of provenance." The jeweller offered two hundred and said he'd give not a shilling more. He and Mr. Todd glared at one another, the way men do when they are itching for a fight. I heard the lamp flame whispering and the sounds of the street coming through the window glass. I turned and saw a constable standing cater-corner to the shop, staring right back at me. What was he doing there? Had the Oakley girl sent him to watch our comings and goings? I gave him a little wave, raised my glass of gin to him. He looked through me as if I was a ghost.

"I've presented you with a perfectly good string of pearls," Mr. Todd said, "and you insult my intelligence by saying they're fakes. Where are you from and where are your papers? How do I know you're real?" He demanded to see the jeweller's purse and the cash in it to prove he was not a crook himself.

Old Beacham acted all offended and looked as if he was

about to jump up from the table and stomp out. But he didn't. He couldn't tell for sure if the pearls were fake or real. He couldn't let them slip away, it was plain enough. He tapped his fingers on the table as he thought about it, then pulled out a fat purse and lay it between them, keeping his hand close in case Mr. Todd tried to spirit it away. Mr. Todd reached across, lifted the purse, felt the weight of it, dropped it back on the table.

"That's barely fifty pounds in there. You planned to swindle me right from the start."

The old man protested, saying that there were many more sham pearls than real ones in London, if he thought they were real he would return with more money, but he had to be sure.

Mr. Todd didn't know what to think. "For all your talk of fakes and shams, you still sit here with my gin on your lips. Have you come to make a fair deal or not?" he asked. "I would hate to think you are wasting my time, for I would want something for the inconvenience." His voice was hard. I thought about the razor in his pocket, with its carved curling handle and fine silver blade. I pictured it snapping open and slashing the old man's throat. Did he have a wife who'd miss him if he didn't come home? A business partner? Had he told a cabman where he was going? As Todd grew impatient, he grew reckless. He wasn't in control of himself half the time as it was.

I stepped forward and said it was true that Mr. Todd's wife had recently departed. Mr. Todd and I were only trying to get a decent Christian burial for her. That she was my own dear sister and I'd rather give her dignity in death than keep a fancy string of beads with no value in her absence. I pulled a wiper from my sleeve and dabbed it to my eyes for good measure.

Mr. Todd watched and nodded as I spoke. We made a good team, we did. And I knew the best way to tell a lie was to make it half the truth.

The old jeweller fingered the pearls again and sighed. "I have sympathy for you both, but I'm a businessman. I cannot pay a thousand pounds for pearls that aren't the genuine article." The low light reflected hunger in his eyes, and his voice was tinged with greed. I could see that Mr. Todd was restless. His hand was in his pocket, fondling something, turning and turning it, and I knew what it was that he turned in his palm.

"You said something about tests," I said. He nodded. There were tests that could confirm if a pearl was sham or real. I suggested he take a single pearl away with him to study in his own home. "When you've satisfied yourself it's genuine, you can come back for the rest. I reckon both you and Mr. Todd will be glad of the outcome."

Mr. Todd stared at me all suspicious. I put my hands on my hips and gave him a look to say he'd best play along. Mr. Todd pulled his razor out of his pocket, sliced the silk above the last knot on the string and freed a single pearl. Todd told the jeweller he had two hours to return with it. If he didn't, we'd send the coppers round his place and have him done for theft. "A thousand pounds and nothing less," he said.

As the old man got up to leave, he reached for his purse, but Mr. Todd put his hand over it. "You'll leave that with me and Mrs. Lovett. To guarantee you return with my pearl."

"There's more money in there than the price of a single pearl!" the old jeweller cried.

"Then you'd better come back quickly." Mr. Todd took the

purse off the table and tucked it into his pocket next to his razor.

I led Beacham out the front door, glad to see the copper wasn't about. The old man left, muttering to himself as he stepped out into the night. I locked the door behind him and waited with Mr. Todd for his return, pouring us each another finger of gin. I don't remember what we spoke of during that time. I found that when Mr. Todd and I weren't dancing around one another, bleeding a man, chopping him up, or disposing of hats and clothes, we had little to say. I know there are stories that I fancied him. Stories is what they are. The one I fancied was at Quince's bawdy house, and she might as well have been a thousand miles away.

Not even an hour later, old Beacham returned and banged at the door. I peeped out the window. The constable was nowhere in sight. I could tell when I let the old man in, I could see in his face, that the pearl was real and he was keen to have the full strand. He was a tricky sort, but Mr. Todd was trickier. He met Mr. Todd at the table in the back, seated himself, and lay the single pearl on the table. It rolled toward Mr. Todd who snatched it up and held it out on his palm. "Well? What do you say?"

The jeweller admitted the pearls were real but said the whole string wasn't worth more than five hundred quid, at least not without the proper documents. He said a string of pearls like the one Mr. Todd possessed couldn't be bought like a tray of old silver. The jeweller said he would have to assure his customers that he had got them with clean hands. If Mr. Todd took the cash, the old man wouldn't question the source of the pearls any further. Mr. Todd called him a villain and accused him of wanting to buy a family heirloom for a thief's price, but I could see in his face that he was caught in a corner. Any jeweller would ask for the same set of papers, and any jeweller would offer a cut rate without them.

Beacham once again told Mr. Todd that if he had proof of rightful ownership, he'd give him a thousand pounds that instant. But Mr. Todd said he had to see the cash first or he wouldn't believe the jeweller was dealing with him fair. The old man hesitated, reached into his vest pocket, then lay two hundred-pound banknotes on the table. He asked again how Mr. Todd had got the pearls, said there must have been a will leaving them to my imaginary sister, or a receipt from a lawyer or from another jeweller, and asked to see it. He knew full well there was no such thing. He was a shrewd old bugger, I'll grant you that, much good as it did him.

Mr. Todd let out a cold hard laugh like a barking dog. The old man flinched to hear it. It were a harsh dark sound that cut right through you. But Beacham soon recovered and went one step further. He threatened to call a beak like Miss Johanna had done. "I'll say Sweeney Todd is a thief, that you stole a string of pearls from my shop worth fifteen hundred pounds. Who would they believe, you or me? Best to give me the pearls for the four hundred we agreed upon." He put down another hundred-pound note. That was three.

Mr. Todd went quiet. As quiet as a cat when a mouse is sniffing about. I knew then the old man was done for. I stared at the sweat on his brow, and his knobby knuckles, and wondered at the life he'd had and how many folk he'd swindled. Calling himself a fair and charitable man. Not many people had wills and letters and proof of ownership. And desperate people would take whatever they could get. I'm sure he thought he deserved what was coming to him. And perhaps he did. But he thought it was a fortune, not his own grim end.

"I can see you are a clever man," Mr. Todd said, standing from the table. "Give me a moment to look through my things and I'll see if I can find an instrument to satisfy you."

The jeweller looked surprised, but not so surprised as when Mr. Todd walked behind his chair and knocked the man's hat onto the floor. Then he grabbed the old jeweller by his hair, tipped his head back, and sliced him across the throat from ear to ear. The slash was deep and gushed with blood, spilling over the man's linen collar and shirtfront, just missing the table with the pearls and the banknotes. The jeweller gurgled and put his hands to the cut, watched in shock as they came up red and wet and dripping. His eyes were wild at first but faded and went blank as his life drained away. He slumped back in his chair as the pool of blood crept towards my skirt.

Mr. Todd stood over the jeweller with his bloody hands on his hips, grinning like the devil. He scooped up the notes, the purse, and the pearls, and tucked them in his pocket, then reached into his sodden jacket and pulled out a few more bills and a fistful of trinkets. "Sorry for the mess, Mrs. Lovett. On the brighter side, I believe you'll have ham on your menu tomorrow, and liver and kidney as well."

I reminded him he'd said the visit would be worth my while, but here he was with the pearls, and the cash, and I had nothing but a blood-soaked floor and a ten-stone corpse in a chair.

"I get my findings. You get meat for your pies. That's our

arrangement. You'd best not forget it." He saw the sour look on my face, then peered down at the little pile of blood-soaked treasures in his palm. He picked one out, wiped it off on the old man's shoulder and tossed it to me. "There," he said in a tone that would curdle milk. "Something for your troubles." He then picked the jeweller up under his arms and dragged him into the back room.

I looked down at the little item he tossed my way. It was a feather brooch wrought out of yellow gold, dotted with rubies and opals. It would need a good rinse, but it was lovely in every other way. I tucked it into my pocket, then grabbed the box of soda from the shelf. I shook it onto the puddle on the floor and got out my bucket and mop, and started washing away every trace of the jeweller. Just like I'd done with the rest of them.

AUGUST 11

> *Proverbs 10:2*
> Treasures of wickedness profit nothing: but righteousness delivereth from death.

By now you will have my letter about the unwelcome visitor at our gate. I must confess she has left me rattled, and Sister Catherine as well. The whole of the Priory is touched with unease, and the Sisters are all on tiptoe around me. I am more alone than I have ever been. I look back and realise that I have never had a life of my own, not truly. I have never walked through the countryside, never dipped my toes in a pond, never climbed a tree to watch the setting sun. My life has been lived in one small dark room after another, many of them prisons, most of my own making. And here I am now, alone in yet another room, with you, my one true friend. When my story is told, will you still be here with me? Or off to chase another waxwork villain?

This evening I returned from supper to find this book pulled out from under the mattress where I've kept it hidden these weeks, pulled out and placed in the middle of my bed. It must have been Augustine, who has the only other key. No matter. I am damned whatever I say and do, and I intend to unburden myself of these terrible thoughts and deeds. I hope you've poured yourself a nice cup of tea.

After I mopped the floor of Mr. Beacham, I went out back to where he was hanging up on the hook, stripped to his skin. A more dismal carcass I hadn't seen since Todd and I started our venture. Even so, I carved and scraped and filled the bucket as best I could, then started my baking for the morning crowd. I was dead on my feet when I unlocked the door, but I had to work through the day till all the pies were sold. Then I scarce had time to rest my eyes before we had to haul the old man out into the darkness and push him into the pit.

Mr. Jennings came by that day, round and jolly and chatty as ever. He didn't seem to notice how tired I looked, and if he did, he took care not to mention it. When he reached for one of the Beacham pies, I offered him a nice Cornish pasty instead, giving him a little nudge and hinting that the meat in the Beacham pies was not the freshest. I can't say why, but I could only ever feed the special pies to strangers. I couldn't bear to see them in the hands of anyone I was fond of. He took the pasty gratefully and gave me a few extra pence with his payment. Such a kind man! I wanted to tell him about my son, to ask for his help, but I knew Quince and the doctor would trace any questions back to me. I asked myself at times, in the wee small hours, what more I could have done, if there was a way I could have kept us together. But none of us knows the twists and turns in our paths, do we? How they bring us together, and tear us apart?

Even when I was alone in the shop, I hardly had more than a moment to think of my past. The butcher shop, the Row, the doctor's house, the brothel, they were all far behind me. It hurt to remember how ill-used I'd been. All I could think of was my son. Everything I did, I did for him. I knew one day I would find him and hold him, if only for an hour. Just to know he was alive, and to let him know he had a mother. Even as I worked all night, stripping and cleaning and grinding and stewing, rolling and shaping and stuffing and baking, I knew we would be reunited, that he would forgive me, and our lives could truly begin.

It was soon after Mr. Beacham's unfortunate visit that fate blessed me with the greatest gift, and dealt the cruellest blow. I was bringing a tray of pies to the front counter when I caught sight of a woman peering in the window, her face shaded by the brim of her bonnet. At first I thought it was the Oakley girl come to torment us again. I steeled myself for what was sure to be a fight, but looked again and nearly fell to the floor when I saw that it was my dear Aphra. Shocked as I was, she seemed ten times more so. What was she doing here? How had she found me? My excitement was mixed with fear and uncertainty. What did she want from me? Who else knew I was there? Outside, the street heaved with people and horses and carriages, circling birds, and yapping dogs. Inside, men chattered and clinked knives against plates. I worried that she had been followed, or that she had been made to visit me, to draw me out of hiding. I would have to bring her inside. I was glad she couldn't hear the awful din. I wondered sometimes how peaceful her silence might be.

I put down my tray, smoothed my apron and waved to her. She slipped through the door, shy as a mouse, wearing one of her prettiest frocks, green and gold with tiny pink flowers all over. Her hair was tucked up under a silk bonnet with ribbons that streamed down, framing her face. It felt like she brought all the warmth and light of spring in with her. I'll never forget how she looked standing in the middle of that shop with men all around her drinking ale and scarfing pies. One by one they cast their eyes over her. How unworthy they were to be in her presence.

Moving her fingers, she said, "Hello, little goose," and I repeated it back. I was surprised at how quick the hand-words came back to me. I saw that her dainty shoes and the hem of her skirt were muddy and asked what had happened, and why she hadn't taken a carriage. She looked down at herself and sighed. She told me that she had walked a long way. She didn't want anyone to know where she was going.

"I thought you had left London," she signed. "I thought I'd never see you again." Her gentle hand reached out to touch mine, rough and raw, and I flinched as she did so. I don't know why. I didn't know my own feelings. She looked hurt and sad, like she thought I didn't care for her anymore. So I told her I was very happy to see her. It had been a shock was all. That seemed to make her better. She made the word for "confused" and asked why I had gone from Quince's house, and why I was at the pie shop. Had I been hired to work there?

I shook my head no and told her that I owned the shop, that I'd taken it over. I didn't know the words for all that, so I spoke slow and gestured what words I knew. She squinted at me in frustration, not catching what I was saying. While we tried to speak, some men finished their pies and left, and others came in. I handed them their meals and took their coins. She watched me as I explained, but she didn't understand. I thought maybe I had gotten my signs all wrong. I held up my finger and told her to wait. I got a paper and a pencil. "This is my pie shop. I own it now." I wrote as neat as I could. She frowned, took the pencil from me, wrote back that, no, it was her father's shop. Now it was my turn to be flummoxed. "Your father?" I wrote back.

"Frank Lovett is my father," she wrote. "Where is he?"

My legs went weak. Her father! I put my hands down on the counter and steadied myself, sure that I would faint dead away. It was too much, my head felt too small to hold it all in. You might not believe me now, as you read this, but it's the truth, as I promised to give it to you. Even now, I barely believe it myself. And this was not to be the last of fate's cruel turns.

There wasn't long till closing and still the men were lingering about, watching us as we spoke. I felt like telling them all to get out, to leave and never come back. As for Aphra. I didn't know what to tell her about her father. She knew he'd jumped on Fanny, that he'd troubled the whores at the brothel, that he'd run up debts, that he'd been banned from the place. Why hadn't I known he was her father? Why hadn't she told me? It wounded me at first, that she would keep such a thing secret, but then I thought, of course she would hide it. No one would want to be known as the child of such a wastrel. She was ashamed, that had to be it. And I winced at the thought of her sharing his name. Lovett! Then remembered it was my own now too. How strange that felt.

In spite of it all, did she love her father just the same? Does every child love their parent, and every parent their child? Is it a feeling you get the moment they're born, or does it come over you slowly? Do you have to wring some affection from a stone-cold heart, or is it enough to carry a child within you or hold it in your arms, to let its eyes gaze into yours?

Aphra stared at my face trying to get the measure of me. Her brow creased as it always did when she fretted about something. How could such a beast as Lovett have a daughter as sweet as her? Whatever she felt about him, she was better off without him.

I lifted my hands, made the words as carefully as I could. "My sweet, sweet love. I'm sorry. Your father is dead."

She stepped back from me, put her hand to her heart in shock. I feared she was hurt, or sad, or angry. I couldn't bear any of those things. She asked me if it was true, how he'd died, when he died, how I had come to be in the shop and what of the barber upstairs? I told her to wait with me until the last of the men had left, then I would tell her everything. I gave her a seat and made another round of the shop, doling out pies and ale till every crumb and drop was gone. At last, I cleared the shop out and turned the sign over to Closed.

I gestured for her to follow and led her to my own sitting room. She slipped the ribbons from her bonnet and took it off. I hung it on a peg for her with her cloak. She warmed herself by the fire while I bustled about making tea. I was ashamed of the bare room, the tatty old furniture, the chipped cups. She was so out of place in such a rat's hole but then I remembered she'd have seen her father living in it.

Finally, I sat myself across from her and, with hand signs and pencil-printed notes, I told her what happened with Lovett: he had sent me a threatening note at the brothel, demanded I meet with him, then tried to brutalise me the way he had done to Fanny. And then, my face burning with shame, I said there had been an accident, a mistake, and that I'd killed him when he attacked me. I dumped his body into the pit out back, and afterwards said I was his wife so I could have the shop. I never told her what he said about my baby that night by the church. Even though weeks had passed, I feared they were lies he told me to turn me against Aphra, against Madame Quince. And what if they were true?

I saw the pain in Aphra's face and it felt like I was looking in a mirror. We both had suffered so. "I didn't know he had kin, you least of all," I wrote on the paper. "I'm sorry." She stared at the words on the page for a long time, then she raised her eyes to mine. "My father he was, but he's gone, and I'm glad," she signed. "A wicked man, worse than you know." My eyes filled with tears, and hers did too. She embraced me and I felt her tenderness warm me from my toes up to my cheeks.

My eyes were filled with the sight of her, the way her hair shone in the firelight. How pink and lovely her cheeks were. Her smile, her lips curling daintily. I went all soft inside. But then she began to speak of her father, and her wretched childhood in his care, and an anger began to seethe within me. Her mother had died when Aphra was only three. "He shouted at me, punched me, kicked me. He beat me about my head and shouted. She pointed to her ears. "Everything stopped. I could not hear anything."

I had thought she was born like that, and when I heard Mr. Lovett had done it to her, I wanted to kill him all over again. When she was twelve, he sold her to Madame Quince in exchange for a bit of money, Aphra didn't know how much. But it had been enough for him to clear his debts and keep the shop. I got the wobbles when she said it. It was too awful to bear thinking about. The shop I'd been running and where I made my money had been bought at the cost of her innocence. She had worked off her own debt with Madame Quince, but remained at the Symposia where she was safe and cared for. She reached into her purse and pulled out a few pounds. "Take it, for the shop," she signed. "All for you."

I shook my head and pushed the paper gently back at her. I knew what she'd done to get it. "It's yours, you earned it. Save it for yourself," I told her. "It belongs to you." I thought for a moment she could come live with me and we could run the pie shop together, if she could bear to leave the luxury of the Symposia. But she wouldn't be happy serving pies with men pawing at her and pushing her about. She would be lost trying to understand them as they shouted their orders at her. And what if one of them recognised her from the brothel? Then there was Mr. Todd to worry about. His razor, and his appetites.

I thought about my father's shop, about working with my mother at the front while Ned worked with my father at the back. The customers never spoke to him, they barely ever saw him. At that moment, I had an idea, a terrible, foolish idea. She could come and live with me, and work alongside me, but not at the counter. Not as a woman. My mind raced around it, there was danger in every part of it. But I could not resist. "Aphra," I wrote. "If you've paid off your debt to Madame Quince, there's a way we can be together, here at the shop. I need someone to fill and clean the pans and to help me with the ovens. But. You would have to be somebody else. You would have to be a boy. We could call you Tobias, after my father. We could call you Toby."

I could see how confused Aphra was, reading what I had wrote and then looking up at me and then reading it again. "A boy?" I made the words for "trousers" and "shirt" and "hat" and "hair" and pointed at her and she started to laugh. I shook my head. "Not a joke," I wrote. As a boy, she would avoid the foulest of the customers' attentions, and Mr. Todd's as well, at least until the worst came to pass. I was no fool—I knew my time with Todd could not last. Something was looming over us like a storm cloud, black and swollen and ready to burst. If Aphra could help me through the worst of it, we could face it together and then together we could escape.

"A boy," she answered doubtfully, pointing to herself. "Me." I nodded and told her she could buy a hat and shirt and vest from Fab's outfitter on Mount Street, as well as some shoes and some loose-fitting trousers with braces. Then she could tell Madame Quince that her father had died of drink at last, and that her aunt in Cornwall had sent for her. Quince had never seen my handwriting. If I was careful and wrote simply, a short message from me could do the trick. Everyone had an aunt in Cornwall, it seemed, and no one ever asked too much about them.

I took my paper and pen and wrote out a sad little note for Aphra as if I was her grieving aunt, then folded it up and handed it to her. Then I stood up and went to the drawer of my dressing cabinet, and took out the gold feather brooch that Todd had pulled from Beacham's pocket. "Take this," I said. "You can leave this with Madame Quince as a token till you return after your father's first mourning. Then you can take one carriage to the train station and another back here to me."

She watched me with one eyebrow raised as I finished telling her my plan. She looked back down at the words I'd written, looked back up at me again. I knew how mad it sounded, but it was the only way I could see our future together. I couldn't go back to Madame Quince, not now. And I couldn't bear to lose Aphra once again. "What do you think?" I asked her. "It's no Mayfair mansion. There'll be no servants, no beautiful gowns. If you say no, I'll understand."

She tipped her head down, cast her eyes to the floor. All bashful, she told me she didn't know how to make pies or keep a kitchen, she didn't want me to think her useless.

"Can you sweep a floor, wipe down a table?" I asked. "Everything else I can teach you. I can do three times as much with you as I can by myself."

She raised her eyes to mine. Tears were budding in the corners. She reached over, squeezed my hand, then signed, "I will try—for you." She gestured at the darkening sky. It was time for her to go. There was no way around it. She would have to return before nightfall, or they would send someone to find her. I made her swear that she would come back to me in one week's time, with the clothes she would wear as Toby. She nodded, wiping the tears from her cheeks.

I took her through the pie shop to the front door. She clasped my hands in hers, then turned and stepped out into the cold evening. I never felt so lonely as when I closed the door behind her. Would Madame Quince let her go? Would she run away? Or would I never see her again?

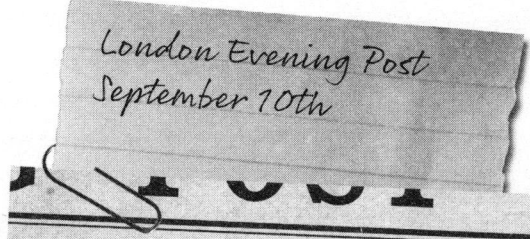

London Evening Post
September 10th

EMBER 10, 1887   10 PAGES   {ONE HALFPENNY

WOMAN'S BODY RECOVERED FROM THAMES RIVER

London: Late Friday evening, the remains of a young woman were pulled from the waters of the Thames, near the site of the construction of the Tower Bridge. Pinned inside a pocket was a note identifying the woman as Sister Catherine Wainwright, an apparent victim of suicide. Sister Catherine had been missing from St. Anne's Priory since Wednesday evening. St. Anne's has endured a number of tragedies of late. Our deepest sympathies to Mother Augustine and the Sisters of the Priory at this sorrowful time.

AUGUST 12

Lamentations 3:47
Fear and a snare is come upon us, desolation and destruction.

Aphra had found her way back to me. Perhaps this is the brightest part of my tale. In those few minutes, to see her again, I was at my happiest. There was only ever her, and now I was watching her walk away, with no way to be certain that she would return.

When I turned back to the shop, Mr. Todd stepped out from the shadows looking dark and suspicious. I near jumped out of my skin. I scolded him for sneaking about and spying on me. He asked who the visitor was, if she was kin to me. Perhaps he didn't know her after all, or perhaps he did but hadn't seen her face. "You two seem awfully close," he said.

A wave of fear washed over me. How much had he seen? I fought to keep the emotion out of my voice. I told him she was my sister, but that she was leaving back to Manchester. His eyes flicked to the front door, then back to me. "It's funny," he said. "Your Mr. Lovett used to cat about with some fancy whores. I thought for a moment she was one of them, maybe looking to see where he'd got to."

My mood went cold. "My sister is the farthest thing from a whore, not that you'll ever know about it." I told him never to speak another word about her and went back to my pastry but he grabbed me by the arm.

"I'll ask what I ask, and I'll say what I say," he warned. "What goes on in this shop is as much my business as yours." He lifted his other hand and touched it to my chin, but he was rough where Aphra had been gentle. "We have to trust each other, we've got no choice. But I don't believe you've told me the truth about who you really are."

"That makes two of us." I yanked my arm out of his grip and grabbed my rolling pin.

"Just be careful, Mrs. Lovett," he said in a low voice. "I've got nothing left to lose. I'm not sure you can say the same." With that, he returned to the shadows. I didn't put the rolling pin down till I heard the back door close and his heavy feet thump up the stairs.

That whole next week I kept my eyes on the shop door waiting for Aphra to come back to me. I looked up every time the bell jangled but it was only ever a customer, and my heart would sink. Mr. Todd kept to himself, as though he was waiting for something too. He saw one or two gents each day, but they all left freshly shaven on their own two legs. I thought maybe something was off, that he'd heard grumblings about the coppers looking for Beacham or maybe foolish Johanna had made some noise about that bloody sailor of hers. As my store of special meat ran low, I knew the urge had to be growing inside him. And that wasn't good for any of us.

In the early hours when I was rolling out dough, cutting it, shaping it and pushing it gently into the pans, I'd think about how Aphra would come back to me, and how we would somehow find a way to get my son. We could leave the shop, leave the city behind, and run away from it all. Maybe we'd go up to Coventry, or over to Bristol, or down to the seashore at Brighton. We could do anything we wanted, be anyone we wanted. The three of us, a family at last. We could open a pie shop. I could sell pies anywhere. I could sell them on the street! But sometimes those happy thoughts turned black when my mind wandered to the viciousness of Quince and Dr. C. I grew rough with the cleaver and thumped down the rolling pin. My hands went bloodless as I worked the meat grinder. There was only Aphra and my child to keep me from slipping further and further into darkness, closer and closer to Mr. Todd. And day by day I grew more convinced I would never see them again.

As I lay in my bed in my little room at the back of the shop, I thought back to my times with Aphra at the Symposia. How lush and golden and magical it all had been. How I would undress her, carefully lifting her gown over her head, the pretty pink one with the little white bows, then loosen the laces down the back of her corset. I'd help her step out of her petticoats and peel off her stockings, then ease her into a bath of hot water I'd heated in a kettle on the stove in the kitchen. Faithfully I made trip after trip to her bedroom with buckets of steaming water, careful not to douse the candles set underneath the copper tub to keep the water warm. After sponging her pale back and her rosy breasts, I'd lift a pitcher of water and pour it over her hair to wash it. I remember her arms and the back of her neck prickling as her skin cooled in the air. Gooseflesh, it's called, funnily enough.

My cheeks would flame as I helped her stand and dry herself off, rubbing down her arms, her back, her thighs. Then

I'd wrap her in a robe and sit her next to a cheerful fire so I could tug the kinks out of her long locks with a horsehair brush. There was always a little pot of tea waiting for us. Aphra would wrap her hands around her cup to warm them, take a sip and close her eyes. We would tell each other stories with our hands. "I love you," we'd say, perfectly quiet. And no one else could hear. Those days had been the best of my whole life.

I was sweeping the floor one night after the shop closed when I heard a little tap-tap at my window breaking into my thoughts. It was so quiet I nearly didn't catch it. Then, I spotted a waving hand out of the corner of my eye. I looked up and caught my breath. There she was, my Aphra, in mourning wear, a black cloak over a black gown, her face veiled, her hair covered under a large bonnet, and a large black valise at her feet. Behind her, a cab pulled away and rolled up the street. The light had nearly left the sky. My heart skipped as I rushed to the door and unlocked it for her. She held a hand up, and looked all about to make sure she was alone. I opened the door wider, beckoned her inside, then she slipped in and put her arms around me.

I pulled her away from the window into the shadows, and hurried her across the shop to my own little room where I closed the door against the world. There was no fire lit, no kettle on the boil, and my dirty breakfast plate was still on the table. I cleared my things away, got a hearty blaze going, and fetched two cups and some sugar for tea. Aphra sat near the fire looking a bit uneasy. I told her I'd worried she wasn't coming back, and asked how Quince took the news of her leaving. I handed her a piece of paper and a pencil.

"Not happy," Aphra signed. Then she wrote, "She was grieved to hear about my father's death. Or so she said. She agreed that my accounts were settled and I was free to do as I wished. But she told me to come back soon. I told her I would be gone a month at least and would send word if I had to stay longer. I gave her the brooch as token. She seemed happier then."

I read the paper then looked up at her. "Was it really as easy as that?" I asked.

Aphra shook her head and wrote that Madame Quince had seemed very sad, more than she should have been. But she didn't argue, she didn't plead, she didn't try to make Aphra stay with the promise of new dresses and shoes and bonnets. She just nodded, took ten pounds from her drawer, and tucked it into Aphra's hand. "Then I hurried here. To be with you."

She looked down at her little purse, reached into it and pulled out a folded note, and something that flashed brilliant in the lamplight. One of the emerald earrings I'd given her that I'd taken from the doctor's house. She pressed it and the folded paper into my trembling hand. It was a receipt, from the Foundling Hospital in Bloomsbury. I looked at her with my stomach dropping through my feet. I read it over and over. There was a picture of a lamb with a branch between its teeth, and across the top it said: Hospital for the Maintenance and Education of Exposed and Deserted Young Children. Beneath it, a date scrawled in a looping hand, and the words: "Received a male child. Newborn." Then the signature of the hospital secretary.

"My son?" I asked, my fingers barely able to form the words. "This is my son?"

Aphra nodded, tears now fully spilling down her cheeks.

I clasped the paper to my breast, too shocked to cry. Lovett hadn't lied after all. My son was alive just as he'd said, safe but locked away, with no mother to love him and a father what couldn't be found. I held up the earring, expecting she had the other in her purse, but she wrote: "The other was left with your son at the orphan house. You will need to match it with this one to claim him." Her face looked blurred through my tears. A sob caught in the back of my throat. "Quince had me bring the earrings and go with her. I was to pretend that I was your baby's mum. She's done it before. She gives them over to be raised until they're five or six years old. Then she takes them back and sells them off. Five quid for a kitchen girl or chimney sweep, eight for a bootblack. I stole back this earring and the receipt from her desk. She won't be able to claim him now. Pray she doesn't notice." She paused, then added, with her hand shaking, "I'm sorry I couldn't tell you about your boy. Quince said it was for your own good, and for the good of the house. Babies are bad luck for us. They always have been."

I could hardly believe it. Kindly Madame Quince had stolen my child, had stolen other children. Monster! I didn't know what to say. Neither of us did, so we sat quietly together. I was happy to see her, but I was also afraid for what was to come. She stared into the fire, her hands still and folded in her lap. I listened to the mantel clock tick the minutes away, wondering how many of them we'd have together. After a moment, she lifted her head and tilted it at me. Her brow creased in its familiar way when she was troubled. "One thing more," she signed. "You are in danger."

"Danger?" I whispered. "What do you mean?"

Aphra sat up straight and her hands moved quickly. So fast that I couldn't catch their meaning. I gently took her hands in my own and mouthed to her, I don't understand. The furrow in her brow deepened. I gestured towards the pencil and paper.

"Three toffs looking for you," she wrote. "They were cross. Asking for the pregnant maid."

My stomach went all queasy.

"They made Madame Quince nervous. She asked us if we knew where you'd gone. One man gave her a card with a picture on it." She drew an eye within a triangle. "They frightened me. Who are they?" She looked up at me fearfully.

I didn't want to tell her, but I had to say something. "Friends of the man I ran from," I wrote. "My former employer. The father of my child."

Aphra sank back in her chair. "Madame Quince told them you ran off with the baby. I said you'd told me nothing," she signed.

I felt a chill run through me. Were we truly alone? "Wait here," I told her. I crept through the shop and cracked open the front door then peered out into the darkness. No Sweeney, no figures in the shadows, no one outside the shop. When I returned to the fireside I asked if she was sure she hadn't been followed.

She shook her head. "Not followed," she signed. "I'm sure."

"Clever goose," I replied. "Let's hope they never find us."

I tucked the earring and the receipt from the Foundling Hospital into my tea tin, and spent that night curled against her in my little nest of a bed. I ran my fingertips over her narrow waist and the curve of her hip, feeling a rush of warmth around us as I did it. Then I put my arms around her and buried my face in her hair. I breathed in the smell of her and closed my eyes, feeling safe for once, and loved. I hope I do not offend you as I tell you of these intimacies that I dared not ask Sister Catherine to transcribe. Aphra turned and pressed her lips to my neck, my breast, and slipped her hand between my thighs and moved it higher, making me feel as I never had before. She then placed my hand on her downy cleft and had me touch her in the same way she touched me, in places where I'd never been touched. Our hands fluttered between us in the candlelight until our words fell away, until I was overtaken with a delicious shuddering that lit a fire within me. She kissed my fingers one by one till I nearly cried. I held myself close against her back and dropped into a deep sweet sleep. The pain and loss that gripped my heart had left me. At least for a little while.

The fire had gone out by morning, but we weren't cold till we put our feet on the floor. I shivered while I built up the coal and kindling in the fireplace grate. Aphra watched me, her flaxen hair hanging loose about her shoulders. I looked over at her valise, which she still had not unpacked. Did she mean to stay? I began to worry. I started to ask, but then I stopped myself, afraid of what the answer might be.

I made some tea and put in a lot of sugar, just as she liked. She sipped it and had a bit of bread with butter. As we sat together, I told her about Mr. Todd. Not everything, of course. She knew he was her father's tenant but had never met him as he arrived after she went to the brothel. I told her he mostly kept to himself but from time to time helped me dump bones and rubbish into the pit out back. I said sometimes he lurked about and that he didn't like strangers. "He's got a temper," I said, "but don't be afraid, he never comes into my rooms."

I told her my head was filled always with thoughts of my son. If I saw a nurse in the street with a pram, or even some poor wretch with a little one in tow, I felt dizzy wishing it was mine. Aphra looked at me with pity, but I didn't want her pity. "Would you help me get him back?" I wrote.

"How? He's locked away in the Foundling Hospital."

"You're his mum as far as they know. We've got the earring, and the receipt. We'll go back there and claim him."

Aphra's brow furrowed. I could see she was frightened.

"They'll tell Madame Quince," she wrote. "She'll come after me."

I knelt before her with the fire warm on my back. I looked up into her face and took her hands. "Little goose. Be brave for me," I said, letting her read my lips. "Please help me."

"I want to," she signed. "But how?"

"Madame Quince thinks you're in Cornwall. By the time anyone figured out who you were, we'd be gone."

"Gone where?"

"I don't know. Anywhere away from here. I promise to keep you safe. Please. I need to have my son with me."

Aphra gazed into my eyes and my heart skipped in my breast.

She nodded, and together, we made a plan.

AUGUST 15

Ecclesiastes 1:18
For in much wisdom is much grief: and he that increaseth knowledge increaseth sorrow.

I look over these pages and ask myself if these are the ravings of a madwoman, if someone could suffer this way and come out of it with her wits intact. Was this all as I remember it? How can a single soul endure so much, at such a tender age? And yet there was more to come, enough to derange anyone and send them into apoplexy. It is a miracle of God's own devising that I am able to write these words at all. And so I must, and quickly, put an end to it.

I was resolved that we should visit the Foundling Hospital, to take back my child or at least learn his location. Aphra had been presented as the baby's mother, so that was the plan we stuck with. We each dressed in our nicest clothes, which wasn't saying much for me. I thought how plain and shabby I looked! We rose early, washed our faces and neatly pinned up our hair. Aphra kissed me softly and squeezed my hand, though her brow was creased and her smile timid.

We hired a cab to take us to Bloomsbury even though it wouldn't have been far to walk. When the cab pulled up in front of the gate I was shocked to see how vast the hospital was. I could see the main building in the distance flanked by two wings, and I wondered how many children they kept there.

We passed through a gatehouse in a high brick wall and came into a wide yard with fields and trees on either side. Aphra and I walked close together in the company of other women holding bundles against their breasts, some mewling and fussing, others quiet and still. A few women had tears coming down their cheeks; most were grim. Not one had a look of hope about them. I felt a pain in my chest as I watched them.

As we reached the main door, my heart began to pound, and all my thoughts flew from me. What if they turned me away? What if he was already gone? I didn't know what I would do. Aphra gave me a smile to comfort me and tugged me along by the hand.

We told a porter we were there to reclaim a child. He showed no emotion as he directed us to the office of the secretary. Inside, we took chairs in a large room with dark wood on the walls. There was a fine Turkey carpet beneath our feet, and portraits on the walls of old men in wigs and red coats. When the secretary came to meet us, I thought I'd be sick all over myself.

As we rose to our feet, he told us to sit down, then took up his place behind a large, shining desk. I had to speak for Aphra, so I explained she was deaf and that I was her cousin. I said she'd left a baby boy at the hospital not two months ago, and she wished to have him back. The paper and earring came out of my pocket, and I laid them on the desk with a trembling hand. My heart fluttered as the secretary fetched a ledger book from a shelf. He flipped it open, and I watched his thick finger run down the pages until, at last, he stopped at the number that matched my receipt.

"Oh yes, I recall," he said. "She came with her mother, Mrs. Quince. A good friend to the hospital. You know her, of course."

"Yes, certainly," I said, not knowing how long I could keep up my lies. "She's from the other side of the family." At that moment, a woman wearing an apron and a frilled cap stepped in the door, startling us. One of the nurses, I guessed. She whispered to the secretary, and I saw her gaze land upon the earring for a moment, shining in the lamplight, before she turned away and busied herself with something in a cabinet across the room.

The secretary fetched a packet of papers and broke the wax seal on them. He unfolded each piece of paper and took from the package the earring that matched mine. "Two months is such a short time," he said. He asked Aphra to explain how her position had changed so that she could care for an infant better than when she had left him.

I signed the question to Aphra, then told the secretary that she had taken a job with me in a pie shop and had a good income, as well as family to help her. I swore I'd do everything I could to support her and the baby. But when I said "pie shop," the secretary wrinkled his nose and looked at us over the rim of his spectacles.

"I don't think you appreciate what is involved in caring for an infant," he said. "Raising a child in a pie shop with no father? Here at the hospital, our babies receive medical care, food, a safe place to sleep and a fine education. They are apprenticed once they are old enough, to secure their future prospects." He asked how a deaf woman with limited means could provide better care than that.

Aphra could see I was worried. She tried to read my lips. She waved at me frantically to ask what was happening. In that moment, though, she was like a moth fluttering against a window in another room.

"I don't doubt you mean well," the secretary said. "And I'm sure you feel great affection for your child, but I'm not satisfied as to your circumstances, and will not be releasing him into your care." The secretary closed the ledger and pushed the receipt and earring back at us. "If you return in the company of Mrs. Quince, I may reconsider," he said. "If she were to come and vouch for your competence, and advise us that your situation is substantially different than it was two months ago, I could be persuaded to release the child. But as it is, you have not shown that you can provide for him. As is customary for an infant, he has been sent to a nurse mother outside the city. It would require significant effort and expense to bring him back, at the cost of the hospital."

"What if we pay you back for all that?" I asked.

The secretary gave a wry smile. "That isn't our only concern."

I took the earring and the receipt from the secretary's desk. Aphra began to weep. My face went very hot, and I clenched my teeth together. There were no tears from me; I felt hollow inside, hollow and black like the pit behind the shop.

"Thank you for your visit," the secretary said. "I believe you know the way out. Please give Mrs. Quince our regards." He scribbled a note in the ledger next to my baby's name, and I felt more hopeless than ever about getting him back. Aphra cried harder when the secretary put the other earring back into the package of papers and resealed the package with a blob of red wax.

My boots felt like lead upon my feet as we walked toward the door. Aphra took my arm to steady herself, her eyes red and swollen. As we walked down the grand hallway, a few girls raced past wearing brown frocks with white caps. I was hardly listening when I realised someone had called out to us. I turned in surprise to see the same nurse from inside the secretary's office walking towards us.

"Pardon me, but I overheard your meeting, and I may be able to help," she said. I knew right away it was the earring that had taken her fancy, but my heart leapt with hope in spite of myself. She took us into an alcove where we could speak frankly.

"Your baby is in the infirmary upstairs," she said. "He has never left the hospital. He has been unwell these past few months, and at one time we thought he might not survive."

"He's here? Not in the country?" I felt a fury rise within me, cold and hard as iron, as I thought about how the secretary had lied to us. I don't know why I was surprised. "Where is he? Take us to see him."

"Now, just a moment. Understand, I can't give him back to you. But I can take you to the infirmary, and you may see him for a few minutes. However, you may not touch him or go near him."

"Can't his mother hold him one last time? Do you not have any heart for a poor young mum?" I asked.

The nurse looked at Aphra's face, streaked with tears, and then back to me. "You don't understand the risk I'm taking just by speaking with you. Now, if she wants to see her child, we can come to terms."

Aphra saw the grim look on my face and tugged on my arm. "What would that be?" I asked darkly.

"I will take that earring from you," the nurse said, "as recompense."

"That is the only thing we have to reclaim the baby," I said, as the icy darkness blossomed in my heart.

The nurse scoffed. "Don't you understand? You'll never get him back." She gestured to Aphra. "She may have plied her trade in Mayfair but she was still a whore. Quince will have that child back soon enough. She and the secretary have an arrangement."

I quivered from head to toe. "We can't give you that earring," I said. "We won't."

"Does she want to see her child or not?"

All of a sudden, I thought of the little glass vial my mother had given me the last time I saw her. I kept it with me always, but what good was it to me now? I took it out and laid it on my palm, then offered it to the nurse. The gold decoration on the glass shone in the light.

She plucked it out of my hand to examine it. She took the stopper off and sniffed. It still smelled of roses.

"Right then, let her see her son," I said. "And you can keep that pretty trinket. It's worth a lot more than one earring. It's the most valuable thing I own."

The vial disappeared into the wretched woman's apron. "All right," she said. "But only for a moment."

All sorts of wild thoughts spun through my mind as we

walked to the infirmary. Could I snatch the baby? Could I trounce the nurse and steal him away? But I looked in dismay at the people walking up and down the halls all around us, and thought of the endless yard in front and the gatehouse. We'd never get away.

It seemed to take an eternity to reach it, but once we were at the infirmary, I found I was strangely numb. A few of the children fretted, but most were drowsy and calm. The nurse put her finger to her lips, so we'd be quiet, and took us inside, where little cots were lined up along each wall. She gestured for us to follow until we stood next to a cot with an infant who was very still. She took the receipt, checked the number against the bracelet on his wrist, nodded, and handed the paper back to me. I hardly dared breathe as I took him in. Just a little scrap of a thing bundled in a blanket. He made a small noise. I was pleased to see him, but as I made my way around to the side of the cot, I caught sight of his flushed cheeks and dark, feverish eyes.

"What's wrong with him?" I asked.

"Debility," she said. "He was born prematurely, and his lungs were not fully developed. He's better than he was. We'll be moving him out of here soon."

I forgot about Aphra, and the nurse, and the whole world, as he looked back at me. I thought he must know his own mum by the way he stared. I was flooded with motherly, warm affection, so powerful it near knocked me over. My eyes brimmed with tears till he grew blurry lying before me. I heard Aphra still weeping. The nurse eyed me suspiciously. I reached my hand toward him, but she yanked a curtain across between us. "That's enough," she said. "You've seen him. Now be on your way."

Everything stopped. The world stopped. A night-black storm thrashed and raged inside me, freezing my heart from within. For so long, I'd thought only men were monsters. But what of Madame Quince, who'd seemed like a mother to me and who I thought cared for Aphra, but who had peddled us both like sides of meat and taken money in exchange for our ruin? Or my own mother, who had abandoned me to fate? She never looked back, never asked after me. Never cared how I made my way in the world. I was as good as dead to her. Then Mrs. Dawson, who did the doctor's bidding, and who would have seen me killed for not giving myself up to her master's twisted urges. And what about that dirty nurse, who made me trade a peep at my own sick child for the price of a shiny bauble, with no sympathy for a mother's longing. Or these nuns who have kept me locked up all these years, who are bound to treat others with kindness and mercy, what kindness and mercy have they ever shown me?

And what of you, Miss Gibson, who would use me for your own ends. Do you have any room in your heart for the wicked Margery Lovett and the abuses she's suffered? Or is her life a grisly tale you'll use to sell some papers and show how much better you are, how much more important, than the dregs of your fine society?

I knew then, and I know it now, that it's every man for himself in this life, and every woman too. I've learned that lesson all too well.

I took Aphra by the hand and led her through the hospital corridors, out of one Hell and into another. She held me up while we walked back, as I thought my legs would give out underneath me. My mind was muddled the whole way, and I nearly got clobbered by a carriage once or twice stepping into the gutter.

As we made our way up Fleet Street, I saw the line of customers outside the shop waiting for me to open. I sent her round to the back door, then pushed through the throng to let myself in. "Sorry lads, closed today. Death in the family. Come back tomorrow." They could see the gloom in my face and moved aside. A few of them murmured their sympathies, for which I was truly grateful. I nodded to them and let myself in, then hurried to fetch Aphra, hoping there were no surprises waiting for us on the larder floor.

AUGUST 16

Psalms 44:14
I live in disgrace all day long, and my face is covered with shame; at the taunts of those who reproach and revile me, because of the enemy, who is bent on revenge.

Once we were inside the shop, Aphra led me to my room, and gently took my cloak off. She bustled about and put the kettle on as I stared blankly into the fire. As the water boiled, she came and sat near me, twining her fingers through mine.

I had lost my son. He may as well have been in the countryside, like the secretary said, for that's where they would send him, and soon. Aphra kissed the back of my hand. She lifted it up to her beautiful golden hair and then said in her hand-words: "I will stay with you. Make me a boy."

"Are you sure?" I asked.

She opened her black valise and pulled out the shirt, waistcoat, hat and trousers that we had discussed before she left. "Fab's trousers," she signed. "Never worn." We both laughed at that.

"There's a cobbler round the corner near Temple Lane, and a haberdasher beside him," I told her. "I can nip round and pick you up some boots and stockings, a young lad's cap. You'll be a fine young man by the time we're done."

Her hair shone in the firelight. Her nose and chin were so

dainty, I wondered if Mr. Todd wouldn't guess right away she weren't a boy at all. Still, it was our best chance, or so I thought. She jumped to her feet and shrugged in agreement, then gave me a mock bow. "For you, I will be a boy," she signed.

Feeling brighter than I had in days, I left her sitting by the fire, hurrying out with a bag full of coins, determined to return quickly with everything we needed to make her mine.

A half hour later, I came back to the shop to find Aphra staring into the fireplace grate. It had died down nearly to cinders. She looked up at me, her eyes shining with tears. I didn't know if she was happy or sad, but she gave me a small smile and sighed. She put her teacup down. "Go on then, do it," she signed.

With my hands sweaty and fumbling, I fetched a large pair of shears I used to cut open bags of flour, then took a handful of her long, pretty locks and began to cut them off. I tried not to pull hard as lock upon lock fell to the floor around my feet. Such lovely waves and curls. It pained me so to do that to her. I sawed and cut the hair till it was close around her ears and the back of her head. I was no barber like our Mr. Todd. Her hair was as choppy as though I'd cut it with a billhook, but no one would know any better with a cap over top of it.

She put her fingers to her shorn hair. It was a sad sight to see, but she smiled. "Breeze on my neck," she signed. When she saw my unhappiness she took my hand and put it against her cheek to comfort me as she often did. "It's hair. It will grow back."

She stood up, close to the fire, and removed her shift, then dropped it on a chair. Her skin glowed like the moon in the flickering firelight. I took up a length of linen and wrapped it snugly around her chest to flatten her breasts. She winced at the tightness of it but nodded at me to keep going. I pinned the end of the fabric under her arm.

Next I passed her the stockings and undergarments, linen shirt and Fab's never-worn trousers, held up with a pair of braces. I watched Aphra pull on each garment and then step, at last, into the boots. They were a bit big on her, but she carried them off well enough, and when I tied a blue kerchief around her neck and put a flat cap on her head, she certainly looked a boy to me. She began to stand differently, walk differently, tramping about in the boots. She tweaked her cap at me and winked, then signed, "Am I a handsome boy?"

"You are not a boy, but you do look like one. Remember, from now on, you're Toby." I made the signs for T-O-B-Y. She nodded and pointed her thumb towards herself, then spelled it back to me. "T-O-B-Y."

I laughed, but then thought about the next body that would drop at the back of the shop. A bloody noggin hitting the floor and splashing blood up her leg. Her screaming and fainting, and Mr. Todd swiping his razor across her throat. I shuddered and took her by the shoulders. I spoke slowly so she could read every word on my lips. "You must never, ever, go in the back room." A bubble of fear had risen up the back of my throat and threatened to burst. "Promise me."

Her brow wrinkled with concern and her eyes widened. "Why?" she signed.

"It's where we cut up the meat for the pies," I said slowly. "It's not something you should see. Just promise, no matter what you see, no matter how tempted you are to set foot in it, never go in there. For me."

"I promise," she signed. Then, untroubled, she took up a broom and disappeared into the shop. She had work to do, she decided, and it was time to get started.

We had a full day and evening together as I showed her what to clean and how, ways that she could help with the baking, how much each pie and patty sold for, and what would need washing up at the end of the day. She saw that it was hard work, and she didn't shy away from it. By the time we went to bed, we had a head start on the morning. Upstairs, Mr. Todd was eerily quiet, like a ghost of himself. I knew we would see him soon enough. The question was when.

We didn't have to wait too long. The next morning, we weren't even open an hour before Mr. Todd appeared amongst the throng of men waiting in line for their pies. He spotted her right away, sweeping near the front door. She hadn't slept well in my narrow bed, so she was yawning and scratching as she worked.

Mr. Todd frowned, then came over to me with a menacing air about him, demanding to know who the boy was.

Calmly I lay a few pies out on a tray. I'd been thinking about what to tell him and had my story ready. "He's my nephew. My poor sister's died, and I've had to take him in. I had to close the shop yesterday so I could fetch him."

Mr. Todd grabbed me hard by the arm and dragged me away from the counter. A few of the men shouted in protest, clamouring for their pies, but Mr. Todd ignored them. He pushed me through the door into the back, squeezing my arm so hard I gasped.

"What are you playing at, bringing a boy into the middle of

our arrangement? Are you mad?" It was exactly the reaction I had expected of him.

I yanked my arm away and rubbed it. "Listen, I'm run off my feet, you can see what it's like up front. I need the help. And the more pies I sell, the more necks you get in your chair. Don't worry. I'll keep him out of your way, for all our sakes. Besides, he's deaf and don't speak except with his hands. He can't hear a thing, and he won't say nothing to anyone."

"I don't like it," Mr. Todd growled. "I don't like strangers mucking around in my business."

"You're not the only one with business here. Do you think I'd bring in someone I didn't trust? He'll never know where the meat comes from. Besides, it'll be better for both of us, we'll seem on the up and up. Nothing suspicious to see here if we've got a boy about the place."

"Deaf and mute," Mr. Todd grumbled. "The less he hears and says, the better."

Mr. Todd still wasn't happy, and not just with the boy. He seemed strange, even for him, then I realised he was afraid. It looked odd since I'd never seen it in his face before. He had been more wary of late, pacing through his rooms all night, always looking out the windows, listening down the stairs. "Pull yourself together or the customers will get suspicious. You're acting like I'm your wife."

His face pinched at that, but he grumbled and followed me back into the shop. I approached Aphra and tapped her shoulder. She spun around in surprise, but relaxed when she saw it was me. "This gentleman's asking your name," I signed.

"T-O-B-Y," she signed to him, while moving her lips.

"Toby," I said.

Mr. Todd asked how I knew the words to communicate with a deaf boy. "Our families grew up together. We all learnt it." He stared at her but she was smart enough to turn away so he couldn't look close at her face. She tugged her cap down on her forehead. He grunted at me again, then left without another word, and trudged back up the stairs.

I was relieved. He wouldn't toss Toby out into the street, at least for now. But just as I was about to tell her, the door opened, and she had to scurry out of the way of the man pushing past the counter towards the tables at the side. I was about to scold him when I saw it was a familiar face, and not one I wished to see again: Mr. Jonas, the doctor's mate. I caught the lick of dark hair hanging over his forehead, the silver-tipped cane, the smell of his tobacco. I rushed back toward the counter, checked on a few trays of pies, trying to catch my breath, and doled out as many as I could to the customers waiting there. Not even a minute passed before men sitting at the tables hollered, but I stayed quiet and hoped Mr. Jonas was gone when I turned around.

As I looked out across the shop I saw that he had seated himself at one of the tables, and sitting with him, staring into his eyes like a moony girl, was Mr. Jennings. Though Jonas was a rat, he was a handsome one. I reckoned that lock of hair had hooked Mr. Jennings's attention.

Aphra tugged on my sleeve and asked what was wrong. I told her I was feeling a bit wobbly was all, the heat from ovens and all the patrons, then I said she looked peaky herself and told her to have a lie down. She often napped in the afternoon back at the brothel, so it wasn't a strange idea. In fact, she yawned as I said it. "Go on," I shooed her. "Everything's fine." I gave her a grin and a pat on the shoulder. After she disappeared through the door, I picked up a serving tray and loaded it with pies. I'd have to deal with Mr. Jonas one way or another.

I shifted the tray and steadied myself as the line of men jumped on the pies like flies to dung. I sold a dozen or so and pocketed the coins, then wiped my hands on my apron and looked all about. Mr. Jennings waved and shouted at me to bring two pies to his table. One for him and one for his companion.

"Mrs. Lovett, a delight as always! Best pies you'll ever eat," he said to Mr. Jonas.

"Pleasure," I said, deepening my voice. I put the pies down on their table and kept my face turned away, but Jonas squinted at me all the same and asked if we'd ever met. My heart beat so hard I thought they both would hear it. I said I'd never seen him before unless he'd wandered past the window.

"I'm only a poor young widow, sir. I run the pie shop since my husband died. I'm here morning, noon and night."

"Perhaps you saw Mrs. Lovett when her husband was still alive," Mr. Jennings offered. "Maybe you had a pie here? Is he familiar to you, Mrs. Lovett? Surely you wouldn't forget such a dashing gentleman." Jennings looked like he'd rather be eating something other than what was on his plate.

I said I was sure I didn't know the gent, begging his pardon. Mr. Jonas asked when my husband passed away. I told him not long ago and excused myself as more men gathered at the counter. As I walked away I heard Jennings say, "She's not usually so brisk."

To my horror I realised Mr. Todd had come back into the

shop. He watched Jonas and Jennings, talking and laughing and tasting their pies. Had he heard what we had said together? Like a mongrel, he'd sniffed out trouble. No doubt he wondered who Mr. Jonas was to me.

Then, as if the whole thing were planned, Mr. Jonas reached into his waistcoat and took out a fat gold pocket watch, engraved on both sides. It let out a little chime as the hour had just turned one. The case caught the light from a nearby lamp, and Mr. Todd, with his eye for jewels and gold, didn't miss it. Just for good measure, I passed close by him and said in a low voice, "That's a fine piece, don't you think? Would look nice in your own pocket."

Mr. Todd moved past as if he hadn't heard me, but made his way to the table. I couldn't tell what he said to Mr. Jonas, but the pocket watch came out again and Mr. Todd was given the chance to admire it. Jonas turned it this way and that, showing him the case and chain. My curiosity got the better of me and I stepped up to the table with a tray of fresh pies.

"You do have a bit of a shadow along your jawline," Mr. Jennings was saying, helping himself to a pie. "I've sat in Todd's chair myself. He gives very good service indeed. You'll be a new man by the time he's done." Mr. Todd could be charming when he wanted to be, so he offered Mr. Jonas his Wednesday Special and said he'd polish him off nicely.

Jonas shook his head and said he'd have to decline, that he was only stopping in for a moment before heading off to another appointment. "Not to worry," Mr. Todd said. "I'll keep my parlour open just for you. Come by when it's quieter, say around seven. The first shave is with my compliments."

"I will consider it." Mr. Jonas got to his feet and nodded to Mr. Jennings, thanking him for the pie. I was never so glad to see the back of a man, but was disappointed he hadn't ended up in Mr. Todd's chair.

"I say," Mr. Jennings said after Jonas had left the shop. "I think your Mr. Todd rather fancies my friend Jonas."

"He might at that," I said as I picked up the plates from the table. "But he does like a fresh face to try out his skills, and a new neck." Mr. Jennings nodded and asked for another pie to take away, and I was more than happy to oblige.

The hour of seven came and went with no sign of Mr. Jonas. I had set Aphra to wiping down some pans while I got to work on my pastry. A quarter hour passed, and I had all but given up hope when a cab pulled up outside and the man I dreaded stepped out, his cape flapping about his shoulders as it caught the evening breeze. I took a step back into the gloom so he wouldn't catch me staring. He stopped for a moment, peered about, then went round to Mr. Todd's stairs. I heard him thump thump his way up, then the door above swinging open and shut. I looked over at my dear Aphra. She hadn't seen, and of course hadn't heard a thing. It was best that I go back to my pastry and act as if it was a night like any other. After all, Mr. Todd might change his mind about polishing off Mr. Jonas. It had been known to happen.

A few minutes later I heard a scuffle above our heads near the back of the shop, like a litter of pigeons attacking some scraps in the street. A gasp and a gurgle, some thrashing about. Then a heavy hard thud in my back room, enough to make the floorboards jump.

Aphra poked up her head and looked at me, her eyes round with fear. "What was that?" she signed, startled. Back at the brothel, Fab would sometimes scare the girls with stories of robbers popping through windows in the thick of the night; Aphra would read his lips and be afraid. I put a hand on her shoulder to calm her.

"It's all right," I told her. "Probably a side of beef fallen from a hook. Mr. Todd can help me with it later. Not like it will get up and walk away!" She saw that I wasn't frightened, so she turned back to the pans and scratched at them with a soft cloth and salt until they were gleaming.

Later that night, long past when Aphra had gone to our bed and shadows were stretching across the shop like cats, Mr. Todd appeared with his hair quite a mess, smelling of sweat and barber's soap. "The boy is asleep?" he asked. I nodded. He nodded back, asked me to fetch a bit of gin. "We should deal with our friend out back." I couldn't help it, I shivered a little. It caught his eye. "No time to get squeamish, Mrs. Lovett. Oh, speaking of time." He reached into his pocket, pulled out Mr. Jonas's watch, twirled it on the end of its chain. "Eye of a magpie, that's what you've got. I might get a new set of blades out of this."

I poured him a thimble of gin and a nip for myself, then we went out back and started our nasty work. Todd had made a mess of Jonas to be sure, his throat slashed up to his ear and a flap of cheek hanging loose. His shirt collar and waistcoat, his whole front, had been drenched with blood. The layers of cloth were stiff with it.

I remember thinking it would be more work to pull off his

clothes than it would be to carve him up. "Go back to the kitchen and bring the kettle," I said. Todd didn't like taking orders from me, but he also didn't want to waste time. He brought back the kettle, the water still hot from the washing, and poured it on the body where the blood was thick. The skin blistered up but that didn't matter to me, I was able to use one of my long meat forks to pull the clothes up, and my shears to cut them off. Soon enough, the bugger was naked and ready for the knife.

"Who was he to you?" Todd asked. "You knew the man and you were glad to see him gone. Was he the baby's father?"

"I don't know what you're on about," I said. "Get him onto the hook." He did as I told him, lifting Jonas up and shoving him onto the meat hook so that it pierced through his back under his shoulder and poked out the front of his chest. Another gout of blood squirted out. I waited till it was down to a trickle then sliced and carved his flesh with Mr. Todd watching. It was the quietest he'd ever been with me.

"He had lots of questions about you," he said finally. "How long you'd been here, how long you'd known me. If you had a sister who'd just had a baby, that sort of thing."

"What did you tell him?" I asked as I dropped bits of meat into one bucket and then another. "I guess it doesn't much matter now, does it?" I could feel his eyes on me, trying to see into my mind, my heart. I had my back to a killer in a room full of knives and cleavers. He could end me if he wanted to. How did I know he wouldn't?

"Will you always be a mystery to me, Mrs. Lovett?" he asked.

I wasn't sure what to say at first. I stopped my work and turned to him, knife in hand, blood up to my armpits, sweat dripping down my brow. "The woman you see is the woman I am, Mr. Todd. My life's what made me. No mystery at all." I turned back to the carcass, just a few more minutes to go. "What about you?" I asked. "What rattles around in that head of yours and keeps you up at all hours?" He wasn't expecting that. He went so still I thought he'd stopped breathing. I looked over my shoulder and saw it in his face as plain as day. He had his own past, and in it, something that pained him deeply. But I wasn't ready for the tale he told me.

He began to speak of a wife and son. His wife had been uncommonly beautiful, his son small in stature but bright and quick. His voice softened at the love he had for them, and the pride he had in his boy. I'd never heard him speak that way before, nor would I ever again. Mr. Todd said he'd worked as a ratcatcher and grave digger to put bread on the table, and his wife had taken in slopwork. Though they didn't have much, they'd been as content as any family could be. I was shocked when he mentioned Ratcliff, and the docks, and spoke of a little flat they kept over a tobacconist's shop because it sounded like one very near to where I'd grown up.

"What happened to them?" I whispered, as though we were speaking of the dead, and it turned out we were.

Mr. Todd said his son liked to play in the gutter with some local boys. There wasn't nothing unusual about that, but one day his son chased a ball into the street and was knocked flat by a carriage. He was taken to hospital, and it was there he bled to death that very night.

The shadows seemed to creep in closer around us, and the blood rushed in my ears as I thought about the little boy whose leg I'd sawn off and the pitiful child's skeleton Dr. C kept in his surgery. Maybe it seems fantastic, but the world is such a peculiar place, I've learned that people you thought you'd never see again find their way back to you. You've been tied to them all along and didn't know it. And others you loved and built your life around were taken from you forever.

"What did he look like, your boy?"

"A little devil he was, quick on his feet with big eyes and chestnut hair like his mum."

"And his name?" I held my breath waiting for the answer.

"Daniel," he said. "His name was Daniel Todd." He spoke so quietly and looked so miserable I could hardly bear it.

I had to say something. And I didn't believe it myself, but all I could think of was, "I'm sure little Daniel is with God now and watches over you." I'd heard priests say the same to grieving mothers, though it sounded empty every time I heard it. But maybe it gave them comfort.

Mr. Todd barked out his wicked laugh and said, "What God takes a man's innocent child, then drives his wife mad with grief?"

I put my knife down and wiped my bloody hands on my apron. "Your wife's locked away?"

He nodded. "She's in Bedlam this very day." He let out a cough to cover a sob. It reminded me of my father. "Enough talk," he said. "Sun's about to rise." I nodded, motioned for him to help me. He lifted the remains of the carcass off the hook and laid it down onto the floor. We wrapped it in sackcloth, not too tight, leaving some room to let the rats in, then dragged it out back and tipped it into the hole.

I looked over at the demon that was Mr. Todd and saw just a hint of tenderness. How queer to see both things in him together. I couldn't help asking. "Do you ever see her? Your wife?"

Mr. Todd shook his head and dropped his chin to his chest.

"Is that why you do these things?" I asked. "You're angry with God?"

He shot me such a hateful look, I thought it would knock me over. "This pit right here?" he said. "This is my God. Don't get too close to the edge of it."

He dropped the grate over the hole and went back inside. As he did, I saw something out of the corner of my eye, a flutter on the other side of the fence. A figure, I thought. I pulled my shawl tight to my neck, went up and peered over into the street. A fidgety little nightjar was perched on an old tin bucket with a fat brown beetle squirming in its beak. I watched it swallow its supper, then when it spied me peeking at it, it whirled about and flew off towards the church. A bad omen those birds were, but bad omens were everywhere in London. Everywhere you turned, every place you looked. I peered around the alley, up towards the street. Nobody. Nothing.

I went back inside to mop the floor and grind and stew the meat before Aphra woke from her sleep. I heard a few creaks above my head. It was Mr. Todd pacing from room to room once more. Then the first light of morning began to warm the skies.

AUGUST 18

Proverbs 17:4
A wicked person listens to deceitful lips; a liar pays attention to a destructive tongue.

I will say I wish to God that Mr. Todd never laid eyes on my Aphra, or Toby as we called her. I thought it such a clever trick to make that beautiful creature into a boy, as if no one could tell by the way she moved and the gentle air about her. I shall write this part as though I don't know what is to come. As though we were happy together for all our days.

In the end Mr. Todd gave in and let Toby stay, as long as the boy kept to the front of the shop and didn't find out how our business was run. I swore I would keep our secrets safe. And so, for a time, Aphra and I were happy together. We were freer than we'd been our whole lives and didn't answer to nobody but ourselves. But we lived on a dagger's edge, always afraid of who might come through the pie shop door. Maybe a customer from Madame Quince's, or another friend of the doctor's, or even that miserable wife of Fiddler's set on another round of screeching.

Those nights when I thought there might be a God, I wondered what he was punishing me for. To have put me through so much, so many things I didn't deserve. But I'm not a crying sort of girl, not anymore, and I won't be starting now.

Even though my eyes are stinging as I think back on my dear Aphra. Would she have loved me the same if she knew what I was, what I had done? She only ever saw the best parts of me. That's the way I wanted it.

I've done penance for my crimes, enough for me and Mr. Todd many times over. I'm ashamed the people closest to me didn't know me at all. My mother, my Aphra, even Mr. Todd. They only saw a smidge of what's in my soul.

The only one who knows the whole of my life, Miss Gibson, is you.

To put my life on these pages has helped to quiet my mind, but it has also opened old wounds, and fed the fire within me to see my son. I've given you what you've asked for. My own true story. Please help me. I must lay eyes on my boy even if it's the last thing I do. I must explain to him that he was wanted and it weren't me who gave him up. Maybe he'll forgive me. It's the only thing I ask for now.

Those last few weeks before our lives fell to ruin, I saw what was coming but could not stop it nor step out of its way. If Mr. Todd's mind bent to a wicked path after the loss of his wife and son, it only grew worse after he spoke of it. His hair was wilder, his laugh more fiendish. He grew suspicious of everyone who came into the shop. He talked to shadows, and hid in the corners. The littlest things caused offence. I feared more and more for my own life, but Mr. Todd never turned his razor on me because he needed me. I was the one who concealed his crimes. That tiny smidge of softness I'd seen in him when he spoke of his family, that was gone entirely.

All that time, poor Aphra swept the shop, greased pie pans,

and put them in the oven, but never knew the meat came from anywhere but the kill-calfs in Barking or the slaughter-men in Smithfield. She rose before me and made steaming cups of tea. She lit the fire in the grate and cleaned the shop while I ground the meat with pork and spices and stuffed it into pie crusts. She fed the fires in the ovens while the pies baked golden brown, and she served them to the customers. Even so, Mr. Todd went dark on Toby, fearing he would betray us. Aphra felt the weight of his stare and grew afraid of him, she could hardly sleep. I said I'd protect her with my life, but she knew Mr. Todd could bring us both down without a sweat.

It wasn't long after we rid ourselves of Jonas that Mr. Todd got the itch again, hovering at the back of the shop and glaring at my customers, looking for one or two to be sent his way. I saw my chance to give him what he wanted, and take revenge on the brute who had brought me to my lowest. I knew the doctor would show up on our doorstep before long, looking for Jonas. Maybe with Mr. Jennings in tow. One morning after the early crowd had cleared from the shop, I said to him, "Mr. Todd, I believe I know someone who would benefit from a visit to your chair. The father of the child we once spoke of. A man of means, with jewels on his rings and a silver-tipped cane. And a purse full of coins, no doubt. He has lived too long by half, in my opinion. If you like, I'll invite him to your parlour. Tonight."

Mr. Todd's grin spread across his face like a disease. "It would be my pleasure, Mrs. Lovett. Anything for a friend."

Once Aphra was awake, I got the nicest bit of paper I could find and had her write out a note for me in her pretty handwriting.

I'm tired of hiding.

You can have our son for your own if we arrange terms.

Meet me tonight, half-eight at Lovett's Pie Shop,

Fleet Street near Chancery Lane. Half-eight, no later, no sooner.

I'll be waiting.

Peggy

Her eyes grew wide as she wrote out each word, looking at me with alarm. I soothed her, told her that all would be well, that I knew how to handle both the doctor and Mr. Todd. She was to wait in my room that night after closing and not open the door to anyone but me. Then I reached into my pocket and pulled out the string of pearls I'd nicked from Mr. Todd's parlour while he was going round the shops looking for new blades. I gave the pearls to Aphra and told her that she was to make use of them in whatever way she wished if something were to happen to me. She was right fearful, but she nodded and stayed in the shadows for the rest of the day.

As I closed the shop that afternoon, I gave the note and three shillings to a cabman on the corner, and told him to deliver the message to Dr. C in Highgate, to be sure he put it in the doctor's hand and not anyone else's. All day I was nervous, but I knew he'd come. Word of our son would draw him out. I was taunting a dangerous cur, but I knew the end was coming and I wanted what I deserved. I'd stand and watch as Mr. Todd opened his throat, listen to him gurgle and gasp. Smell the hot wet blood as it gushed out of him like a fountain. I'd carve him up with my cleaver and then kick him into the pit, feed all his best bits to the customers for free.

This villainy is what brought you to my doorstep, isn't it? If I hadn't been a monster, you wouldn't have looked for me. You wouldn't care a whit for my story. But now I've given you most of it, we're almost there. And so, like Mr. Todd with a neck in his chair, I'll pull out my own sweet blade and finish it off.

Aphra didn't know what I was plotting, and I couldn't tell her. I didn't want her to see what was in the most poisonous part of my heart. The part that didn't have her in it. I asked her to make us a bit of supper while I tidied the trays and tins for the morning, then sent her off to sleep, stroking her hair till her breathing slowed. I waited for the doctor with a candle at my elbow and a bottle of gin. One glass, two glasses, and the room went a bit soft at the edges. But my mind was keen.

At half-eight sharp the doctor hammered at the door. When I opened it, he crossed the stoop, bringing in a cold wind that made my candleflame leap. He took in the room, to make sure we were alone, then turned a menacing glare upon me. He still had a mark across his face where I'd whacked him with the poker.

"What, no hello?" I said, trying to act like my heart wasn't about to hammer out of my chest. He looked like he wanted to wrap his hands around my throat and throttle me.

"Let's get on with it," he snarled.

I gestured towards an empty chair then sat opposite him and poured two glasses of gin. One for us each. He tossed his back all in one go. That was good. I had a mind to get him fuddled so Mr. Todd could shave him that much closer.

"Where's the boy?" he asked.

"Somewhere safe."

"I didn't come here to play games. Give me my son."

"I got a few things to say first." I poured more gin into the doctor's glass. He stared at it as though it was poison. "You'd best be polite and drink it," I said.

He drank the whole lot in one go then slammed the glass on the table. "You stole cash and jewellery from my wife, split my face open when you were caught, and murdered an innocent girl, whose body we found in the ice house after you fled."

The cheek of it! "Ain't you the clever one, pinning your crimes on me! Like I wouldn't have a story or two to tell about you."

"And who do you think they'd believe? A raggedy thieving housemaid, or a respected doctor from Highgate?" He sneered at me, very pleased with himself.

I poured him another gin. "What about your wife?" I asked. "What did she do to deserve being carved up like that?"

"She married me," he snarled. "Sacrifices must be made in the name of science, not that I expect you to understand. I'm preparing a lecture for the medical school about the circulatory system and the chambers of the heart. I'll show them hers. Or yours."

My skin prickled. "You killed her?"

"Perhaps. Or perhaps she died of natural causes. She was in poor health for years." The leering grin he gave me was awful, and I knew he'd finished her off at last. At least she was out of her misery, poor thing, but my heart chilled as I thought about her standing in the window with her eyes plucked out.

Mr. Todd would get revenge for her, for me and my baby, for the girl in the ice house, for Mr. Todd's son, for everyone he'd ever hurt.

"How's your friend Mr. Jonas getting on?" I asked.

Right away my question made him suspicious. I thought I'd pushed too far and near kicked myself for it. His face was stone, he didn't know what to make of it. "I haven't seen him lately, though he often travels to the continent. I imagine he's catting about in Paris or Rome."

I raised my glass as if to make a toast. "I suppose you'll see him again before long."

He grabbed my wrist across the table and gripped it very hard till I yelped. I dropped the gin glass onto the floor where it smashed to bits. "Where is my son?"

"Ask the barber upstairs," I said, my teeth clenched tight, with sparks of pain shooting into my hand.

"Stop taking the piss and let's get on with it," he growled as he released his grip on me.

"Mr. Todd made arrangements for the boy to be raised in the countryside. But don't fret. Toss a few quid my way and I'll have him send the boy to you," I said. "Those are my terms. I reckon he's best with his father. What a grand life he'll have in your posh house. I'm sure Mrs. Dawson will be as kind to him as she was to me."

The doctor stood up so fast he knocked his chair over and ordered me to take him upstairs to the barber or I'd pay the price for crossing him. I played the frightened, simpering girl and led him up the stairs, half dizzy with excitement. I knocked on Mr. Todd's door and announced our arrival. He let us in, appearing with a fresh apron over his nice waistcoat, like he'd dressed up for the occasion.

"Tell me where my son is," the doctor said, very rude.

"What an unpleasant start to our conversation," Mr. Todd said. "Never mind. You look like you've had a long day." He patted his chair. "I reckon you could use a shave. Let me polish you off while we talk, eh? No charge for such an honoured guest."

"I don't want a shave. I'm here for information."

"And I will give it to you, of course. I have no wish to keep your son from you. In fact, I am the one who persuaded Margery to contact you. A boy needs his father."

I nodded. "If it weren't for him, you'd have never heard a whisper from me."

The doctor didn't know what to believe.

"Mrs. Lovett, could you leave us?" Mr. Todd said. "If the gentleman and I speak alone, I think everyone will get what they want."

I felt so much fear in that moment, that all the horrors of the world were on my doorstep. I wanted to laugh, to cry, to fold myself up tight and disappear. But I could not show any weakness. I had to be strong and I had to be sharp, for my son wherever he was, for Aphra and for myself. I walked out of the barber shop but left the door ajar and peered through the gap. I couldn't hear what they were saying. The doctor waved his hands about while Mr. Todd nodded sympathetically. He helped the doctor into the chair, easy as anything, then hung a cloth over the doctor's shoulders, and leaned him back. "That treacherous bitch," the doctor finished, I heard that clear enough. Mr. Todd just nodded and grinned his awful grin.

He turned away to mix up a cake of shaving soap in a bowl while the doctor railed on about something. "The stars were aligned!" he shouted at one point. "My son is destined for greatness!" It was maddening, not being able to hear more. I stepped closer, had my ear to the crack of the door as Mr. Todd put down the bowl, as though he'd thought of something. When he reached into his pocket I saw a flash of silver. He stood behind the barber chair and made to draw his shining blade across the doctor's throat. I leaned in closer to see the brute's bloody end and stumbled against the door. I froze as it swung open with a loud squeal. The doctor looked at the door in shock and jumped up just as the gleaming razor sliced into his flesh.

Ruby blood splashed onto the cloth, the chair, the floor, the wall. I thought Mr. Todd had done it, but the doctor sprang out of the chair, howling. There was a gash across his cheek that stretched up into his eye, piercing it. He had his hand to his face with blood running through his fingers. Mr. Todd lunged at him again, but the doctor fought back and knocked the razor from Mr. Todd's hand. I watched it skitter across the floor. Snatching up a walking stick from inside the door, I raced at the doctor with a shriek and swung that stick with all my might. The silver end of it cracked his temple and the skin split open. It was deeply satisfying, and though he howled in agony, it didn't take him down. He looked ghoulish, with blood running down his face, one eye blind and the other wide with fear.

Mr. Todd tried to pick up his razor, but when he leaned over the doctor kicked him in the face and legged it towards the door. He ran past me with his cheek gaping open. The bloody wound went through the flesh to his teeth. The doctor was so frightened I could almost smell it on him. Mr. Todd snatched up the razor blade and gave chase.

When the doctor got to the stairs Aphra was standing there, dressed as Toby of course, come to see what was the matter. She looked like a ghost, white as chalk and filled with terror. She let out a brutal scream the likes of which I'd never heard before, then attacked him with her candlestick. But she only landed a glancing blow before he grabbed her roughly and threw her down the stairs. Her skull cracked on the steps as she fell, and she tumbled till she was in a heap at the bottom. I felt each hit in my own bones, and I screamed, though I barely heard myself for shock.

Aphra lay on the floor, all bent and deathly still. The doctor ran past her like she were rubbish, with his hand to his cheek trying to keep the flesh together. He couldn't see properly from all the blood, and he'd hurt his leg. Mr. Todd thundered down the stairs and went after him again. The doctor was as furious as a trapped animal. He turned over tables and chairs, pushing them at Mr. Todd. I knew it was the end. We'd never get out of it unless Mr. Todd finished the doctor off, but a chair caught him across the chest, and he staggered to his knees.

I crouched close over Aphra and saw her eyes were wide and full of tears. Her breathing was ragged, her hair all wet and red. "Come on, love," I said. "We'll get you all fixed up." I knew it was hopeless, but I wouldn't let her go without a fight. If God had any mercy at all, he'd have spared her and put me out of my misery. It was cruel to take her life and leave me behind without her. I put my arm around her and hauled her to her feet. We stumbled through the pie shop, past the men battling like dogs. I'd hurt my foot and winced with every step. I tried not to think about how badly hurt Aphra was or I'd have collapsed.

Mr. Todd wrestled the doctor to the ground and put his knee on his chest. He drew back his hand to make another slash across the wretched man's throat when the front door crashed open and Miss Johanna rushed in like a banshee, her teeth bared, her hair untied and wild. She had a pistol in her hand with a long thin barrel.

"Mr. Todd!" she shouted. She pointed the gun and cocked it. I heard my own breath, and Aphra's gasping. The shop was dark and murky, the candle flames bright points of light. I smelled blood, and rotten pig's meat, and the muck of London streets, and my mother's oil of roses. I didn't know if it was real or not. I didn't know if anything was.

Mr. Todd looked up in shock. He saw Miss Johanna and he saw the gun, and he laughed his wicked laugh. It filled the pie shop and rang in my ears. The loudest, cruellest sound I'd ever heard.

Miss Johanna pulled the trigger and the pistol fired, throwing back her hand. Mr. Todd's laugh stuck in his throat and he dropped like a stone. I saw a spot of blood on his shirt where his heart would have been. I watched it bloom. "That's for Arthur Thornhill," she said. "The man I was to marry." She threw the gun down and wiped tears from her eyes. "That was his pistol, from when he served in Burmah. And now you'll not ever hurt another soul."

I didn't know if Miss Johanna was in a state to shoot me too so I hurried to the back door with Aphra, fast as I could. The doctor was on the ground next to Mr. Todd, holding his face and bleeding all over the pie shop floor. I'd never be free of him, long as he knew where to find me.

Aphra could barely walk, weak and heavy she was as I dragged her towards the grate. I lifted the iron cover and pushed her into the pit as gentle as I could. She landed on the bodies below. I couldn't see nothing in the dark hole. I dropped down after her.

I felt the pile of corpses under me. All arms and legs, wet and stinking, soft flesh slipping off bone. Sweat and rot and blood. A shaft of moonlight came through the hole up above. I felt for Aphra in the dark and pulled her into the light so I could see her pretty face. "My little goose," I whispered. Cradling her head to my breast, I kissed her forehead. She gasped and murmured. I shushed her and pressed her fingers to my throat and said I loved her and that I was sorry for all she'd gone through. I was sorry I couldn't protect her. Then she went limp and still, and was gone. Just like that. In the end, her death was on my hands, and the heartbreak of it is always with me.

Up above I heard shouting. It was Miss Johanna and the doctor. My heart jumped. I peeled off Aphra's boy clothes and struggled out of my frock. I tugged on the shirt, trousers, and jacket, and piled my hair under the flat cap. I pushed my fingers into Aphra's pocket and found the cursed string of pearls and, to my shock, the paper from the Foundling Hospital and the earring. The shouting got louder. The doctor leaned his head in the hole. He shouted for me. I glanced up. His face was a mask of blood. I knew he couldn't see me in the dark. I jammed everything in my pocket and scrambled off the pile of bodies, their bony hands clawing at me as I twisted myself free. I ran off through the underground tunnel towards the underside of St. Dunstan's, best as I could remember it. I left behind the pie shop, the doctor, Mr. Todd, and dear Aphra. I never looked back.

I climbed up into the churchyard and ran into the night, hurrying through the crowded streets. "Hey, you, boy!" someone shouted, but I never turned round. I never shook the feeling that the doctor was on my heels. My lungs burned, my legs were weak with shock and fear. I saw Aphra's face, staring up into nothing, dead in the pit with all those butchered men. She never deserved an end like that, and it was all down to me. I have never forgiven myself to this day.

September 15, 1887

Dear Miss Gibson,

I am afraid I owe you the deepest of apologies. Months have passed since our last correspondence, and I neglected to pursue your enquiries with the diligence that I promised. Had I done so, I could have located your mysterious doctor so much sooner. As it transpired, several of our older members received word of your research through other channels and were able to piece together the identity of the gentleman you seek: Sir Charles Cornell, 1st Baronet. He was what was known at the time as a hobby surgeon: not an accredited physician and therefore not a member of our college but a keen practitioner of the surgical craft and in particular the treatment of women's troubles. In earlier days, he was a close acquaintance of Sir Henry Halford and Sir William Gull, Physicians-in-Ordinary to the Royal Family, and was called upon to consult on cases arising among the ladies-in-waiting and others in Her Majesty's retinue, administering pessaries and unguents, performing examinations and minor surgeries. He may have been known informally as "the doctor" to his patients, close friends, and possibly his staff.

Sir Charles did indeed have a well-appointed house in Highgate village where he held medical offices of some sophistication. He had a wife, a frail young thing. She bore him a son, sadly stillborn. The ordeal left her barren and bedridden for much of their marriage despite his many ministrations and interventions; eventually her heart gave out and she died. Interesting though: a young maid in his employ found herself in the family way as sometimes happens. In her shame and remorse she left the household, and by all accounts ended up in dire straits. When the time came, she gave her baby over to the Foundling Hospital. She went quite mad, it seems, and disappeared from view, but Sir Charles was able to locate and claim the boy, and raise him as his own.

Sir Charles is no longer with us; he passed more than fifteen years ago. However, his son is now a fine gentleman, Dr. James Cornell, a physician of considerable repute who lives at the family home in Highgate. And so it was that yesterday I received a message from Dr. Cornell, who is very eager to meet with you. I enclose his card, which he urged me to pass on to facilitate your acquaintance. Please be kind enough to convey my very best wishes when you see him.

On a much graver note, please allow me to offer my sincere condolences on the death of your father. He was a great man, revered and respected by all in his acquaintance. Although he left our circle many years ago, he is remembered by the Masonic fraternity as a man of tremendous compassion, integrity and discretion. His tragic and senseless loss must be devastating to you, your mother, your household and your family. I am certain that the criminal responsible for this vile deed will be apprehended in short order.

Yours very truly,

Dr. Philip Montague

THE ROYAL COLLEGE OF PHYSICIANS
THE REGENT'S PARK, LONDON

AUGUST 19

Psalms 41:7
All that hate me whisper together against me: against me do they devise my hurt.

This will be goodbye, Miss Gibson. One of the kitchen maids has come to my door, I do not know her name. She was badly burned in a fire as a child; one side of her face is scarred and mottled. She came to tell me that she heard Augustine talking with one of the other Sisters. The gate is to be left unlocked. I'm to be taken at dawn. I thanked her, then asked if I could touch her cheek. She said she wouldn't mind if I did. I ran my fingertips across the scars and asked if they hurt, and curiously she said, "Only in my dreams." This is true for me as well. I dull myself while I'm awake, but in my dreams the pain I've hidden springs to life, fresh and sharp as ever.

As I ducked and dodged through the alleys and shopways along The Strand, the thoughts whirling through my head slowed and fixed themselves upon one thing, one place: Wilfred Street. In my early mornings at the pie shop with Mr. Jennings, when he would keep me company as I pulled the pies from the oven and cooled them on the counter, he spoke of where he lived, a house on Wilfred Street, round the corner from Buckingham Palace. He asked me often to join him for tea or for supper, but in the evenings I was either too tired or too caught up in preparing for the next day's customers. Wilfred Street. I had nowhere else to go, I had no one else to turn to. He had told me once he'd defended monsters, and I felt like a monster then. But Mr. Jennings had never shown me anything but kindness. I was pulled to him like we were attached by a thread. I skittered in and out of the shadows, alert to any ringing bell or burst of shouts that might mean that I'd been sighted. Wilfred Street, was all I could think. Wilfred Street.

It took me close to an hour I'd say but in the end I found the address: a modest house of yellow brick near the end of a long row, with his name engraved on a small brass plate beside the door. It was late and the lights were out, but I knocked and knocked. I knew I looked a fright so I straightened myself as best I could. A witchy old maid with a candle opened the door and turned up her nose at me. "Get off the stoop, you dirty wretch," she spat, and made to shut the door again.

I put my hand against the door to stop it from closing. "Mr. Jennings knows me," I said. "Tell him I've come with a message from Margery Lovett."

She asked me for the message, and I told her it was for him and him alone, then added that Mr. Jennings would be vexed if he learned I'd been turned away. She ordered me to step inside the front door and not an inch further. "You ain't setting foot in my clean parlour looking so filthy." She went off to fetch Mr. Jennings, scowling back at me as she climbed the stairs.

I glanced at myself in a looking glass, and wiped a smudge from my cheek. Then realised I had splotches of blood on me that were hid by the darkness of my jacket and trousers. What would Mr. Jennings think of me? At last, he appeared wearing a fancy smoking robe and a round red hat with a yellow tassel. He frowned when he saw me. "Young man. What has happened? What news have you of Margery Lovett?"

I took off my cap and let my hair fall over my shoulders. "Don't you know me, sir?"

Mr. Jennings was as shocked as I'd ever seen him. "Good heavens. Margery?"

Even though I wanted to be strong, and not one for weeping, I sobbed my eyes out then. "I'm so ashamed to come to you like this. You've no idea the trouble I'm in. I've got nowhere else to go."

Mr. Jennings tut-tutted and told the maid to pour me a bath and give me one of her plain dresses to put on. She weren't too pleased about it but she did what she was told. He said I should go upstairs and clean myself up and we'd share a spot of tea. I could tell him all my troubles over a nice hot cup and a plate of crumpets. I couldn't hardly think of all I'd been through and how I'd tell him any of it.

But once I was all soaked and scrubbed and wrapped in a dressing gown, we sat down together in front of a roaring fire that warmed my face and feet. I slurped the tea and scarfed the crumpets and told Mr. Jennings what I could without him throwing me back out into the street. I said what I knew of Sweeney Todd's history, which may or may not be true. I told him that the doctor who once employed me had come looking for me and our baby, but Mr. Todd attacked him and slashed his face. Then Miss Johanna came in like a bull looking for her missing suitor, and shot Mr. Todd on the spot. I said my shop boy, who I was very fond of, had been cruelly murdered by the doctor, and I told Mr. Jennings how I'd put on Toby's clothes to make my escape, and run through the night to find him. He was the only friend I had in the whole city, I said. He was touched by my tale, and he believed me. I daresay most men wouldn't have.

Mr. Jennings let me stay in a spare room that the maid did up for me. She was cool to me at first, but in time we grew fond of each other, and she kindly kept our secrets.

There was a bit of a stir in the papers, MURDERS and BODIES and MEAT PIES in big black letters, so I kept inside the house for fear of being snatched up and jailed. Then we read in the Times that a woman's body had been found with those in the pit under the pie shop, and that it must have been the monstrous Mrs. Lovett. Aphra's final gift to me, to take the name of Lovett off my shoulders.

Mr. Jennings and I, which is to say Theo and I, were married at the courthouse six months later. I knew he was less inclined toward the ladies, so we never shared a bedroom. But it didn't bother me a whit. As friends, we were happier than most who marry for love or money. I managed the staff, the household, and the accounts, and was as good a wife as any woman ever was.

The week before we married, I showed dear Theo the earring and the receipt for my son. He went to the Foundling Hospital and enquired after the baby. He said he was there for a client that for shame didn't want to be known, but she was the child's last living kin. The hospital searched their files and said they had no matching earring, no such record, and no baby like that had ever been turned in. Ever more determined, Theo arranged a carriage to Highgate a few days later and arrived unannounced at the doctor's house to pay a social call. His plan was to present himself as a collector of unusual objects, with hopes of adding to his collection. It was all for naught. A cautious young woman received him at the door. Yes, it was the doctor's house, she and a small housekeeping staff were preparing it for new tenants. He had been transported to Inverness where his wife's family had an estate. He was not expected to return, the move was thought to be permanent. She knew nothing of his collection, and had not heard tell of a child. Perhaps if he left a card, she could arrange a correspondence and an eventual meeting if he returned for a visit? Theo declined, begging her pardon, and wishing her a good day.

Then, just a few short months after, we read in the evening papers that a Mrs. Antoinette Quince had died in her sleep at the age of seventy-five. A benefactress to the arts and to young women of the Empire, it seems, known on either side of the Channel for her kindness and generosity. With her demise, the whores of Mayfair were scattered to the winds. The Symposia was no more.

Every evening after that, for nearly twenty years, Theo and I sat by the same fire. He wore his smoking robe and cap and read a few chapters from one of his many books, while I took up my embroidery hoop and thread. We shared pots of Earl Grey and plates of fancies while he told me about the goings-on at court. Once or twice a year we had a few of Theo's friends to the house for supper or a little party. Once we made a trip to the seaside, a windy and gloomy journey by train that brightened as soon as we set our feet upon the shore. We made a happy family together, Theo and I, though of course we never did have a child.

How I missed my son in all that time! The tiniest thing would bring him to mind, swaddled in his hospital blanket, his wisps of black hair, his flaming cheeks and dark feverish eyes. Did Madame Quince lay claim to him without the precious items, or had he been raised by a family somewhere in the countryside? Had he even survived? I told myself he had, for the other outcome I couldn't bear to think on.

Many years later, I came down one morning for breakfast to find Theo at the bottom of the stairs, flat on his back, gaping at the ceiling. I thought he'd taken a tumble, but in the end it turned out his heart had failed him. I put his head in my lap and told him he was kinder and gentler to me than any man had ever been, and I couldn't thank him enough for it. When the undertaker came and spirited him away, I found my life empty once again.

I gave him as lavish a funeral as I could manage. Theo deserved all that and more. I'd had a lovely headstone with his name carved on it. I wanted to give him a weeping angel, but it would have cost a sum that could run his household for a year. In the end I gave him an urn and a drape. The stone mason said it showed sorrow, and the veil between Heaven and Earth. That was fitting, I thought. I felt the veil between us was thin, that his hand was always on my shoulder.

When all the other mourners left and it was just me by myself, I knelt down at the edge of his grave and dropped in my black silk wiper wrapped around the sailor's string of pearls. They fell onto the coffin with a clatter like bones. But my final mistake was being the last to leave and letting my face be seen. For though I'd just buried my husband, and was walking and weeping alone, a pair of hands grabbed me from behind and threw me into the back of a large black carriage parked at the cemetery's edge. I got a glimpse out the window as they carried me away. A dark figure stood at the side, a tall stern man in a silk top hat and mourning cloak with a black satin patch strung over his eye: it was none other than Dr. C.

The doctor had never forgiven what Todd and I had done to him. Twenty years he waited! He had me locked up in this Priory to perish here, forgotten, to live out the rest of my wretched life. Why he never snuffed me out and stuck me in a pauper's grave, I will never know. The will of God, or maybe the devil? It hardly matters now. You've found me, Miss Gibson, and now I leave with you the emerald earring, and the receipt for the Foundling Hospital which I have carried with me since the day I took them from Aphra's pocket. For the last time, I beg you. Please find my son. I don't know what the future holds. The Sisters here are my jailers and will never let me go beyond these walls. They will hide me until the end of my days.

That is all, Miss Gibson. You have my whole story. Heaven only knows what the future holds. It's all in the Lord's hands, and your hands, now.

September the 18th, 1887

Dear Miss Gibson,

I am sorry you will never read this, but I wanted to write you all the same. I'm so grateful for all you've done for me. And I'm so happy that in your final moments, you got to meet my son.

He's a fine strapping lad, isn't he! Takes after both his father and his mother. Your enquiries were what led him to me. He's the one who pulled me out of that terrible Priory and back to the physician's house in Highgate. He owns it now, and I'm the lady of the house—fancy that! And after all these years I still have that brass key, and still it opens every door. Including the ones not opened but in secret.

He's a proper doctor, he is, he has his papers and everything. And he has all his father's clients and connections. His father was a hard man, and he raised a harder son, but still he has room in his heart to love and forgive his old mum.

He took me to a show the other night, a penny gaff. It was a huge surprise. I couldn't tell what he was on about. He had us dress in pauper's clothes, then led me down this narrow passage, Finamour Lane, a stone's throw from St. Paul's. Near the end was a hole in the wall with a heavy oak door and a red lantern shining beside it. I didn't know what I was in for. The room was full to the rafters with drunken men and rowdy women, with grubby children running up and down the aisles. It was so hot and close I thought I might faint. And then the show started! It was a bawdy spectacle, what with pipers and dancers and clowns and ladies with their dugs out getting coins tossed at them. "What are we doing here?" I asked him. This was worse than any music hall, closer to watching a dogfight. I thought we'd be rolled and robbed for sure. "Just you wait!" he said, with a gleam in his eye.

Finally, this plaintive lass came out onto the stage and sang a tune that I had known since I was on my mother's knee, and that I sang to my own dear lad before he was born.

Last night I did dream that my lost love came in.
So softly she came that her feet made no din.
And she turned her head to me, and this she did say:
"It will not be long, love, till our wedding day."

As she finished her pretty little song, an old rude woman in an apron hollered from back of the stage. "Pies!" she shouted. "Get your fresh hot pies!" And then a tall mustachioed ruffian wheeled a chair onto the stage, a crude wooden joke of a barber's chair, and I knew just then what we were there to see.

The crowd jumped and cheered; they knew nearly every word and shouted along when they could. The singing girl was Johanna who had lost her sailor lover. The mustache was Sweeney Todd, a barber who had lost his wife. And the old lady with lines drawn deep in her face was Mrs. Lovett, a lovesick baker that had lost her wits. There I was, sitting there in secret, watching my own life played out in front of me. Except it wasn't my life, not really, it was all comical until it were bloody, and then all bloody until it was tragic. And then with everyone dead, including Mrs. Lovett, it came to an end. As the crowd clapped and stomped, and the actors stood and took their bows, my son leaned over to me and whispered into my ear. "Look how famous you are, Mum," he said. He were beaming as much as any light on the stage. "Everyone knows who you are, and what you've done. One of these days, I'll be as famous as you."

You've met him, so you know: he can be impulsive like his father. He needs his mother's gentle hand to guide him. And that is why I'm writing this, to thank you. You've made a proper mum out of me at last. We had ourselves a pie last night and toasted you by name. What a dainty dish you were! As tasty as anyone could hope.

I don't have many days left, but each one is a miracle now, and that's all thanks to you. And, soon enough, all of London will know the name of my son, Jack.

Forever in my heart,

Margery Lovett (Mrs.)

Dew—

I appreciate your assembling this dossier. I have examined it thoroughly and can find nothing here that will help us in locating Miss Gibson. This all just shows that she fell into the thrall of some deluded widow peddling fairy stories. If I may be frank, it's what I would expect from some spoiled bluestocking hoping to place herself in a profession where she doesn't belong.

I expect she's run off with some bloke she doesn't deserve, poor sod. She'll turn up in her own time, of that I have no doubt.

Burn all these pages, and our back-and-forth as well. Save nothing. See you tonight, Turk's Head, half six.

With hearty good wishes,

Insp. Abberline

Corinne Leigh Clark's
Acknowledgements

I must start by thanking David Demchuk for bringing me along on this dark Gothic journey and for his kindness, wisdom, and generosity with his time and his knowledge. David, you have changed my life, and I will be forever grateful. To our intrepid agent Barbara Berson, who knew that the best way to tell the story of Margery Lovett was to bring David and me together. Thank you for your friendship and for believing in me from the day we met. I wouldn't be here without you.

To our US editor, Nick Whitney, many thanks for your insightful feedback and passion for this project. Thanks also to the Hell's Hundred/Soho Press team and to our UK editor, Rufus Purdy, and everyone at Titan Books for enthusiastically embracing Margery and her story, which waited more than a century to be told.

Francis Sealey, your early reading and discerning comments on the manuscript were enormously helpful. And thanks to my kindred spirits in the UK. A piece of my heart is always with you: Lois, Francis, Tanya, and Mark Sealey; Dominic Wood; Edward Field; Leila Kalbassi; Sharon Baker; Allan Vaughan; and Alison Burrows.

For the heartfelt encouragement since I first put words on paper: Deborah Amador, Joe Cappadocia, Jane Dougan, Elana Robson Down, Bruce Duncan, Debbie L. Dunn, Jacey Evans, Geri Lalach, April Tyler, Erica and Joyce Weste, Gale Willgoss, and AZ, thank you. Thanks also to my mentors Kelley Armstrong and Brian Henry.

To my mother, Beverley Clark. Thank you for sharing with me your love of books and for steadfastly believing I would be a writer one day, despite many detours along the way. To the rest of my family, whose support and love mean the world to me: Grant, Alana, Gavin, and Sarah Clark; and Chuck Gadbois. To my two gorgeous, smart, and loving stepdaughters, Erika and Natasha Cappadocia, and to my husband, Perry Cappadocia. All the ways you support me are too many to list. None of this is possible without you. I love you.

David Demchuk's
Acknowledgements

First and foremost, my deepest gratitude to my partner in literary crime, Corinne Leigh Clark, who was kind enough to join this wonderful project and bring her very best to it every single day. This book would simply not exist without her.

Profuse thanks as well to our mutual agent, Barbara Berson, who shepherded this book from its conception and brought Corinne and I together for this collaboration. Whatever success this book may achieve, it cannot reflect the gratitude I feel for Barbara's efforts with my work.

I am very thankful for the participation of fellow author Hayden Ira May in considering our depiction of deafness and disability, and in particular the character of Aphra. His contribution was invaluable as we hurtled towards the final draft.

I am grateful to my good friend and architectural consultant Christopher Lauzon, who provided much helpful advice about the construction and layout of the various houses and shops depicted throughout the book.

Many thanks to our US editor, Nick Whitney, and the entire team at Hell's Hundred/Soho Press, and to UK editor, Rufus Purdy, and everyone at Titan Books. You have brought our words to life in ways we could not have imagined.

All my love to my husband, Chris Poirier, who married me and left me to move across the country as I wrote this book (don't worry, I followed), and endured untold horrors as a result. He will have his chance for revenge, I am sure.

My dearest friends: Asif, Laurie, Anthony & Alex, Dom, Kevin, Jake, Lynn, Ian & Greg, Dennis, Fran & Ron, Steve, Kim & Gardenia & Casey, Ann & Ali. You all have supported me so much and I am ever in your debt.

Finally, many thanks to my esteemed compatriot Kelly Robson, whose conversation with me on social media shortly after the death of Stephen Sondheim inspired this book. I urged her to write it, she urged me to write it, and I am the one who blinked. Thank you, Kelly, for setting me on this wild adventure.

Nota bene: We are grateful for the many historical reference materials that we consulted in shaping this book. They are too numerous to mention. While we have strived for accuracy in many of the book's finer details, our depictions of such institutions as the Fleet Street press, the nascent medical profession, the Metropolitan Police, the brothels of Mayfair, the Anglican Church, the British monarchy and the Freemasons are, as you might hope, entirely fantastical. All of the names, characters, businesses, organizations, places, events and incidents are either the product of our imaginations or are used in a fictitious manner. With hearty good wishes.

About the Authors

DAVID DEMCHUK has been writing for print, stage, digital and other media for more than 40 years. After many years in Toronto, he now lives by the sea with his husband in St. John's, Newfoundland (Twitter/X: @david_demchuk; Bluesky: @daviddemchuk.com; Instagram: @spo0ky_dad).

CORINNE LEIGH CLARK is a writer of gothic stories that reflect the human condition in a historical context. She is a graduate of the creative writing program at the School of Continuing Studies, University of Toronto (Bluesky: @corinneleighclark.bsky.social)

Mrs Dawson's household recipes

Almost all of the following pie recipes are made with either a shortcrust pastry or a puff pastry.

The measurements used in Mrs Dawson's cooking are different to the ones we're familiar with now. So, to avoid confusion, here's a list of conversions.

1 ounce = 28.3 grams (so 8 ounces is equivalent to about 225 grams; 9 ounces is equivalent to about 250 grams)

1 pound = 450 grams (so 1½ pounds is equivalent to 680 grams)

1 dessert spoon = 2 tablespoons

1 kitchen spoon = 1 teaspoon

1 pint = 568 millilitres (so ½ pint is equivalent to just over 250 millilitres)

TO MAKE A SHORTCRUST PASTRY

INGREDIENTS
8 ounces plain flour
4 ½ ounces butter, diced
½-1½ dessert spoons milk

1. Sift the flour into a bowl then add the butter and rub it into the flour with your fingertips until the mixture resembles fine breadcrumbs. Add a pinch of salt, then ½ dessert spoon milk, and mix again. Keep adding milk until the mixture comes together into a dough, then shape this into a flat circle and put aside in a cold place for at least 20 minutes.

TO MAKE A PUFF PASTRY

INGREDIENTS
9 ounces plain flour
8 ounces butter

1. Sift the flour into a bowl then add a pinch of salt and then ¼ pint water, and mix until the dough comes together. Shape this into a flat circle and put aside in a cold place for at least 20 minutes.

2. Put the butter between two pieces of baking parchment and tap it with a rolling pin to soften it. Cut the butter in half and repeat this action, making sure the butter is easy to manipulate yet still cold. Flatten the pieces of butter until they are the size of a small photographic plate.

3. Lightly flour a surface, then roll out the dough into a circle. Put the butter in the middle of this circle, then fold over the left and right sides of the dough so they overlap in the middle.

4. Lengthen the dough by rolling it out, then fold the bottom third up to cover the middle third, and fold the top third down over these. Seal the dough gently by pressing down on the edges with your rolling pin. Give the dough a quarter turn.

5. Repeat this action four times. Once this done, set the pastry aside in a cold place for at least 1 hour before using.

—

BEEFSTEAK PIE

INGREDIENTS

For the stock
Beef bones
1 carrot, peeled
1 onion, peeled
1 bay leaf

For the filling
1-1½ pounds lean beefsteak
Flour seasoned with salt and pepper
2 onions, peeled and finely chopped
Shortcrust pastry (see page 413)
1 egg, beaten

1. First, make a beef stock. Put the bones into a large pan and cover with water. Bring to the boil and skim off the fat. Add the carrot, onion and bay leaf, and simmer for 2-3 hours, continuing to skim off the fat every 30 minutes. Season to taste with salt. Remove the bones and discard, then strain the liquid and set aside in a warm place.

2. While the stock is simmering, wipe the beefsteak, remove the skin and fat, then cut the meat into small cubes.

3. Coat the beefsteak cubes in the seasoned flour and place them in a pie dish, piling them up more generously towards the centre. Sprinkle the onions between the cubes of meat.

4. Add the beef stock so that it comes a quarter of the way up the pie dish.

5. Roll out the shortcrust pastry until it is ½-¼ inch thick and wide enough to cover the pie dish. Cut a ¾ inch strip from around the edge of the pastry to cover the rim of the pie dish. Wet the rim with your finger, then position the pastry strip around the edge, allowing it to overlap the rim a little.

6. Damp the join and the rest of the pastry, and cover with the pastry lid. Press the edges together, then brush with beaten egg.

7. Make a small hole in the lid and bake in a hot oven for 15 minutes at 425-450°F, then reduce the heat to 350°F and bake for another 1¼-1¾ hours or until lightly brown.

8. When the pie is cooked, reheat the remaining beef stock, then widen the hole in the lid and pour it in before serving.

EEL PIE

INGREDIENTS

For the stock
1-1½ pounds good-sized eels
Butter, to thicken
Flour, to thicken

For the filling
Puff pastry (see page 413)
2 pinches dried sage

1. First make an eel stock. Remove the eel heads and tails, add to a pan and season. Pour in 1¾ pints of water and bring to the boil. Reduce to a simmer, then thicken with butter and flour. Set aside in a warm place.

2. Roll out a thin pastry base to cover the bottom and sides of a pie dish. Cut the remaining sections of eel into 1½-2 inch pieces, rub over the dried sage and combine. Then add the eel mixture to the pie. Pour in as much eel stock as will cover them, then place a puff pastry lid over the top.

3. Make a small hole in the lid and bake at 350°F for 1-1½ hours or until lightly brown.

COLD CALF'S HEAD PIE

INGREDIENTS

For the stock
Remains of a calf's head (to produce 1-1½ pounds meat)
1 carrot, peeled
1 onion, peeled
1 bay leaf

For the filling
½ pound bacon
2 hard-boiled eggs
Forcemeat
¼ kitchen spoon mixed herbs
Rind of ½ lemon, grated
Pinch ground mace
Pinch grated nutmeg
Puff pastry (see page 413)

1. First, make a stock. Put the calf's head into a large pan with the carrot, onion and bay leaf, and cover with water. Bring to the boil and simmer for 2-3 hours. Remove the head to a separate pan, then strain the liquid and set aside in a warm place.

2. Remove the meat from the calf's head and cut into small, thin strips. Do likewise with the bacon. Cut the eggs into thin

slices. Mix the forcement rather stiffly with a little raw egg and shape into balls.

3. Put a thick layer of calf's head meat onto the bottom of a pie dish, then cover with a thin layer of bacon and a few egg slices. Add a generous sprinkling of salt, pepper, mixed herbs, grated lemon rind, mace and nutmeg. Repeat the layers until the dish is full, then pour in ½ pint stock and cover with a puff pastry lid. Set the rest of the stock aside to cool and form a loose jelly.

4. Make a small hole in the lid and bake at 350°F for 1 hour or until lightly brown. Pour in a little jellied stock through the hole in the lid and set aside. Serve cold.

PARTRIDGE PIE

INGREDIENTS

For the stock
1 chicken carcass
1 carrot, peeled
1 onion, peeled
1 bay leaf

For the filling
1 partridge
1 ounce butter

½ lb veal
2 rashers bacon
1 hard-boiled egg, thinly sliced
2 mushrooms, roughly chopped
1 small shallot, sliced
½ dessert spoon chopped parsley
Puff pastry (see page 413)
1 egg, beaten

1. First, make a stock. Put the chicken into a large pan with the carrot, onion and bay leaf, and cover with water. Bring to the boil and simmer for 2-3 hours. Remove the chicken and discard, then strain the liquid, season generously and set aside in a warm place.

2. While the stock is simmering, take your partridge, and pluck, draw, singe and wipe the bird with a damp cloth, then joint it neatly. Fry the joints in the butter until lightly browned.

3. Slice the veal thinly, then lay the pieces in the bottom of a pie dish and season well. Lay the partridge joints on top, along with the bacon and slices of hard-boiled egg. Sprinkle on the mushrooms, shallot and parsley, then pour in stock until it is halfway up the dish. Cover with a puff pastry lid. Set the rest of the stock aside in a warm place.

4. Make a small hole in the lid and bake in a hot oven for 15 minutes at 425-450°F, then reduce the heat to 350°F and bake for another 1¼-1¾ hours or until lightly brown. Glaze the pie with beaten egg 15 minutes before it is ready to come out of the oven.

5. When the pie is cooked, reheat the remaining stock, then widen the hole in the lid and pour it in before serving.

HARE AND POTATO PIE

Ingredients

For the stock	For the filling
1 chicken carcass	½-¾ lb hare meat
1 carrot, peeled	½ lb streaky bacon
1 onion, peeled	4 ounces breadcrumbs
1 bay leaf	Dash Worcestershire sauce
	1 lb creamed potatoes
	1 ounce butter, cut into small pieces

1. First, make a stock. Put the chicken into a large pan with the carrot, onion and bay leaf, and cover with water. Bring to the boil and simmer for 2-3 hours. Remove the chicken and discard, then strain the liquid, season generously and set aside in a warm place.

2. Once the stock is ready, cut the hare into small pieces and fry. Cut the bacon into small strips and add to the hare meat, along with the breadcrumbs and enough stock to moisten well.

3. Place a layer of this mixture onto the bottom of a greased pie dish, then season well and add a little Worcestershire sauce. Cover with a layer of seasoned creamed potatoes, then repeat the layers until all the mixture has been used up. Top with a layer of seasoned creamed potatoes. Scatter the butter on top.

4. Bake in a hot oven for 20 minutes at 425-450°F, until browned. Serve with a good gravy.

SIMPLE MUTTON PIE

INGREDIENTS
1-1½ pounds lean mutton
Shortcrust pastry (see page 413)
2 onions, finely chopped
1 egg, beaten

1. Divide the mutton into pieces of a moderate size and season them well.

2. Roll out a thin pastry base to cover the bottom and sides of a pie dish, then pile the mutton on top, along with the onion. Pour in water so that it comes halfway up the dish.

3. Roll out the shortcrust pastry until it is ½-¼ inch thick and wide enough to cover the pie dish. Cut a ¾ inch strip from around the edge of the pastry to cover the rim of the pie dish. Wet the rim with your finger, then position the pastry strip around the edge, allowing it to overlap the rim a little.

4. Damp the join and the rest of the pastry, and cover with the pastry lid. Press the edges together, then brush with beaten egg.

5. Make four small holes in the lid and bake in a hot oven for 15 minutes at 425-450°F, then reduce the heat to 350°F and bake for another 1¼-1¾ hours or until lightly brown.

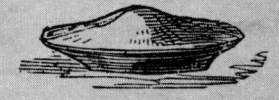